A MEMORY RETURNS

He stood, hovering menacingly over her. "Send me back right now!"

"No," she said evenly. "The experiments are finished. I thank you for your cooperation, Mr. Hersh, but I think it is time to terminate our relationship."

"No!" Hersh screamed. "What's wrong with you, Silv? Wouldn't you trade *this* for all that we could have?" He gestured around the cubicle, his face settled into a posture of disgust. "The whole world is ours."

"No, it's not," Silv replied, afraid of his temper. "These have been simple, psychotropic experiments in aggression retardation. The other thing is merely a side effect."

He laughed then, throwing back his nearly square head. "You might have got a hothead out of detention for your 'experiments,' but I'm no idiot. You're old, Silv, ready to die—but not me. I want to live up there on the surface. I want to breathe real air—"

"And kill," Silv said harshly. "And change things."

M E M O R I E S

M I K E   M c Q U A Y

BANTAM BOOKS

TORONTO · NEW YORK · LONDON · SYDNEY · AUCKLAND

MEMORIES

A Bantam Spectra Book / June 1987

ISBN 0-553-25888-5

Published simultaneously in the United States and Canada

Bantam Books are published by Bantam Books, Inc. Its trade-
mark, consisting of the words ''Bantam Books'' and the por-
trayal of a rooster, is Registered in U.S. Patent and Trademark
Office and in other countries. Marca Registrada. Bantam
Books, Inc., 666 Fifth Avenue, New York, New York 10103.

PRINTED IN THE UNITED STATES OF AMERICA

O   098765432

To Russ Galen—friend, agent, banker, confidant—
nothing but good memories

The Ruins of Time build mansions in Eternity.
—William Blake

Most of what follows is true. . . .

A neurotic is the man who builds a castle in the air. A psychotic is the man who lives in it. And a psychiatrist is the man who collects the rent.

—Anonymous

"What's happening now?"

"My father is holding me on his shoulder, raising me above his head so I can see. The hall is so crowded, so many people pushing in to see the great man. I've never seen a room so big. My father is telling me that this man is more important than any man in the country, but I can't understand how anyone could be greater than my father."

"How old are you?"

"I am four years old."

"Who is the great man?"

"I don't know. I'm happy because it's like a holiday—so much excitement. Thousands of candles are lighting the hall and I feel they are the stars in the sky."

David Wolf sat back and uneasily watched the woman half sprawled on the faded couch. He had been here before with her, had touched this nerve with his practiced hand many times. Institutionalized for thirty years she was his, and everyone else's, practice subject. That's what State Hospital was for—practice.

"And then what happens?"

"I see my Uncle Philip who brings me sweets when he comes to visit. I call to him, but . . . he's talking, arguing with another man."

The woman was called Sara, but no one knew her real name. All the old records had been destroyed in the fire of '53, and after all these years, anyone who knew her by her real name was long gone. She was Sara, the guinea pig. Shock treatments had taken most of her conscious memories. Somehow she had managed to escape the stainless steel scoop when lobotomies were the craze back in the late fifties. David was using another kind of scoop—hypnosis.

He persisted, trying to push her to catharsis. "What are they arguing about?"

"I—I don't know, but everyone around us is getting angry. I'm scared and hold tight to Papa." Sara began crying, shaking slightly.

"Please," David said, forcing down the tension in his own voice. "Try and stay calm. I'm right here with you. It's all right. You can get through this. What's happening now?"

"It's horrible. The man has taken out his sword and puts it in my Uncle Philip and he falls down. I call for him to get up, but the crowd is yelling now, pushing against us. I'm crying. A man hits Papa and he almost drops me, but we push through them . . . they're all around, all screaming, screaming! I put my hands over my ears but the sound won't go away!"

She began shaking uncontrollably, losing it. Her withered face was sweating profusely, her eyes wide and hysterical. This was where David usually brought her out of the trance, when the dystonic reaction began; but this time he was going to go ahead. He stood quickly, moving to the old wooden desk and the hypo that lay upon it. A sense of guilt welled up in him, but it was drowned by waves of excitement. After years of trying regression therapy, he had come up empty. Until Sara.

Oklahoma twilight streamed pink through the dirty fourth-floor window of State, lighting the cold bare room to a surreal glow. David thought to turn on a light, decided against it. He soaked a cotton ball in alcohol, then picked up the hypo and moved to the woman.

"Hang on, Sara," he said low and swabbed her shaking arm just above the elbow.

"Run, Papa!" she screamed. "Run!"

She was all over the couch, vibrating wildly. He grabbed her arm and threw himself over her body just to steady her enough to give her the injection. He pinched up the flesh then jabbed her with the needle, hurrying to give her less time to break the thing off in her arm.

He plunged the pale liquid through the tube and jumped off her, moving away, surprised to find himself breathing heavily. He'd done it, 25 mg of chlorpromazine, and now he'd have to live with whatever happened next.

So would Sara.

She thrashed for another minute, then settled down, though her face was drawn tight, strained.

"Are you there?" he asked.

"Yes," she answered in a faraway voice.

"What's your name?"

"Elise."

He let out a long breath. She was still under. He had never gotten this far before, and now a whole world was opening up to him.

"The man has stabbed your Uncle Philip."

"Yes. Now all the people are chasing us. I can hear Papa breathing in my ear. I'm so frightened, I can only hold tight."

"Where are you running?"

"Our house. Mama and little Jacob are there. Everyone is very frightened and I fear because I know my Papa is not the greatest man in the world for he can't protect us."

"Where are you . . . what city?"

She spoke in a child's singsong, memorize voice. "I live at Four Three One Ironmonger Street, London. My papa owns ten stalls in the Cheape Market."

"What is the year?"

Her voice faltered. "I—I don't know."

David looked down and checked the tape recorder that sat on the floor beside his chair. It was still going, still capturing the electromagnetic vibrations of memory.

"What's happening now?"

"They're trying to break in our door, our windows."

"Who?"

"The crowds . . . our neighbors."

"Why?"

"I don't know. I'm so frightened. Mama is crying and holding Jacob. She has a knife in her hand and is going to cut my little brother."

Despite the injection, Sara was shaking again, a horror of such immensity overtaking her that David fought with himself over bringing her out of the trance. What was happening to her? What incredible fantasy had eaten away at her soul like this? He was caught in it himself. He had to go on, clinical or not.

"What's happening, Elise? What now?"

Sara jerked to a sitting position, her eyes vibrating. She opened her mouth and screamed, "Fire!"

"What fire . . . what fire?"

"They can't get in our house. They are setting it on fire. The flames so big . . . Mama, no! Don't!"

"What's happening?"

"She's stabbing Jacob, over and over. She's covered with blood. Smoke everywhere. I'm coughing, falling on the floor. Papa is praying *Vaddui*. Mama is coming near me through the smoke. She still has the knife! No, Mama! Mama! Mama!"

Sara was convulsing wildly, tongue out, gagging. The horror was real, absolutely real. And it was taking her away.

"Damn!"

David grabbed her as she fell off the couch, holding her, trying to bring her back. "When I count to three," he said loudly, trying to get above her animal sounds, "you will be Sara again. You will be yourself..."

Someone was knocking loudly on the door.

"Go away!"

The knocking persisted, louder.

"You will not remember anything about Elise and the other time."

"David?"

A female voice. Liz? What was she...

"Wait, please wait!"

"David, I've got to speak with you."

"One...two...three." He tapped her on the forehead, the method he had used in inducing the hypnosis. She immediately relaxed in his arms, slumping, falling into a drugged sleep.

He lifted her, so light, like a feather, and placed her gently on the couch. He was still vibrating inside with a mixture of guilt and triumph. A breakthrough, but at whose expense?

"David, open up!"

"Just a second!"

He took a minute to compose himself, straightening his tie and running fingers through his loose black hair. The tape recorder was still going. He bent to it and shut it off, slipping the cassette tape into the pocket of his sports jacket.

He opened the door, his sister Liz staring at him, a look on her face he had never seen and couldn't place. She had never come here before, not to State.

"How did you know to find me here?" he asked without preamble.

She walked into the office just long enough to see the old woman on the couch, then moved back into the waiting room. "I'm not here to fight with you, David," she said, voice neutral. "I need to talk to you about something very important."

He walked out of the office with her, closing the door

behind him. "Sure," he said, moving to the vacant nurses' station just off the waiting room to pick up the phone. If Liz wanted to talk to him it could only mean trouble. He was already late for rounds as it was. He'd have to get rid of her. He punched up the numbers for the head nurse, waiting the ten rings it took to get her to the phone.

"This is Dr. Wolf," he said. "I need a couple of orderlies and a stretcher up on four. No . . . no problem. I had to sedate Sara. Okay."

He hung up the phone an looked at Liz. She was staring at herself in an old dark mirror that hung on the yellow stone wall.

"How much do you need?" he asked.

She continued to stare into the mirror, bringing her fingers up to gingerly touch her face, as if she were seeing it for the first time. "This face," she said, "reminds me something of mine when I was young. My nose was almost exactly like this. Fascinating."

"What are you babbling about?" he said, and took off his sports jacket. "Tell me how much you need, Sis, and dear God, don't tell Bailey. She'd string me up by the balls."

She stepped away from the mirror, staring at him darkly. "I've lived your life from a distance," she said, shaking her head, clucking like an old woman. "To be this close . . . to breathe your air with healthy lungs . . . it's seductive, almost frightening."

He walked up and took her by the shoulders, staring into her soft blue eyes. "Are you all right?"

"That's a matter of opinion, Dr. Wolf. I need your help desperately."

He released her arms and walked to the old, maple-stained coatrack, hanging up the jacket and taking his long white lab coat off the peg. He transferred the tape into the lab coat.

"The last time you came out to our house, Liz," he said, putting on the coat, "you threw the best part of a tequila sunrise on Bailey and called her a whacked-out, pill-popping floozy who didn't have the morals of an alley cat."

"Wrong, David," she replied, her face seeming to physically change form. "I gave her every bit of credit for having the morals of an alley cat."

"There's my loving sister. Now, how can you ask me to help you when you treat my wife like a typhoid carrier?"

"You're miserable with her. You can't expect me to not react to that, I—"

The double doors burst open and the orderlies came in, pushing the gurney in front of them.

"In there," David said, pointing to the office.

"David, please," Liz said, face suddenly grave. "I'm sorry . . . Please, we've got to talk before it's too late."

"Too late for what?" David replied, looking at his watch again. He was going to miss part of Bailey's dinner party now, and would have to spend the better part of the evening repenting. "I'm really busy, can't this—"

She looked at him fiercely, a fire in her eyes he didn't know she possessed. "This is more important than anything you could possibly be doing," she said, her voice strained with cold sincerity.

"David, we're late," came a voice from the door. David turned to see Dr. Frankel framed in the doorway, white gloved hands holding open the swinging doors. With his smooth, contemplative face and soft white hair falling down over his ears, Mo Frankel was the father that David had never had. He was David's friend and confidant, ready even to scold with love. "Even I like to get out of here sometimes."

"I'm sorry, Mo," David said, motioning the chief of staff inside. "I was working with Sara . . ."

The stretcher was wheeled out of the office, the old woman thrown carelessly upon it. One arm dangled off the edge of the thing, Sara's flower-print dress crumpled way up, exposing her legs.

"I see that you were," Frankel said, in his always-soft, slightly accented voice. He stopped the orderlies and arranged the woman's dress for her. Then he pulled her arm up and lay it across her chest. He looked at the orderlies, his stare an X ray. "That could be you lying there."

David watched as they carted Sara off, back to her pen to wait for the next experimenter. She was ambulatory meat, the behavioral scientist's voodoo doll always ready to be stuck with an assortment of psychological straightpins. It was her lot, her job, to be the repository for all the mistakes and frantic doomed brushfire efforts of learning psychiatrists who would mature after her use to go on to be the Freudian salvation of any number of people who could afford a hundred dollars an hour for their time. Sara was a professional victim, and was quite accomplished at her work.

Frankel turned and looked at David, who sensed a certain disappointment on his face. The man started to speak, then stopped, looking at Liz. "My name is Frankel," he said, extending his left hand, the glove that covered it immaculate, bright white.

Frankel had been a victim of experimenters himself once, behaviorists whose goals were something less than altruistic. For that, he was doomed to sympathize terminally with those too passive to protect themselves. His life had been given totally to understanding and compassion, a vocation not nearly as fulfilling as it seemed on surface.

Liz started to put out her right hand, then put out her left to meet the doctor's. "My name is, Si..." she began, then stopped, shaking her head. "I'm sorry... Liz Wolf."

"My sister," David said.

"You have David's eyes," Frankel said, nodding. "Am I interrupting?"

"We were about to speak of something very important," Liz said. "A... personal matter."

Frankel raised an eyebrow, his smooth face betraying no emotion. "Perhaps I should—"

"No," David said harshly. "I was just explaining to Liz that we can talk after rounds."

"David..."

He glared her to silence. "There's nothing we can't talk about later."

Her eyes spit fire again, but she tightened her lips and didn't speak.

He walked quickly to the door, moving Dr. Frankel along with him. "Call me," he said to Liz over his shoulder.

"Wait!" she said sharply, a command.

David jerked around to face her, his own face hard. It had always been this way with them, one confrontation after another. But there was something different about her this time, something harder.

"Just a few seconds of your time," she said.

"I'll hold the elevator," Frankel said, and wandered off.

David walked back to her. "Now, why did you want to go and make a fool out of yourself in front of Mo."

"I'm not your sister," Liz said, and David stopped, waiting for the punch line. Instead she said, "I am inhabiting the body and mind of Elizabeth Wolf, but I am not her."

"I've really got to go," he replied. "When you stop

playing around, call me at home and tell me what you're so worked up about.''

"I am not your sister," Liz said resolutely.

David walked back through the door, then turned to look at her again. "Okay, I'll bite. Who are you?"

Liz Wolf smiled, a smile that made her face look different again. "I am the dream of your childhood," she said.

David hurried to catch up with Frankel, his footsteps echoing down the long fake-marble hallways. The hospital had been a WPA project in 1933, and looked like all public buildings erected during the Depression. It had been built psychologically, to appear rock solid and stable during a time when everything else was falling apart. It was built to resemble Greek buildings of the fifth century B.C., apparently with the thought in mind that if the Acropolis was still there after so many millennia, so too would State Hospital stand.

Frankel was holding the creaky old elevator, waiting patiently for David, who hurried in and pulled the metal accordion safety gate closed after shutting the outside door with the "4" painted on it.

"Sorry about Liz," he said.

Frankel shrugged, pushing the up button. "She seems very nice," he said absently, then casually pulled out his pipe and began loading it from a black leather pouch.

"You're angry about me working on Sara," David said, not even bothering to frame it as a question.

"What are you doing to her?" the older man asked.

The elevator shuddered, starting up slowly, brick wall moving past outside the safety gate. "Regression therapy," David said.

Frankel laughed around the stem of his pipe, then lit it on a disposable lighter. "You're too good a doctor for that nonsense," he said, then drew deeply on the pipe, a smell like burnt cherries assaulting David's nose.

"I think I've hit a breakthrough," David said, and put his hands in his pocket, the feel of the tape in there bolstering his confidence. "I think I've sent her back to a previous life."

"David, this is unscientific. Whatever reactions you got could be anything—fantasies, something she read once—you know as well as I do that hypnotic subjects want to please their hypnotist while under."

"I'm just trying to help her, Mo."

The elevator shivered to a stop on nine. They stepped out on the psych floor and moved down past the nurses' station and through the double doors to Nine West and its barred windows.

The psychiatric ward contained fifty beds. The high walls and ceilings were painted pale green and echoed spoken words as if one were shouting down a well. Old, art-deco light fixtures hung from the ceiling like scalloped dough, their shades crisscrossing the room with well-defined shadow. The noise was nearly overpowering, the patients reacting loudly to the nighttime soap opera they were watching in the attached rec room.

"We lost Willy last night," Frankel said as they strolled toward the ring of people at the far end of the room.

"What happened? The gallbladder?"

Frankel nodded. "Reynolds opened him up last night and decided to wipe it out and drain it instead of taking it out."

"Sounds like Reynolds," David said.

"Yeah. When he closed he decided to do it with one row of wire stitches."

"What about closing the peritoneum?"

"Too much trouble," Frankel said, bitterness edging his voice. "When the night nurse came in to check post-op, she found him eviscerated, the wound wide open and his intestines spilled out of the abdominal wall. She called Reynolds, and you know what he told her? He said to put a heavy dressing on it and tape it up to hold the intestines in. Then he 'looked in' this morning and found Willy dead."

"State Hospital," David said.

"Don't be cruel with Sara," Frankel said, putting a hand on his arm to stop him from walking. "A long time ago I diagnosed her as schizophrenic and anal retentive. Try and set up some transference with her. Stick to basics."

"Mo, she's got no mind to work with," David said. "No conscious mind, anyway. You know that."

"I didn't say it would be easy. Psychiatrists specialize in their own abnormalities. Think about that. Put yourself in her place. Don't treat her like the others do. Don't be like Reynolds."

David went into his pocket and pulled out the cassette. "I'll make a deal with you," he said "You listen to this tape, and if you still think I'm on the wrong track, I'll stop the hypnosis and do what you say."

Frankel held out a gloved hand and David placed the tape in it as if it were a newborn baby. "I really do want to help her."

Frankel seemed to look a million miles through David. "And maybe help yourself at the same time, too. Eh?"

> *A simple Child,*
> *That lightly draws its breath,*
> *And feels its life in every limb,*
> *What should it know of death?*
> —Wordsworth

Davy Wolf sat in front of the television listening to the President of the United States, and felt the cheating hand of Death on his shoulder. His fears threatened to overpower him; the unfairness of it all. They couldn't stupidly take his world away, his chance for a future. It wasn't right. They had lived their lives. Why couldn't he live his?

"... Aggressive conduct, if allowed to grow unchecked and unchallenged, ultimately leads to war." President Kennedy looked directly at the camera, his voice clear and firm. "This nation is opposed to war. We are also true to our word. Our unswerving objective, therefore, must be to prevent the use of these missiles against this or any other country and to secure their withdrawal or elimination from the Western Hemisphere."

"Would you turn that damned thing down?" his mother called, her voice belligerent with alcohol. Didn't she understand?

"Momma, we're blockading Cuba . . . the Russians . . ."

He reached out a trembling hand and fiddled with the volume. He understood what nuclear war meant; he'd been dreaming about it for months, huge mushroom clouds bursting through happy lives, and in his dreams he was always running, running, but never running toward anything—and that was the scary part.

"As a necessary military precaution I have reinforced our base at Guantánamo, evacuated today the dependents of our personnel there, and ordered additional military units to be on a standby-alert basis."

He flexed his legs and hugged them tightly to him. There would be huge firestorms and you couldn't drink the water. All the food . . . poisoned. What kind of world is that? He'd never drive, or know what girls had under their clothes.

The front door burst open and Jerry, his mother's boy-friend, staggered in. He was dressed in an old army uniform that was much too small for him. His face was flushed, eyes glazed.

"I'm ready," he said. "We'll all be called up before this is over."

"What the hell happened to you?" his mother said, her voice flat, guttural.

"We're going to war," Jerry said, falling to his knees beside Davy. "We'll all be called up." He slapped Davy on the back—hard. "We're gonna kick Russian butt, huh, boy?"

The man's breath was rank with booze, overpowering. Davy felt all closed in. "No," he said. "No, you don't understand . . ."

"I understand," Jerry said, getting back to his feet. "We shoulda kicked their asses after we took Berlin."

"The path we have chosen for the present is full of hazards, as all paths are; but it is the one most consistent with our character and courage as a nation and our commitments around the world. The cost of freedom is always high—but Americans have always paid it."

"You're drunk!" his mother yelled.

"So what?" Jerry said. "So fuckin' what? A man's entitled . . ."

"You were going to take me to dinner."

"I'm going to war!"

"And one path we shall never choose, and that is the path of surrender or submission."

"Get out of my house, you goddamned asshole!"

"Aw, come here, Naomi. Come on, give me some sugar."

It was swirling around in Davy's head, pounding on his skull, trying to get out.

"Get your hands off me."

Jerry had grabbed his mother, was pulling her hard against him, his hands all over her. "You can't send me off without a little somethin', honey. Come on, you know what you're good for."

Davy was up, confused, moving toward them.

"No, Jerry!" His mother was really fighting the man. "Not now . . . the children."

Jerry's face was dark, mean. "Fuck the children!" He ripped down the top of her housecoat, pushing her roughly to the sofa.

"No!" Davy said, grabbing Jerry's arm. "Leave her alone!"

Jerry turned to him and his face was like an animal's, like a wolfman's. He swung out with a large hand, and Davy flew across the room, his mother's screams filling his ears. He tried to sit, his head spinning where it banged the wall, and just as he felt filled to bursting—

his mind expanded.

There was a voice and a vision.

The voice tried to reason with him, to calm him down. But the vision. The vision was everything. Crystal clear it was, and fraught with understanding. It showed him the history of the world, his world, and beyond. There were no bombs in this world. There was only the gradual deterioration of self-indulgence. It was the inevitability that wore him down, the monster of selfishness that waits to destroy everything. The visions crammed out everything else. Poisons in the land, in the water, in the air, in the populations—a world worn out, unable to support itself. Life in the dark, underground, far underground. The vision was bleak with despair, without hope, like his dreams. But he knew, really knew, the vision was real. There was no hope. There was no future.

Davy Wolf was twelve years old, and hope was his mainstay. Realization brought an inner pain that he found intolerable in all respects.

He closed in. He couldn't even hear himself screaming, even after they had come and taken him away.

> *The French are highly individualistic and ungovernable and the extraordinary thing is that, although they project great leaders about once a century, those leaders rule effectively but bequeath chaos.*
>
> —C. L. Sulzberger

General Napoleon Buonaparte stood beside his pair of eight-pound cannons and stared through the drizzle along the length of rue Neuve Saint-Roch, the church of Saint-Roch proudly facing him at the end of the long, cobbled block.

He was wet, soaked through from sixteen hours of Paris fall rain, his threadbare uniform affording no protection from the cold or the rain. It was the afternoon of 13 Vendémiaire—5 October—and he waited, patiently, to defend the Republic.

The sky rolled gray above, a symphony of grays as the wet

stone buildings and streets reflected their drabness back to the pregnant clouds. Thunder rolled, the horses rearing under the sounds.

"Were those drums?" Barras asked from beside him.

Buonaparte looked up at the man who sat beside him astride a magnificent gray stallion, his uniform and demeanor marking him with the unmistakable look of command. Unfortunately, looks could, indeed, deceive.

"No sir," Buonaparte said, sharing a look with his gunners.

"Perhaps you were wrong about this," Barras said.

"They will come," the young general said. "They must come to us. They have no other course."

And come they would. To the Tuileries, the seat of government, the Royalist and anarchist troops, numbering thirty thousand, would have to inevitably make their way. In the aftermath of the Revolution, the taking of the Tuileries could be the only real and definite sign of taking power. And Buonaparte had every avenue of approach sealed off with the guns he had rushed in from Sablons during the night.

The rumble again, French troops all along the street coming to attention.

"Thunder," Barras said gruffly.

"No, citizen," Buonaparte said. "Drums."

The shouting started almost immediately, then the gunfire, as rebel troops with fixed bayonets charged the barricades erected by Barras to protect the rue Saint-Honore a block away.

"Now we'll see," Barras said, trying to hold down the horse that had gotten skittish beneath him.

"They will come," Buonaparte said, then nodded to the gunners. "Load with case shot."

The men rushed to comply as the sounds of battle grew louder around them. Buonaparte watched wordlessly as chains and kegs of nails were poured down the muzzles of the eight-pounders, their trajectories leveled to the streets. The Revolution had provided him his commission and his life, and he meant to protect it and its Constitution. Being a Corsican, he had been spared the decimation that had torn through the ranks of army officers of noble birth. He had been promoted from captain to brigadier general in four months, based solely on his command of the artillery brigades at the battle of Toulon. And now he stood beside the commander in chief of the forces of the interior defending the government, the commander himself never having risen above the rank of second lieutenant.

These were the times of flux, of change. These were the times of dreamers who could be kings if only they had the courage and imagination to reach out and take what was ripe for the taking. The old ways had died in a bloody froth, and everywhere fresh air blew in to fill the vacuum. Buonaparte had an advantage in this struggle of newness, however—he had the guns. When every other artillery officer in the French army had emigrated, he was left the only man capable of defending Paris. He waited for the rebels with delicious anticipation, his pale blue eyes locked on the empty street, his insides bursting with the excitement to come.

He was twenty-four years old.

A cheer arose in the unseen distance, Buonaparte looking up at Barras who was already staring down at him, his lean, handsome face set hard as granite. The man's defenses had fallen. All that separated France from the hands of the mob were Buonaparte's forty guns.

The young general smiled a thin smile. He felt the surge of history and rose to meet its thrust. "Prepare to fire!" he called, a handful of blue-coated regulars taking to the doorways and bushes.

And they came, a screaming mob pouring onto the streets in front of the church, firing wildly, pumped up by their overwhelming numbers.

"Steady," Buonaparte said to the gunners as the crowd charged the street toward them. They were like a wave rolling over the wet, slick cobbles. But they weren't quite close enough yet.

"Fire!" Barras ordered, skittish as his horse, and the gunners opened up, lengths of chain and nail shrapnel ripping a bloody swath through the front ranks.

Buonaparte stared fire at his commander, but held his peace. There'd be glory enough for all after this day. "Reload!" he called through the black smoke and gunpowder smell.

The crowd charged again, and Buonaparte could hear his other batteries firing on the rue Saint-Honore a block distant. All at once a pain shot through his head and he doubled over, his initial thought that he had been shot. But the pain eased in an instant, leaving behind a rush of strange and alien sensations.

"Fire!" he heard himself say, the words followed by a burst of laughter that was swallowed in the roar of the cannons.

It was as if someone, some *thing,* had taken possession of his body. A demon? Nonsense.

His sword was in his hand. He tried to put it away, but he had no control over his own body. He waved it above his head, a gesture sure to infuriate the vain Barras. "Fight, my children! The Revolution! The Revolution!"

They fired another volley, the gray streets now red with blood and bloated with bodies. The rebels fell back, regrouping immediately for another charge.

His mind filled with thoughts he couldn't understand, of other wars in other times. He feared for his sanity, but it all seemed so clear, so crystal clear.

"Fire!"

The guns roared, church facades crumbling in a haze of white dust a long block away. He had absolutely no control over himself or his surroundings. Whatever had possession of his mind had it absolutely.

One of the soldiers broke away from his cover and came across the street, directly between the guns and the mob. He was weaving slightly, his face fixed in perplexity. He found himself watching the spectacle, wondering if it was Silv.

Silv? Who was . . .

"Fire!" he called, before the soldier had even been able to get across the street. But the gunners waited, just an extra second, and the soldier cleared the muzzles as they spit hot death into the charging crowd.

The soldier pushed himself, face now angry, between Barras and General Buonaparte. "You can't do this," the soldier said. "You have no idea what you may be setting in motion."

"I'll do what I please," Buonaparte heard himself say, then he laughed at the soldier. "There's nothing you can do to stop me. Fire!"

The guns bellowed again, the soldier grabbing him by the lapels. "Please, you must listen to me. You can't . . ."

Napoleon Buonaparte, the Corsican, broke the hold on his jacket and shoved the soldier into Barras's horse, which broke and ran. Barras went nearly to the gates of the Tuileries before getting it back under control.

"What happens if you change something, Hersh?" the soldier yelled, keeping out of arm's reach. "You've taken this man's body and mind and you're leading troops. What happens if you change the flow of history?"

"I don't care, Silv!" the presence yelled back. "And you can't touch me! I'm here now, and I'm going to stay."

"We'll see," the soldier said, eyes narrowing. Suddenly the soldier's face went slack and pale, and he crumpled to the pavement unconscious.

The thing in Buonaparte snorted with contempt, then turned again to the gunners. "Fire!" he yelled, case shot ripping once more through the ranks.

This time, when the mob broke, it didn't regroup. The people fled, hysterical, into the surrounding streets, leaving several hundred bodies behind.

"Go after them!" Buonaparte yelled to the cavalry. "Keep them at bay!"

And five thousand loyal troops broke the back of the thirty thousand, chasing them through the city streets and, finally, through the sewers.

> *Psychology which explains everything*
> *explains nothing,*
> *and we are still in doubt.*
>
> —Marianne Moore

David Wolf drove his white Porsche out of the parking lot of State Hospital and onto Thirteenth Street and the maze of teaching-hospital structures that were lumped together there. He called it Blood Alley, the place where people who couldn't afford to be real patients came for medical care to learning doctors who couldn't afford to make mistakes on real patients and so practiced on the freebies.

This wasn't the case with David. He had his own practice, his own slate of dependable, ambulatory cases of neurosis and depression, enough to buy him a new couch and an office redecoration every year. No, David Wolf didn't fit the mold. He had other reasons for spending time at State, and though he tried, as always, to think of himself as an altruist, it didn't really line out that way.

The evening was late spring hot and dry, the dependable Oklahoma wind the only thing keeping it from being stifling. He loosened his tie and took a breath, thoughts of Sara filling his head. Mo had all but accused him of unethical behavior in dealing with the woman. Was it true?

He didn't know. Sara had been pegged as a hopeless victim years before. He could certainly make a case for desperation measures with her that made sense. Only that's not what Mo had meant. The old man wondered about David's real motives. Was he actually trying to help the woman, or was she simply his experiment? Was the pleasure he had derived from the results of today's session on her behalf or his own? Was it even a fair question?

He turned onto Lincoln Boulevard, heading toward the state capitol building. The answer to his question was perhaps the answer to a riddle of his life. For David Wolf was a man of contradicting feelings and actions. Like an animal, he sniffed the ground for answers without knowing the questions. Capable of great compassion, he was driven to heights of viciousness that surprised and frightened him when he chose to examine them, which he usually didn't. He wanted a reason for things, yet fled in the face of all reason. David Wolf was a man to whom frustration was like air, a great deal of his frustration centering on his wealthy patients.

He used his regular patients the way a rapist uses his victims, taking pleasure in drawing out their inner fears and then humiliating them. For rich people, he had discovered, love to be humiliated. It's a way of alleviating guilt over their selfishness and the conspicuousness of their consumption.

But at State, things were different. Mo said that psychiatrists specialized in their own disorders. At State, David dealt completely with schizophrenics, throwing himself into their lives and confusions with a depth and caring that stood in total counterpoint to the rest of his life. But was it the patients he was trying to cure, or himself?

He felt that Sara was like a bridge between his two selves. He wanted to help her, but the thought of a breakthrough in regression therapy was like a shot of B-12 in the ass. His own mind was a jumble of past and future occurrences, his own conception of time something that never traveled in a straight line.

He passed the capitol, its flat, domeless roof unfinished for nearly a hundred years. He drove Lincoln Boulevard, past the capitol hookers who peppered it, to old 66 then turned south, heading for the new money.

He had looked for Liz after rounds, but she wasn't in the building. She had been acting crazy, but his sister had never been famous for her stability. Well, if she had anything to say to him, she could catch up to him some other time. If she wanted to brave Bailey, it was at her own peril.

He took the scenic route home, through the old-money Nichols Hills neighborhood, and wondered how much trouble he'd be in for being late to Bailey's party. She was his third wife, and the best screamer of the lot. For some reason, she thought that communication could only occur in the upper decibel levels, somewhere between heavy metal music and atomic explosions. He didn't mind, really, except he wondered what effect it might have in the long haul on his hearing.

Of course, David's wives never seemed to be around for the long haul.

He passed through the stately houses of the long-term wealthy, places owned and operated by many of his old in-laws, then made the short trip down May Avenue toward his neighborhood, the kind built around golf courses by people who hadn't yet learned that money meant responsibility. Actually, there were three kinds of money in Oklahoma: old, new, and squirrelly. The squirrelly moneyed were by far the worst. They were all lower-case oil wildcatters who had made their fortunes in the kind of dirt real rich people hired gardeners to soil themselves with. The oilies had no respect for their cash. They built huge, barnlike palaces on the wrong end of town and drove their Lincolns as if they were Sherman tanks. The men drank beer in the bottle and their wives drank tall things of odd color. They all worshipped blue jeans and boots and built themselves stadium-sized clubs and dancehalls where they wouldn't have to take their cowboy hats off at the table.

David Wolf had never worn a cowboy hat. In the squirrelly money neighborhoods, that was tantamount to a confession of homosexuality.

He drove past the entrance to the golf course and up the long, winding hill that overlooked the seventeenth green to his house.

The wide, semicircular driveway was already filled with cars, forcing him to park out on the street. His house was huge, squared-off and boxlike, with a tall cement wall that closed in everything but the front. It looked alternately like a penitentiary or a squat skyscraper.

The party was in full swing when he opened the front door. Like the runoff from a leaky waterbed, it soaked the living room and spilled out into the backyard where, apparently, some sort of cookout was taking place. On surface, this one looked worse than most. It was a combination of Bailey's artsy-fartsy college literary friends and her south-side oil-patch buddies, leftovers from her own squirrelly money dabblings.

Like oil and watercolors, the two groups had segregated themselves, the artsy-fartsies inside to be near the bar, and the oilies in the backyard, apparently close to the great outdoors that had spawned them.

Like some perverse Tinker Bell, Diane Bailey Wolf flitted between the two groups, blond hair flowing behind her, hostess gown billowing, her eyes lit up like Buick headlights—that is, until she saw David.

He made a beeline for the bar, moving quickly through the crowd as she hurried to head him off at the pass. He beat her, though he had to practically knock over a roller-derby queen who called herself a poet to do it. He made it to the Spanish bar where Max, their pool man, stood looking uncomfortable in a starched white domestic's jacket.

"What'll it be, Mr. Wolf?" Max said, his eyes focusing on the tiles of the bartop.

"Scotch," David said, looking to see where Bailey was. Good, she had gotten held up talking to a squat, bald man dressed in a T-shirt and sports jacket. "Double 'em up, and hurry."

"Yes, sir," Max said, and held up a bottle. "Is this Scotch?"

"No," David said, frowning at the bottle of Canadian whiskey. 'The chubby bottle over there. What the hell are you doing back there, anyway?"

"Don't know," the weathered man said gruffly. "Guess the missus couldn't find any niggers quick enough."

"It's rough, all right," David agreed.

David stole a glance. Bailey had gotten away from the bald man and was moving toward him again. He took a breath and promised himself not to take it seriously. Bailey and the drink arrived at the same time.

"You're late," she said. "I've been worried."

He couldn't resist. "You haven't worried about anything since the invention of the fake Gucci bag."

"You rotten, lousy son of a bitch," she said in a hoarse whisper. "I hate your fucking ass."

"I'm fine, thank you," David said, taking a long drink. "The day was a little rough, but knowing I'd have my loving wife to come home to, I—"

"Blow it out your ass," she said. "Where the hell have you been?"

"I got held up at State," he said.

"On the night of my party," she said, building to a mini-crescendo, "the biggest night of my life, you desert me for . . . for . . . nonpaying clients!"

He nodded. "Guilty," he said, and drank again. "Though I thought that *last* week's party was the biggest night of your life."

Her eyes slanted and glazed, the prelude to the big tears, the gully-washer. "How could you?" she sobbed. "How badly do you hate me?"

"Oh, come on," he said, laying a hand on her arm.

She jerked away.

"Diane, please," he said, and finished the drink, nodding quickly to Max for a refill. "I couldn't help it. I didn't want to be late, honest to God. I'm a doctor. I have responsibilities."

"You're never late for your *own* parties," she said. "Isn't my life as important as yours? Your life matters to me, but mine is useless to you."

"Now, Diane. That's not fair . . ."

"You just think I'm stupid, don't you? A stupid, ugly cow. Well, Jeffery doesn't think I'm stupid. He thinks I'm a really talented writer."

"I'll be he doesn't think you're ugly, either," David said, and regretted it immediately. The second drink arrived and he began downing it as quickly as was humanly possible.

"What's that supposed to mean?" she said, louder now. "Is that what this is all about? Are you late because you're jealous. You petty son of a bitch!"

As if on cue, the bald man began walking toward them. Yeah, he had the look—detached savoir faire—that Bailey went for every time. This could only be Jeffery, the writing teacher.

David finished the drink and could sense the layer of numbness blissfully deadening his brain. Good. He was getting Baileyized. Another drink or two and he would be able to feel almost human in this house. The crazy part of it all was that he had known, really known, what she was before he married her and that he brought out the worst of it.

"You must be Dr. Wolf," the man said, sticking out a soft, pudgy hand. "I'm Jeffery Truitt."

David smiled at the man, then at Bailey, whose face had turned radiant and angelic again. "So, you're the writing teacher," he said, shaking hands.

"Oh, Jeffrey's more than a teacher," Bailey said, eyes sparkling. "He's a published author of prose and poetry. He wrote a novel about a Polish private detective who had stigmata."

"Maybe I've read it," David said, eyes wandering to the bar and his new drink. "What is it called?"

The man looked at the floor for a minute. "Well, I called it 'The Passion of a Haunted Man,'" he said, "because it was very metaphysically oriented. But the publishers never understood, and retitled it *The Power and the Gory*."

"Was there a sequel?" David asked politely.

"No," the man said with deep-seated vehemence. "I was too original for the New York establishment. I guess you're pretty proud of your lovely wife here."

"On occasion," David replied. "It depends on what she's done."

"She's quite a little writer." He patted her fraternally on the shoulder, his hand lingering a second too long.

"Oh . . ." Bailey said modestly. "David doesn't want to hear this."

"No!" David said loudly, getting a good start on the next drink. "Tell me about it. What's the big news?"

The man's face got serious and Diane's got serious. David tried, but it didn't work with him. "She's just finished a novel that rips the lid off political corruption in the state of Oklahoma."

David raised his eyebrows and stared at Bailey. "I thought you had promised your father you'd never write about him," he said.

"My father never took a dishonest dollar in his life," she said, forever the apologist over the fraud indictments of two hundred county commissioners.

"That's the problem," David replied. "It was the honest money he grabbed."

Just then, the doorbell rang.

"More company?" David said. "Goody!"

Bailey looked at him suspiciously, and the bell rang again. "You two get acquainted," she said. "I'll be right back."

She turned and walked off, David left staring at a man nearly a foot shorter than him. He got a good look at the top of the man's hairless skull, marveling at the ridges and valleys. "So, are you fucking my wife?" he asked Jeffery.

"I beg your pardon?" the little man said.

"No, you should've done that *before* you fucked her."

"I'm sure I don't know what you're talking about."

David smiled at the man. "My wife couldn't write a good obituary and you know it," he said. "She fucks all her teachers. It's the closest she gets to true art."

"Get out!" Diane screamed from the doorway. "Leave this instant!"

David turned to see Liz standing on the threshold looking determined, her handbag clutched tightly to her bosom.

"The gang's all here," David mumbled, and held up his drink. "Cheers."

He drained the Scotch and winked at Jeffery, who didn't know whether to crow or run for cover. David looked at him, shaking his head. "If you lay down with pigs," he said seriously, "you're going to get trichinosis. Think about it."

He picked up the remnants of his drink and moved to the door in time to hear an uncharacteristic gesture from his sister.

"I'm sorry for the things I've said to you in the past," Liz was saying. "I hope that you'll forgive me."

"When the sky rains money, sweety," Bailey said. "Now get out of here, you fucking lezzie, before I have Max toss you out."

"Don't you dare," David said, moving up to briefly hug Liz. "We have some family business to discuss."

Bailey turned angrily to him. "Don't push me, David," she said. "If that woman steps in this house, I'm leaving."

"What about your party?" David asked.

"Fuck the party."

"Be my guest," David said, reaching out a hand to draw Liz into the house. "When you do, make a videotape. I'll watch it later."

"I'm telling you not to do this," Bailey said.

David nodded, feeling too sober all at once. "I know," he said. "I'm sure you'll find a way to get even."

Davy Wolf walked taller because of his visions. Like someone who existed in the light of absolute certainty, he knew, really *knew,* the message of life, the pristine, crystal-clear heart of the matter.

It was simple and direct: people were stupid. They were stupid and selfish and devoid of any foresight when it came to the affairs of their planet and, indeed, their own species.

The white-robed doctors surrounded him on all sides, moving him rapidly down the caverns of State Hospital. He had explained to them the problems with life and with people, and they had responded with denial. He had shown them Truth and they had retaliated with arrogance. Doctors were as stupid as everyone else—perhaps more stupid, because along with the usual human failings, they thought they were God, too.

"It'll be fun," tall Dr. Morgan said, the smile on his face only. "You'll be supercharged and be able to run faster."

His mother and Jerry walked the long fake-marble halls with him, but they were kept outside the group of white, walking pillars, Naomi sobbing into a small lace handkerchief that was scented with jasmine.

The smell was of alcohol and Davy felt that everything he touched had come out of a refrigerator.

"It's the water," he said, staring up at their rubbery faces, trying to get them to listen. "The water will go eventually. It'll go everywhere, very slowly, but once it's gone, it's gone."

"You're going to feel a lot better after today," one of the pillars said.

"Oh, do you think so?" Naomi asked between sobs.

"Oh yes," Dr. Morgan said, moving his black-frame glasses higher on his nose. "This machine's the biggest breakthrough since the invention of tranquilizers."

"I feel fine," Davy said.

"This way, son," Dr. Morgan said, all but shoving him into a room.

"He just likes the attention," Jerry said, his arm around Naomi's hip, massaging gently.

"If there's nothing to drink," Davy said, "life dies—all life. We can stop that. If we all just show a little concern..."

"Here we are, Davy boy," a red-haired, red-faced man said. "In just a little while, all those bad dreams will be a thing of the past."

"They're not dreams," Davy said. "I can see...see the future."

Dr. Morgan lifted him to sit on a rubber-padded table, even though he was perfectly able to do that himself. There was something that troubled Davy about the man. It was as if he were some kind of professional maid, always trying to make sure everything was tidy and perfect.

"Nobody can see the future, son," he said, face fatherly, voice soothing. "We have enough trouble understanding the present, now, don't we?"

"But sir . . ."

Dr. Morgan squeezed his arm hard. "Don't we?"

"Yes, sir," Davy said and got real quiet, wondering why people had begun flinching when he talked and why they had taken to talking about him as if he weren't there.

He looked abound the room. It was all white and cold like everything else here. The table he sat on was directly in the center of the bare room; the only other thing in the whole place was a small machine that had two plastic knobs on the front and a needle gauge of some kind between them. The machine frightened him.

The men in white turned to Naomi and Jerry.

"You'll have to go now," said Dr. Morgan firmly. A command from Olympus. "Just leave everything in our hands."

"Come on," said Jerry, pulling Naomi by the arm. "We'll go get a drink and come back."

"Are you sure this is the right thing to do?" Naomi asked.

Dr. Morgan nodded confidently. "I assure you, Mrs. Wolf, that by the time we're finished with Davy, his problems with reality will be a thing of the past. Our therapy will rid him of all delusions."

"I don't need your old machine!" Davy called from the table. "I'm all right. I just . . . understand things, that's all."

The men in white all laughed, and Dr. Morgan, face fixed in a slight smile, hurried his mother out of the room, closing and locking the door after her.

He turned and walked to Davy. "Take your shirt and pants off," he said.

"It's cold," Davy said. "I don't want to."

Dr. Morgan smiled, then nodded to one of the other men. The aide, a lean Negro, moved to Davy and began unbuttoning the boy's shirt.

"This is really for the best, son," Dr. Morgan said, his eyes opened wide.

"What are you going to do?" Davy asked as the Negro pulled his shirt off and began working on his belt.

"You like to talk about the future," the man said. "Well, see that machine? It *is* the future. We'll hook you up to that thing and before you know it all the bad dreams will go away."

"They're not dreams," Davy said.

"Of course they are," Dr. Morgan said, with the same certainty that Davy had about things. The boy wondered if the doctor had heard a voice, too.

"If we could only take steps to not contaminate our water supplies, we can live on the surface for a long time to come. It's at the very least a matter of proper waste disposal. Do you know that even now canisters of nerve gas left over from World War Two are beginning to deteriorate and seep into water supplies. Without water, everything dies."

"It rained yesterday," the Negro said, slipping Davy's pants off right over his shoes. "In fact, it's been raining for weeks. I don't think we're running out."

"There's water," Davy said. "But what about the quality?..."

"You're going to have to lay down now," the Negro said, and pushed him prone on the table. The rubber padding was freezing and made him jump. All the men in white took that as a bad sign and rushed over to him, three of them holding him down.

"Lemme up!" Davy yelled. "What are you doing?"

"Now, take it easy, son," Dr. Morgan said. "No need to get excited. Besides, no one outside of this room can hear you."

"Where's my mother?"

"You'll see her soon," the doctor said and walked to the machine. He picked up a metal ring with wires dangling from it and walked back, bending down to be close to Davy's face. "This little thing is going to help make you normal again, Davy. Won't that be nice?"

"I'm normal already," Davy said, struggling now under the confinement. "Let me up!"

"This is like a wonder drug, Davy, and State Hospital is one of the first places to have it." The good doctor fitted the chromium ring on Davy's head, adjusting it down to fit him. Two metal pads stuck out slightly from the ring and rested, secure, on each side of his temple. "This will chase that other person inside of you away. Won't that be nice?"

"I need to warn everyone about the water," Davy said.

All the men laughed.

"Life is a fine and wonderful thing. You need to start enjoying it. President Kennedy and the scientists are going to put us on the Moon in a few years. They certainly have the future under control. You'll understand."

"Bad things have always happened," Davy said. "No one can protect us from us."

Dr. Morgan straightened and walked to the machine, nodding quickly to the other white suits, all of whom increased their pressure on him, forcing him tighter onto the table.

He became really frightened then. What were they doing? "Momma!" he screamed. "Momma!"

One of the men shoved a small rubber hose into his mouth, gagging him, and told him to bite down.

He saw the doctor's hands reach out to turn both knobs on the machine at the same time. He saw the needle begin to rise, then his insides lit up like a million flashbulbs popping—hold it, I think you're going to like this picture! There was no pain, no sensation of any kind. He was aware of his body coming up off the table despite all the men trying to hold him down. And there was a scream, lost somewhere within the vortex that swallowed him down, down, down into the numbing darkness where there were no dreams and no futures.

Hersh's vacant body sat relaxed on the folding chair, his head lolled back making his Adam's apple hump prominently up from his neck. His face was slack, eyes rolled up showing only the whites. He could have been dead. Silv wished he were.

She stared at him for several seconds, letting her own mind settle down, then used her index finger to shove the guidance button on her chair in the direction of the lab table.

Her breathing was raspy, despite the steady trickle of oxygen that hissed into her nose from the canister strapped onto the chair—too much excitement. She had to try and calm down enough to get the RNA inhibitor into him.

Her wheeled chair moved silently up to the low table. The room was tiny, barely a cubicle, the dirty cinder-block walls all closing in on her. This was insane. She'd bring Hersh back, then stop this nonsense before everything went to pieces.

Quad Ops wouldn't understand—this was too large for them—but she'd worry about that when the time came. One thing she was sure of: they'd never get the comps on this one. She was too smart to be convinced and too old to be frightened.

The key hung around her neck. She tugged at it, breaking the string, then reached for the lockbox, the external skeleton that supported her body creaking slightly under her wildly shaking hands.

With a great deal of effort, she got the key in the lock and opened the metal box, the syringes within lined up in a neat little row. She reached in for the darker syringes of diaminopurine, her grasper locking around one and clamping solid the way her withered gray hands never could.

There was no time to lose. She wheeled quickly to Hersh and injected him in the carotid artery of the neck in order to get the RNA-destroying fluid to his brain as quickly as possible.

She wheeled backward then, bumping the table behind her, and watched. The reaction began within seconds. Color seeped back into Hersh's deeply pitted face as life returned, in waves, to his body. He shook his head against consciousness, the dreamer not wanting to awaken. A word squeezed hollowly from his lips, almost as if it were echoing through a cave: "Nooooooo!"

He jumped in the chair, snapping straight up, his eyes wide and angry. "No!" he said again. "What am I doing here?"

She regarded him warily across the short distance that separated them. His breath came in short gasps as his own oxygen bottle hissed into his nose. He was tensed, a nightmare waiting to happen, and she realized that in her haste to bring him back she hadn't dwelled enough on *his* reactions.

He stood, hovering menacingly over her. "Send me back right now!" he demanded, each word a shout in the enclosed room.

"No," she said evenly. "The experiments are finished. I thank you for your cooperation, Mr. Hersh, but I think it is time to terminate our relationship. I'll get in touch with your unit and you can—"

"No!" Hersh screamed. "What's wrong with you, Silv? Would you trade *this* for all that we could have?" He gestured around the cubicle; his face settled into a posture of disgust. "The whole world is ours."

"No, it's not," Silv replied, afraid of his temper, of his lack of control. "These have been simple, psychotropic experiments in aggression retardation. The other thing is merely a side effect."

He laughed then, throwing back his nearly square head. "You might have gotten yourself a hothead out of detention for your 'experiments,' but I'm no idiot." He walked a circle around her, making her feel small and trapped. Control was Silv's specialty. Take it away and she was merely a frail, frightened creature. "You're old, Silv, ready to die—but not me. I want to live up there on the surface. I want to breathe real air, eat red meat and walk in the rain . . ."

"And kill," Silv said harshly, ". . . and change things."

He stooped to get in her face. "So, that's it. You don't want me to bugger things up. Well, let me tell you something about that." He straightened, his eyes searching the room. She could call for help, but feared letting anyone else know what was going on. She realized now, too late, that she should have hidden the syringes before bringing Hersh back.

The man pointed a stubby finger at her. "Why should I care about changing things? The assholes who destroyed the surface with their insecticides and their chemical and atomic wastes sure as water never cared about how they were changing Earth for us! So, generation after generation, we burrow like moles and live with the pain, pain caused by our ancestors. And we regulate our bodies with drugs because we were never meant to live like this. Well, I want what they have—what we're all entitled to—and I mean to get it."

"You're not thinking, Mr. Hersh," Silv said, trying a different tack. "Suppose you change something around back there that would affect your ancestors? You could, in fact, uncreate yourself."

Hersh laughed again. "I'll take that chance." He leaned down to her again, putting a thick hand on either arm of her wheelchair. "Now. Tell me where the juice is. I've got an appointment and I'm already a thousand years late."

"There isn't any more," she said, but her eyes darted quickly to the lab table and gave her away.

He smiled, sputtering, and gave her chair a push. She slid several feet and banged hard into the wall, waves of pain washing over her as she felt ribs crack with the impact.

He moved to the low table, drawing a vial of clear liquid out of the box and holding it up. He relaxed immediately, drawing the syringe up near his peeling lips to kiss it. "I've only got one problem now," he said.

"You're right," she replied, moaning, clamping her right arm tight against her ribs. "How much time you'll spend in detention over this outrage."

"That's not my problem," he said. "You wouldn't dare tell anyone about this. Just think what Quad Ops could do with something like your magic potion. No, that's not the problem. The problem is you."

"What do you mean?" she said, voice small.

"I mean that as long as you're alive, you'll bring me back."

She straightened in the chair, her pain telling her how serious he was. She could see the determination in his face, the deadly determination. "All right," she said, a wave of pain making her flinch. "Go ahead. I promise I won't bring you back anymore."

"Too late for that, Silv," he said, and gently laid the syringe on the lab table. He chuckled softly. "I've lately learned some lessons in self-assertion."

He began looking around, she didn't know why, but when he bent to the lab table and began unscrewing one of the legs, she knew it was a weapon he was after.

"Please, Hersh," she said. "I'm your friend. How can you?..."

"Yeah," Hersh said, pulling the leg off, the table still standing on three. "When you pulled me out of de-ten and put that stuff in my arm, we were friends, too. You didn't know what that could've done to me."

She closed her eyes and nodded, letting her head fall forward, chin resting on chest. It was useless to argue any more.

It comes to all. It comes to all.

She could hear him standing above her, hear the hiss of his air. Strangely, she was thinking not of herself, but of a young boy who was frightened of her world.

"I'd like to tell you I'm sorry, Silv," she heard him say. "But, to be honest, I couldn't care less."

Senses acute, she heard the rush of air as he swung the metal bludgeon. There was no sensation at all. She drifted—a second, an eternity—a tuneless melody bringing her back.

She opened her eyes and was looking sideways at Hersh's legs. She was on the floor, her own blood spread everywhere. She was dead and knew it. How long before her body confirmed the fact she could only imagine.

Hersh was humming happily, a melody without tone, as he destroyed the syringes one by one, smashing them on the table.

He walked back to his chair and sat down, the clear syringe in his hand. He filled her line of vision. He smiled at her open eyes, saluting that which was dead in her. "For a smart lady, Silv, you sure were dumb." He injected himself in the neck, grimacing with the entry. "Maybe you were just too damned old to remember what it was like to enjoy life."

His eyes fluttered then, his body sagging in the chair. He sighed, a long, relaxed outbreath, and was gone.

She lay that way, watching his body, waiting for her own to take its final journey. Her thoughts weren't profound, nor were they particularly directed. A variety of life experiences slipped through the memory holes, losses mostly, emotions gone beyond recapture, pleasures and opportunities wasted. It was a melancholy death as these things went, the violence of it in counterpoint to its reality.

A tear filled her eye, a bitter tear that burned. She wasn't crying. Could it be blood?

Her conscious mind began to jumble, images unconnecting and restating themselves. Another tear in her eye.

It wasn't tears or blood. It was something dripping off the edge of the lab table onto her face. Though she couldn't move, she could blink, blink the tears in and hold them.

She was filled with a floating sensation.

The want of logic annoys. Too much logic bores. Life eludes logic, and everything that logic alone constitutes remains artificial and forced.

—André Gide

David Wolf held a deathgrip on his Scotch as he watched, from his second-floor study, Bailey's oil-patch buddies whooping it up in the backyard. They had had enough beer, and the barbecue sauce was running down their chins, so they had just entered the next mandatory phase of any oily party—they were pushing one another into the pool, careful to remove their cowboy hats first.

David shook his head, smiling. Max would have a field day tomorrow scooping change off the bottom. "You've got nerve, I'll give you that," he said, then turned to face his sister. "Not many can engage in a firefight with Bailey and walk away unscathed."

"You're drunk," Liz said. She had taken his easy chair in the corner, and was huddled up in it, looking very small and breakable.

"Drunk!" he yelled, jumping up on his desk chair. "Of course I'm drunk!"

He jumped to the top of the large walnut desk, papers and pen sets flying all over the room. "I'm deliciously, exuberantly, painstakingly drunk and I don't care who knows it. I'm so drunk, I think that you should get drunk, too. At least we'd be in the same world."

He jumped off the desk, stumbling over an antique wooden chair and falling, with the chair, to the floor.

"Jesus Christ!" He jumped to his feet, examining the chair from all angles, breathing a sigh of relief. "If that had broken," he said, looking deadly serious, "Bailey would have taken it out of my butter-and-egg money." He sat on the newly examined chair and began looking around for his drink. "I'm almost drunk enough to think that all this is somehow natural and right."

"It's not," Liz said.

David got up and retrieved his drink from the windowsill. "I know," he said, sitting back down. "You remember how Mother used to scrimp for months to save enough to take us to fancy restaurants?"

Liz thought for a moment, smiled. "We'd dress up and pretend we were rich and act snooty to the waiter."

"We'd send things back and make them recook them."

"We'd treat them like shit, then leave a big tip."

They both laughed, David taking a drink. "Hell, I'm still pretending," he said.

"We have something of grave importance to discuss," Liz said.

David reached over and set his drink on the desk, bending to begin picking up the stuff he had scattered on the floor. "I'll be honest with you, little sister," he said. "I don't think there's anything of any importance in this whole fucking world."

Liz made herself smaller in the chair. "Do you remember when you were sick when you were thirteen?"

"Not much," he said. "I know something happened to me that reached a peak during the Cuban missile crisis . . . I remember that very clearly . . . but after that, several months after that, is all a blur."

"You were given shock treatments," Liz said.

"I don't believe that," David replied, and took a drink. "Had I been sick enough mentally, they would have never let me into medical school."

"Nevertheless, it happened."

"Is this what you wanted to talk about?" David said. "For the sake of argument, I'll agree that I was sick and had shock treatments. Now what?"

"You weren't sick," Liz said.

David stood. She was beginning to irritate him, the same thing that happened every time she talked about the old days. He walked to Liz, taking her hand and drawing her out of the chair. "What the hell are you getting at?" he asked, anger edging his words. "Just say it out."

They stood there for several seconds, staring into one another's eyes. The room was quiet and elegant all around them while the yahoos from out back drifted in and out like the calling of distant gulls.

Liz tightened her lips, seemed to win some inner battle, then spoke. "You were given shock treatments because you heard a voice inside you, a voice that showed you the future. I'm the one who put that voice in your head. I was trying to calm you down because you were frightened, but I didn't realize the effects a glimpse of my world would have on you."

"My sister, the ventriloquist," he said.

"You should have figured it out by now, David," she replied calmly. "I'm not your sister."

"I've got it now," David said, tweaking her on the cheek. "You've discovered some long-lost diary that Mother kept. In it, she talked about my illness and the fact that you were actually a foundling." He grabbed her in a bear hug. "Congratulations! You're not infected with the insane Wolf genes." He picked her up and began swinging her around.

She screamed—shrieked. "Put me down! My God! Put me down!"

He set her back on the floor and she was trembling. The

terror in her voice was real. He'd been swinging her around like that for as long as he could remember.

"What's going on?" he said.

She put fingers to her temples. "I—I'm sorry," she said, and sat back down, shrinking in the chair again. "It's an old habit pattern, I—I can't explain right now."

"You're serious about all this, aren't you?" he asked.

"If I tell you my whole story, will you promise not to laugh at me until I'm completely finished?"

He moved away from her, automatically sitting behind the desk. Somewhere inside his brain he was getting into his professional mode. Something was, indeed, wrong with Liz. "I promise I won't laugh at all," he said.

The room seemed too large now. Wood paneling and shag carpet a length of miles between them, the floor-to-ceiling bookcases awkward distractions.

"Come sit here," he said, directing her to the chair he had almost broken.

She nodded absently, her mind wrapped up in the words she was trying to say. She moved to the new chair, turned it to face him.

"I'm usually a direct woman," she said. "Walking around things is a new phenomenon to me."

"Then, be direct," he said. "I'm listening."

"My name is Silv," Liz said. "I live in Quad-14, deep under the surface of the Earth in an area you know as Surinam. There are a number of quads in my geographical area, but we think we may be the only humans left alive on the planet."

"Why is that?" David asked.

"The environment cannot support life," she said simply. "The only fresh water left on Earth comes from snows high atop the Andes Mountains. The quads are built on the banks of an underground river that is fed from there. We have lived this way for nearly a millennium. We love, we hate, we wage our little wars to feel important, we feel confined. We do all the things that you and yours do."

David watched her carefully. She wasn't kidding. He began to worry for her. "When did you begin...living in this world, Liz, I mean, Silv?"

"Please don't analyze me, Doctor," she replied, eyes hard. "We don't have the time for it."

"Fair enough," he said. "Go on with your story."

He wouldn't be able to treat her himself. Maybe Mo would take a look at her. He was more understanding than most.

"I work for Quad Ops—that's the government. I design psychotropic drugs for them that help keep the population well balanced chemically. We don't use psychiatry in the quads, Dr. Wolf . . ."

"David," he said.

"David. We maintain a certain . . . balance in our society, and drugs are a necessary component of that."

"When you talk about psychotropic drugs," David said, "you're speaking about such things as Thorazine . . . or Mellaril?"

Liz frowned. "No, not exactly." She thought a minute. "Have you ever heard of a drug called LSD?"

"You know I have, Liz," he replied. "We took it together once in the late sixties."

She nodded, satisfied. "We work on the electrical synapses. LSD is a psychotomimetic derived from ergonovine, the basic research on which forms the core of our culture. In fact, another ergonovine derivative is the reason I'm here."

"Go on."

"I was working on the channeling of aggression. In other words, I was trying to develop a short-term drug that would curb the soldier's aggressiveness when he wasn't on the battlefield, yet not render him docile when he needed to be aggressive."

He watched her in disbelief, her delusion far more advanced than anything he'd previously encountered. She spoke with such authority, such knowledge of her subject, that it was difficult *not* to believe her.

"I spent several years developing some threads," she said. "Finding the proper beta blockers is a hit-and-miss effort at best. I finally got something that looked good in the comps, and they gave me a soldier to work with who had been put in de-ten for fighting."

"A subject for your experiment," David said.

Liz nodded. "Something went wrong," she said. "Now bear with me. Here is the strange part."

Here is the strange part, David thought and looked at his drink. It was sitting forlornly on the corner of the desk. He thought about reaching for it, but basic professionalism kept him from it.

Liz leaned up, putting her arms on the desk and fixing

David with her stare. "The drug didn't work the way it was supposed to. Somehow, it managed to open up the gates of Time."

David laughed. He couldn't help himself. "I'm sorry," he said quickly. "You'll have to admit, this is getting pretty far out. How could a drug affect time?"

"Well, to begin with, there's no such thing as time," Liz said.

"How so?"

"Time is a concept we invented to help us move around in our world. Time is meaningless quantity, a simple function of the speed of light."

"Einstein's theory," David said, fascinated despite himself.

"Time itself, as a quantity that is measurable and exists, I have proven wrong by being here today. But bear with me. What is a memory, David, where does it come from?"

"No one knows," David replied. "It's past information held within our cells, our genes, that we can sometimes recall and sometimes not. No one knows where or how it's stored."

"Why do we remember certain things and forget others?"

David shook his head. "I don't know."

Liz reached down to the floor and picked up her handbag, withdrawing from it a number of syringes, filled with liquids. Half the liquids were clear, the other half reddish colored.

"Where did you get those?" he asked.

"I took them from the hospital while you were making your rounds. I used a vacant lab to mix up my batch of drugs, then filled the syringes."

"You . . . you stole this stuff?"

She nodded, holding up one of the clear vials. "If you take my drug," she said, "you can travel into the past, as far as you'd like to go for as long as you'd like."

"Travel . . . how?"

She smiled. "I don't know much more than you do about the reasons, but I've got a theory. You see, each cell in our body contains all the information it needs to create a new human being. This information is as old as the species. In fact, while in the fetus state, we go through changes that suggest all the evolutionary levels from the dawn of time."

"Yes," David said. This was weird. Liz, who had bragged about the *D*s she had gotten in science as a kid, was now quite happily advancing genetic evolutionary theories like she was born with them in her mouth.

"When we hear something, or see something, or read something, it filters through the brain's electrical apparatus and gets compartmentalized someplace. All the information must go in; it's only in the retrieval that we have problems. Well, my drug does away with all that. When you take it, you remember, quite literally, *everything*. You remember everything that you've ever known or done, you remember all the things your father and mother had ever done up until the time you were born. You remember what their fathers and mothers knew, and what *their* parents knew. You can remember, in the simple clarity of perfect and total recall, *everything* about your bloodline, all the way back to the primal sea."

This time David did reach for his drink, finishing it with one long pull. "Okay," he said. "I'm mesmerized. I have no idea what's going on here, but let's talk for a second. Now, you're telling me that you somehow have invented a drug that affects the amino acids, the RNA, that carries memory, and that it can induce a state of total recall that not only encompasses the life of the taker, but also can open up the memories of previous generations?"

"Ad infinitum," Liz said, smiling. "You're quicker than I had hoped. You can travel your bloodlines in your mind."

David put his hands in the air. "That's great," he said, "but . . . Silv, it doesn't explain why you are sitting here, in my study, in my sister's body."

"I'm not . . . really doing that," she replied. "Stay with me. As a professional in the field of the mind, tell me what reality is."

"Real reality or philosophical reality?"

Liz smiled. "Both."

David loosened his tie and leaned back in his chair. If Liz was totally insane, which she certainly seemed to be, she was far more interesting as a psychotic delusional than she was as a sane person.

"Well, to any individual living on the planet, reality is the solid ground and the life they see around them, but medically, it's a lot more complex than that. A great deal of what we think of as real is created right up here." He pointed to his head.

"The human mind has evolved to three times its original size during the course of the species' existence. Speculation currently holds that the reason for this was the creation of language to express our world, then expansion to include all

the abstract notions that encompass that expression. Reality is
a result of that evolution. What we create in our brains, is
what we call 'real.' "

"But is it?"

"In a sense, yes," he said, beginning to get her point.
"We all believe things that aren't true; we remember events
that never happened, or remember them differently than they
happened. When we read a book of fiction, we create that
reality in the most literal sense. The book will be real, every
bit as real as the other information we take into our brains."

"This is all the result of the smattering of things that we
remember," she said. "Yet the realities we create can be very
strong."

"Of course," he said. "That's what psychiatry is all
about, readjusting realities."

"Suppose you had absolute recall. Suppose that you could
remember *exactly* the way events transpired and bring that
reality in its full detail to the forefront of your mind."

"In a sense, you'd be recreating it."

"In a very large sense, David Wolf," Liz said, her face
rapt. "I remembered you, and I am here."

"You've come back to my time," David whispered.

"I *am* your time," she said. "I've created it in my mind. I
gave you a vision when you were thirteen and it's infected
every second you've lived since. Do you know how long ago
that was?"

David did some quick calculating. "Twenty-three years,"
he said.

She shook her head. "To me it was a couple of hours ago,
and most of that time has been wasted here in your sister's
body. Remember Einstein and forget time. Moments are only
moments while you are living them."

David stood slowly, his mind a jumble. He walked past the
window. Outside, two of the oilies had hoisted their wives on
their backs and were running around the yard playing chick-
en while most of the others, fully dressed, splashed happily in
the pool. Some of the artsy-fartsies had come into the backyard
to study the spectacle.

He walked to his bookshelf, the battleground of his life.
There, Bertrand Russell and George Bernard Shaw nestled
comfortably next to psychic and occult literature, philosophy
played tag with science, Reason slept with Religion. There
was a section on death, a subject of fascination to him his

whole life. And then there were the books and pamphlets, all
jammed in together, all talking about the same topic, the
dwindling water supply. Something, *something,* was going on
here.

He turned abruptly to her. "Why?" he said at last. "Why
have you come here?"

"I need your help," Liz replied, as if it were the most
natural request in the world.

"Bingo!" he screamed, and laughed loudly. "You've broken down the boundaries of time and space, traversed the
bloodlines of the ages, inhabited the body of my sister, and
you need *my* help!"

"You, of course, don't believe any of this," she said
quietly.

He walked up to her and put an arm on her shoulder. "I
think you've shaken me up like nothing has ever done before,
I'll say that. You've known right where to go for me. You're
apparently more brilliant than anyone ever imagined, Liz, but
you're not a time traveler. No one is. But you've come to the
right place for help."

"Give me ten more minutes," she said, shrugging his hand
off her shoulder.

He went back to his seat, wishing he had another drink. On
top of everything else, now he had a crazy sister to contend
with.

She started right in, undaunted. "The man I experimented
with has gone into the past and refuses to come back."

"What does that mean?"

She shrugged. "I don't know. He's currently inhabiting the
body of a distant ancestor who's a military leader."

"Do you know the name?"

She nodded. "He is called Napoleon Buonaparte at first,
then changes the spelling of the last name to Bonaparte to
sound more like those he lives with."

"Napoleon?" David said.

"You've heard of him, then?"

David laughed. "Of course."

Liz nodded. "Good, that will help. This is all new, this
time traveling. Up until now, I've only just inhabited bodies
for short times and never interacted with the host body for
fear of changing something."

"You mean, changing history?"

"Yes," she replied, curling into the chair. "I've tried to

get Hersh to come back, but he refuses. I'm afraid he'll . . . do something.''

"What's that got to do with me?''

"You're a psychiatrist,'' she said, gently fingering the syringes she had laid on the desk. "We can't force him back, but perhaps you can talk to him, analyze him, help him to realize that he can't stay where he is.''

"Why me, though? Why pick me?''

"I don't have that many direct ancestors who are psychiatrists, for starters,'' she said, looking intently at the syringes as if she were trying to make her mind up about them. "You've understood all we've discussed . . .''

"And,'' he said when she sputtered.

She tore her gaze from the syringes and met his eyes. "And I've already screwed you up, haven't I?''

He reached for one of the syringes. She jumped, startled, face fearful. Then she backed off, letting him pick one up and study it. "You're holding something back,'' he said.

She responded curtly. "I've told you enough.''

"What's in here?'' he asked, shaking the mixture.

"The drug,'' she said. "You must promise me not to analyze it.''

"And if I do?'' he asked.

"The results will be on your head, not mine.''

He picked up one of the darker vials. "What's in here?''

"2, 6-diaminopurine,'' she said. "It's an RNA inhibitor and acts as an antidote. If you ever want to come back, think yourself to the present and inject it.''

"Wouldn't the drug wear off by itself?'' he asked, setting it gingerly back on the desk.

"You could live for eons of other time before that would happen,'' she said. "Will you help me?''

"If you're asking me if I'll put that stuff in my veins without finding out what it is, the answer is no.''

"You'll change your mind,'' she said.

"I doubt it,'' he replied.

"Your life is at a crux,'' Liz said. "An event will transpire tonight that will help you change your mind. That's why I'm here. When you take the drug, meet me where your father heard about Pearl Harbor. I'm leaving now. There is much to do.''

Exactly then, Liz's eyes began to flutter, her face paling to milk white. Then she slipped off the chair and fell to the floor.

Carla James laboriously cranked the large clockworks, tightening the spring that would turn the new Fresnel lens at the Portland Head lighthouse. One tight cranking would hold the lens for all night, a good thing since Carla was small enough that even that was a major effort. It had been thought, when they installed the lens, that she would have to vacate the light in favor of a man, someone stronger, but she had worked to build up those muscles, surprising even herself when she was able to crank it the first time unaided.

She stood, a hand to her strained back. The new lens was a godsend, its bull's-eyed glass prisms magnifying the oil fire-light, enabling the light to be seen as far as twenty miles away. Not that it would do any good tonight: a spring mist was already rolling low on the Maine waters, threatening to blow in thick and heavy, and even Mr. Fresnel's invention plus the fog bell would be useless in the fog.

She opened the door to the outside ramp, taking her logbook with her. A hundred feet in the air, she stared out over a wild and empty sea, salt breeze whipping her face, fluttering the many layers of her dress around her stockinged calves.

Carla had once been fearful of the great height of her lonely perch, but that had been long ago. Now it was her pedestal, her platform upon which to view the world. Before her lay the infinite sea, raging wildly against the stoic, pitted rocks of shore, waging never-ending battle with always fresh resources. To her right, in the distance, the sleepy city of Portland prepared, as she did, for the approaching night. She glanced at her logbook. There was nothing expected by her tonight. Good. Already the encroaching mist had totally obscured the horizon.

"Is anybody there?" came a voice from far below, echoing up the spiral stairs. An involuntary chill made her shudder.

She walked back into the light, moving to stare down the length of the stairs, to the face smiling up at her like a sunnyside egg so far below.

"May I come up?" the man called, and without waiting for an answer began the long climb.

"No," she called down. "Come back another time."

The man laughed, paying her no heed. He whistled a sea chantey as he climbed, Carla looking frantically around her for an exit, or an answer. Neither were available to her.

"Please go away!" she called.

"I'm coming up." His voice was a little harder this time, and a great deal closer.

She circled her enclosed shell twice, thrice. Trapped in her own tower, she could only wait. He reached her within minutes. He smiled broadly as his head crested the top of the stairs.

"A long climb," he said.

"Who are you?" she asked.

"It doesn't matter," he replied, climbing up to stand beside the light, studying it casually. He had the bearing of a sailor and wasn't from Portland. He nodded toward the light. "Never saw one of these up close . . . only from the other side." He indicated the sea.

"Your name," she said. "Your name. Is it Silas Luper?"

He cocked his head. "Now, how could you know that?"

"I've known . . . and I've dreaded your coming for years."

The man looked at her, his eyes taking her full measure. She felt embarrassment creep up her neck, then fear as he moved toward her, his eyes dark and intent, his lips dry.

"What are—" she began, then he lunged at her, grabbing, his hands running over her body.

"No!" she screamed, pounding his back with ineffectual fists made strong from cranking the Fresnel lens. He laughed, moving against her.

She stopped fighting, easing in his arms. Then, as he released his tight grip, she shoved away from him hard, jumping to her feet.

Carla tried to make the stairs down, but he got there first, blocking them off. She ran outside, right up to the rail, and she was staring straight down at the spray-foaming rocks far below.

His hands were on her, spinning her around. She looked deeply into his eyes. "Could you love one already dead?" she asked.

He pulled her away from the rail, laughing loud, and drew her to the floor beside the Fresnel lens.

Liz sat on the floor of David's study, trembling in his arms, tears streaking her cheeks. "W—what happened to me?" she asked in a small voice.

"I honestly don't know," David replied, holding her tight, comforting. "What are you feeling right now?"

"I'm feeling silly on the floor," she replied, pulling a bit away from him and wiping at her eyes. "Help me up?"

He got up, weaving, still drunk, and reached out an arm to her. She hoisted herself to her feet and stood, a hand to her head. "There was someone else inside of me," she said, "controlling my actions."

"Do you remember any of it?"

He led her to the couch and sat beside her, a protective hand on her shoulder. She was trembling, truly frightened. "It was like a dream," she said, puzzlement denting her features. "I was there, in there, but it was like I was someone else or someone else was controlling my actions." She shook her head, long brown hair sliding across her face. "God, do you think I *wanted* to come here and have to face down Bailey? I just had no choice."

"What makes you say it was someone else?" he asked.

"Another life, other . . . memories were in my brain. They're fading now . . . Christ, David. I could sure use a drink."

"In a minute," he said. "We need to talk about this while it's fresh. Are you game?"

She nodded, taking a deep breath. "Just for a minute," she replied, then looked at him, her eyes liquid and frightened. "Am I crazy?"

"Do you feel crazy?"

"Don't psychoanalyze me!"

David laughed. "That's what the other person said, too."

"She's my descendant, isn't she?"

He stared at her. "You believe it's real, don't you?" he asked quietly. "I mean everything: the possession, the revelations about my childhood, the story about the drug—all of it."

She tightened her lips. "Does that mean I *am* crazy?"

He hugged her, feeling a blood bond that had long ago been covered over by many layers of emotional scar tissue. The closeness made him uneasy. "Of course not. What do you remember about the woman inside you?"

"Her feelings mostly," Liz replied, and leaned her head back on the couch, relaxing somewhat. "Apprehension, fear concerning her role in all this. She comes from a bleak place. Her world—our world . . . is the culmination of all that has gone before. People from her time look upon themselves as the suffering children, condemned through the guilt of the fathers. Silv's world is every dire prediction you've ever heard about the future. It all came true; every lousy thing we ever did is mirrored in our future.''

He stood, confused, and walked to the desk. Whether or not he wanted to believe what had just taken place, he still had a piece of physical evidence—the syringes were lying on the desktop. He picked one up and held it up for her. ''Where did these come from?''

''Silv told you,'' she said. ''We found an empty lab at State and she mixed up some chemicals.''

''Then you did steal this stuff?''

She shrugged. ''I didn't want to. Do you believe me?''

He stared down at the syringe, realizing that the answer to all of his questions resided in the clear fluid that shimmered within the glass tube. ''How can I believe you?'' he asked. ''You've come to me with the impossible. You've brought me something that no rational human being could ever believe. On the other hand, how can I *not* believe you? What has transpired here tonight is totally outside of my experience. *Something* is going on—but what?''

''You'll know soon enough,'' Liz replied, standing tentatively. ''Silv said that something will happen tonight.''

''Do you know that it is?'' he asked.

She looked at the floor. ''Yes.''

He moved to her, taking her by the shoulders. ''What?''

She continued staring down. ''No,'' she said. ''I won't tell you. That would ruin everything.''

He moved to his desk, getting into the top drawer with his paper clips and stamps, pulling out paper and envelope and shoving them across the desk to her. ''Write it down and seal it. We'll check it later.''

She took the pen from his desk set and did what he asked, sealing the envelope when she was through. ''Maybe I should leave,'' she said. ''I've caused enough problems tonight.''

''Nonsense,'' he said, taking the envelope from her and placing it in his desk drawer. ''I promised you a drink. The least I can do is follow through like a good host.''

''Or like a good doctor keeping the patient under observation.''

His eyes lit up. ''Something like that.''

''Okay,'' she answered. ''But I want to avoid Bailey if I can. I've had enough strange experiences for one night.''

''That's fine by me,'' he said. ''We'll sneak down to the kitchen, then get the booze and sneak back up here.''

She hugged him quickly. "Maybe we're both crazy," she said. He nodded broadly, smiling, but inside his mind was spinning. He had two choices. Either his sister was telling the truth or she was the most advanced psychotic he'd ever seen. Neither solution made sense. Had she been sick, it seems he would have recognized it a long time ago. If she were telling the truth, it meant that the entire world had just been turned upside down. But things like that didn't happen, did they, and certainly not to people like him.

They left the study and moved down the long, dark stretch of hallway leading to the back stairs and finally to the kitchen.

"I don't mean to fight with your wives," Liz said as they made their way along the hall. "I can just never seem to help myself. You're so talented, so . . . deserving. But you always marry bitches who don't appreciate you."

"Correction," David said, turning on the stairway light and starting down. "I always marry *rich* bitches who don't appreciate me."

"You're not happy," she said.

"Who is?" he replied, stepping into the large kitchen. "You've never married. Are you happy?"

She looked him straight in the eye and shook her head, no. "Our momma didn't raise us to be happy."

"She raised us to look out for ourselves," he snapped, surprised at his own vehemence. "She did all right."

She held his stare. "You wanna talk or drink?" she said.

"Drink," he replied.

The kitchen was modern, with a large chopping-block table set in the center of the room and lots of stainless-steel fixtures and mixing utensils that were never used hanging on the walls. Through the window he could see the party still going strong outside. The artsy-fartsies had joined the oilies now and they were all undoubtedly discussing the realms of higher mathematics. A bottle of good Scotch, the kind he didn't give to company, was nestled on a small shelf above the stainless-steel refrigerator. He took it down and poured them each a glass. "You think I should take the drug, don't you?" he asked.

"I believe my vision," she said, "so I believe in the drug. But whether or not you want to commit yourself to helping Silv is entirely up to you."

"What if I don't take it?" he asked, handing her the drink.

"I don't know what," she answered, and drank the entire glass. "I really should go."

"No," he said forcefully. "You just don't want to be around when . . . it happens."

"Bailey and I hate one another," Liz said. "God knows, it's probably my fault. But my being around here is not going to help anything."

He poured them both another drink, the renewed influx of alcohol loosening him up again. Hell, he'd just flow with it. What difference could anything make?

"Let's take the bottle upstairs," Liz said, finishing the second drink.

David took a long drink right from the bottle before recapping it and sticking it under his arm. "Lead on—" he began, but was interrupted by the telephone ringing.

He turned his head. A red wall phone hung near them in the kitchen. Funny, he had lived here three years without realizing there was a phone in the kitchen. Shrugging a question to Liz, she nodded unhappily, not wanting to meet his eyes.

The phone rang a second time. He moved to it and answered.

"Wolf's nut house."

"David? It's me, Mo Frankel."

"Well, hi, Mo, I—"

"Just listen for a minute," the doctor said. His voice sounded excited and agitated. "I want to say this before I change my mind. That tape you gave me, the recording of Sara, I just finished listening to it and doing some checking. I—I didn't realize how . . . real it would seem. Do you know what she was talking about?"

"No," David answered. "Can't say that I do."

"It rang a bell with me," Mo said. "I went back and started checking history . . . my history, Jewish history. The event she was referring to actually took place. September third, 1189. After the coronation of Richard I, who they called the Lion-Heart, there was a massacre of Jews in London. The Cheape Market marked the edge of the Jewish quarter at the time. The Jews built their houses of stone so the Christians couldn't come for them, but it didn't stop the celebrants from burning down the whole quarter, and a good bit of Christian London while they were at it. Everything fits, including the suicide. Back then, Jews would rather have killed themselves than submit to Christian indignities.''

David opened the bottle and drank again. ''Are you saying that you believe I have a real case of regression to a past life?''

''I don't know what I'm saying,'' Mo replied. ''We've got to talk about this, to interview Sara some more. I don't know how she could have gotten this information. She's been at State for forty years.''

''David,'' Liz whispered harshly, and pointed out the window.

David looked. Bailey and her writing teacher had broken away from the crowd out back and were heading toward the kitchen door to the outside.

''Can we talk tomorrow?'' David asked. ''I'm free for lunch.''

''Yes,'' Mo agreed. ''I want to listen to the tape again and think about this. Tomorrow would be good. Do you want to meet somewhere?''

''I'll come get you at State,'' David said. Outside, Bailey and Jeffery were nearly across the lawn. ''I'll just find you.''

''Good,'' Mo said. ''I really think you've come upon something here.''

''Maybe,'' David said, watching Liz make faces and shake her arms around. ''Good-bye.''

''Sure,'' Mo said, disappointment in his voice. David hung up.

''I don't want to see her now,'' Liz said urgently.

''Right.''

The two were crossing the patio, cutting off any escape routes. David looked quickly around, his eyes resting on the walk-in pantry.

''Here,'' he said, taking her by the hand and drawing her into the small room. He looked at her with great seriousness. ''We'll wait out the storm.''

He closed the door all but a crack, the barest light seeping in with them. The top was still off the bottle, but they had no glasses. David took a drink and passed the bottle to his sister. It smelled stuffy in there, like old bread and vaguely Chinese spices.

Sometimes, when he and Liz were young, their mother had used to make them hide in closets if she was having a new gentleman caller over who didn't know she had children. She always broke the news later, if there was a later, but she had always wanted to try her wiles on them first—the carrot on the stick.

"I feel like—" Liz began.

"I know," David said. "Déjà vu. Shhh."

David took the bottle back from Liz, drinking deeply. He heard the door open, then Bailey's high-pitched laughter.

"Oh God," she said. "Come here."

There was silence for a minute, David resisting the impulse to throw the door open and confront it. He felt Liz's hand on his shoulder, squeezing gently, trying to reassure. He drank again.

"I could hardly stand it," came Jeffery's voice. "Being so close to you, but not being able to touch you or hold you."

"I was so hot before," Bailey said, "that I went into the bathroom and masturbated."

Shit, thought David. She'd used that line on me before we got married.

"Really?" Jeffery replied. "Did you really?"

David heard movement. Then, through the crack in the pantry door, he saw them. Bailey was leaning against the cabinets, Jeffery pushing against her, his hands all over her.

"I can't stand it when we're apart," Bailey said, her arms going around the writing teacher's head, pulling him down to her chest. "I love you so damned much."

"Ah wove ou somunch, oo," Jeffrey said, his mouth filled with the material of Bailey's blouse.

"Son of a bitch," David whispered, insides shaking. He knew that Bailey screwed around, but to bring it into his own home . . .

Bailey pulled the man up, sucking greedily on his mouth, her hands going to his buttocks, then moving around to the front of his pants.

"Your husband's such a pig," Jeffrey said as he bucked himself against her. "You were so right about him."

"He's made my life hell on earth," Bailey replied, unzipping the front of his pants. "You're the only bright spot in the desert of my existence."

"Writer's talk," David mumbled, and drank again. At least all the lessons were being put to some use. A darkness was descending upon him that scared him a little.

"We can't here," Jeffery said, backing away slightly from Bailey. She had his erect penis in her hand and was working it like a taffy pull. ''What if someone . . . your husband . . . should come in.''

''I want you right now,'' Bailey said huskily. ''I can't stand it anymore.''

''Not here . . . I couldn't.''

''An honorable man,'' David whispered, and tried to drink again, but found the bottle empty. He was surprised he had drunk so much. It had settled his brain into some sort of crystal realization of events that transcended mere thought processes. He was feeling moved to action, and he knew the feeling would manifest itself somehow. He just didn't know how, or care.

''I know a place,'' Bailey said, moving away from him as he hurriedly zipped himself back up. She took him by the hand and led him out of David's vision.

''Where does this lead?'' David heard him ask.

''The garage,'' Bailey said, and the voices disappeared.

David pushed the pantry door open and walked into the kitchen, Liz right behind him.

''David?'' she said, a plea.

He looked at her, his face set, his mind locked into that place of absolute clarity that was untouched by propriety or understanding or civility. ''It's okay,'' he said, voice surprisingly lilting in tone. ''It's all in fun, right?''

Liz looked at him, concerned, but didn't speak.

David set the empty bottle on the counter and raised a finger. ''Right back,'' he said. ''I have something I must do.''

He turned and walked through the house, surprised that he was finding walking so difficult when everything else seemed so sharp and clear. He waved broadly to Max as he passed the bar, and found his own front door difficult to get through.

The lawn was large, the evening alive with cicada and the smells of the cookout. He weaved across the lawn to his car, feeling the warmth of the Oklahoma wind tingling through the numbness of his body.

What he was looking for was clipped to the visor on the driver's side. He put it in his pocket and went back to the house.

Liz was standing in the wide living room when he got there, her face torn between resignation and fear.

''Don't say anything,'' he warned. ''This is all part of the game, I know it is. You're part of this, too. You can't enter in. It's my move."

He walked to the sliding glass doors to the outside. His backyard was huge, the pool barely taking up a fourth of it. There was a concrete basketball court off to one side, the rest immaculately clipped green lawn.

They were all out there: the lesbian poets, the overbearing fiction writers, the rough-faced oilies and their pudgy wives, the white-jacketed servants, the dead cow dripping barbecue sauce over the hickory fire.

"My friends!" David shouted, opening his arms wide. "Welcome to my home!"

There were shouts of acknowledgment, and David, smiling in his crystalline clarity, walked into the crowd. His people, they were there to make the evening memorable.

As he made his way through the expansive crowd, he waved and shook hands and said all the right things. "Hey, saw your story in the last faculty anthology. Loved it!" Or, "Hey, saw you brought in those Canton wells! Money to burn! Money to burn!" Or, "Hey, Mack better watch out for you, Rosie. I might just steal you away. Looking good!"

It all flowed in and out for several minutes, Liz following in David's wake making sure he said nothing to get himself hurt, jumping in when he approached dangerous territory. Somewhere along the line he had acquired a cowboy hat that was too large, and it rode way down on his forehead, covering his ears. A barbecue sandwich had found its way into his hand and he waved it around like a flag as he made his points.

Finally, he climbed atop some wrought-iron furniture that had come with the house and addressed the crowd. "My friends," he said. "Gather 'round. I have something of tremendous import to show you."

"Hey, cowboy!" someone yelled from the group.

"Yahoo!" David screamed, and waved his sandwich above his head. "I know the secret of Western civilization, the single thing that has made the world what it is today!"

"Oil!" someone responded.

"No fair, guessing," David said, pointing the sandwich. "You all will have to follow me to find out."

He jumped off the chair and waved his sandwich for them to follow. Dutifully, the thirty or so people lined up behind their host and marched across the yard. He took them over the manicured lawn, past the red-brick outdoor grill with the gas jet to help burn the hickory, past the kidney-shaped pool and attached hot tub in matching tiles, finally to stand before the garage.

"Gather 'round, no shoving," David said, and they formed a semicircle before him. He pointed behind him, toward the garage door. "Within that garage lies the secret of the world, the one single thing that has affected more change, more politics, more art, than anything else. Would you like to see it?"

"Yes!" they all called, laughing and holding up their beers. His people. Good.

He reached into his pocket and withdrew the automatic door opener he had taken from his car. "Ladies and Gentlemen, I give you, the Answer!"

He dramatically pointed his little box toward the door and clicked the button. So easy, better living through technology.

The door rose dramatically to showcase Bailey and Jeffery, both naked, lying on a blanket atop the trunk of her white Lincoln. She had her legs wrapped around his ears as he pounded frenetically in and out of her.

"Perpetual motion!" David announced as Bailey screamed and scrambled out from under poor Jeffery, all the while trying to cover her body with an inadequate number of arms.

The crowd reacted according to their will, the lesbian poets turning away while the others gawked, the writers taking notes while the oilies whinnied like Arabian horses.

"Poetry in motion!" David said. "The pinnacle of artistic self-expression!"

"Stop it!" Jeffery screamed, and jumped off the back of the car, Bailey grabbing up the blanket and covering herself with it.

The man walked toward David, his deflating erection bobbing up and down in front of him. "Seen enough?" he asked the crowd. "Would you like a side view? A back?" He turned a full circle, the writers taking the hint and turning away, while the oilies poked one another and whinnied some more.

Jeffery walked right up to David. "You're a sick man," he said. "You need to get some kind of help."

"Wait a minute," David said, anger clouding everything. "I'm the injured party here, asshole. In case you haven't noticed, that's my wife you're playing hide-the-stick with."

Jeffery jabbed an index finger in David's chest. "She came to me because she needed something to make her feel like a human being again. She came to me because you make her feel cheap and worthless."

"Who the hell do you think you are?" David said. "My life . . . my wife's life are none of your business."

"You're a killer," Jeffery said. "Only you don't use a gun or a knife. You kill slowly, from the inside out, starting with the heart. You take away someone's humanity to make them fell empty . . . useless. You degrade them emotionally. You poison them intellectually. You grind them up spiritually."

"I could shoot you," David said, "and not a court in the country would convict me."

"Do the world a favor," Jeffery said. "Shoot yourself."

With that, the man turned calmly and walked back into the garage for his clothes. Bailey had already run off, Jeffery, casual, slipped into his T-shirt.

David stared at him for a minute, his crystalline clarity gone now, the confusion of life settling in again. He pushed the button on the hand opener, closing the door, then turned to those crass enough to be still standing there.

"Party's over," he said softly, Liz moving up close to embrace him.

He broke the embrace and ran for the pool, jumping into the deep end and sinking to the bottom. The quiet was overpowering. Swimming had been the universal curative for him since he was small, the exercise a catharsis, the peace a salve. But not tonight. Instead of taking calm from the waters, he only felt he was bringing filth to them. He didn't deserve the water tonight and he surfaced, climbing out to find Liz still waiting for him.

He looked at her, saw the tears in her eyes and knew they were for him. Then he remembered.

Dripping wet, he ran back into the house, charging drunkenly, falling into things. He got back up to his study, the recent events that had taken place there still embedded in the atmosphere.

The desk drawer stood partly open. He slid his hand in and pulled out the envelope containing Liz's prediction. With shaking hands, he tore it open and read:

You will publicly expose your wife's infidelity.
I'm so sorry, David.

He crumpled up the letter and held it in his fist, squeezing tightly. Then he laid his face in his arms and began to cry.

"Do we hafta go back in there?" Davy Wolf asked his mother as they walked the cold hallways of State Hospital.

"We're just here to pick something up," Naomi said. "Dr. Morgan has something that belongs to us."

"They won't make me ... make me ..."

Naomi Wolf put her arm around him and hugged him close. "No dear. No more treatments."

Davy didn't understand. He hadn't been here for a month, and his mother was dressed in the kind of clothes she usually wore for her gentlemen friends. Her perfume was strong and hung on her like fog, and her cheeks were so red it looked as if someone had hit her.

Davy looked around, fearful that they stood out too much in the sterile hospital atmosphere, fearful that perhaps they had simply forgotten about him and that seeing him again would make them put him in the room with the machine some more. But they didn't. Everyone walked past, going about their business as if he weren't there at all.

"Here we are," Naomi said. "Come along, Davy."

They walked through a frosted glass door with DR. MORGAN—PRIVATE written on the glass. They were in a small waiting room that opened into an office in the back. Davy felt a chill go through him when he saw Dr. Morgan sitting at his desk, a pipe in his mouth.

The doctor looked up in surprise when they walked in, rising to meet them in the waiting room.

"What a pleasant surprise," he said, reaching down to shake Davy's hand. "And how have you been?"

"Perfect, Doctor," Davy said as sincerely as he knew how. "I'm fine, really completely better."

The man tousled his hair as if he were a baby, then straightened a bit to look at Naomi. "Mrs. Wolf," he said, shaking her hand, holding her hand too long when he shook it.

"I hope we're not disturbing you," Naomi said in the soft, put-on voice she sometimes used that drove Davy crazy.

"Not at all," the man said, and pushed his glasses a bit higher on his nose. "What can I do for you?"

"Could we ... talk for a few minutes?" she asked.

"Certainly."

He led them into his office. Diplomas filled the walls, along with pictures of a family and their activities. Davy let Dr. Morgan's wall transport him to a life that included picnics and family meetings and the same people sitting across from you at the breakfast table every morning. A dream world.

"Sit down," the doctor said.

They sat, Davy staring in wonder at the incredible array of knickknacks that tried to make the coldness of State seem somehow human.

"Now what can I do for you?"

"I was wondering," Naomi said sweetly. "Now that Davy is all recovered and has nothing more wrong with him, it seems like his records here should be turned over to me."

Dr. Morgan leaned back in his desk chair and lit his pipe, puffing madly to get it going. "I don't understand," he said at last.

"He's not a sick boy," she said. "He's fine, normal. He just had an . . . episode, that's all."

"Yes?"

"It just seems a shame that there should be a file on him that says differently. I'm his mother. I'm responsible for him. I should have his file."

Naomi kept her voice sweet, her eyes never leaving the doctor's. The man fidgeted slightly in his seat, Naomi leaning over, the top of her loose blouse exposing her breasts. Davy picked up a photo cube and studied it intently, watching the young boy who smiled back go through fifteen years of growth on the cube's six sides.

"State law requires us to keep those records," the doctor said through a haze of gray-blue smoke. "I would be subject to criminal penalties if I did anything to them."

"It seems so unfair," Naomi pouted.

"I'm sorry, Mrs. Wolf . . ."

"Naomi."

"Yes. I'm sorry, but there's really nothing I can do."

Naomi smiled, then reached out and took the photo cube from Davy's grasp, setting it back on the desk. "Go wait outside for a few minutes, dear," she told the boy. "Mother needs to talk to the doctor privately."

"Can't we just go, Momma?" Davy said.

"There's really nothing—" Dr. Morgan began.

"Just a few minutes, Davy," Naomi said. "Then we'll go have some ice cream at Kaiser's."

She stood, looking sternly down at him. The famous you're-really-in-trouble look. Davy rose and walked into the waiting room, Naomi closing the door behind him.

He sat for a while, watching the dark shadows glide past the opaque door glass. The furniture was leatherette and metal, torn in many places. He moved around the furniture, counting cigarette burn holes and finding the most comfortable chair. Then he picked up a copy of the *Saturday Evening Post,* going for the back first, the Ted Key "Hazel" cartoon, then relentlessly making his way through the whole magazine, reading only the cartoons.

He finished the magazine, the fear still there in the pit of his stomach. It seemed he had been sitting there for hours. He got up and walked around the room, stepping only on the white tiles of the checkerboard linoleum floor, finally ending up near the door to Dr. Morgan's office.

A noise, like crying, was coming from the other side. He was immediately worried. Reaching out a tentative hand, he opened the door a crack and peeked in.

Dr. Morgan, fully dressed, was sitting on his desk chair, while Naomi, naked, sat atop him, moaning softly as if she were in pain. The doctor's mouth was filled to overflowing with her breast, and he looked like a baseball player with a huge wad of tobacco in his mouth. His hands ran all over her as she moved up and down.

He knew what it was, he was old enough to know that, but he couldn't figure out why. He backed away from the door, tears inexplicably coming to his eyes.

He sat back down, hating himself for crying, but not being able to stop. He tried reading the cartoons again, but the tears still came. It frightened him, because he thought if Dr. Morgan saw the tears he might put him in the room with the machine again.

That did it. The tears dried, the resolve strengthened. He sat stiff in the chair, putting all of it out of his mind. He had to control it. He had to.

Within minutes, his mother appeared at the office door, a file folder under her arm. "Now that wasn't so long, was it?" she said.

"No," Davy replied, and stood.

"How about that ice cream?"

"I'm not hungry."

He waited, tensed, for Dr. Morgan to come out of the office and know right away that he had to go back to the machine. But he didn't. In fact he never saw Dr. Morgan ever again.

"I'll bet you'll be hungry when you see that ice cream," Naomi said happily, leading him back out into the corridor.

"Yes," Davy said automatically.

On their way out of the hospital, they passed a nurse's station, Naomi throwing the file into a large trash bin nearby. But Davy was off having a private picnic somewhere and recognized neither the activity nor its intent.

From that day forward, Davy's "episode" was never mentioned again, and Naomi, if it were put to her, would deny that it had ever taken place.

David had been having a dream. It took place in a palace of ice that glittered like a million diamonds in the light. He was young, maybe nine, but was dressed in tails, with a top hat and black cane with a white top like Fred Astaire had used in his movies. His shoes shined like mirrors.

He was walking through the palace, room after room, looking for his mother so he could show her his outfit. He found her in the corner of a room as large as a football stadium, admiring herself in a full-length mirror. She wore a floor-length gown made from a million icicles that tinkled like tiny bells whenever she moved. Her lips were as red as blood.

When she saw him, she held her arms out to him, but he couldn't get close enough to hug her through the curtain of ice. That's when he heard the distant screaming.

"What's that, Momma?" he asked.

"That's your sister, dear," Naomi replied, fixing icicles to her ears like dangles. "She's in the boiler room, paying the freight."

He could hear growls mixed with the horrible screams. "We've got to save her!" he said loudly.

"Oh no, dear," Naomi said, shaking her head to the sound of millions of tiny bells. "If I went to the boiler room, my lovely gown would melt."

"I'll save her!" David yelled, and ran toward the screams. He ran and ran, through an infinity of rooms, finally coming to a rusted iron door. He threw it open to a blast of hot air.

The boiler room was dank and rusty, a huge furnace blazing intently at its rear, large piles of money stacked up beside it with a shovel buried in the pile. Liz, barely more than a baby, was tied up on the floor, screaming. A large scaly snake, bigger than a man, with human hands, was slithering toward her.

"No!" David yelled, and the snake turned and looked at him. It had a human face, like one of Mother's boyfriends, and it began laughing as it slithered over Liz.

David ran to help her, but he wasn't getting anywhere. The harder he pumped, the heavier his legs became. Her screams were horrible, heartrending. He put his hands to his ears, but they wouldn't go away, they wouldn't . . .

He sat up, drenched in sweat, his own breath loud in his ears. He was in the study, still sitting at the desk where he had passed out. His clothes were still damp and clammy from his earlier romp in the pool. It was dark in there, the only light filtering in from an O.G.& E. pole in the backyard. His head was pounding, and he smelled like booze and sweat.

The desk lamp was arm's length away. He reached out and clicked it on, straining to see his watch through sleep filled eyes. Three A.M.

The evening flooded back to him, the shame of it nearly overpowering. Sleep had helped nothing. Liz's prediction still lay crumpled on the desk. The syringes still lay in a neat, military line before him.

He wondered where Bailey was, and exactly what all this would mean. Whatever there had been to the marriage was undoubtedly shattered tonight. A three-time loser.

It wasn't as if he intentionally screwed things up. He had entered every one of his marriages with high hopes. He always looked out for himself, true, but he hadn't wanted any of the relationships to end.

The crumpled paper sat before him like an undissolved lump of flour in gravy. He frowned and picked it up to toss in the trash can. Then he thought better of it and stopped. He unfolded it, rereading its message, then flattened it out as much as he could and folded it neatly.

He opened the drawer to put it inside for future perusal—and he saw the gun. He drew it out, slowly, lovingly. It was a small gun, a .25 caliber, the kind they called a lady's gun.

It had been Naomi's, and he had had a surprisingly difficult time getting it back from the police. They had all thought it odd that he would want returned to him the weapon his mother had used to blow her brains out.

He had had no interest in guns before or since, but this gun, *this* gun, was different. It was the very personal family murder gun, the one you used when it was time to leave. The gun was his bridge to sanity. If he could look at it and not want to use it, he was all right.

Jeffery, the writing teacher with the published novel about detective stigmata, had told him to kill himself. God knows, the man probably knew more about it than he did; maybe he was right. He was guilty as charged, wasn't he?

The clip containing the bullets was buried under piles of papers and loose clips. He found it, and slid it gently to click into place in the butt of the pearl-handled semiautomatic.

He stared at the now lethal weapon, but the urge to use it wasn't there. For David Wolf had a choice. There was something fundamentally wrong with him, something dark and virulent, he was convinced. Removing himself seemed to be the thing to do, if only to end the nightmare. But there were ways and there were ways.

The gun went back in the drawer and the drawer was shut tight. David reached out and drew one of the syringes toward him, a rush of illicit anticipation surging, like the first time, in college, he had ever tried marijuana.

Why not? What in God's name did he have to lose?

He stood, the pain in his head centering behind his eyes. He'd need aspirin and maybe a hot bath. And Bailey. He should see how and where she was. Fidelity had been nothing but a joke between them through most of their relationship. She hadn't deserved the humiliation he had put her through.

His black leather physician's case lay years untouched and dusty in the study closet. He opened it, fishing around until he came out with a small black leather case holding tongue depressors and otolaryngoscope with attachments. He pulled all that stuff out and used the case to hold the syringes Liz had given him. He zipped it up and put it in his wet back pocket.

He found Bailey in the bedroom. Dressed in a nightgown, she sat reading, her eyes and nose deep red from crying.

"What the hell do you want?" she said when he came in.

"This is my house, too," he replied.

"Don't think you're going to sleep in here. Don't think you're ever going to sleep in here."

He moved into the room, going to his walk-in closet to get out his big terrycloth robe.

"Don't worry," he said. "I just want to take a bath, then I'll leave you alone."

"Take a bath somewhere else."

"All my stuff's in this bathroom."

She slipped out from under the covers and stood. "Then *I'll* go somewhere else." She moved for the door.

"Diane," he said.

She stopped, turning to him. "My first name," she said. "You must want something."

"Just to say I'm sorry. I didn't need to wash out our dirty linen in front of all those people."

"Those 'people' were my dearest friends," she said, eyes flashing, and David could feel it starting all over again. "How will I ever be able to face them now?"

"Look. I said I was sorry," he said, feeling stupid for getting angry again. "Can't we just leave it at that? You have some responsibility here, too. You didn't have to bring your fuck buddy into my garage."

"You can make anything sound dirty, can't you?" Her tears were starting again. "Oh God, David. What did I ever do to you? What horrible thing had I done that you wanted to punish me by marrying me?"

He took a step toward her. She backed away. "Diane," he said again, his voice choked. His mind was whirling. He had played out scenes similar to this one with two other women. It all twirled giddily around him, a merry-go-round of pain. "You didn't do anything. You were handy."

"I had loved you so much," she said, wiping at her eyes, leaning against the doorframe for support. "I listened to you tell me about what bitches the others had been, and I wanted to hold you like a baby, comfort you, and tell you all women weren't like that. Now look at me. I can't talk to you unless I'm screaming. I hate myself, what I've become."

She looked at him, eyes bright red, staring intently. "And I hate you for what you've done to me. You and your prenuptial agreements and strange money deals. You think I don't know? I've got lawyers, too, David. You've drained me like a leech. Taken my money and done God knows what with it. Don't you understand? I'd have given you everything I had . . . everything. If only you'd have loved me."

David Wolf, lover of nothing, lowered his eyes and admitted the truth. "I know that," he whispered.

"Bastard!" she screamed. "Why me? Why did you pick me to destroy?"

He turned away from her then, unable to tell her that he had no reason. "I'm going to take a bath," he said.

"I hope you drown!" she screeched, and slammed the door, leaving him alone with the bad energy of the room.

David stripped out of his wet clothes and put on the robe, slipping the leather case into the pocket. The large bedroom couldn't have seemed emptier had the furniture been gone. The house was worth three mil, its note in the name of some obscure corporation that David owned. When they split, Bailey wouldn't get it. Amazing the things that people will sign when they trust someone.

David went into the bathroom and surprised himself by locking the door. He'd never done that before. Paranoid? He drew a bath, the water as hot as he could stand it.

While the tub billowed steam into the Mexican-tiled, double-sink room, he took four aspirin for his head. His stomach was bad, too. He forced himself to throw up, then dropped the robe and climbed into the tub.

The water was so hot it turned his skin red. He sank down, letting the heat clean his system out. He was too old for this shit. The morning was going to be awful.

The morning. . . .

He sat up, reaching out of the tub to root through the pocket of his robe, the feel of the leather case strangely reassuring. He took it out and unzipped it. Ten syringes stared back at him; five clear, five red. He wondered why she had given him so many.

He took out a clear syringe and lay the case on the edge of the tub. He took the stopper off, the needle glinting harsh bathroom light. Liz had told him not to analyze what it contained. It would take an idiot or worse to shoot an unknown substance into himself. He was worse.

He'd had a patient once, a manic depressive who had lived a seminormal life by chemically balancing himself through injections of dopamine. He had gone to David because of an urge to suicide that never quite went away and made his life a living hell. David had done what he could, but Death will have its way, and the man eventually jumped from the top floor of a Marriott Hotel in full view of a playground full of schoolchildren next door, splattering himself all over the top of an airport limo. He had left a note stating simply that it was all for the best, and strangely, David knew that it was. That's how he felt now.

He sat there in the tub, thinking of another David and a painting called *The Death of Marat*. It depicted the leader of the French Revolution, his skin blue in death, sitting as if asleep in a tub full of blood. That David, like him, was a gentle artist who ground his colors in gore, sentencing thousands to die in Dr. Guillotin's famous equalizer.

He laid the syringe gently on the case and reached again for his robe, pulling out the sash. He wound it around his arm just above the elbow and knotted it tight.

He thought about the meeting place as he clenched and unclenched his fist, pumping up the veins in his arm. Where his father heard about Pearl Harbor, she had said. How strange. All he had ever gotten from his father was a last name. He had deserted Naomi while she was still pregnant with Liz and he was just a toddler.

It wasn't possible, of course, for him to actually go back to 1941, but the point was, David didn't give a damn anymore. If they found him the next morning, blue and peaceful like Marat, what difference could it make to anyone? David Wolf had spent a lifetime making sure no one would miss him when he was gone. In that, at least, he'd been spectacularly successful.

He brought the needle to his arm and found a good-sized vein. Yesterday, it had been Sara getting the shot for almost the same thing. He stuck it quickly, grunting, and pumped the fluid into his arm.

Even with a slow injection, the liquid went in hot. He pulled out the needle and sighed, then tossed it across the room to land in the wastebasket. While he waited for it to circulate through his body, he got out one of the red syringes and readied it for use. If something went desperately wrong with his body, he'd try the antidote if he could.

He lay back in the tub, thinking about Liz and the drug, remembering the time when they were children that she had filled a dish with rich, dark mud and told him it was chocolate pudding. The memory seemed so fresh that he could taste grit on his tongue. He could see her chubby little face so plainly, giggling as he spit mud over everything and began chasing her.

The room seemed different. All the angles seemed sharp and well defined, the colors bright and true, but if he didn't concentrate on it, he drifted, everything disappearing in front of him, changing shapes, becoming other rooms, all sharply defined, all real. They ran past him like motion-picture film, each frame different, each flickering shadow real, but shadow nonetheless.

His head was spinning, his concentration drifting more and more. Liz, four years old, stood before him, laughing at the mud on his face. He could almost reach out and touch . . .

He could! His hand held flesh, his fingers wrapping around the small arm.

"Let me alone, Davy!" she squealed, trying to pull free. "I'll tell . . . I'll tell . . ."

He pulled away, the bathroom now his dorm room at med school. The smell of aftershave was strong in his nose as he dressed in his best suit. He had a date with Jeri, the rich girl he had met at his roommate's parents' cookout. He needed money for tuition, and Jeri'd been hinting around about how she'd really *loooove* to be a doctor's wife . . .

"No!"

He pulled himself back to the bathroom, head still spinning. What had Liz told him? Pearl Harbor. Pearl Harbor. Pearl Harbor.

It was warm for December, and the hickory-nut and blackjack trees of southern Oklahoma hadn't given over all of their leaves yet. Red and gold, rusty-brittle fellows fluttered gently before Sonny Wolf's Chevy pickup as he drove the dirt road to Lake Murray, just a few miles south of Ardmore, the leaves wobbling as they fell, totally covering the road like flower girls dropping blossoms before the wedding party.

The voice of the Reverend Billy Clyde blared out of the tinny radio, his voice wrapping around the creaks and wheezes of the old gray truck, the hellfire and brimstone rising with the shocks as they bumped in and out of potholes camouflaged by falling leaves.

Sonny was ecstatic. Naomi Wheeler was sitting beside him, the prettiest girl in Ardmore. She sat with her feet up on the dash, her blue gingham church dress hiked way up over her knees. He tried to act nonchalant as he talked to her, but his eyes kept drifting to her legs, perfectly formed, shining in silk stockings that had come all the way from New York.

He knew about the stockings because his father had ordered them special at the store. Naomi and her mother had lived in Ardmore for nearly two years, had shopped in his pa's store for all that time, and that was exactly how long he had been in love with Naomi. He had heard that she had had a brother who'd died, but no one ever talked about it.

"Do you believe everything the Reverend Parker says about sin?" she asked him, turning to smile slightly when she saw his eyes appraising her.

"Well, I don't know," Sonny said, feeling embarrassed about the funny feelings he was having in his stomach. "My pa says that religion was invented to make people good. So, I guess you got to know what's bad first."

"But how could he *know?*" she persisted.

"He reads the Good Book, course. It's all in there."

"I'm not sure," she said, stretching, the movement pulling her dress even farther up her thighs. "Sometimes I think the Good Book is just a bunch of stories. How about you?"

Such a thought would never occur to him in a million years, but he didn't want to seem unsophisticated to her, so he said, "Yeah. I've always wondered about Jonah and that fish."

He couldn't believe that she was there with him. It had taken him over a year of seeing her in the store just to get up enough nerve to talk to her, and then it was just to say hi, or help her to find something. Probably it would have gone no further than that had war not been imminent. Out of high school now, he was going to enlist and would be gone in a week, maybe forever. That, plus the nice weather and the fact that both families walked out of church at the same time, had forced him into stammering, agitated action. Impulsively, he had asked her to go for a drive with him, and just as impulsively she had said yes, that she was tired of the "boys" she had been seeing.

She licked red lips, her eyes devilish. "I don't think kissin' is a sin, do you?"

"N-no," he said quickly, the word catching stupidly in his throat. "I ain't never thought nothin' like that."

"How about French kissin'?"

He wasn't exactly sure what French kissing was, but it sounded fun. "No, not that either."

She reached out and put a hand on his leg. "Well, just where *do* you draw the line, Sonny Wolf?"

This was it as far as Sonny was concerned. He had shot the dice and rolled sevens all the way around. He was a week away from the military, a beautiful girl sat beside him with her legs sparkling in the noon sunshine, and an incredible erection was stretching his jeans tight across his crotch. It was time to shoot the bundle. "I'm a man of the world," he said, the best line he would ever use in his entire life.

Suddenly the lake loomed up before them, not large, but fine for around here. It shimmered brightly, all fifty acres of it, the peaks of small wind waves catching rays, glinting like thousands of Zippo lighters being lit and extinguished. Murray was a man-made lake, just as all Oklahoma lakes were man-made.

He pulled off the road, feeling a slight dizziness. He put his hand to his head. The lake was deserted despite the nice day. After all, it was December. A strange rush of thoughts jumbled his brain for a second.

"What is it?" she asked, sliding up close to him, touching side by side. She put a cool hand to his head, her eyes so wide, innocent one minute, scandalous the next.

"Something . . ." he said, and reached for the radio, turning it up.

David Wolf sat lightly just off the edge of Sonny's brain, his own mind too shocked to believe what was happening. He was there. He *was!* He could feel Sonny's body, could know his thoughts, but wasn't close enough for Sonny to recognize him.

This can't be real. This man my father? This gangly hick the man who ruined my momma and wrecked our lives? It's insanity . . . the drug has torn out my mind. The drug. I still remember the drug. Haven't lost everything. I'll weather this. Jesus Christ. . . .

The host body turned and looked at the woman. It was Naomi at about fifteen years. He could recognize her. *The dream, so real.* She was so fresh, so young and beautiful. The body he was in ached for her with longing stronger than he could remember—*This is crazy!*

She knelt up beside him, beside Sonny. Her full breasts were pushed tightly against his arm, the body's longing swelling like a tidal wave. "What does a man of the world do when he's alone with a woman?"

But the boy had already been altered, already had a

premonition. "Listen..." he said, pointing to the now blaring radio.

"...We interrupt the Reverend Billy Clyde to bring you this special announcement. The United States Naval Base at Pearl Harbor, Hawaii, has just been attacked by Japanese aircraft. Details are still comin' in, but so far it looks like nineteen of our ships have been sunk, and the death toll could reach into the thousands. Among the ships that went down, the battleship *U.S.S. Oklahoma*, lost with all hands. Remember Pearl Harbor! More details as soon as we get 'em."

"It's war," Sonny said. "They just blasted our whole damned Navy."

She threw her arms around him. "You're goin' off to war, my brave Sonny! Will you protect me?"

"Naomi, I..."

The host body had put its arms around Naomi, its hands running freely all over her back, occasionally slipping down to her wide hips or the side of her breast. She pulled closer, a leg slipping up over its thigh, touching him... there.

No! I can't... not... this.

The host found her lips, its brain flashing patterns of color and texture, not thinking. A large callused hand came around to tentatively cup her breast, then grab when she didn't resist.

No!

"No!" David sank in full and pulled away from his mother, hitting the doorhandle and tumbling out of the truck. Sonny's mind was screaming to David's in confusion and fear as all of David's life opened up before him.

He stood on shaky legs, feeling the full measure of health and agility of the eighteen-year-old host, the crispness of the day, the sweetness of the air—all of it overwhelming.

Naomi was out of the passenger side of the truck, the host body stumbling all over the road, trying to coordinate movements with the brain patterns of another boarder.

"David!" Naomi said. "Is that you?"

David?

The girl his mother was ran up to him, reaching up to take him by the shoulders. "David, give over. Listen to me!"

But David was beyond listening. His mind, faced with the all-absorbing landscape of the totally irrational, took flight. His brain bolted in panic, flying the dark, endless corridors of total recall.

*   *   *

Smoke, drifting with the wind. Genetic fear of fire overcoming all other instincts.

Flight.

Trees. I must stay in the trees.

The screams of frightened animals filling the paths, crashing the brush below. Behind, the fire's crackle, racing with the wind. Fly before the flames.

Monkeys around me, chattering. Hairy arms, heart pounding, beating my chest. Flee. Distance the flames. The trees turn orange and feed the heat. No safety! Get control. Home . . . home . . . home . . . home.

He was ten years old, sitting in the old free standing tub, a bar of Lava soap in his hands. The water was murky, dirt gritted beneath his toes. He'd been playing King of the Mountain on the dirt pile by the new addition. Sunlight filtered through the cheap plastic curtain. The wall was stained with concentric brown rings beneath the tearing paper. The double sink was bright white, the counter long.

Home.

The paper faded to Mexican tile as the tub dissolved, changing shape all around him, flattening, narrowing as his legs grew.

A zipper case with a syringe sitting atop it took shape on the side of the tub, forming into solid life on the information supplied by his brain. A shaking hand reached out to touch the thing, first going through it, then grabbing when it became more solid.

Without pumping up a vein, he watched his arm through blurry eyes, stabbing at himself when he thought he had something. He injected the burning fluid into himself, then sat back, shaking uncontrollably, trying his best to hold his created reality together.

Within minutes, the room solidified on its own, its reality substantial enough that he no longer needed to hold it together himself.

David relaxed slowly, by degrees, his body untensing completely when he was sure it was over. Everything around him was solid, real. He could believe again that it wasn't going anywhere.

What in God's name had happened? A powerful drug, no doubt, one that could make dreams so real. Dreams? Could he really pragmatize away his experience that easily? It was more than a dream, much more.

The water in the tub was still hot, still steaming. He couldn't have been gone but a matter of seconds, long enough to inject the drug, then the antidote; yet that's not how it felt to him. Silv had talked about the nonexistence of time. If only she had prepared him more. Now he had come back and totally messed up the experiment. What now?

He got out of the tub and dried off, slipping into the robe. He was a doctor, a believer of cause and effect. It would be too easy to pass off his experience as merely a dream. His brain had been too alive, the experiences still too vivid and too real to have been anything else.

One thing he was absolutely sure of. He was in possession of the most powerful drug ever invented on the face of the Earth. Its reality made the hallucinations of other psychotropics seem silly. He'd need some help sorting this one out. Mo Frankel might be the man to see. Mo was much more level-headed about such things.

Water.

In Quad14 the words *life* and *water* were synonymous and interchangeable. The branch of the mountain stream that emptied into Quad14 had a twisting brick pathway to run over, falling down patterns of steps and small falls before wending its way to the treatment plant and on to the ration center.

Silv sat in her chair by water's edge, her blue robes covering most of her hardware. The path was three feet wide and four feet deep here at the grotto. Pilgrims gathered all around her, segregating themselves by the colors of their hooded robes. They came to the water to pray or simply to humble themselves before the mystery of life. They gave the woman in the chair a wide berth, however, her advanced age marking her as one of the Immortals, one of the important ones kept alive through chemistry to serve the quad in a special capacity. Her stature brought her nothing but loneliness, however. The Immortals were treated as demigods, feared and avoided by the citizens as a whole. Silv had lived her last sixty years as an outcast of her own importance.

The grotto was large at this place, by far the largest open area in the entire quad. Its high, smooth rock walls were

painted in the lush greens and golds of what the outside must
have been like, the images of trees and flowers and sunshine
constantly reminding them of all they had lost.

"Chemist?" came a tentative voice from behind.

She pushed the button that turned her chair to face the
voice. A soldier in rock camouflage addressed her from a
distance of ten feet.

"Do you have him?"

"Yes'm," he said, jerking a thumb behind him.

Silv looked up the wide stairs leading down to water's
edge. At the apex, two tall, burly men in camouflage robes
held a smaller man between them as pilgrims flowed past
going up and down the steps. The man stood stiffly, resenting
the hands upon him, smart enough to keep his mouth shut.

"Good," Silv said. "Have your men bring me up the
stairs."

"You mean . . . touch you?" the man asked.

"Now, Sergeant."

"Yes'm."

The man went up and took control of her subject, while his
charges came down and carried Silv, chair and all, up the
stairs to face her experiment.

"You're Hersh," she said to the small man. He looked like
a rodent with small head and long nose. His dull eyes, half
lidded, jerked continually back and forth.

He nodded his answer, his eyes never resting on Silv.

"That will be all, gentlemen," she said. "I'll take him
now."

"But, ma'am," the young sergeant said. "This is a
dangerous—"

"Push my chair, Hersh," she ordered, the man falling
quickly behind and taking the chair with both hands. "Green
sector."

They moved off, leaving the soldiers, in confusion, behind.
Hersh moved her away from the open grotto area, into the
honeycomb of tight, cramped hallways that formed the bulk
of the quad. Walking the colors, he turned down a hall
marked with a green stripe painted along its length

"I hear you can get me out of de-ten," he said in a flat
voice once they were walking the hall.

"You killed your lieutenant?" she asked.

"He was a slug, miss."

"Call me Silv."

"He was a slug, Silv. He deserved it."

"How long are you in for?"

"Too long. You can get me off?"

"If you cooperate."

They had moved rapidly through the residential doorways and were entering a zone of government offices, the doorways numbered and named. People hurried past in both directions, some carrying loaves of breadsub under their arms.

"I'll do anything," Hersh said. "I can't hardly stand it in de-ten. They keep the lights off all the time. It's pitch-dark. After a while your head starts makin' up stuff. You start dying for light, any light, a little light. I can't stand it."

"I'm going to ask you to take something," she said, "—a shot."

"What kinda shot?"

"One that will make you stop hurting people," Silv said. "I can't guarantee anything, but it might even be enjoyable."

"And if I take this shot, I won't have to go back. You've got the power to do that?"

"I've got the power," said Silv. "Here we are."

The office had her name on it, though an illiterate Hersh couldn't know that. He helped her with the key, one of the only doors in 14 that had a lock, and wheeled her in.

It was tiny. Just enough room for a work table, cabinet full of materials, and a couple of chairs. Silv buttoned out of his grasp and moved to the slate table.

"Sit in that chair," she said, preoccupied. "Roll up your sleeve."

Hersh did as he was told without thought. Too slow to be frightened, he simply gazed around the room, taking in the wonder of test tubes and glass bottles, things such as he had never seen.

"Have you always fought?" she asked him as her metal pincers grasped the syringe full of clear liquid and brought it to her lap.

"You know," he said, looking all around, "you got to look out for yourself. It's a tough world."

She turned the chair and whirred toward him, stopping with a jerk beside his exposed arm. "Your files show you've been put in detention three times for fighting."

"None of them was my fault."

"I see."

She took the alcohol vial and poured it on his forearm, then used her pincers to pluck up the skin. "You'll feel a slight prick," she said, then jabbed the needle in. "This may burn a little."

"What are you giving me?" he asked, not out of concern but rather just curiosity. "It burns."

She ignored his question and looked into his dull eyes. "I won't keep you under long this first time," she said. "Just try and remember whatever happens, whatever . . . feelings you experience. We'll stay down longer next time."

"Sure, I—" he began, then his eyes widened. "Hey, what're you doin' here?"

He began thrashing in the chair wildly, then suddenly collapsed, falling limp, head tilted back.

"Damn," Silv said, and raised her withered hand, weak index finger finding a fluttering pulse on his neck. "Still alive, anyway."

She turned from Hersh and moved to the table, taking up the syringe containing the universal antidote she had designed fifty years before. Her mind was filled with thoughts of the drug. It wasn't supposed to do this. She had figured on mild hallucinations combined with an overall feeling of well-being that could keep Hersh docile as long as he was under the influence. Unconsciousness had never figured into the scheme. The patient was supposed to at least be ambulatory.

She wheeled back to him with the antidote. Maybe the dosage had been too strong. If anything happened to this one, the next would get half dosage, for starters.

She watched him for a moment, hoping he'd come out of it on his own. When he showed no signs of doing that, she sighed and injected him with the red liquid, then backed off and hoped for the best.

Within three minutes he began to stir, moaning softly, then jerking up when his senses crystallized. He looked at Silv in confusion.

"Who are you?" he asked.

"Don't you remember me?" she asked.

"Who are you?" he demanded loudly.

"Silv, the Chemist. Surely you remember."

He stood, looking around as if he'd never seen the lab. "This place, somewhere . . ." He put a hand to his head, then looked at Silv again.

He smiled. "Of course I remember," he said. "You brought me back, no?"

"That's right, you had lapsed into unconsciousness. Do you remember anything after you took the drug?"

He smiled wide then, laughed despite his best efforts to hold it in. "How long have I been under?" he asked.

"Just a few minutes," she said.

"Amazing."

"Do you remember anything?"

"Well . . . yes," he said carefully, as if he was weighing every word. "I remember a feeling of well-being, and . . . nonaggression."

"But you were unconscious."

He paced the room. "Everything's so cramped here, so dreary. No wonder people get depressed." He clapped his hands together. "So. Let's try it again. I promise not to pass out this time."

"We'll have to wait now," Silv said. "Make sure you have no adverse reactions. When we try next time, I'll put you on half dosage, and see if that helps."

"No!" he said loudly, then softened. "Don't do that. I'm sure I was just . . . tired or something. It'll work better this time. Come on, let's go."

"You're so anxious," Silv said. "Why?"

"I want to be cured," he said. "The sooner the better."

"And you don't remember anything except a feeling of well-being?"

"What else is there?" he asked.

"No hallucinations?"

"What makes you say that?" he asked, a strange timbre to his voice.

"I've reserved a room for you next to the lab," she said, wheeling back to the table and setting down the syringe containing the antidote. "We'll keep you under observation tonight, then go back to the experiment tomorrow if you're fit."

"Never felt better," he said. "Never."

She wheeled around to face him. He was staring hard at her, his eyes bright and clear and deep.

Something was desperately wrong here. This wasn't the same man she had injected just minutes before.

The great law of culture is: Let each become all that he was created capable of being; expand, if possible, to his full growth; resisting all impediments, casting off all foreign, especially all noxious, adhesions; and show himself at length in his own shape and stature, be these what they may.

—Thomas Carlyle

David reached State Hospital at fifteen minutes until eleven. It was raining, a phenomenon peculiar to Oklahoma only in the spring and the fall. Summer rain was unheard of.

He parked out front, in the "Emergency Only" slots and headed right up to the psych ward. He had made it to his office for his eight o'clock and his nine o'clock, but had been unable to concentrate on his patients, even stepping out of his transference role once to tell his nine o'clock that something she said was "stupid and crazy."

With the session ruined, he called it off, then cancelled his ten and eleven o'clocks, something he never did.

His mind was still a jumble. Bailey had left sometime during the night and he had no idea of where she could be. He had been calling Liz every fifteen minutes since seven that morning without success, and had even gone to her house after his abortive nine o'clock, but she wasn't there. So, he had driven aimlessly around north Oklahoma City, not too surprised when he found himself making the turn on Thirteenth into Blood Alley.

He walked to the nurses' station on nine. Christine Beckman, the head nurse, was busy reprimanding one of the RNs, a girl of no more than twenty, for giving out a whole day's worth of medication all at the same time.

"But Miss Beckman," the girl said, "the patients prefer that I do it that way."

Christine stared daggers over the top of her half glasses. She had been at State since emigrating from Germany in 1945, and knew more about medicine than most of the doctors who stumbled their way through its fake-marble halls.

"Listen, Bobbi—"

"Barbi," the nurse corrected.

"Whatever the hell . . . of course the patients like you to do it that way. You've got most of them so high you could tie strings to them and *float* them out of here. This is a hospital, young lady, not a hippie crash pad."

David reached over the high counter and picked up a telephone, dialing an outside line, then Liz's number.

"Lighten up, Chris," the young woman said. "We're understaffed and I'm busting my ass as it is. Hell, the more I pump them up, the more docile they are, anyway."

"I could have your license and your job in a minute for remarks like that," Beckman said coldly.

"Go ahead," Barbi said, hand on her hips. "It'd be another loss to attrition, another body that wouldn't get replaced because of the budget."

Beckman shrugged. "You're right, Barbi," she said. "So instead of firing you, I'm going to bump you down to nurse's aide for a while. We'll see how a few weeks of mopping floors and cleaning bedpans will improve your outlook. That's all."

The woman didn't say it, but the word *Nazi* was on her lips as she turned and stormed away.

David heard the phone ring, once, then again. Christine turned and looked at him, anger puckering her wrinkled lips. "It's you," she said.

The phone rang a third time. "Would you try and find Dr. Frankel for me?" he asked Christine.

"Hello?" came a voice on the other end.

"Thank God I finally got you," David said.

"David!" Liz said. "Are you all right?"

"I don't have to look for Dr. Frankel," Christine said. "He's in ICU with Sara."

David pulled away from the phone and stared at the nurse. "Sara?" he said softly.

Christine glared at him. "She never came out of the coma you put her in last night."

"David?" Liz said again.

"I—I'm here," he replied, shaken. "Listen. I've got to talk to you. Where have you been?"

"You won't believe this," she said. "I've been to a shrink."

"Who?"

"I really don't want to tell you his name yet," she answered. "Okay?"

David looked at Christine again, but the woman turned away from him and began filing charts.

"Did you talk about . . . last night?" he asked, his throat suddenly dry.

"No," she replied. "Though I might sometime."

"Then, why?"

"Silv made me . . . think about some things that I need to talk out with a professional. That's all I can say right now. As soon as I understand it myself, I'll tell you about it."

He rubbed his face, feeling lousy. "I want to talk to you," he said. "Later. Maybe dinner?"

"Sure," she said. "Only this time you come to my house. I'm not ready for Bailey again."

"Okay," he said, glancing at his watch out of habit. "Seven?"

"Sure. I've got nowhere to go."

He rang off and stared at the wiry little nurse's back. "Christine," he said.

She turned around and faced him. "Yes, *Doctor?*"

"Tell me about Sara."

She shrugged, aging fruit under a starched white rind. "Nothing to tell. You put her to sleep. She stayed that way."

"I was trying to help her," he said.

Her expression didn't change. "Whatever you say, Dr. Wolf."

He searched her eyes for compassion, but it was all reserved for the patients, the victims. He turned and strode back to the elevator, taking it down to intensive care on four.

An atmosphere hung over ICU, nothing physical, just a general malaise of emotion that seemed to move through the whole floor in waves, making you put your feelings away, hide them somewhere, lest they be lost forever. There was hope here, but very little; recovery, but usually partial.

The halls here were quiet, the light somehow dimmer. David Wolf walked the open ward, checking each little curtained cubicle, looking for the one that was *his* problem. He found it.

Sara lay on a gurney, surrounded on three sides by a beige curtain wrapped on a metal frame. She still wore the dress she had worn the previous night. IVs fed each arm. Electrodes were attached to her temples, their wires strung to the EEG that Mo Frankel was bent over.

"How is she?" he asked, stepping into the cubicle and checking the pulse on her carotid artery.

Frankel straightened, groaning. He looked tired, his expression unhappy, but not condemning like Christine's.

"I don't know," he said, his Polish accent thicker when he was worn down. "She's fine physically. She just won't wake up."

"What's been done so far?" David asked, pinching the skin on her arm, watching the color return.

"Not much," Frankel said. "Nobody exactly knows what you did, so we haven't known how to counteract it."

David leaned down near her ear. "Sara, this is Dr. Wolf. You've been in a deep sleep, but when I tap you on the head three times, you'll awaken feeling refreshed."

He straightened. Frankel moved in close, leaning down, watching intently. David tapped her head and spoke again. "Wake up," he said. "Forget Elise. You are Sara, and it's 1986. Please. Come on, old girl."

Nothing.

The two men shared a look, and David tried again without success. Frankel removed his glasses, using a white-gloved finger to wipe a smudge off the lenses. He seemed weary to David, a weariness that rest couldn't help.

"She tested positive to chlorpromazine," the old man said. "Reynolds turned some interns loose on her, and they really did their homework: gastric lavage, ephedrine . . ."

"How about her blood pressure?" David asked. "Is it low?"

Mo replaced his glasses. "High, believe it or not. It's the damndest thing I've ever seen." He pointed to one of the IVs. "Apresoline, forty milligrams to keep it down. And look at this." He walked over to the EEG, tapping the screen, jagged lines jumping across the green CRT. "Normal to agitated brain-wave activity. She should be wide awake, running track . . . but look at her."

David bent to her ear again. "I'm sorry, Sara," he said. "I had no idea . . ."

"We've got another problem," Frankel said. "I've already had to fight to keep her in ICU. The nurses here want to stick her in a med-surg unit and I'm not so sure that administration won't go along with it."

"She won't get the proper care in med-surg," David said.

"She's a lifer from the psych ward, David," the man said, the tiredness in his voice again. "They want the space for patients who have some chance of recovery."

"They don't want to spend the time it would take to care for her," David said, the bitterness evident in his tone.

"Would you?" Mo asked quietly. He shook his head. "To think that last night you seemed so close to something . . . extraordinary."

"I have found something extraordinary," David replied, and met Frankel's eyes, "—something beyond belief."

A tall red-haired nurse walked into the cubicle, moving to take out the IVs. "Time to flip her over," she said, bored. "Excuse me, Doctors."

David moved aside as the woman performed the every-two-hour chore of turning the patient over to avoid bedsores and to keep fluid from pooling in the lungs and extremities. A long-term coma took an incredible amount of care, David thought, and no, he wouldn't want to be the one to do it.

"Massage her limbs and back," David said. "Exercise her."

"We won't have her that long," the redhead replied. "They're preparing an NG tube in med-surg to feed her right now. We can't spare the space or the time."

"While she's here, Nurse," David said, angry, "you'll do as I ask."

"Yes, Doctor," the woman said coldly, and began to run a range of passive-motion exercise on Sara's arm.

David watched her for a moment, making sure she at least stayed on it for a time, then looked at Mo's drawn face. "Can we talk in my office?"

"*Ja,*" Mo replied, moving up to Sara's head to stare at her closed eyes, the lids bobbing with movement beneath. "Look at the REMs, David. What's going on inside her brain right now?"

"London," David said, and walked out of the cubicle.

They made the trip to the office blocks in silence, each dealing with Sara's condition in his own way. When they reached David's, Mo threw himself down on the couch Sara had lain on the night before.

"What a strange and dichotomous world we live in," the old man said, and he looked as if he could sleep there. "We like to call ourselves healers, but what do we really heal? Sara? Ourselves? Nothing ever changes. We play at medicine to make our world seem orderly and important. So someone gets sick and we take blood for testing, then we take more blood, and more. We prick and prod and subject the patient to every form of indignity known to man, then we prescribe drugs that change the system and cause more symptoms that we prescribe other drugs for. Are we really so much different than the medieval barbers who drew their blood with leeches instead of needles?"

"The quality of life has changed," David said. "We keep getting closer."

Mo sat up and rubbed his eyes. "Do we? Last night, Sara relived a pogrom that took place in the twelfth century. In the forties, I lived a pogrom that took millions of useful, productive lives. And, perhaps, Sara has been undergoing a slow, 'humanitarian' pogrom called modern medicine that's inexorably robbed her of her nature, and now her reality."

"Mo, I—"

"Wait," he said, and held up a gloved hand. "I was a teenaged boy when they took me from the Warsaw ghetto on the train to Auschwitz. You could see the smokestacks from miles away belching fire into the black night, smell the burning flesh." His face had taken on a masklike set, his voice sounding mechanical. "When we got off the train, we were divided into two groups by Mengele, the angel of death. The first group was stripped and taken immediately into the gassing rooms and killed, climbing over one another, fighting for a last breath. The rest of us weren't so lucky."

The sob came from deep inside, hands going to his face.

"Why don't we talk later, Mo," David said. "Rest now."

The man's face came from behind the curtain of hands, his eyes red, his wrinkles a thousand years old. "No. I must say this out or else I'm afraid I'll end up resenting all this."

"Resenting me?" David asked.

Mo looked at him tenderly. "David, I've loved you like a son. But there's a well of anger that lives within me that you could never understand. It must have some release or...or..."

"Go on," David said quietly.

"Those of us left alive had a job to do. We had to carry the bodies to the ovens and cut any gold fillings out of the teeth before we burned them. The things I did. I carried my own mother's naked body to the ovens to burn, cut the gold right out of her mouth...God help me...I did it to stay alive."

"She would have wanted that," David said.

"Don't smooth it over!" Mo yelled, tears streaming out of his eyes. "Where do we draw the line? How much humanity do we barter away to preserve our miserable shells, our destructive existence? Well, I have a reminder."

He stood, agitated, holding his right hand out to David. "Did I tell you what happened to my hand?"

David shook his head, his throat dry. He'd always secretly wanted to know, but had never had the bad taste to ask.

"I did my job, for the Nazis," the old man said bitterly. "I did it well, so well I forgot what was happening and decided to get in on it. I began taking some of the fillings for myself...no more than one a day. I buried them in a tiny hole out behind the barracks that no one else knew about. I would be rich after the war, I thought."

He laughed at that, shaking his head. "One day an SS officer saw me palming a gold tooth and decided to teach me a lesson. He put a foot on my wrist and pinned my hand to the floor. Then he took the butt of a rifle and pounded me on that hand, over and over, thirty, forty times. He broke every bone in my hand, shattered them, then just left me.

"I still had to keep up my end or I'd be killed, too. Later, as the Allies approached, they gave up the ovens and started burning the bodies in huge pits; whole tree trunks served as firewood. Then we scattered the ashes. The area around the camp was all swamp back then, as far as you could see. It isn't that way today. We reclaimed that swamp with human loam twelve inches thick."

He lay back down on the couch and stared at the ceiling. "I couldn't talk about the war at all for twenty years. They did as much reconstruction work on my hand as was possible. I became a doctor to try and undo some of the wrong I'd done. Psychiatry was my field for I didn't need a great deal of manual dexterity for that."

He held up the hand again. "My hand is my badge, my reminder of the monster that lies within each of us. It's horribly scarred and deformed...but I don't think it's taught me anything."

"What do you mean?" David said. "You're the finest man I know, the most loving, caring individual I've ever met. You've lived a life of total giving...to your friends, your patients..."

"My patients!" Mo said, and laughed, a horrible, self-destructive laugh. "Sara was my patient, and now we've institutionalized her to death. We've spent years and years reconstructing her brain and teaching her to live here in our little concentration camp by going along...just by going along. I've seen it happen before. That woman's in a coma down in ICU because she thinks we *want* her to be. *That's* what a caring individual I am." His hand was shaking. "Even with this! Even with this, I could allow that to happen, because, just like the Nazis, I was absolutely convinced it was for the best.''

"She came here because she was mentally disturbed," David said, and he took Mo's deformed hand in his own, the hair standing up on the back of his neck when he felt its awkward contours. "We didn't cause her problems. We tried only to alleviate them the best ways we knew how. We've made mistakes with her, horrible mistakes, but never out of a desire to hurt. We're not like the people who did this to you, not at all."

"But the end result is the same, isn't it?"

"Not necessarily," David said, releasing Mo's hand. "Not necessarily."

"What do you mean?"

David stood and walked to the window. The rain ran in sheets down the government approved earthquake-proof glass, running like a small river down the hill that was Thirteenth. The sky was large and rolling gray, occasional thunder bumping the distance. Darkness like night hung in the middle of the afternoon.

"I disagree with your assessment as to what's wrong with Sara."

"You have another theory?"

David knew of no logical way to approach Mo with this, so he just started in. "When I regressed Sara yesterday, and many other times in the past, it wasn't as I thought then, a past-life regression. It was more fundamental than that. It was genetic. I think we knocked so much out of her brain with our shock treatments, that this . . . memory is all she has to draw on."

He turned from the window then, to see if Mo was laughing at him. Rather, the man was staring in interest. "You've changed your opinions overnight," Frankel said. "Why?"

"It'll take a little time to explain," David said.

"My time has been borrowed for forty years," the old man said. "I can spare you some of it now."

David moved back and took his seat across from the man. He told the story, all of it, Frankel sitting quietly, listening to every word without comment. When he was finished, he reached into the inside pocket of his sports jacket and pulled out the zipper case. He showed Mo the syringes, the eight that were left.

"That's why you were so strange on the phone last night," Frankel said as he examined one of the needles.

"Yes."

"And you won't test the chemical to see what it is?"

"No," said David. "I've thought about this a lot. I've been where this takes you, and I'll be quite honest—I don't want the responsibility of knowing how to make it."

"And what has this to do with Sara?"

David took the syringe back from Mo and put it in the case with the others "If I'm right about Sara," he said, "she's trapped now in the only reality she can remember. Perhaps, if I could give her a shot of this, it would expand her mind and break the pattern. If I brought her back then, it could perhaps even restore normalcy of some kind."

"You're asking me," Mo said sadly, "after all I've told you today, to give my permission for still another experiment on that poor woman, with a totally untested drug at that."

"This is different," David said.

Mo stared at him for a long time, then he took off his black-frame glasses and wiped residual tears from his eyes. "There's only one way I'd ever conceive of giving Sara this drug, David."

"What's that?"

"Test it on me first. I'd like to move through time and space. I'd like to see for myself the origin of the universe."

"You're making fun of me."

"Did you believe it before you took the drug?"

David smiled. "No, of course not. I just felt I had nothing to lose by taking it just to see."

"Borrowed time, remember?" Mo replied. He removed his white jacket and rolled up his long-sleeved shirt.

"Now?"

Mo nodded. "Before I lose my nerve. Besides, it only takes a second, right?"

David got into the case and prepared a syringe. "You're absolutely sure of this."

"It may be *my* salvation," Frankel said. "I feel responsible for that woman lying there in ICU. I've supervised hundreds of doctors who've come in here and used her like a human voodoo doll. I've got to believe there's still hope. Go ahead, expand my mind."

He held his arm out, David going for the alcohol bottle in his desk. The old man's arm was pale as milk, his veins jagged and purple under translucent skin. Livid red scars snaked their way from under the heel of his glove, his body a roadmap of the horrors he had lived through.

David took the man's arm, so thin he could wrap his hand around it. "This will burn a little going in," he said, and swabbed the area just below the elbow with alcohol. "Pump it up for me."

The old man made a fist with his good hand, flexing up the vein. David injected, watching Mo's eyes, distant pain bleeding through in never-ending measure.

Mo sighed when David pulled out the needle, and laid his head back on the couch.

"It'll take a minute," he said.

"I understand," Mo replied.

"And Mo?" David said.

"Yes?"

"Just visit back there. Try not to fuck with anything. I'm not sure where our reality and the reality of the drug intertwine, but I think it's best not to . . . Mo?"

The man was gone.

David watched him for a moment, then drew a syringe of the antidote out of the pouch. It seemed silly to inject him so soon after giving him the drug, but he didn't want to strand Mo for too long in his past.

He took the limp arm, swabbing again, injecting again. Then he sat back and waited. Within a moment, Frankel's eyes began fluttering. He sat up quickly, shaking his head. The first thing that crossed the man's face was pain, his arms folding across his chest. Then puzzlement strained his features. He looked around the office as if he were seeing it for the first time.

"Mo?" David said.

Frankel's eyes rested on David. He looked at him as if trying to place him, then said, "David? David Wolf? Is it really you?"

"Of course it's me," David replied. "Who else?"

"But that was . . . so long ago. How is it possible that you . . . that this place . . ."

"I only injected you a minute ago," David said. "You've only been gone a minute or so."

Mo sat back, his features relaxing. "It's going to take me some time," he said, shaking his head. "I have a great deal to readjust to. This old body, for one. I'd forgotten what it felt like to live in it.''

"It worked, then," David said.

Mo's face brightened. He laughed, spontaneously, freely. David had never seen him this loose. "Yes, my dear friend. It worked."

"Where did you go?"

"Can I have some water?" Mo asked.

"Sure."

David went to his desk and took out a bottle of distilled water he kept there because he couldn't stand the taste of Oklahoma water. He poured Mo a paper cup full and brought it to him.

"Thanks," Frankel said, taking a small sip, then a deep breath, grimacing again with the pain of his body. "Where did I go, you ask. Well. I went to many places and did a great many things." Mo drank the rest of the water.

"Many places?" David said, taking the empty cup and wadding it up in his hand.

"Listen to me," Frankel said. "I've been wandering for a long time. I spent ten years alone studying Kabbala in the body of a Jewish scholar."

"Ten years?"

"I've wandered for lifetimes, David. The first few years I used to wonder about you, about . . . all this. But I soon enough forgot about it and went about my wandering with my people. I left Egypt with Moses . . ." He laughed. "It wasn't exactly like Cecil B. DeMille told it. The parting of the Red Sea was actually a flash flood. The plagues were real enough. They simply took a lot longer to occur than the Bible implies. And it was the Egyptian seers who blamed the Jews for them. Moses was smart enough to get us out of there while we argued among ourselves."

"I still can't believe this," David said. "Now I understand what Silv meant when she said you wouldn't want to wait for the drug to wear off by itself."

"The paths I've walked," Mo said, standing. "I knew King David, and Solomon. I had long talks with RaMBaM, Moses Maimonides, one of our greatest scholars." He walked a circle around David, tousling his hair. "I even knew Jesus."

David found himself smiling with Mo. "Really?"

Mo shrugged. "Yeah. One of my ancestors was one of his followers—Simon Peter, the one they called the Fisherman."

"And what was Jesus like?"

"He was okay," Frankel said. "A typical radical rabbi of the time. There were plenty of them, but he had real charisma. When the crowds got too big, and the talk got too revolutionary, the Romans got rid of him as a public nuisance."

"What about resurrection?"

"Aah, shadow chasing." Mo got himself another drink of water, downing it in one swallow. "We thought we saw him on the road one night, at least we wanted to think we did. Whoever it was sure looked like him, anyway. It was all very scary and mystical.

"By this time there was a pretty large congregation built up, so Peter learned to speak, and kept it going with the others."

"Did you ever interfere with anything?"

Mo sat again, stretching out with a grimace. "This body," he said, then turned to stare at David. "Not really. Once I kind of did with Peter. I couldn't resist playing psychiatrist. The man had some real problems. He had gone to Jaffa to preach. Things hadn't been going well. Jews were not amenable to conversion, especially to someone who claimed to be a messiah but had died without fulfilling the covenant. Anyway, Peter stopped for the night at Simon the tanner's house, right on the Mediterranean. He was hungry as hell, but didn't have any money, and Simon was serving shellfish for dinner. Well, Peter was deathly afraid of eating *traif*, nonkosher food. He went to bed hungry, almost deliriously so. It was stupid. So, I gave him a dream. I wrestled with him like God wrestled with Jacob, and Saul. I gave him a vision of wonderful nonkosher foods all dancing around in his head. Needless to say, he got up and ate. Harmless enough. You brought me back shortly after that."

"Simon the tanner," David said.

"What?"

"There's something familiar about that."

Mo was up again, pacing the room. "I feel so confined," he said, "so closed in. Moments ago, the entire history of the world was my playground; now I'm stuck between four walls in a failing body with no escape."

"What do you think about Sara?" David asked, turning to watch the man roam the office like a caged animal.

"Who's Sara?"

"She's the reason you took the drug."

Mo stopped walking and stared at David, his face falling. "Oh," he said quietly, lowering his head. "Let's wait a day or so for me to get myself together before we go injecting this in other people. Right now, all I want is to go back myself."

David picked up the pouch and zipped it closed, sticking it back in his sports jacket. "What do you mean?" he asked, slightly alarmed.

"I mean I want out of this shell again," Mo said, voice authoritative. "I mean I want you to send me back and leave me back." Mo looked at his deformed hand. "I had a cousin in Germany who passed as a non-Jew. He joined the SS and ultimately became one of Hitler's aides. It occurred to me that I could travel to his mind and kill that maniac before things like this—" he held up his hand—"could happen."

"You mean, change history," David said.

Mo shrugged. "Why not? This is not history, it's barbarism."

"You're not thinking clearly about this," David said. "Let's keep some sense of balance. You took a mental ride for a minute. You never left this room."

"That's not true and you know it," Mo said, harshness lacing his voice. "I was there. I was a participant in the unfolding of the world. Send me back, David."

David stood, moving toward the office door. "I've got to think about this," he said.

Frankel moved around to block the door. He reached out, taking David by the arms. "I'm asking you as a friend. Send me back."

David shrugged off the man's hands. "I can't give that responsibility to you," he said. "Not like this."

He moved out of the office then, through the waiting room toward the outer door.

"David, please!" Mo called, his voice broken and pitiful. "Don't leave me trapped here. Just send me for another minute, that's all I ask."

This was insanity. David walked out the door without turning around, his insides a cement mixer.

"David."

Mo Frankel's pleading voice followed him down the hall, drifting on the echoes of memory.

"David!"

* * *

"That'll be eight seventy-three, with tax," the teenage girl said as she hooked the aluminum tray to the window of David's Porsche.

She stood, leaning over at the waist, her unlined innocent face lewdly smacking gum as David straightened in the seat so he could get his hand down into his pocket for the money.

He pulled out a handful of bills, wadded and wrinkled, and found a ten amidst the flotsam and jetsam. He handed it through the window. "You keep the rest," he said.

"Thanks, mister," she said, her face, like any teenager's face, looking as if there were nothing more for her to learn in the entire universe. She had it all, all the answers—sex, music, and the right clothes. Immortality.

She moved off, her features blanched pale by the neon lights of the Sonic Drive-in. David watched her hips swaying in the short uniform skirt she wore, and remembered a time when Sonic carhops used to wear roller skates.

"What you're thinking is illegal," Liz said from beside him.

"Sin of omission," David said, giving her a hamburger from the tray. "I'm nothing but an old fart to girls that age. Did you order fries?"

"No," she replied. "But if they gave us some, let's look at it as Destiny." He handed her the cardboard boat and the Coke she had ordered.

"Bailey would never come here with me," he said, and took a sip from his own Coke. "She was afraid someone would see her."

"Still got the best burgers in town," Liz said around a mouthful. "Have you heard from her yet?"

He half turned in the black leather bucket seat, resting an arm on the steering wheel. "No. She's probably off shacked up with Jeffery somewhere. Guess I've screwed up another one."

"You just marry the wrong women, that's all."

"I think it's been kind of like another job," he said, and reached around to the window tray for his hamburger. "Psychiatrists are the poorest doctors there are. At a hundred bucks an hour, there are still only so many hours in the day. It seems my wives have always been income supplementers." He bit into the burger.

"I hate it when you talk like this," Liz said. "Don't sell yourself so short all the time."

"Maybe I'm just being realistic for once in my life. You've always taken up for me, and I love you for it, but I'm not a victim of circumstance. I've made my own problems and have to live with them."

"Maybe you didn't make all your own problems," she said softly.

A car pulled up two slots away from Liz's side, the carhop running out immediately. A pimple-faced boy with long greasy hair rolled down the window, the girl poking her head in and kissing him as his hand fondled her ample hip. No accounting for tastes.

"What do you mean by that?" he asked, and the suspicion was heavy in his voice.

"You already know what I'm going to say, you've got that tone in your voice again."

"You're going to talk about Momma," he said.

"I told you I went to a shrink today," she said. "It was because . . . because . . . Silv made me remember things that happened a long time ago, things I've tried to put out of my mind."

"About Momma," he said low.

"Listen to me," she said. "I know how you feel about her, but I can't share that, David. You remember when she killed herself . . . how old were you?"

"Seventeen," David said.

"Well, I was twelve." She ate some fries and washed them down, putting her paper cup up on the dash. "You remember her 'friend' Bert?"

"Yeah . . . the last one."

Liz's eyes had misted over. She took her head and drew it back. "He abused me, sexually abused me, for over two years."

"What? I—I never knew."

"We tried to keep it from you."

"We?"

"Mother and I," Liz said, and simply stared at him.

David put his food on the tray and reached out to take Liz's arms. "Mother knew?"

She shook her head slowly, her lips quivering. "It was M-mother who let h-him," she said, and this time the tears wouldn't hold back. She started crying, her whole body shaking. David leaned across the console and took her in his arms, letting her cry into his jacket. "I felt s-so ashamed, so responsible. He'd come into my room late at night, smelling of booze, stinking of sweat.'' She shuddered with revulsion. ''He'd call me his little doll baby at first, but when he was . . . doing it, he'd curse me, call me every name he could think of. Then he'd leave some money on the night table when he was done. Mother would come in later and clean me up and hold me. Then she'd take the money.''

''No!'' David said, pulling away. ''How can I believe what you're telling me?''

''The last time,'' she continued, her cheeks shining wet, ''it wasn't enough for him to have sex. He beat me, too. He beat me with a belt and with his fist. Mother got hysterical when she saw it. She threw him out, and . . . and that night she was dead.''

She stared at him, and he knew she was looking for his compassion. He was all tightened up inside. Naomi had been cursed. Deserted by a no-good husband, she had been forced to support herself and two young children without any help at all. He remembered. She had worked hard as a waitress, but that could never be enough. She had loved them both, he was more convinced of that than in anything in the world. The story that Liz told him simply couldn't fit that picture.

''I've always felt responsible, like all of it . . . all of it was my fault,'' Liz said. ''I've been afraid of men ever since, I think. I always have excuses for why the ones who come around are never good enough. But I'm beginning to think that maybe they're just excuses.''

''It's not your fault, Liz,'' David said, but his mind was busily rejecting her confession. He tried to move into a professional gear, but it just wasn't possible with this.

''Why are you pulling away from me?'' she asked.

''I'm not,'' he said.

''You are. I can feel you closing up.'' Her voice rose in pitch, her lips a slash. ''You've got to start facing up to this, just like I'm having to. You've always had a blind side on this. You can't—''

Suddenly she put a hand over her mouth, her eyes widening in fear.

''I can't what?'' he said.

''Nothing,'' she replied. ''Forget it.'' She turned in the seat, facing out the windshield, both hands shaking even though she had them tightly clamped together.

''Liz . . .'' he said.

"Take me home now, David."

"We have a lot to talk about," he said.

"Please, David. Take me home, I . . . aahhh . . ." Her hands went to her temples, grabbing. Then her body threw itself back against the seat and she took several deep breaths.

"Liz?" David said, alarmed. "Are you all right?"

She turned calmly to him, her face somehow different. "I'm back," she said.

"Silv," he breathed.

Silv looked down at her lap, at the hamburger that sat there in its white wrapper. "What's this?" she asked, picking it up.

"Food," he said. "Try it."

She tentatively brought it to her lips, looking at him before putting it in her mouth.

"Go ahead," he urged.

She bit into it, unsure, then began chewing, slowly at first, then with more confidence. She took another bite. "What is it?" she asked.

"Hamburger," he said. "Ground-up cow."

She began choking, spitting out the food. "You eat flesh!" she yelled.

"Yes. You don't?"

"Never," she said, taking the whole thing and handing it to him. She saw the glass and grabbed it, taking a drink of Coke. She washed it around in her mouth, then opened the car door and spit it out, the teenaged boy in the next car staring with his mouth open.

She closed the door again. "This drink isn't bad," she said. "It's sweet to the taste."

"I'm sorry I panicked at the Pearl Harbor thing," he said. "It was all so . . . strange."

"Forgivable," she said, but didn't look as if she meant it. "I gave you extras in case you felt the need to experiment before getting the confidence to really make the jump."

"The power of this," he said, "is more than I think I can handle."

She nodded. "Then you must know why I'm so desperate to get Hersh back. The responsibility of this is so awesome that no human being should be able to use its power . . ."

"Its seduction," he said.

"You *do* understand," she said, and laid a hand on his arm. "This was never meant to be discovered. I have no idea what will happen if someone on the drug changes history. If reality is, after all, an illusionary state, then with this drug we could potentially tear its fabric apart completely."

"On one hand, what you said makes no sense," he replied, and went for his burger again. He started to take a bite, but Silv was staring at him in such horror that he put it back on the tray. "On the other hand, I've been there and your logic is inescapable. It seemed real, down in Ardmore, as if it was happening right then."

"It was," she said.

"I gave the drug to someone else," he said.

Her shoulders squared and she turned to him, angry. "You did what?"

"I was afraid . . . confused. I needed help. I needed advice. He was amenable."

The woman in Liz's face had strained it ugly with rage. "Don't you see what's happening here, you idiot? I invented the means of the world's destruction. I'm trying desperately to undo what I've done, but now it's all getting out of hand. How could you do that?"

"What do you expect?" he returned, just as angry. "You come into my house, in my sister's body, with some cock-and-bull story about time travel and genetic drugs, and you expect me to just fall in with the program just like that. Why in God's name did you come to me at all? I never asked for this. I don't want it now."

"I need your help," she said.

"There's more than that. There's got to be more."

She started to speak, but turned away instead. "What about the person you gave the drug to?"

"One of my colleagues," David said. "He's back now."

"Then he's dangerous," Silv said.

"Dangerous?" David laughed. "Mo's the sweetest man who ever lived."

"If he's had it . . . if he knows you have it . . . if he's felt its power, knows its addiction—he's dangerous." She looked at him again. This time her face was fearful. "Come with me now. You know how the time dilation works. I've been with Hersh. He still won't leave the body. He's gone to Egypt to wage war against the Turks. We can catch up to him there."

"Egypt? Now?"

"1798," she said. "We have ancestors there. Come with me. Help me." She half smiled. "It will only take a minute."

He was half fear, half excitement. He didn't want to make

a decision like this on the whim of a second. "I don't have it with me," he said.

"Your life is misery," she said. "Look at this as a great adventure. Come with me."

"I've told you..."

"Of course you have it with you," she said. "You know the power by now. No one who knows the power could leave it out of his sight. Get it out." An order.

He reached into his jacket pocket, slowly drawing out the zipper case that now contained six syringes. She took the case from him and opened it, immediately taking out one of the needles.

"Don't hold that up in here!" David whispered harshly.

She looked startled, then thought with Liz's brain. "Drugs are illegal," she said, almost comically, and lowered the syringe, looking around.

"I'll have to take my coat off," he said.

"Don't bother," she said, kneeling up on the seat and bending across the console. "I can get it to you quicker."

Like a flash she moved on him, pushing the needle into his neck and plunging quickly.

"There," she said, and sat back.

He began to feel strange almost immediately. He closed his eyes and leaned his head back. "Why did you take me to Ardmore?" he asked.

"I wanted you to be hit with everything at once," she said. "So you'd understand. So you'd believe. Remember Napoleon... remember Egypt. Remember. Remember."

Whoever walks by the way and sees a fine tree and a fine field and a fine sky and leaves them to think on other thoughts—that man is like one who forfeits his life!

Give us back our fine trees and fine fields! Give us back the universe...

—Berdichevsky

Heat.

Blinding light.

Infinite blue.

David squinted, as if the eyes he squinted through were his own. Blinking, he slowly opened them wide to find himself standing in the midst of a vast desert that stretched out as far as the eye could see. The sun glared off the sand, making it glow, the atmosphere dancing in shimmering waves.

He was hot and thirsty, and had a nagging pain in his left leg, a deep pain that made him wince. He felt incredibly dirty, in need of a bath, and knew he must smell terrible.

His name was Louis Cuvier, and he was a farm boy from Aix. He had joined the army at seventeen to get out of the fields. He was uneducated, and was now in total withdrawal from his own body under someone else's command. Louis Cuvier had already decided he had gone insane, but, apparently unable to do anything about it, had simply wimpered emotionally within his inhabited shell.

An army stretched around him, their woolen blue jackets and white cotton britches totally unsuited to the harsh Egyptian climate, but Bonaparte was a stickler for discipline and bearing and refused to let them out of uniform.

Louis's first action was against the Mamelukes under Murad Bey, the Circassian who could decapitate an ox with a single blow of his scimitar. Then they faced the Egyptian infantry at the Battle of the Pyramids, Napoleon using his heavy artillery, muskets, and battle squares to superb advantage, defeating the army of 24,000 in less than two hours, with the loss of barely two hundred men. French democracy had come to the Holy Land.

David stood, turning, simply taking it all in. There was a headiness here that went beyond understanding. He was here, two hundred years in his own past, watching history unfold. He had borrowed a body that had been dead for centuries and was reliving the moments of its life. Silv had said that reality was illusionary, but the reverse was also true. He had no idea of what any of this could mean, but he was excited as hell to be involved in the process of discovery.

A half-mile in the distance, the great pyramids of Giza thrust into the bright blue sky. Stone monoliths, a family: Daddy, Momma, babies. They were massive, even from a distance. He had come to Egypt once with Jenny, his second wife, but had stayed in the hotel and gotten drunk the night the tour bus came out for the pyramid show. He wasn't sorry now. Nothing could ever replace this first magnificent look from the viewpoint of history and of an eighteen-year-old French boy with a bayonet wound in the left leg from chasing Egyptians into the Nile.

"Louis," someone called to him in French. He spoke

French! Without a lesson in his life, David Wolf spoke fluent, if peasant, French. He wondered what a quick mind would be like to inhabit.

He turned confidently to his name, though a sudden pang held him back. *What if they can recognize me through my disguise?*

"Gerard," David said, recognizing Louis's cousin. "Were you able to find anything for the pain?"

"Only this," Gerard said, pulling a bottle of local wine from inside his coat. "Perhaps it will do you, eh?"

Louis reached instinctively for the wine, David recoiling when he pictured the open market it must have come from. He remembered the smells—pumpkins, fly-blown dates, camel cheese. He pulled his hand back.

I need it!

Not now.

"Something wrong with the wine, David?" Gerard asked in English.

David started at his name. They *could* see through the disguise. "No, I . . . I . . ."

"It's me, Silv," Gerard said. "David?"

"Silv," David sighed. "You're a man?"

"You can be anything you want," Silv said impatiently. "Now listen. He's in the shade of the pyramids, having some sort of party. We'll start on him now."

"We're not allowed to go over there," David heard Louis say.

Silv stared at him, her bushy red moustache highlighting a ruddy complexion. He had gotten used to her as Liz. He hardly felt comfortable with this blue-eyed, stringy-haired wild man. "We don't have time for your nonsense," she said. "Just come with me."

Silv turned and strode off, her blue uniform tattered and stained with wide rings of sweat. David took a step, pain searing his left leg.

We need it now. Now.

"All right," David mumbled, and jerked the cork from the dusty bottle. He started to wipe the lip on his coat sleeve, then thought better of it when he saw the mites crawling there. He took a drink. It tasted like charcoal starter smells.

But the second sip wasn't so bad.

He hurried after Silv, making his way through camp, the men looking for shade and fighting the swarms of black flies that continually plagued them. They drank and complained and sang *"La Marseillaise,"* or *"Les héros morts pour la liberté."* But it was misery he felt in Louis, and in all of them, a sense of uselessness, and sense of being used.

This was only one regiment of the 55,000 troops who had come to Egypt with the general. The rest were in Cairo on leave or scattered through the provinces being ambushed by Bedouin.

Silv had already moved out of the camp area and was trudging across the sand. David hurried to catch up, the pain in Louis's leg nearly unbearable. It had to be infected. If the boy wasn't careful, he would lose the whole leg, maybe worse.

No!

He took another drink, feeling Louis's fear rising up in him also. He was jolted. A connection. Why did he understand Louis's fears of joining?

"Our policy has been one of patience and restraint, as befits a peaceful and powerful nation, which leads a worldwide alliance . . ."

Twelve years old, he sits in front of the television, listening to a president tell him that nuclear war might be close at hand. His hands are trembling with the unfairness of it. How can the world do this to children?

He watches in horror as Jerry, in a too-small uniform, grabs Momma. He jumps to his feet.

No!

"No!"

"David," Silv said sharply. "Would you be quiet?"

"You came to me when I was a child," he said, taking another drink, the pain ebbing somewhat. "You screwed up my life."

"I already told you that," she said.

"But I didn't get it."

He tilted the bottle back again.

"Don't drink any more than you need for the pain," she said, raising an eyebrow.

"Come on," he said. "I'm a big boy. I've been handling my liquor all by my myself for a long time now."

"I'm not amused," she said.

"I don't give a fuck what you are, lady," he replied. "This

is my dream, not yours. And I'm going to have to get my young friend here some medical help pretty quick."

"What do you mean?"

"I mean he's hurt. I mean I'm a doctor and know how to fix things like that. What the hell you think I mean?"

"We don't have time," Silv said casually. "And what if he's destined to have trouble with the leg? Leave it be, David. If the body stops working well, get another. I feel many presences here."

"You callous bitch," he said. "Don't you have any feelings at all?"

"You're a good one to talk about feelings," Silv said in French, then switched to English. "React as little as possible with the body you inhabit. It isn't our place to direct their lives. If the pain gets too bad, abstract yourself from it."

"I took an oath when I became a doctor."

"I know you too well," she said, switching back to French. "Don't try and put something like that over on me. Just do as I say."

David laughed and took another drink. "Don't push me, Silv. I don't need any of this. I can jump out on you anytime."

"You won't, though," she said. "You're standing at the gateway of existence right now with your mouth hanging open. I saw the look on your face when you crossed over before. Besides, it's not every shrink who gets the chance to psychoanalyze Napoleon Bonaparte."

"Never thought of it that way," David said, realizing she was using Liz's speech patterns to lull him. He didn't completely trust Silv, and determined to keep an eye on her.

"There he is," she said, pointing.

"Anything I should know?" David asked.

Silv thought for a minute. "Hersh has changed the name since the last time I saw him," she said finally. "Dropped the U from the spelling of Buonaparte."

"Interesting," David said.

"How so?"

"That's the spelling of the name that sticks through history."

Silv shrugged indifferently. "Perhaps it was the host's idea, then."

"Perhaps," David replied, surprised Silv was willing to let such historical analog slide away so easily. He filed the notion away for future reference.

They had come within fifty yards of the pyramids and the several hundred people who milled around their bases. The late afternoon sun was already down beneath the peaks of the monoliths, creating large areas of shade where tables full of food and drink were set.

Arab sheiks and their entourages mixed with Egyptian and European citizens and Bonaparte's officers. Camels bleated and walked freely through the crowds, while veiled women peered out from the flaps of brightly colored tents, giggling and scurrying back inside from time to time to share something with their sisters.

"Incredible," David said. "I still can't believe it."

"Look at him, strutting around and poking out his chest," Silv said with contempt.

David recognized the general immediately. He easily addressed a large crowd that had gathered around him, laughing and gesturing as he told a story. He was a small man, but his face betrayed a much larger stature. It seemed to glow from within with power and confidence—all self-generated. His uniform was not much better looking than David's, but he wore it like a god—bright clean, buttoned all the way up to the neck, his boots polished to reflection.

Once in David's life he had been in the presence of true greatness in the person of a renowned microbiologist who had pioneered and perfected the science of bone marrow transplants. The man was gentle and soft-spoken, but anyone who ever came in contact with him knew that he shone with an inner light that was far brighter than their own. He had the same feeling now.

"Come on," Silv said, and led him right into the crowd, despite Louis's protestations. The smells were nearly overpowering. David had never realized how olfactorily anesthetized his culture was until he walked into that crowd. Reluctantly, he found himself abstracting as Silv had suggested, guiding Louis from a distance. Both the pain and the smells subsided to background annoyance. Whenever his charge showed an inclination to bolt and run, he slipped back in and guided again, like riding a horse.

They had pushed their way right up to the inner circle. Strangely enough, Napoleon was in the process of acting out a ghost story, playing the parts like an actor, and a ham actor at that. Silv didn't give him the opportunity to finish.

"Hersh," she said.

The man stopped talking and stared at the red-haired, red-faced corporal who had spoken to him.

A general with too large a head and frizzy hair strode up and laid a hand on Silv's shoulder. "Return to the regiment, Corporal," he said in a nasal voice, "and turn yourself in to your commanding officer."

"No, Berthier," Napoleon said gently. "I must have words with these... gentlemen. If you will excuse me, we will continue with the stories later."

He turned and walked immediately from the group, Silv angrily marching right out with him. David hurried to catch up, Louis still protesting within.

The pyramids rose magnificently around them, the Sphinx nearby, all but the top of its head buried in the sand.

"Why can't you leave me alone?" Napoleon/Hersh said to Silv in French.

"You don't belong here. This world is the domain of others. You have no right."

"We've been through this before," he spat, rage just under the surface. "The whole universe is yours. Leave this part of it to me."

"I can't do that. You must return with me."

The man laughed. "Will you return, Silv? Return to what?"

"Don't," Silv said quickly.

"And who's this?" the man asked, jerking a thumb in David's direction.

David hurried to walk next to them, feeling foolish at being shy to meet a legendary historical figure. "My name's David Wolf," he said.

"From where? What quad?"

David shrugged sheepishly. "From... Oklahoma City."

"What century?" Hersh asked, his features dark.

"Twentieth?" David said.

Hersh looked at Silv. "Don't give me a hard time while you go dragging people here from all over the damned universe."

"I'm a doctor," David said. "Silv asked me to—"

"Not now, David," Silv ordered.

Hersh narrowed his eyes. "What's the game, Silv? What are you and your *boy* trying to pull here?"

She stopped walking and pointed a finger at him, David

taking another drink. "We're here to convince you to give up this stupid charade and go back where you belong."

"I belong here!" he shouted, and drew a small sword from his side, sticking the point in Silv's neck, pushing her back until she was flattened against one of the mammoth stone slabs of the Great Pyramid of Cheops.

"Listen to me," he hissed, the point of his sword drawing a small trickle of blood from Silv's neck. "I was brilliant in Italy, victory after victory, republican government instead of the domination of the bloody holy vandal Pope in Rome. They wanted me to attack England. Instead, I came here, a small step from India where I can wrest away from them their economic livelihood—much better than attacking them directly.

"We've a Destiny here, to bring ideas of Justice and government and art and science to this backward land. I have a hundred and fifty civilian scholars with me to help advance this place. I've set up postal service, and a mint. I've put streetlamps in Cairo and built its first hospital. The first books printed in this country were done by me, pamphlets on how to treat bubonic plague and smallpox. The name Napoleon means Lion of the Desert, and the Egyptians call me Sultan El Kebir, commander in chief." He pointed to the Sphinx, its face glowing complacently in the declining light. "I'm digging that great art treasure out of the sands of superstition. Me. I'm doing it. Now, tell me where I belong."

Silv never flinched. "You promote the very ideas of progress that you say destroyed the world we came from."

"I don't care, Silv," Hersh said. "I'm housed in a magnificent mind with grand ideas. My existence is important and useful, and nothing either you or your skimmer friend can say is going to change a thing. The only reason I don't kill you right here is because you'd just jump to another body and I'd be out a couple of good soldiers."

"Then, kindly lower that that pig sticker," Silv said.

Hersh threw his head back and laughed deeply. "Pig sticker!" he howled. "Stay with that body long enough and we'll make a good republican out of you!"

He lowered his sword and sided it. "Hell," he said, and turned to smile at David. "I can't get rid of you, and you can't get rid of me. What do you say we return to the festivities and be civilized about the whole business."

"You've never known a civilized day in your life," Silv said.

"Don't get tedious," Hersh said, then winked at David. "Right, skimmer?"

"Right," David said, secretly happy to see Silv put in her place. The wine was doing its job; the approaching evening was cooling things down; the setting was magnificent; the company was incomparable. "Let's party."

Hersh smiled widely. "That's the fellow," he said; and reaching out, he pulled David's ears, laughing the whole time. "Come, my friend, let's go make a speech. I just love making speeches."

Arm in arm, Hersh and David, Napoleon and Louis, made their way back to the head table, leaving Silv behind. Everyone rose at their approach, the general waving them back to their seats. "We're all free men here," he said.

A sheep's head was set on a large silver platter in the center of the table, its meat piled beneath it, the whole thing set atop a layer of rice. Everyone used their knives to carve off pieces.

The table consisted of the nine ruling sultans who Napoleon used as his buffers between himself and the Egyptian people, plus his officers, and a handful of civilians.

"Gentlemen," Napoleon announced. "This is my friend…" He looked at David.

"Louis," David said. "Louis Cuvier."

The general reached out and tore off part of the sheep's gum and handed it to David. "Louis will be joining us tonight. My young friend is quite an extraordinary man. He can foretell the future."

"Like a gypsy?" asked an old man.

"That's Tallien," Napoleon whispered. "Very stern man."

"N-no," David stammered. "Not like a gypsy."

"Louis is a visionary," Hersh said, winking. "He can tell the futures of science and government."

"What is the future of disease?" asked a middle-aged man with a fleshy face. "Will smallpox or the bubis take us all?"

"Gaspard Monge," Napoleon said. "A good foil. He saved the Republic by showing us how to turn church bells into bullets."

David smiled. "Smallpox, the plague, typhus, consumption— all the diseases that take your lives now will be virtually eradicated by mid-twentieth century, thanks to understanding of the body's own immunological systems and a drug called penicillin that was developed from bread mold."

Everyone laughed at the bread mold, no one taking him the least bit seriously. Hersh nodded knowingly to David. Somewhere during the discussion, Silv came to stand near the table, in David's plain sight. Unmoving, unspeaking, she stared at him with deep, pained eyes.

"And transportation," Berthier said, tugging on his drooping moustache. "Will we replace the horse?"

"Yes," David said. "Horses won't even be allowed on most city streets."

Everyone laughed again, making David feel the butt of it all. He carried on, his face getting red.

"In the twentieth century, horses will be replaced by an invention called the automobile, a wheeled carriage that has an engine to turn the axle. When one wants to go a long distance, there's always the airplane, a winged vehicle that can cross the ocean from America to Europe in a matter of hours. Men even journey into space in rocket ships."

"And do they hit their heads on heaven's floor?" a captain said, the whole table laughing. "The young fool thinks he's been there!"

"Give him more wine!" Berthier yelled. "Perhaps he'll live in the thirtieth century."

David stared at the laughing faces around the table. He had forgotten and fallen into his own viewpoint. "Just a dream," he said sheepishly.

"A dream of Utopia?" Hersh asked.

David stared at him, aware of what he was getting at. "No, not Utopia," he said bitterly. "Advances in technology mean advances in ways to kill. Weapons of unbelievable power that can destroy whole cities and make their lands uninhabitable, environmental sicknesses that poison the air and the water for everyone, a world population of nearly eight billion with no way to feed them. Misery in massive doses, life only for those who can afford it."

"Like now," one of the Moslems said, pulling his robes tighter around himself. This one not laughing.

David looked at him. "Maybe nothing ever changes."

A pall fell over the table. Napoleon stood immediately and banged his wine goblet with his knife. "Enough predictions. I have something to say."

He waited until all nearby had quieted before reading from a piece of paper he pulled from his pocket. "Cadis, Sheiks, Imams—" he read loudly, "tell the people that we too are true Moslems. Are we not the men who have destroyed the Pope, who preached eternal war against the Moslems? Are we not those who have destroyed the Knights of Malta, because those madmen believed that they should constantly make war on your faith? We must work together for the unification of our brotherhood. We all worship the same God; we are all of one flesh. I beseech you not to look upon us as conquerors, but as your brothers. I ask that you go to your mosques and tell the people that the French are Moslems like themselves. Advise all Egyptians to take an oath of loyalty to your new government. Only then may we all be free to live in peace here in the Land of all Lands."

He sat then, winking at David and taking a sip out of his goblet, Berthier hurrying to refill it from a pitcher.

One of the muftis stood, lost in the folds of his black robes, his eyes alive, dancing through the tangle of his white beard and leather face.

"Sultan El Kebir," he said. "We will be happy to issue a proclamation to our people concerning our deliverance by your hand from the horror of the Turks. A friend of the Prophet, yes, my lord. But should the French wish to truly be called Moslem, you must first renounce wine, then submit to the rites of circumcision."

The Frenchmen at the table groaned loudly, Napoleon trying hard to keep the grin off his face. He stood, bowing deeply. "A friend of the Prophet it is, Honored One."

David laughed with the rest of them, beginning to feel comfortable at the right hand of Power. Silv stood watching him intently, but it didn't bother him at all. He'd had wives pull that one on him all the time.

They sat, talking of war and drinking until well after dark, until the pyramids were black, looming gods of silence, watching their every move, as they had watched others.

David had finished his bottle, and had helped with several pitchers, recounting events of the world to come for the amusement of the guests. No one, of course, believed such fantasies. And after a time, David stopped believing them himself.

And through the night Silv stood her lonely vigil, never moving, never speaking. Finally, as the festivities began to wind down, Napoleon took David aside under the pretext of seeing the sheiks to their tents.

"My friend," he said in David's ear, "let's slip away. I have something to show you."

Then, like a child, Hersh wished many good-nights in his grandiloquent way, then ran around a red-and-white striped tent, hiding behind.

David hurried after him, the man taking him by the hand and charging across the sand to hide around the edge of the smallest pyramid.

Putting his back against the stone, he peered around the corner to observe the activity. He came back smiling. "Good. No one has seen us. Come on."

David followed giddily. Louis was shitfaced, but David, an older and far more accomplished drinker, was simply transported, floating on butterfly wings, no cares, no responsibilities. Hell, if Louis got sick, he could just remove himself and wait it out.

They began to move through the monoliths, David beginning to realize some discomfort from the wine. "Where does a man go to take a piss around here?" he asked.

"The world, my friend, is our pissoir," Hersh said, gesturing toward the pyramids. "Just pick a convenient rock."

So both men unbuttoned their britches and pissed upon the pyramids, Hersh muttering, "*Mon general* is unfortunately small in all departments."

Both David and Louis sighed with the relief. Napoleon, who drank very little, finished before David and, turning to him, said, "So, what does it all mean, David Wolf? Now that the universe is yours, what will you do with it?"

David watched his urine run down the rocks hewn five thousand years ago to soak in the ageless sand. "It's too overpowering," he said. "Too new. I can't..."

"We'll talk," Hersh said. "But not here. Come, I have something to show you at the officers' bivouac."

David buttoned up and they walked on beyond the monoliths to the other side, where the officers would be shaded from the morning sun. The sky was magnificent overhead; a starfield two or three times greater than anything he had ever seen twinkled through a clean, clear atmosphere unhampered by pollution or city lights.

God's country. God?

They walked into the neatly laid-out rows of officers' tents, past the picket of sentries to a huge tent, stopping before it.

"Yours?" David asked.

Hersh simply smiled and shook his head, siding the flap for David to enter. He moved into a perfumed haze, amid a silent, sputtering glow of candles.

"Berthier's shrine," Hersh said, low, almost reverently. "Come here."

The smoke of frankincense hung like a shroud, braiding through the thick smell of the orchids that adorned small tables and vases set all around. They moved toward the altar at the back of the large room. It was set with many kinds of flowers, all crowded together. Between two large flickering candles was set a portrait of a woman with deep, dark eyes and hair relentlessly black that fell past her shoulders.

"It takes three mules to carry this setup," Hersh said.

"Who is it?" David asked.

"Giuseppina Visconti," Hersh replied. "Berthier met her while we campaigned in Italy, and has been a slave to his own passions ever since. He daily threatens to resign as my chief of staff and return to her there. At night, he goes out and stands beneath the Moon at the exact moment that she is seeing it in Milan."

"Incredible," David said.

"No," Hersh answered sternly. "We all have our ruling passions, our reasons for being. What are yours, Mr. Wolf? What makes you go wander out under the Moon?"

"I should ask you that question," David said, falling into his professional mode. "You seem to have an answer for it."

Meditation cushions were scattered around the tent floor. Hersh gathered several together and made a small lounge for himself, reclining on it. "He gets so angry when I do this," the man giggled, then lay flat on his back. "You turn my question around on me, Twentieth Century. But I will answer it for you."

He put his hands behind his head and stared upward, as if watching the sky instead of dark canvas. "I have lived many lifetimes, done things you couldn't even imagine—acts of supreme kindness, acts of unspeakable horror. My happiness is in the doing, I've found that out. When I realized I could jump from death, that I was, for all purposes, immortal, I began to look for the right world to house my godhead."

"Godhead?" David asked, amused.

"Call it what you want," Hersh said, abruptly sitting up and staring. "I've found no other god but me. Neither will you."

David sat on the carpet-strewn floor. He tried to cross his legs, but the pain was too intense. He straightened them out in front of him. "Don't you feel a sense of responsibility toward the lives you take over, the lives you may screw up by changing things?"

Hersh laughed. "The man who lived here before I showed up hates my guts," he said, "but he's never turned down my advice, either. You see, I found him as child at a military school. He was involved, of all things, in a snowball fight with a great many other children. I was jolted, when I passed through the mind, by its power and its limitless desires, and I determined to stay in this one and ride it out to see where it could go. You are beginning to see the results around you."

"But you have no right to do these things, especially with your knowledge of the future."

"I have no knowledge of this future," Hersh said. "I have no idea where this will take me. I discovered many years ago that when skimming it's always more fun to not know in advance."

"Are you trying to tell me that Napoleon is not known in your culture?"

The man raised a hand, eyes flashing in the jumping candlelight. "Say no more about it. I will not hear anything concerning this man's future, do you understand?"

"Why does this point bother you so much?" David asked.

"I will answer your other question," Hersh said, standing, pacing with his hands behind his back. "Concerning my rights. You see, I've discovered that there is no right, no wrong, no ethics. I can make life what I wish. After all, this is just a fantasy, anyway. There's no reason, David Wolf. There's no rhyme, no point, here. Lives come and go, passing before our eyes like the shadows of orchids jumping in the light on the side of the tent. I live for the honor of the moment, the glory, the rush of accomplishment.

"I've found a mind after all my travels that lives as huge as my own desires. We're capturing a profusion of moments here, reaping memories. Ask the body you're in how he felt when the Mameluke cavalry charged us on July thirteenth."

David didn't have to ask. "The Arabian horses," he said, "prancing, carrying their riders lightly, snorting. The riders with arms inlaid with gold and precious stone, their costumes brightly colored, wearing turbans surmounted by egret feather, some with gilded helmets. It was glorious, a moment like no other, a moment to remember. We fought for France; we fought for riches.''

''There, you see?'' Hersh said.

''I also remember that we would have died of thirst had we not taken Alexandria. I remember promises of villages with food and water, and finding nothing but desert and ruined hovels, cisterns filled in by the Bedouin. I remember men being trampled to death when we finally found a well. I remember men shooting themselves after losing their wits. I remember us desperately needing rations and medical supplies and getting nothing but reams of your proclamations. I remember Nelson sinking the fleet, including *L'Orient* with all our ecus, cutting us off and stranding us here.''

Hersh put up his hands. ''My friend, you will learn soon enough that pain is not a cumulative commodity. The moments . . . the moments are everything.''

''But these are your moments,'' David said, pointing a finger, ''at the expense of the rest of the world.''

''Yes,'' Hersh said with authority. ''My dream, my moments. I ask you again, David Wolf, what is it you seek with *your* godhead?''

David stared up at one of the most loved and hated figures ever to walk the face of the planet and felt the man's eyes boring into him like a spoon digging out bitter grapefruit. ''An end to the pain,'' he said quietly, both of them turning to the sound of the tent flap being sided.

Silv stood there, outlined by the night, her visage stern and uncompromising. ''Are you coming, David?'' she asked.

Silv picked the place, David knew, for several reasons. Hersh could not find them there to eavesdrop, for one, and certainly a place like this could not be conducive to causing any disturbances in the timeline. But as he rose from the chair, shifting his brown habit, the heavy rosary beads he wore as a cinch clicking against his legs, he knew that she had also picked it to humble him, to keep him off balance.

He walked to the window of the tiny, damp room. The walls were bare, the furniture plain, the atmosphere spartan. This was a place of prayer and meditation, all comforts selfish and useless and sinful. Sister Mary Teresa's withered, liver-spotted hand sided the curtain to look out at the effects of two weeks of overcast and rain on Woodstock Abbey.

The grounds winding down to the Oxford forests were a pale, vibrant green; all the vegetation, all the myriad shades of green and brown glowed from a surfeit of water in unnatural, garish hues. Compelling but unreal. Dogs bayed a distance down the forest paths, a hunt in progress. Castle Woodstock and its environs, including the abbey, had once been a hunting lodge, but Henry I had forced its larger constructions simply by spending time there, the machineries of government having to move with him. Outside of the imprisonment of the teenaged Princess Elizabeth by her sister, Mary, at the abbey the year before, nothing of any import had happened there since the time of Henry II and his great love affair with Rosamund Clifford.

David dropped the curtain and turned, not surprised to see Sister Jude standing in the doorspace. Sister Mary was surprised, however, to find she had a relative at the abbey.

"This tomb doth here enclose/ The world's most beauteous rose," Sister Jude said.

David answered, smiling, with, "Rose passing sweet erewhile,/ Now naught but odor vile."

Jude nodded and entered, closing the door. The words they spoke, from Rosamund's tombstone, were said to have been written by Henry himself. Though the nuns all secretly knew the verse, not one of them would ever be caught dead reciting it.

"So, how does it feel to be a woman, David?" Silv asked, stretching out on Sister Mary's cot.

"Strange," David replied. "Different, but the same. Does that make sense?"

"It'll be vespers soon, we don't have much time," Silv said. "What do you think you're doing with Hersh?"

David sat on a rough, wooden chair, the woman inside him convinced she had been possessed by demons. She seemed very afraid of men because of childhood traumas and David, very unprofessionally, sent her into acts of contrition by filling her head with all manner of vile thought.

"You've got a great way of ingratiating yourself to people, Silv," he said, hugging himself against the chill.

"We've got no time for what your sister Liz calls 'chit-chat,'" Silv said, picking up the cross on the huge rosary and turning it over in her hands, studying it idly. "I brought you back for a reason, and now it seems you're turning on me."

"You want me to analyze the son of a bitch, don't you?" David said loudly, exasperated.

Silv jerked up in the bed, waving her arms for silence. "This is a cloister, you idiot. Not so loud. We may as well take it down to the chapter house and invite everyone to hear our talk."

"What difference would it make?" David asked. "Come on, Silv. Loosen up. We're going to have to be a little bit flexible on how we do this. This whole thing does qualify as extenuating circumstances, don't you think?"

She stared at him, her face in conflict. "Where I come from," she said, "people do as I say. It's been that way for . . . for a long time. I'm having a difficult time adjusting to your ways."

"And you're scared," David said.

"I'm what?" she rasped, unable to yell.

"There's no shame in that," David answered. "I think I know how you feel. You've set wheels in motion that you have no control over and you're afraid of the results."

"I'm a person used to control," she said.

David stood, feeling all the aches and pains that accompany a fifty-year-old body that has spent half that time mortifying its own flesh. The room smelled of mildew and decay. He moved to sit beside Silv, wanting to scratch underneath the tight hood he wore. "You're going to have to take this as it comes," he said, patting her leg. "If you want to succeed, it's the only way."

"Does that mean you're going to help me?" she asked, the body she inhabited pursing its wrinkled lips.

He looked away from her. "I—I honestly don't know," he said. "I'm not even sure what it is I'm supposed to be doing."

Silv started to respond, but David put up a hand to silence her, the sleeve of the Benedictine robe sliding down his arm. "Let me say a few things out, first. Then you tell me where I'm wrong." He gestured around the room. "I know that this . . . all this, is real. I can believe that because I believe what I see, what I touch, what I think. But I have a difficult time believing that the entire situation is real. I'll just wake up sometime and be right back in the Sonic Drive-in and say, 'Wow, what a dream.' And the crazy part of it is that's exactly what *will* happen. Time past is time passed—gone, a memory.

These *dreams* that we're manipulating might be nothing but that.''

"I came to you," she said softly, "as a child. I adversely affected your life. That was no dream, David. A few seconds' worth of outside contamination in your twelve-year-old mind and you were altered, perhaps for good and all. No, this is no metaphysical-hypothetical discussion we're having. Hersh would like you to believe that because it voids him of any responsibility in the matter. He's merely justifying his actions.''

David breathed out, fingering the rosary. "You're right," he said. "I'm not adjusting well to all of this.''

"Understandable," she replied, her features softening. "New rules, new game. But the same ethics apply, and that's where our concentration should center. Think about this: If Hersh is wrong and he appreciably changes historical imperatives, he could destroy all life on this planet. He could end bloodlines, promote others. And what possible effect could the dichotomy of unmatched historical perspective have on the timeline itself? Any possible scenario short of Hersh's dream is likely to be genocidal.'' She jabbed a finger at her chest. "I don't want that responsibility on my head, all right?''

"And do you think that I want it?" he said, loudly again, then quieted. "Look, this is your deal. I'm not cut out for this sort of shit. I've never known an unselfish moment in my whole life. You're a fool to expect anything out of me.''

She stood, angry, and moved to stand right in front of him. "And you love to feel sorry for yourself, too," she said. "How many times do I have to tell you that given your special connection to this whole thing, you were the only possible choice? Let's try it another way: You have the chance, because of who you are, to help save humanity's future. None of us wanted it. We just got stuck. Why don't you just stop crying about it and do what your own ethics demand?''

The logic was inescapable. David was there. His purpose was all locked up with Hersh and Silv now. There was no one else. He walked to the window and stared out, horses, and riders in red coats farther down the pathway recreating the first hunt. Recreating all hunts. Sister Mary was praying in the back of his mind. He let himself swoon into it and rode with her for a moment. He was right when he had said he hadn't known an unselfish moment. Maybe it was time, for once in his useless life, to give back some of what he had taken. He smiled. Bailey wouldn't believe this. Hell, he didn't believe it himself. He broke from Sister Mary's internal novena and turned to Silv.

"I'm worried about Hersh's mental state," he said.

Her lips tightened, her eyes staring deep, an undoubtedly unknown gesture to the little old lady in whose spirit house she now resided. "What do you mean?"

He couldn't stand it. He pulled back the hood and scratched his head, using both hands. Sister Mary obviously had head lice, but didn't scratch them as part of her mortification exercises. "He shows some evidence of psychosis," he said, still scratching. "His delusions about the Egyptian campaign nowhere near match up with Louis's reality. His boldness is, I'm afraid, a result of these delusions. His mood swings, his introspection, his refusal to deal with reality on any level . . . including his time skimming—all these point in the direction of relatively severe psychosis. Couple that with the fact that he's a leader of men . . ."

"How about the person whose body he inhabits?" she asked. "What is his mental state?"

"Give me a break," David said, pulling the hood back into place and automatically tucking a few wisps of hair beneath it. "I'm sticking my neck out a mile to make the statements I've made on the basis of one session. This is no quick study."

"How long?"

"To diagnose him or cure him?"

"Cure."

"To cure him . . . years, maybe more than a few. Psychosis is usually more difficult to deal with, and more dangerous, than neurosis."

She clasped her hands in front of her, probably a gesture common to Sister Jude. "Anything could happen in a matter of years," she said.

He laughed. "Don't you know about the history of Bonaparte?"

"No," she said, her face darkening. "Back in the quad, I found the name in Data, but it was classified. After I found him, I haven't wanted to know, or I'd drive myself crazy trying to help things along."

"Well, I *do* know," David said, "—a little bit, anyway. Enough to tell you we're in very deep shit."

"Tell me no more."

He nodded. "I'll honor your wish," he said, and envied her lack of knowledge. "One thing. I don't know about the Egyptian campaign, but as his doctor, I fear that his delusions will keep him from any victory. Things may fall apart in the desert very quickly."

"Why don't we meet back there and continue watching him?"

"Sure," David answered. "One thing, though. If I'm to be his psychiatrist, I must be a friendly and, above all, neutral presence in Hersh's life. You'll just have to bear with me on that."

She said nothing. Seconds later, Sister Jude's eyelids fluttered and she fell to the floor in a heap, groaning softly. Silv was on the move.

David, enjoying the solitude, stayed in the body, studying, quieting her fears, until the bells rang the call to vespers. He wanted to share the prayers, but the body he was in had to relieve itself, and he simply got too embarrassed to pee *that* way, and ended up jumping back to Louis in Egypt.

Time is a fluid condition which has no existence except in the momentary avatars of individual people.
—William Faulkner

David stumbled, naked, out onto the magnificent balcony just off his suite in the Mameluke palace, the whole of Cairo spreading out before him like an elaborate Christmas garden, the blue life-giving waters of the wide Nile cutting a sparkling swath through the decay of the city. A low rosy haze hung in the air, dissipating with the morning sun that glinted off the golden domes and towering minarets of the three exquisite mosques that presided over the hovels that made up the capital city of Egypt.

The scene was like a picture postcard, fragile and pristine, delicate to the eyes. David drew in a breath of chill morning air, then leaned over the balcony and threw up.

He'd done it again, let the body he was inhabiting drink far too much and render itself incapacitated. It had been a good one, too, twenty years old, lean and handsome. The night before, he had used his own considerable wiles along with the natural charm of the host body to seduce one of the European seamstresses who had accompanied the expedition to Egypt, her soldier husband away tax collecting in the provinces. It had been a pleasant enough diversion, especially when David found that he could control and keep using the host body even after its mind had drunk itself to the coherency of Jell-O. But, unfortunately, it was time to clean up and move along.

He felt the stomach heave, though nothing was left in it, and removed himself while the body threw up again. This wasn't going to do. He wasn't about to spend an entire day recuperating from someone else's hangover, even if it was his own insistence that had kept the wine flowing.

The host moved away from the rail, back into the huge bed-and sitting room that was hung with filmy gauze of the palest blues and yellows. The walls were tiled, the bed as large as his office at State. Josef, his name was Josef, was walking an erratic course, and stumbled against a brass incense brazier, knocking it to the floor, sweet jasmine embers glowing as he stepped on them with bare feet, so out of it he didn't even notice. David found himself disgusted with the host, his position as outside controller easily acclimating itself to the righteous posture.

Josef stumbled again, falling half on the bed, the upper part of his body sinking into the perfumed softness of the sleep cushions. Near him, the woman—an F name . . . Fanny—lay on her back, her own naked body rich cream against the stark white sheets. Her chest rose and fell evenly in sleep, her powdered wig half tilted across her face, makeup smeared across her cheeks. Josef took a look, his insides stirring despite his condition. He tried to rise, then tumbled for good. The mind fell to rest, that black empty night that preceded the onslaught of dream sleep.

David had waited out the eternity of darkness until dream sleep many times, finding in the moving pictures of the dreaming brain every psychological demon ever imagined by even the most imaginative surgeon of the mind. Sexual fears dominated all, just as Freud had predicted, but there was something else that crept into every brain, something insidious that colored every thought, every action on the subconscious level, even, and especially, sexuality—fears of death.

The death fear formed the core of the id. It was the reason for every human aspiration and every gross inhumanity. The thinking brain's inability to deal with the eventuality of its own death subconsciously dominated every human action to the point that it controlled all, making the human merely an extension of his own fears. The French had an expression that summed it up perfectly: *raison d'être,* the reason for a thing's existence. Humans existed in order to die. In the playhouse of the subconscious mind, everyone understood this, but every conscious thought and action formed a desperate denial of the absolute belief. The extension into psychiatric terms was fascinating. Denial of the basic belief and escape into the fantasy called reality meant that each and every human being was a victim of his own psychosis. Aristotle would have put the proposition syllogistically: Psychosis is insanity; all humans are psychotic; therefore all humans are insane. The concept was simple and direct. It explained everything, even how he could time travel: Reality, all reality, is an invention of the conscious brain; therefore, nothing's real.

He pulled away from Josef, drifting, in search of another mind. He had learned slowly over the last several months the trick of skimming, searching for just the right light to settle into. He practiced it often, taking mind after mind, sometimes settling like a dust cloud in the very back, simply letting things be and watching them like a movie. Other times he would take control, using the host body for his own ends, then leaving it. Hersh, of course, had been right. They *were* gods. Freed from Death's awesome power and responsibility, he wandered like a metaphysical vampire, searching out the peak emotions, the perks, he called them, and draining them for himself.

Death held no sway over David Wolf. He was free to go anywhere he wanted, anytime, in nearly any body. The genetic tentacles ran deep; ancestry ultimately traced itself back to the first ancestries, many branches shooting off from a few trunks. He shared genes with many minds, enough so that his feelings of freedom were total.

He had already given up probing the dream state, instead choosing to flit during the sleep ritual, usually traveling to the other side of the world where it was daytime, plundering other emotions, raking the hottest coals of human activity, always looking for the new thrill, the untried sensation. He could do anything that was possible within the human ken.

Except find happiness.

He settled into the mind of a sergeant of the guard who was just coming on duty at the morning shift change. His responsibility was Bonaparte's suites and the sleeping quarters of the palace VIPs. He was handy and convenient, and David had used him before.

Hello, Jon.

What, you again? You'll take me from my responsibilities.

Just for a little while. You're growing a beard.

Don't want to, but the damned Arabs think that you're a slave if your face is shaved.

Unlike the others, Jon Valance had never reacted much to David's intrusion into his life. He was a dull-witted but likable man who had the unique ability of accepting as a given whatever life ordered for him. A highly religious man, Jon found life a never-ending mystical experience to be viewed with awe and wonder. He thought that David was an angel of some kind, come to use him as an instrument to speak to his commander, proof enough that the Lord Almighty favored the manifest destiny of France, something he had been convinced of for many years.

David took the body fully, leading it down the ornate, sculpted hallways toward the suite that everyone called the Hall of Strangers, because so many different bodies were allowed to inhabit it.

He picked out the first two uniformed men he saw of lesser rank. ''You two,'' he said, pointing. ''Come with me.''

He led them to the double doors, moving quickly through them without preamble, and walked up to the woman to wrap a beefy hand around her slender calf.

''You,'' he said, shaking her. ''Get up! Get up!''

Her eyes flew open in a panic as she tried to cover herself the way Bailey had done at the party, the young bluecoats laughing and moving up close.

Valance gazed around the room, finding her clothes in a heap on the floor beside the bed. He grabbed them up and threw them at her.

''Get dressed! Get out!''

How many times David had wished he could have gotten rid of women that way. While Fanny hid behind her protective wall of clothes, Valance turned to the unconscious form of Josef, whose inert body almost seemed to be kneeling in prayer.

''Get him out of here,'' David said. ''Take him back to his regiment.''

The men, used to strange goings-on in this suite, did as they were told without question. They took the limp body under the arms and knees, carrying it out past Gerard Cuvier, who was walking in. Silv had arrived.

Unlike David, Silv refused to inhabit any body save the one she was already in. Within her scope of feelings, she had a duty to perform that included leaving everything tidy and normal. She was driven to undo what she had done, and any suggestion, any thought, of enjoying the experience, or of using it in any way other than to perform her duty, was totally beyond her ken. That David did what he did caused Silv no end of grief; that Silv did what she did left David in a state of humorous perplexity.

Silv watched the woman dressing and the sotted body being carried out, her face an unreadable mask. She walked up and stared at Jon Valance. "David?"

"Good morning, Silv," David replied in English just for fun. "I trust you passed the night in an agreeable enough fashion."

"I see how you passed the night," she said.

He sat on the bed, putting a hand to his stomach. Valance was, unfortunately, afflicted with acute gastritis, the symptoms bothersome to David when he was sunk in too deeply. "Spare me the lecture this morning, all right? I'm really not in the mood for it."

"You make me sick," she said.

He belched loudly. "Apparently you have the same effect on me."

"How can you throw away everything we're trying to do here and act like this?" she said, exasperated. "What if that woman gets pregnant?"

David pointed toward the doorspace through which Josef's inert body had just exited. "He did it."

"How can you go tinkering with lives this way? Don't you have any sense of decency or ethics? This is wrong, David. Wrong!"

The woman had thrown on just enough clothes to get herself out of the room, and hurried past them, running, without a word.

"Nice girl," David said.

Silv grabbed his arm, shaking. "Stop it!"

He pulled his arm away, staring fire at her. "I'm just having some fun," he said, "—entertainment. I don't fuck with things the way Hersh does, I just help them along. Where I come from we have recreations to keep ourselves occupied all the time. Here there's booze when you can stand it, and sex when you can get it. And there's fighting . . . and killing.''

"And books and contemplation and philosophies. You're just making excuses.''

He stood, taking several slow, deep breaths to ease his stomach. "All right," he said. "Let's try this: I can't help myself. This is the experience of a lifetime. We have the power to do anything we want, and I can't help but use it.''

"To use it, you're using others.''

"Just like I've always done," he said angrily, scratching the stubble of Jon's new beard. The man's feet were bad, too. They hurt like everything.

Soak these things in saltwater, Jon.

Too busy. Don't have time.

"You knew what I was when you brought me here," David continued. "I'm a sociopath. I use people.''

"I've been around you long enough to know that sociopaths have no conscience. That's not true with you.''

"What makes you think it's not?''

Gerard stared at him balefully, moustache twitching. His voice quieted. "There were more executions last night," Silv said.

"Another thirty heads, I know," David replied.

"Could you do nothing to stop it?''

"The executions were in retaliation for the massacre of French troops in the Cairo garrison," he replied, standing, the pain centering in the pit of his stomach. He'd have to dump Jon soon enough. "Many of those killed were the ringleaders. They *are* fighting a war here, Silv. It can't be done without harshness.''

"You sound like him.''

"Look. I'm sorry if all this offends your sensibilities. But what do you want me to do? These things take time. I work with Hersh whenever he allows me close enough to.''

"I saw you working early yesterday evening," she said bitterly. "What was the game—canasta?''

"Keeping in touch with Hersh as an individual is an important part of the therapy.''

David moved to the door, heading toward the general's chambers. With any luck he could still catch him at his toilet, which was usually the only time during the day that Bonaparte was free to talk casually. Despite all, David was absolutely devoted to the task of freeing Hersh from Napoleon and vice versa. As the reality around him made less and less sense, David was drawn more and more to the concrete accomplishments of his profession. If he had to believe in something, it was himself in relationship to his job. He sometimes thought that his solid anchor in Dr. Freud's philosophies was the only thing keeping him from falling into the same delusional whirlpool that had sucked up Hersh. Perhaps that's why Silv locked herself so tightly to her own mission.

"Just convince him of how stupid it is to hang on to this fantasy," Silv said, following David into the hall and down its scented length. "Why do you baby him?"

David belched loudly, relieving some of the pain in his stomach. "Because he's crazy," David said. "Remember? He's a delusional paranoid, unable to face any kind of reality save the one he's created in his own mind. It becomes difficult, though, to acquaint a patient with reality, when everything's a dream. If it were easy, you could have done it without me."

"You should spend more time with him, instead of indulging yourself in your own fantasies."

"What do *you* do when the body you're in gets horny?"

Gerard's face reddened. "Sex is all in the mind."

David laughed. "Where do you go when he masturbates?"

"You're disgusting," Silv said.

He turned and jabbed an index finger at Silv's chest. "Stay out of my life, Silv. I'm a highly qualified professional and I'm doing the best job possible under the circumstances. The reason I play cards with Hersh is that if I don't try and stay in simple contact with him as an individual, he's going to follow the classic regressive course and lose himself completely in the fantasy. Back home, they hospitalize people like Hersh so as to totally control their atmosphere to avoid just such a descent into madness. Right now, he's exercising at least some basic controls over his behavior. If you want to see him go *really* nuts, just let him totally absorb into his host body. At that point, he'd be capable of anything . . . anything his imagination could dream up. So, get off my case, lady. I'm good at what I do, and I'm doing the best I can."

Silv's response was clipped, icy. "I've never interfered, Dr. Wolf, only questioned. Your behavior has been something less than exemplary and professional, so I think my fears are not without ground."

"Blow it out your ass."

Silv stopped walking, David continuing. She called down the hall to him. "Remember your own background," she said in English. "How much humanity do you give over before you fall into the pit, too?"

He ignored her, but her words stung nonetheless. He was pushing, pushing the experience, what Hersh called the "rush of moments," trying desperately, through indulgence and variety, to bring some kind of peace to his own life, to no avail. The experience was addictive, all addictions being debilitating and fatal if fed unchecked. Silv was smarter than he liked to admit, her strength of character a point of envy and, perhaps, salvation.

Was he addicted? He didn't know. He had spent four months in Cairo, experiencing every possible human activity: murder, rape, birth, malnutrition, gluttony, drugs and alcohol, the touch of death, scholarship on every level, prayer. He had had sex in both male and female bodies, one night indulging himself in forty separate sexual experiences within a period of several hours. But all of it was done lightly, without controlling the person—in effect, voiding himself of any responsibility in the matter. In his more reflective moments, of which there were many, such uninvolved excess seemed debased, worse in its way than actually performing the activities himself. Such voyeuristic pleasure could only be viewed as a sickness.

Of his own life, there seemed little left except for the work. He barely thought of home, relegating feelings about his own life to the farthest corners of his psyche. He most times tried to ignore the other man, David Wolf the twentieth-century human; for that was a fragile, frightened person, not a god, a man of one confused life with a termination point at the end of it. Unfortunately, such an approach failed to take into account the fact that he still had the thought patterns of the other person, still had the problems. He realized these things, but, in his godlike fashion, chose to ignore them.

He reached the general's apartments, his uniform allowing him to brush past the guards and enter. He had managed to spend a great deal of time with Hersh over the course of the last several months, trying to establish himself as a neutral presence in the man's life, hoping to stand later as a model for transference, at which point real treatment could begin.

It was difficult, if not impossible, to consider treating

Hersh. Tranquilizers would have helped; a stable, quiet environment could have helped a great deal. Hersh was going to have to realize that he needed help before anything positive could happen. Hersh liked him, he thought, and trusted him as much as he could anyone, and that was a step in the right direction. He had found that he liked the man in his more rational moments, and that he liked Bonaparte, the real one, who also resided inside the general's shell. But he didn't speak much with the real general; it was Hersh he needed to keep in contact with, Hersh's mind that he feared losing. He tried every approach he could think of to keep Hersh thinking about his own life back in the quad, though he had yet to have any luck drawing Hersh out about it. David felt like a cheap magician, continually reaching into the top hat, wondering what he was going to pull out.

The huge connecting suites that formed Bonaparte's quarters looked like the inside of a museum of Egyptology. Art treasures unearthed during the various expeditions were scattered everywhere, along with reams of paper: Villoteau's research into Arab music; Larrey's of ophthalmia; zoologist Saint-Hilaire's treatises on Orang-outangs, the crocodile, the ostrich, and the hitherto-unknown fish, the Nile polypterus—studies that later gave weight to Darwin's theories. It was difficult to think of Hersh/Napoleon as totally destructive. From the scientist's point of view, the invasion of Egypt was nothing less than miraculous. He heard the sound of splashing water and loud voices, and moved through a scalloped alcove beside which hung a huge map of Egypt overlaid with Napoleon's dream plan of reopening the ancient canals that connected the Nile to the Red Sea near the Fountains of Moses at Suez.

"Get away from me, Pekingese dog!" Hersh screamed, and seconds later, the general's close friend, Gaspard Monge, cursing and fuming, passed him, dragging a wagon containing a large black stone filled with hieroglyphics they called Rosetta. His fleshy lips sputtered as soapy water ran down his face and the front of his frilly white shirt.

"Don't go in there," he warned Valance. "To go in there is to be murdered . . . or worse."

David thanked the man and moved to the toilet. Napoleon sat in a huge wooden tub, the bowl spun with gold. Around his head, covering his hair, was a madras knotted on the sides. But it was already wet from his incessant twisting and turning. Two brightly dressed, turbaned Mameluke servants attended him, boys no older than seventeen, probably brought from Africa as chattel to satisfy the Mameluke homosexual taste. One shaved him while the other kept his water hot from a boiling brass kettle. The room was large, all tiled in intricate patterns, and opened onto a large veranda much like David's, affording the same view of the Nile.

Napoleon's features, so intense and pristine at rest, were now strained ugly with anger. His pale eyes flashed when he saw Valance standing in the doorway. "I'll have your balls if this isn't important, citizen."

"Doesn't matter to me," the gruff man replied.

Hersh sank back in the soapy water, getting the madras wetter. "David," he said, "I don't have time for you today. Go away."

"I passed Monge on the way in," David said, walking into the room and leaning against the wall. "It looked like he was trying to share your bath with you."

"He cares nothing for me," Hersh said, animated. "All he's interested in is his precious rock. I'm surrounded on all sides by betrayal." He made to shake his sponge-filled fist, but he jerked his head against the razor, opening a tiny cut. He grabbed the boy with the razor, shaking him. "You, too? You betray me, too?"

"It wasn't his fault," David said calmly. "Let him finish or you'll go through the day half shaved."

"I don't care," the man replied, wiping at his bloody face with the sponge. "I've been made to play the fool anyway."

"What happened?" David brought a straight wooden chair draped with towels in from the veranda and moved it up close to the tub. He nodded to the frightened Mameluke to continue shaving Hersh.

"The Turks have declared war on France because of my invasion," he said.

"But I thought Talleyrand . . ."

"Yes, I know. Talleyrand was supposed to go to Constantinople and negotiate peace to keep this from happening. One of our ships finally got through the damned English blockade last night with dispatches. Our beloved foreign minister never left Paris."

"Why?"

"*Why!*" Hersh screamed, both boys jumping away, horrified. "Is there any reason? Can there be any reason? We're cut off here, strangled, and it's his fault. Everything that happens from this moment on is his fault. History will vindicate me!''

''Is that important to you, the vindication of history?'' David asked, slipping easily into the professional mode.

Hersh ignored him, and picked up a sopping wet newspaper from the floor, throwing it at Valance to splash onto his lap.

''And if that isn't enough,'' Hersh said, ''I'm the laughing-stock of Europe.''

Valance looked dumbly at the English newspaper. He couldn't read a word of English, but David could. On the front page of the *Morning Chronicle* was a drawing of several seedy-looking French scientists attacked by angry crocodiles: one was being bitten in the thigh, the other in the rump. The scientists were credited with the authorship of treatises on ''The Education of Crocodiles'' and ''The Rights of the Crocodile.'' Beside that, though, was something far more inflammatory. A letter, captured by Admiral Nelson from a blockade runner, from Napoleon to Josephine in which he accuses her of a public love affair with Hippolyte Charles. It was written in Hersh's typical style of tirade: irrational, accusing, grossly exaggerated, and promising a ''glaring public divorce.''

David put the newspaper on the floor and tried to mop up Jon's uniform with a towel hung on the back of the chair. ''You knew the possibility existed that this might fall into the wrong hands when you sent it,'' he said.

''What are you trying to say, that I wanted this to happen?''

''Not consciously,'' David said, watching the boy finishing up the shave. ''But the affair hurt you deeply, and sometimes people like to compound their hurt to add to the guilt.''

The pale eyes narrowed, and David wasn't sure who it was that was listening to him. ''You mean like saying, 'Now she'll be sorry?' ''

David smiled. ''Something like that.''

Napoleon let himself slide under the water to rinse the shaving soap off his face, totally ruining the madras. When he came up his demeanor was hard. ''Well, I hope the whore *is* sorry. I should have known better than to marry someone who had been passed around the Directory like a croquet mallet.''

''Why did you marry her, then?'' David asked.

Hersh pointed to his head. "*He* says it's because she's the only sort of woman I've ever known."

"Is that true?"

The man just stared at him, the little knots of his head-covering dripping water onto his pale shoulders.

David tried again. "I take it, Hersh, that the choice of a mate was yours, then?"

Napoleon laughed. "Had I chosen, the marriage would have been a lot more politically expedient." Then his face strained again. "I never saw you turning down the sex, though, did you?"

David sat, fascinated, watching Hersh have a conversation with himself. While they argued, he thought about the timeline. If Hersh had chosen Josephine and not Napoleon, what did that do to Silv's conception of historical imperatives?

"Then, you wouldn't have married Josephine?" he asked, breaking up their one on one.

"Never," Napoleon said, then Hersh added, "Don't let him fool you. He likes it better than he says."

Napoleon stood, stepping out of the tub. One of the dark-skinned boys took the sopping madras off his head and replaced it with a fresh one, as the other dried him off.

"See this?" Hersh said, pointing to a crescent-shaped birthmark on the general's hip. "I've got one just like it on the body I left at the quad."

"Really?" David said, picking up the discussion. "Then, your routes here must be direct. It gives you quite a long line of ancestors, Hersh."

"Yeah," Hersh said. "In fact my Da, he . . ."

The man stopped talking and simply stared, sadly, his eyes unfocused.

"Your father," David said. "You've never talked about him before. What did—"

"Don't have no father," Hersh said, his voice laced with deep intent. "Don't talk about it."

"No problem," David said quietly, and sat while they got the general ready. The boys carefully trimmed his nails, then rubbed his body with a silk brush in preparation for the eau de cologne which was then massaged into him.

David watched as they dressed a now silent and sullen Hersh, first in silk stockings and linen drawers. His britches were of white kerseymere with a white shirt. The general sat to get on his riding boots with the half-inch spurs that he insisted upon.

"What are you going to do?" David asked at last, knowing he'd be losing Hersh for the day soon.

"About what?" Hersh asked, holding out his arms for the blue jacket.

"The expedition. It's as good as over, isn't it? Your army grows smaller. The English have kept you from supplies and reinforcements. Now, with the Turkish threat . . ."

"You would have me withdraw, is that it?" Hersh asked, taking his silver snuff box and his tortoise-shell licorice box and putting them in his vest pockets.

"There's no shame in it," David said hopefully. "It's not your fault, Hersh. Talleyrand is the one who messed it up. Go home. Everyone will understand." David reasoned that time away from Egypt might give him the therapy time he needed in controlled surroundings.

Hersh looked at him evenly. "So, you betray me, too," he said low, his voice filled with contempt. "You would have me run back to the Directory with my failures and have them laugh me right out of my commission." He pointed a shaking finger at David. "I'm going to show you all, from my whore of a wife right down to dear Silv. I'm going to show you that I have the power to do what I want and make it stick. Let the Turks come! I'll meet them in Syria and drown them in the Sea."

"That's a march across the Sinai Desert," David said. "You can't—"

"Yes!" Hersh screamed, raising his arms to the heavens. "I can do whatever I want, and nobody . . . nobody can stop me!"

The Mamelukes began screaming, covering their heads and falling to the floor. Napoleon and David shared a look, then gazed through the opening to the veranda. There, floating just above the city, a large hot-air balloon drifted slowly past.

"Ha!" Hersh said, running out onto the veranda, David right behind. "That's Condé. Condé!"

The balloon drifted past at a hundred-yard distance, its color a solid republican blue. All around on the streets and in the buildings, the Egyptians were crying and pointing, many of them tearing at their clothes and beating their breasts, so awesome and frightening was the sight to them.

Hersh banged on David's back and pulled his ears happily,

then waved to the man in the wicker gondola, who called back through cupped hands, "My general, my general!"

Hersh turned to David, taking him by the front of Valance's uniform. "Look at them on the streets," he whispered loudly, "cowering and bowing down." He fixed David with deep, brilliant eyes. "That's how I intend for this whole continent to be."

Silv had to sit for nearly a quarter of an hour at the door to her room watching an Army detachment march by before the hallway was clear enough for her to move into it with her chair. Quad 23 was apparently mounting another offensive, taking the waterworks of quad after quad, expanding their territory to allow their warlords more space. Quads 13 and 19 still acted as a buffer between them and 23, but it wouldn't last forever. Eventually the two superpowers would have to confront one another.

She had awakened in great pain. Her diagnosis was that her pancreas was going out again, the third time in the last seventy years. She hated the thought of another operation. Recovery took longer and longer, and pain was already a way of life for her.

She hurried her chair down the hall, red and green robes stepping aside to let her pass. She wondered if Hersh was up yet, or if he had tried to run away. The hope had been that a night's thought would help put her on to Hersh's actions of the day before, but she had drawn a blank. Perhaps the drug was so good that he simply wanted to go back under immediately.

It was half past the hours of eights when she pushed open the lab door to see him already there, fiddling with her lockbox.

"What do you think you're doing?" she demanded.

He turned casually, a smile on his face. "Just killing time," he said. "You're late."

"Convoy," she said. "Quad 9 has fallen."

He shrugged. "All the neutrals will fall."

"I've heard that they're putting everyone to the sword."

"Well, that makes them just as bad as us, doesn't it?"

He moved to the experiment chair and sat down. "I'm ready," he said.

"Let's talk first," she replied, moving to the lab table to

retrieve her box and put it on her lap. She rolled over to face him. "Why are you so anxious to take the drug again."

"I like it," he said, his face wide and innocent. "It's euphoric."

"There must be more."

"Why?"

"If we don't talk, Hersh, I'm never giving you the drug again."

His eyes widened. She saw, impossibly, *fear* in them. "Please," he said. "What do you want to know?"

She held the box on her lap, just out of his reach. He barely took his eyes from it, for he knew it contained the drug. She sensed power in him, determination as hard as the rock walls.

"You were only under for a few minutes," she said. "What could you possibly have experienced in so short a time?"

"Time," he said. "You used the right word."

"I don't understand."

He sat up, agitated, hands shaking. "I experienced time, through dreams, through other lives. A great deal of time passed. I saw many things."

"This isn't what you told me yesterday."

"I lied yesterday," he said, forcing himself calm. "I was afraid you wouldn't put me under again if you knew."

"That you dreamed? Why?"

He gave her the innocent look again. "I don't know. I just did."

Silv experienced a momentary rush of disappointment. The drug wasn't designed to put people to sleep or to make them dream. As a violence controller, it was going to be completely useless. She'd have to scrap it and start all over now.

"Are you going to give it to me now?" he asked.

She thought about saying no, but it wouldn't hurt to test it just one more time. Maybe someone over in drug design could find a use for it.

"Why not?" she said, unlocking the box with the key that hung around her neck.

His face lit up like that of a child being taken to the grotto for the first time. "I'm ready," he said, rolling up the sleeve of his fatigue shirt.

"This time," she said, opening the box of syringes, "we'll leave you under a little longer. Then, when we bring you back, we'll put you through a battery of cognitive tests to see the effects, all right?''

"Fine, fine," Hersh said impatiently. "Anything."

Something still seemed wrong. There was something about Hersh's behavior that genuinely disturbed her. She withdrew a syringe from her box, but her wall screen began to buzz before she could inject him.

She rolled to the table and set down the box, then moved to the small cathode screen inset in the wall, its red "Message" light flashing angrily. She punched it up, meeting a smooth, bureaucratic face on the other end.

"What can I do for you?" Silv asked. "We're in the midst of experiments here right now."

"Are you Matriarch Silv?" the young man asked.

"Yes, yes, get on with it."

"I'm the computrol shift supervisor," he said without giving his name. "We've noted heavy usage from your lab terminal this morning in unauthorized areas and were wondering if we could help you somehow."

"I haven't used my terminal this morning," Silv said.

"Someone with your access code did," the man said. "They've tried ten different ways of getting into the unauthorized section of the history records. I think you could get that information if you fill out the proper requisition and request forms..."

"I didn't make any requests!" Silv said, and turned to Hersh. He had taken the drug already. He sat, relaxed, on the chair, a used needle lying on the floor.

"Our information is quite correct, I assure—"

"Wait!" Silv said. "Wait a minute." Hersh *was* into something. As was her usual rule, she lidded it right away. "Oh, yes, I understand now. Exactly what information were you unable to give us?"

"There is a top clearance code put on the file marked 'Bonaparte, Napoleon.' The name is flashing across your screen now. You don't have the clearance for this access, but it is within your authorization to request special access if you—"

"That will be all," Silv said. "I appreciate your help. We'll make it over to regs today and fill out the necessary requisition. Thank you."

"Glad to be of service ma'am," the man said, and blanked from the screen.

Silv turned her chair around and rolled over to Hersh's inert body. This was his doing. Just dreams, he had said. It took more than dreams for a grunt like Hersh to overcome a lifetime of training and become a terminal thief. She had to get to the bottom of this.

The name kept flashing in her mind the way it had on the screen. She could bring him back, but it wouldn't solve anything. The only kind of knowledge she could use would have to be firsthand; the only person she could trust with knowledge was herself.

Another syringe sat waiting for her on the table. She wheeled over to it and picked it up with her metal clamp fingers. *Napoleon, Napoleon Bonaparte*. What did it mean?

She pushed up the sleeve of her robe and jabbed the needle in without any prep. That something strange was going on, she was certain. That Hersh was dangerous, she could only imagine.

> *We have been told that there is a "present world" and a "world to come." That there is a "world to come" we must believe, for that is our faith. And maybe someplace there is a "present world"—though I am sure it could not be this hell we are living in now.*

> —Rabbi Nachman of Bratzlav

Citizen Private Joseph Gouraud made the final assault with the 69th, Bonaparte standing atop the ramparts, screaming, urging them forward as they crossed the trenches filled with the rotting dead of six weeks and many previous assaults. The walls of the citadel loomed large before him, thick white stone, sprouting cannons, many of them French cannons. The city was protected on three sides by water. This was the only way in.

The Turks, the ugly Turks, held Acre—black teeth grinning as the Frenchmen ran afoul of their gleaming scimitars with which they beheaded their prisoners upon capture. The English under Sidney Smith reinforced them in the fortress they had held since Richard who was called Lion-Heart had taken it from Saladin eight hundred years before.

Gouraud charged the stone citadel through the smoke and fire of the two hundred guns that pounded them from the walls. There was movement but no thought as his insides screamed back the fear and the urge to bolt. The sun was as hot as the cannons, the taste of his own sweat as acrid as the fetid haze of the dirty smoke. Men fell all around him, crying out for help, as medics ran through the littered field, ignoring the wounded, picking up expended cannonballs to bolster the sagging French artillery.

"Close ranks!" the general called, and Gouraud followed blindly as the gates to the citadel's courtyard loomed nearer. In the past weeks they had breached those gates four times, only to be driven back by the insane fury of the Turk and his flashing steel. But this was the last charge and everyone, except possibly Bonaparte, knew it. English reinforcements had arrived in the harbor, and if they didn't take Acre now, right now, they would never have another chance—Syria, and possibly Egypt, would be lost.

Battlements of stone littered the field, Gouraud charging with held breath through the last corpse-filled ditch. He made for a series of ramparts on his left—just a second of surcease, an instant of safety, before screwing up his courage to make the gates.

No! a voice inside him called, but it was already too late.

He made the ramparts gasping for breath, felt his second of safety just before a red-turbaned head poked up from the other side of the stone parapet, laughing, and drew down his gleaming blade.

Gouraud watched it in slow motion as it blurred a pathway to his face. He felt it enter his head painlessly, the heavy blade sinking deep. Then he slipped quietly under the shroud of night, his life spinning away, water down a drain. He expressed neither outrage nor resignation. He simply died. . . .

David Wolf pulled reflexively from the mind just as he felt it making its plunge into oblivion. He had felt that attraction before, that irresistible quicksand sucking the spirit into the dark warmth. He had felt it in other minds, had, oddly enough, felt it in his own life. The one thing they had never overcome or explored in the time frame was death. It was the one barrier he couldn't cross and come back from—and hence his fascination for it. He had made innumerable charges in hundreds of minds since coming to Syria, had felt the death well up many times, not unlike the darkness of dreamless sleep, and had escaped it just as often. What would happen if he chose to not abandon the dead mind, he couldn't imagine. But the fear of it kept him out.

He hit the timestream on a dead-run escape, slipping through realities, touching down lightly, like a stone skipping on a lake, until he was able to collect his thoughts enough to search for the light at the battle of Acre.

He flowed back softly, touching many minds. In what was left of Hersh's army, he still had over two thousand ancestral possibilities; two thousand chances of glory or death. He was angry at himself and angry at Gouraud. The man had had much to live for and was an excellent mind companion. For the most part, David had backed off and let him have his own head in most matters, including matters on the battlefield; but why had he forgotten the Turks at the battlements?

A stupid slip, a mental error, and a life was lost—for what? So Hersh could keep alive his delusions of conquest and glory.

David had developed an odd attitude concerning life and death during the Syrian campaign. Upon looking at it from the outside, from beyond the experience, it struck him as a sad sort of grasping. Humans were like the flowers that grow in the warmth of a false spring just before the end of winter. They try desperately to live, to withstand nature's onslaughts, yet are doomed by their very nature. So beautiful. So fragile. So condemned. People rush around trying to give meaning to their few moments, yet all the rushing robs them of the contemplative time they need to truly appreciate what they have.

David had discovered that being a god was, indeed, an addictive experience. He would not want to be human again. The thought frightened him. Far better to use these flowers, to cut them and put them in a vase to provide beauty while they lived. To think of them any deeper brought depression.

He chose a private named Dupree to come back in, a young man of seventeen years and a little over three months. Bonaparte had picked the young man to run dispatches between him and Kleber, who defended his flank, and the young man stood beside him now, his uniform as threadbare as his vision of life.

Bonaparte stood atop the parapet, his eye glued to the telescope, his face set in a scowl. David took the young host quickly, against his usual rule when entering a new body, and stared up at Napoleon.

"I fear we're looking at the final moments of this adventure," he said, surprised at the squeakiness of his voice.

Hersh looked at him in surprise, then bemusement. "It must be you, David. Silv would never get this close to the battle."

"You've lost nearly everything, Hersh," David said. "What the Turks haven't taken, the plague has. You've got to fall back with what you have left and leave this damned place before you lose yourself, too."

"You're a fool," Hersh said, then pointed toward the citadel a hundred yards distant. "There! They've breached the gates. Victory is ours!" He jumped from his stone wall into the protection of the ramparts, facing Dupree. "Now you'll see. We've deprived fucking Nelson of his best port and opened up a clear channel to Constantinople. The world is ours!"

"And Smith's reinforcements?"

"Have you no faith, man? I've the most loyal and best trained army on Earth. The English will be no match for us. Now we'll teach old Djezzar some lessons in French."

They both turned and watched the gates, David trying to ignore the turmoil that was boiling within Dupree at his intrusion. The battle raged for several cannon-punctuated moments, David knowing he was watching the culmination of the eight months he had spent trying to be Hersh's friend and physician.

The march across the Sinai had been deadly, Hersh's already diminished troop strength wearing away even more. Without food or water, they had been reduced to eating their own pack animals, David grateful that he could abstract and know neither hunger or thirst. His army at low ebb, with no chance of reinforcements, it took the full strength of Hersh's delusions to continue onward, spreading himself and his men ever thinner, his own confidence growing ever stronger the harsher the odds against him became.

Amazingly, the first thing they had encountered in Syria was victory. The fortress of the ancient city of Jaffa had fallen in three days. But the exultation was short lived. After leaving a force in Jaffa, Hersh marched up the coast to Acre, hoping to take the citadel there and deprive Nelson, who had dogged him since leaving Paris, of his best port. But it wasn't to work that way. Week after week, the siege dragged on, assault after assault stopping short of victory, as the bodies in the ditches continued to pile up, raising a stench that could be smelled for miles. And now seventeen ships full of Turks were landing to reinforce the garrison. The dream had shattered. Even Hersh's delusions would have to be faced—and David worried about it.

The outcome of this charge was preordained. The Frenchmen withdrew slowly, trying to retain their foothold against the onslaught of English Marines and regular sailors fresh to the battle. But it was of no use, they were mastered. To a man, they turned and ran, breaking ranks as English muskets tore dark tribute through their flight. The Marines poured through the gates, their red jackets a spreading pool of blood, followed by the barefoot sailors with their black-and-white-striped shirts and their waist-long queues bouncing on their backs.

"Rearguard!" Napoleon called, taking control. "Cover their retreat!"

"When the rest of the English fleet lands," David said, "they'll attack in force. You're going to have to get out of here."

"Those cowards," Hersh said without pity. "Little children running from their mamas. This is all their fault."

"They were far outnumbered," David said. "They did their best."

"Cowards!" Hersh screamed, and strode in the direction of their retreat.

David hurried to follow through the thousands of men moving through the smoke all around him. Like a dream they charged in and out, specters appearing only to disappear seconds later in the haze. He caught Hersh just as he found the remnants of the 69th regrouping behind the ramparts.

"I'll ring you out in skirts!" Hersh screamed to the beaten and bedraggled men who lay panting and bleeding on the ground. "Pull down their breeches. You've got cunts between your legs, not cocks. Pull the breeches off those sissies!"

David ran to him, trying to calm him, but not forcibly enough. Berthier joined him, taking Napoleon by the arms and leading him away from the hapless 69th.

"We've got to think about leaving this damned place," Berthier said. "If we're to survive, for the good of the Republic, we've got to forget Syria and fall back to Egypt."

"I haven't given up on a fight since Maddelena," Napoleon said, his wispy hair sweat plastered to his head. "I'll not give up on this one. We'll regroup at Jaffa and try again."

"We can't," Berthier said, his voice heavy. "I've had new reports of plague outbursts. Jaffa is rife with it."

"It's not plague," Hersh said.

"But, sir, I—"

"It's merely a fever with buboes," Hersh said with finality. "And I'll hear no more about that. These babies will simply have to gut up and face it like men."

"Yes, sir," Berthier said.

They walked across the remnants of the battlefield to the tent city behind the lines, David looking sadly at the bodies, crushed flowers, that littered the field haphazardly. Minds sucked into that black void—gone. A water boy caught them, sloshing a bucket with both hands, all of them drinking back what they had lost to the heat and the battle.

Hersh fell silent, brooding, walking quickly with his hands behind his back.

David watched him, hating and respecting him at the same time. He had run Egypt with brilliance and with stupidity. Cut off from his homeland by Nelson, he had run a country without relief or money, enduring hardships that would have sent ordinary men to flight, yet had been able to write to the Directory: "We lack nothing here. We are bursting with strength, good health, and high spirits." It was either true heroism or absolute madness. Knowing both of the inhabitants of the body of General Bonaparte, David knew that both inclinations were present in equal measure. Yet he was unsure where Hersh's paranoid psychosis left off and Napoleon's heroism began. It was legends that were being created here.

Silv waited at Hersh's tent, still quietly inhabiting the body of Gerard Cuvier. She watched them reproachfully, eyes accusing, as always, never giving an inch. She guarded her own body like a shrine, never letting it near the fighting, always watching Hersh.

Bonaparte stopped in front of the tent, standing silently for several embarrassing moments. Then he shook his head, as if emerging from a dream, and turned to Berthier. "Assemble the officers," he said. "I'll meet with them in fifteen minutes."

Berthier nodded tiredly and walked off, Hersh turning his attention to Dupree. "David," he said. "Come in, I want to talk to you." He looked at Silv. "Alone."

He sided the flap and moved into the stuffy darkness of the tent, David following. Soft moaning filled the room. Napoleon lit a candle, its flicker illuminating Gaspard Monge, who lay delirious on a cot.

"Poor fellow," Napoleon said. "His dysentery was so bad, I had them move him in here so I could care for him myself."

David moved to the man and did a cursory examination, holding his breath against the smell. The man was comatose, his arms wrapped painfully around his stomach. At home, wherever and whenever home was, David would have hospitalized him and brought in broad-spectrum antibiotics, but here, there was nothing.

He straightened. "Keep putting fluids into him. A mixture of boiled water, sugar, and salt should help with rehydration," he said, Napoleon nodding idly, not really listening.

He was sitting at the desk from where so many Egyptian proclamations had originated. David pulled up a chair and sat quietly, waiting.

"What's going on here?" Hersh asked, confusion evident in his features. "It was there, right there." He held out an open palm, then angrily closed it into a fist. "It's that damned rabble who call themselves soldiers." He pounded the fist on his knee, hard, painfully. "It's their fault. I should ring them all out, every—"

"Not all of life can work out the way we want it to, Hersh," David said quietly, reaching out to take the man's closed fist in both his hands. "You did what you could in a bad situation. You did better than anyone else could have done, better than you could have expected. You're a man, and to be a man is to fail sometimes."

"I'm not a man!" Hersh yelled. "I'm a dreamer. This is my dream!"

"You're a soldier of the quad," David said, Hersh pulling his hand away. "You are a visitor in another time, but you are not of this time. Because you can control this man doesn't mean you can control everything."

"Yes, it does!"

"You can't control me. You can't control Silv. You can't even control Talleyrand."

The man looked at him with deep, knowing eyes. But he let the remark pass. "An Asian empire could have been mine," he said softly after a few minutes, and David was beginning to think that Hersh had retreated totally and left Bonaparte to his own devices. "We could have marched to

India and taken it from the English. The wealth of the trade empire could have set us on a whole new course.''

"Is Hersh in there?" David asked.

"He's pouting," Napoleon said.

"Hersh," David said. "You've done as well as could be expected. You have nothing to be ashamed of. The gains have all been your gains, the problems unforeseeable. Why don't you leave this mess behind? Go back with Silv. She's promised that nothing will happen to you. She doesn't want this to get out any more than you do.''

Napoleon shook his head. "He's shut himself off. He's not listening to you. I really can't picture him in Paris in his state.''

"We have the present to worry about now," David said.

Bonaparte smiled. Reaching out, he playfully pulled on David's ears. "Always the pragmatist," he smiled. "Yes. We do have present problems." He turned and began writing at the desk. "I'm ordering the evacuation of Syria.''

"Perhaps 'strategic withdrawal' would be a better term," David said.

"Yes, excellent." He wrote for several minutes, finally scrawling his name with a flourish and blotting the whole thing.

He folded the order, sealing it with his personal symbol, the bee, rather than the official seal of the Republic. "Berthier will probably be happy for this," he said, and tied a ribbon around the order. "This will put him a step closer to his beloved angel.''

"Berthier is a good and loyal soldier," David said, standing.

"He's a self-serving bastard," the man said, and David felt the return of Hersh. "But he amuses me. Come, let's break the news before I change my mind. Tonight, we return to Jaffa.''

They left the tent, Napoleon hurrying to greet the assembled officers, walking with a swagger, his head high. It was difficult not to admire him.

David moved off with Silv.

"Another new body," she said with implied criticism.

David ignored her dig and walked her toward the stables, past row upon row of dirty tents, wet laundry hanging from the stays. In the eight months they had been together, David and Silv had never found common ground on which to meet and exchange ideas. It was as if the three of them were some monstrous gauge, with Hersh and Silv as opposing extremes and David as a wildly fluctuating needle jumping between the two. He disliked the body she inhabited, he knew that much, but whether that extended to Silv herself, he wasn't sure. How much are our feelings about people tied up in what they look like?

The whole camp smelled of death and decay. The grand scheme was just so many broken pieces on the ground. It was time to be thinking of home. David picked it up from the soldiers, but the melancholy extended to him also. Afraid as he was of the frailty of one life, could he really exist as a specter? He thought a great deal about Sara and the reality she was trapped in back at State Hospital.

They passed Louis Cuvier as he hobbled past on his new pegleg, carrying water. He saw, but didn't acknowledge, his cousin Gerard and the new host that walked with him. His eyes held a certain longing that made David feel almost guilty, for the sharing of minds worked both ways.

"We're finished here," he told Gerard. "Hersh is falling back to Egypt. Perhaps he's had enough."

"You don't believe that," she said.

"No," he responded. "In fact, we'll have to watch him closely now. I'm not sure how he'll handle a collapse of his dream."

"Could he give up the dreams entirely?"

"Probably not. He's got some others to blame. If he pulls himself out of this depression, he'll probably just readjust the dream state."

"An interesting word," Silv said quietly.

"What?"

"If."

They arrived at the small stable in the occupied part of the city, no more than thirty horses for the officers confined in a small grain shed. No cavalry had come on the expedition.

The sentry passed them on recognition of Cuvier. Since Hersh couldn't do anything about them, he chose to give them whatever they wanted.

They outfitted a pair of Arabian mares and led them from the shed into the late afternoon sunshine. "We may as well be ready," David said. "Once he makes up his mind, he doesn't like to wait around. Look."

He pointed. The Corsican, followed by Berthier and several officers, was moving quickly toward the stable. "You anticipate me, David!'' Hersh called from a distance, then doubled his pace until he arrived before Silv and David, his officers forced to keep up with quick, mincing steps on the cobbled ground, holding their sabers tightly against their sides.

"We're going to get our belongings,'' David said.

"Good,'' Hersh replied. "We take a detachment of fresh troops and leave immediately. The rest of the army will follow and cover our rear.''

They were underway within an hour, moving southward under ever-darkening skies. Hersh was already pumped up again, having explained away his defeats, and was busy dreaming up new conquests. He laughed and joked with his officers, while David and Silv rode a few paces behind. But David wondered if it were Hersh, or Napoleon, who led the army now. He feared that Hersh was still indrawn, still brooding.

A long double line of blue stretched out behind them on the dirt road, clouds of thick dust rising to hang like fog in the air. Fields of grass and grain stretched out on either side.

And then the smoke came.

"What is it?'' Silv asked.

"He's burning the fields,'' David replied, holding the saddle pommel and turning to look behind them. In the distance, the darkness was beginning to cherry in an unbroken line to the horizon.

"Why?''

David turned back, already feeling some pain in his butt. This body wasn't used to sitting a horse. "Probably to discourage the Turks from following.''

"What now?'' she asked.

He looked at her, Gerard's weathered face flickering in craggy light. He wondered what the face he was inhabiting looked like. He hadn't even had the chance to look in a mirror. "You tell me,'' he said. "So far, I've done everything you've asked. I've sat here for eight months of my life . . .''

"No,'' she correcred. "Eight months of other people's lives.''

"All right,'' he replied. "Hersh has been my patient for eight months, and I think, under the circumstances, I've done a pretty good job of establishing a rapport with him. I've had an interesting time all the way around.''

"But you think that if he was going to change history, it would have already happened.'' She took a gourd off her pommel and took a long drink, handing it to him. "The same thoughts have crossed my mind. If my theory is correct, the future may already be lost to us."

He pulled the stopper out of the jug. "And what if your theory's not correct?"

"We'll worry about that after we've finished with Hersh," she said. "Meanwhile, just keep working on him."

"I didn't sign on to be your boy," he said. He drank, then splashed a small amount on his face. "It may take a lifetime to make any headway with Hersh. His delusion is so convenient, there's really no reason for him to reject it."

"Then, give him a reason."

David felt himself getting angry. It was always this way with Silv. "It's not that easy," he said, too loud, exasperated. "He's got everything a man could want right now. What would motivate him to return to the rat hole you call home?"

"Back at the quad, we would simply adjust his behavior with the proper drugs," she said, twitching her moustache.

"You'd put him in a Skinner box if you could."

"Skinner?" she said, brightening. "The philosophy of Skinner forms the cornerstone of our society."

He nodded. The entire sky behind them was a bright, throbbing red. "That's probably part of Hersh's problem. Environmental control doesn't allow for genetic input. It's a great way to raise a society full of repressed lunatics."

Silv laughed. "Of course a psychiatrist would say that. You'd have no means of making a living in my world. Drug readjustment accomplishes what you get paid thousands for. In my world, environmental control is absolutely essential to maintain order and sanity. In such close quarters, we need it to survive."

"What exactly was Hersh's upbringing like?"

She shrugged. "How should I know? He was a soldier, wherever the hell they come from. I think they breed them."

"Breed them?" David said, leading his horse off the road. "I've got to get off this thing for a while."

Silv, bemused, moved into the grass beside the roadway, the troops passing, bedraggled, sleepwalking in a never-ending line.

David climbed down, rubbing his buttocks with both hands. "Something in Hersh's background is causing his delusions, something he's escaping from. It may be a single event. It may be the sum of all his training. He was violent back in the quad, even on your drugs. Whatever it is, he's sealed it away where he won't have to touch it. You were just kidding about breeding soldiers, I take it?''

"The problem with humans," Silv said, "is that they've always flown in the face of evolution and natural selection by sending their best and brightest off to be killed in wars. In the quad, we breed for menial and dangerous work, thereby insuring a future for our best brains, while building a fighting and work force that takes orders and doesn't think independently.''

"That's inhuman," David said.

She got off her own horse, leading it by the rein to walk in front of him. "What could be more inhuman than the total madness we've seen so far?" she said, her voice strained. Gerard's face reddened with Silv's anger. "Stop babying him, David. Are you his doctor or his collaborator? We stood on the beach in Jaffa and watched him execute three thousand prisoners, including children clinging to their fathers in death.''

"He couldn't feed them," David said defensively, his own buried guilt rising with Silv's accusations. "His own army was starving. If he'd have turned them loose they would have rejoined their forces.''

"Listen to you!" she screamed, veins standing out on Gerard's neck. "You're justifying his actions!" She grabbed the front of his uniform, popping buttons. "Don't you see what's going on here? You're just like him! You've fallen into it, too!''

"No!" David screamed, anger and shame washing over him as he shoved Silv away, knocking her to the ground. "You're wrong! I'm not like him, I'm not!''

"That's why you haven't helped him yet," Silv hissed from the ground. "You don't want to.''

David was shaking, the words cutting like a knife. "You bitch! You fucking bitch!''

Gerard jumped back to his feet and charged, banging Dupree hard in the chest, both of them falling. They rolled, scrabbling at one another's faces, trying to tear the inner self out into the open as the sky blazed above them, turning the darkness to the lowest levels of hell.

David levered his younger, stronger body, kicking free and slamming Silv on her back, knocking the wind out of Gerard. Face set in a sneer, he cocked a fist, wanting to smash that damned red face, wanting to shut her up for good and all.

He stopped, holding back the fist with tremendous effort. "What am I doing?" he said, rolling off Silv and sitting on the ground.

Silv struggled to her knees, gagging, gasping for breath. He looked at her, at the body she inhabited.

"I know I've got problems," he said, lips trembling. "I know that I'm weak. But dammit, Silv, I swear to you I'm trying my best." He felt tears stinging the young eyes and realized that Dupree was crying for him. "It's so damned lonely and confusing. I feel like a shadow, not real, but tied to reality. Hersh has his dreams. You have your strength. Me, I don't belong here, but I've nothing to go back to. I don't know what anything means anymore, and I don't even have sleep to escape to."

He stood, dusting himself off, while Silv sat staring intently at him from the ground. "There's the experience, isn't there—but without meaning, without a . . . point, it's ultimately hollow." He looked at her, shook his head. "I guess I just can't see the point. I'm lost, Silv, drifting, and you've been no help at all. Why couldn't you have given me some of your strength, instead of cutting me down in my work, the only thing I have faith in?"

"You're a professional," she said curtly. "A little goading should bring out the best in you."

"A little goading?" he replied. "This isn't the classroom. These conditions are hardly clinical. I'm a human being caught up in a situation beyond my understanding or control, and I'm scared. Maybe you're right, and the addiction has taken me, too. God knows, I'd like to be swept up by *something* right now."

He gestured around him, turning a wide circle. "Everything's in turmoil, as far as you can see. Hersh *is* God. He controls the fantasy, and you'd best get used to it."

He walked away from her, retrieving the large black horse that had wandered off and was standing, snorting and pawing the ground, the proximity of the fire frightening it. He picked the reins off the ground and took them back to Silv, handing them to her. She stood, face quizzical.

"What are you going to do?" she asked.

He looked at the ground. "I'm leaving," he said. "I've had enough. Go find yourself another fool."

"David!" She took his arms, forcing their eyes to meet. There was urgency on her face. "Where are you going?"

He shrugged. "I don't know. I'm afraid to go back to David Wolf. I don't think I'd know him anymore. Maybe I'll wander for a while..."

"No," she said in a small voice, her hands clamped on him like vises. "Please don't leave me. I'm begging you."

"There's nothing more I can do here," he said, surprised at her vulnerability. "This is beyond my control."

"Wait," she said, and it was her turn to look at the ground. "I—I'm... grateful for all you've done. I know I don't express it very well, but..." She looked up at him. "I've been alone for a very long time and have forgotten the courtesies, the protocols, of life."

"You're as scared as I am," he said, surprised by the fact that he was surprised.

"It's why I act the way I do," she answered. "My aloofness has always been a wall for me, a way of keeping people at a distance. Here it's the only protection I've got. I've always depended on *your* strength. Please don't take it away from me. I don't know what to say. I have no idea how to handle any of this."

David looked at Gerard and felt Silv's sincerity peeking through, almost like a child peeking from behind his father's trousers at a stranger.

"There's a lot we can talk about," he said. "I'm not so bad."

Silv nodded, moustache twitching. He put out his hand, Silv staring at it, then, slowly bringing hers up. They shook hands.

"Glad to meet you," David said.

"Please don't hurt me," Silv replied, smiling tentatively.

"Let's not hurt each other," David said.

They mounted up and rejoined the column, David unsure as to whether he would actually have left or not. As slim as his own hold on reality was, it was tied directly to his work with Hersh. He feared the total letting-go, the weightless free-fall into the void of life that was so much like the attraction of death. Something had to matter, and until something better came along, his relationship with Hersh was it.

As for his possibilities of success with Hersh, he didn't hold out much hope. Silv's revelations about Skinner just about clinched it. A behavioral scientist, Skinner believed that the concepts of freedom and dignity were metaphysical myths that held no real meaning, that government and civilization needed environmental control over human beings to help them live harmoniously. If Hersh, a violent offender even in a closed society, were to be turned loose from that kind of control, his mind couldn't help but run wild. But the conditioning was certain to backlash. Hersh was trying to control the world because he felt inferior to it, all a product of his early conditioning; and every setback, every loss, drove him further inward—the last place he needed to be.

They rode all night, David splitting his time between calming the body he inhabited and trying to make conversational inroads with Silv. Hersh didn't want to talk with him, and that bothered David. It meant he had something on his mind that wouldn't be pleasant and was afraid David would talk him out of it.

Hersh's friendship with David was the only note of hope in the entire business. Somewhere inside, Hersh knew that David wanted to help him, and that, perhaps, he wanted that help. It wasn't much, but it was all either of them had.

They arrived in Jaffa by midmorning. The general headed directly toward the mosque that his surgeon general, Desgenettes, had converted to a hospital.

The city was ancient, even in Napoleon's time. Set on a hill overlooking the blue-green waters of the Mediterranean, it had seen empires fall and rise for thousands of years. The Crusaders had held it for a long time, fortifying it in the medieval style, centuries later to be refortified by the Turks. David smiled and thought of Mo Frankel. This was the same city Mo had visited nearly two thousand years previously, in the guise of Simon Peter the fisherman.

Hersh had taken the city six weeks previously; David's first stop upon entering it then had been at the house of Simon the tanner, where Mo had given Peter the nonkosher vision.

The streets of Jaffa were not meant for horses. David tied up outside the gates and entered on foot. Dead men lay at the gates, French soldiers, hordes of black flies attacking the bodies. The smell told him more than a look ever could. The buboes. Black plague.

Silv stayed outside the gates, leaving David to enter alone. The narrow stone streets were barely wide enough for a man to walk. Steps mostly, they purposely twisted and turned through blind alleys and cul-de-sacs to confuse invading armies. They were working well with David.

Eyes stared through darkened slits as he went by, eyes that watched the shadow of death as it passed by their doors. In David's world there were treatments for *Pasteurella pestis* infections. Here, only a cold winter or total attrition could save them.

After several wrong turns, David realized he was hopelessly lost. He stared up at large stone edifices that stretched into the sky, and open stairs that rounded turrets to doors set in the middle of towers. Then he got an idea. He closed his eyes and followed the smell. He found the hospital within ten minutes.

Berthier, dark eyes glaring, stood outside the mosque, young Murat, Napoleon's favorite, talking with him.

David walked up to them. "Where is he?"

The men stared at him. They didn't know him. But most of the officers had become accustomed to Napoleon's recent fascination and friendship with enlisted men.

"He's inside, lad," Berthier said, running a hand through his frizzy hair. "Get him out of there if you can."

David nodded and pulled a handkerchief out of his pocket, tying it around Dupree's face. He walked up to the ornately tiled doors, stepping over the entry and into the structure.

He gagged going in, the stench nearly overpowering. Several hundred men lay on pallets on the beautiful tiled floors, pillars like twisted rope rising around the open worship area to support the high ceilings. Most of the men were naked, ugly black festering boils decimating their bodies—in the genital area, under the armpit, finally to the throat; after which death was soon a blessed termination. The men gagged blood and mucus, their moans a low hum that filled the large room continuously like some machine. The sadness of escaping life, of little bits of uniqueness slipping forever out of the world, nearly overpowered David. He could feel the life draining away, his doctor's training useless in this land of the dead. What good was he?

Dupree's panic was all-consuming at this point, despite David's attempts to reassure him. He had to take total control of the body to even keep it there, which meant he left himself open for total experience, including the smells, including the sadness.

Heavily masked and gowned doctors moved through the room of death, doing what they could, which was exactly nothing. Their main function was in ferreting out the dead ones and having them carted away to be burned.

He spotted Napoleon at the far end of the room, walking among the sick, inspecting them. Desgenettes, in uniform with a handkerchief to his nose and mouth, walked with him, speaking loudly above the moaning.

David picked his way carefully through the sick and dying to reach the general, who was arguing with his surgeon general.

"Citizen General," Desgenettes said, voice muffled through his handkerchief, the little man's posture rigid with his own fears. "You must leave this place. The plague is highly contagious."

"Nonsense," Hersh said. "It isn't the plague."

An orderly was attempting to drag a living victim onto a pallet just vacated by one who had died. Hersh rushed over to help him, taking the poor man's shoulders, while the orderly took his feet.

"Please, General," Desgenettes implored. "I beg you . . ."

"Stop with that!" Hersh ordered. "I assure you, General, that these men do not have the plague. Now, we will be marching out of here soon. How long will it take to get these men ready to travel."

"They can't travel," Desgenettes said. "They can't stand, much less march."

"What do you suggest?" Hersh asked, putting his hands on his hips. "Would you leave them for the Turks?"

"I can only tell you, citizen, that these men cannot march."

Hersh turned a circle, his eyes focusing on David. "Do you have any suggestions?" he asked.

David nodded. "Yes. You outside, right now, unless you want that great brain you talk about to die from the plague."

"It's not the plague!" Hersh said loudly.

"It not only is," David said, "but you know it is."

The man took a breath, his face frozen in concentration. Then he broke it, as if awakening from a dream, and turned back to Desgenettes. "They either march or get left for the Turks. We must withdraw immediately."

"They cannot march," Desgenettes said.

"You have drugs here for pain, do you not?" Hersh asked.

Desgenettes regarded him with suspicion. "We have laudanum," he said softly, "a tincture of opium."

"Large doses of laudanum, what would they do?"

Desgenettes took his handkerchief away, his mouth strained to a frown. "Laudanum is fatal in large doses," he said.

Hersh nodded, his eyes turning to look past David, to the distant door. "Those that can't march will be given laudanum in fatal doses," he said simply.

"General Bonaparte!" Desgenettes said. "I'm a doctor, I can't—"

"You will do as you're told," Hersh ordered. "I will not leave my men for the Turk."

"This is unthinkable," David said, horrified.

"I resist this idea," Desgenettes said, and David recognized a good doctor when he saw one. "I will not disgrace my country or my profession by murdering my own kind."

"Then, I'll have someone else do it," Hersh replied, and started walking toward the door. "And you will consider yourself under arrest for failure to comply with a direct order."

Desgenettes stood there, his eyes wide, his mouth open, while David hurried after Napoleon. He caught him as the man was stepping across the high threshold. He grabbed Bonaparte's arm. "You can't do this," he said. "You really can't do this."

Hersh jerked his arm away and continued through the doorway, joining Murat and Berthier by the well in the courtyard. David hurried after.

"Laudanum in fatal doses is to be administered to those who can't march," Hersh was telling Berthier. "See to it."

"No," Berthier said. "That's unthinkable. I never—"

"You will obey a direct battlefield order!" Hersh screamed childishly. "Or I'll have you arrested, too!"

He turned and strode away, his officers watching after him.

David was right there. "You've gone too far, Hersh," he said, hurrying along the narrow streets to keep pace with the man. "A commander who kills his own troops can't possibly survive long."

"The Turks would declare a holiday to figure out what to do with those men in there," Hersh replied. "Believe me, the death I offer is far preferable."

"Bullshit," David said. "You can't speak for the Turks, only for yourself. And I think you've got reason far beyond the present situation to explain your behavior."

"You've got a reason for everything, don't you?" Hersh said. "I think I'm beginning to tire of your reasoning and your constant bickering. Leave me. Take the old woman and get out of my sight. If you don't, I'll strike you down in whatever incarnation you choose to come back in."

They were approaching the gates, winding down a narrow street that faced the sea, the ancient port a hundred feet below them.

"I'll tell you why you went into that hospital," David said. "You did it because you wanted to be exposed to the buboes."

Hersh laughed. They reached the gates and moved through, the bodies David had seen coming in already being carted down to the great burial dump of the sea.

Hersh moved to his horse, untying it from the iron post set into the short outer walls. Silv sat a distance away, beneath the shade of a banyan tree. She stood when she saw them, but David waved her back to sit again.

"Why would I want to expose myself to the plague?" Hersh asked, leading his horse to a close water trough.

"Because you hate yourself, Hersh. You feel like a failure in an unreal world, the King of Nothingness."

"How can you hope to know what I feel?" Hersh said vehemently, his face strained in anger.

David met his eyes, held them. "Because you're not the first to feel this way," he said softly. "You do this and you condemn both of us. I know what I'm talking about."

"You know nothing!" Hersh screamed.

"I know why you've sentenced those men to death," David said.

"Just get away from me!" the man said, pulling his mare's head away from the trough and leading her off.

"It's your own death wish!" David called after him. "You're trying to fix it so it can be done to you!"

Hersh stopped walking, his back still to David. He turned slowly, frightened eyes staring back. David moved to him and took him by the shoulders. "Think about it," he whispered harshly. "Please. Think about it now, before it's too late."

Hersh, the frightened little man that Hersh was, looked pitifully at David, his eyes distant, trying to cope. David increased the pressure on his shoulders, hoping the warmth and reassurance of his reality could somehow help.

Suddenly, Hersh jumped slightly, like a shock had gone through him. He looked at David with wet eyes. "My God," he whispered. "What have I done?"

David let out a breath. "You've taken the first step toward helping yourself," he said, smiling.

"Go to Berthier," Hersh said, "tell him to stop the poisoning. Then have him gather every horse, every mule, every cart that can be pulled or pushed. Those that can't march, will ride. We all go out together."

"Now you're talking," David said, the smile consuming his face.

The general looked at his own horse, at the reins he tightly held. He handed the reins to David. "Start with this horse," he said.

David took the animal from him, turning to lead it away.

"And, David . . ." Hersh said, the man turning to him. "Thank you."

"I'll send you a bill," David said.

> *The tongues of dying men*
> *Enforce attention like deep harmony.*
> —Shakespeare

Ibrahim Khit sat in his home, at his small wooden table, and contemplated the end of his own life. It was the heart of the black night in Cairo, the moonless sky a mirror of his heart.

He had built his home with his own hands, built it several times from Nile mud, whenever the river overflowed its banks, leaving rich silt for the crops and homelessness and dysentery for the city.

The night was so dark that the single candle burning in the center of his table cast a pale half-light around the one-room dwelling, making the body of Reena, his wife, nothing more than the shadow she now was. She lay in the corner, wrapped in a white spread; the small shrine of flowers and orange embers of the joss stick glowing, for he was using their only candle on the table.

His face strained, a sob escaping as he stood abruptly, his chair falling over. He moved to the window, shifting his robes, staring into the darkness, unbroken to infinity by even a single light. He stared at the houses of his neighbors, dark bumps moving up the sloping hillside to the imposing shadow of the palace of Sultan El Kebir, who had recently come riding back to Cairo from Syria led by marching bands and proclamations and captured flags waving. The great Napoleon had also brought a present for the Egyptians back with him from Syria. It rode a dark horse and spoke only in terms of finality—the black death.

It took little Abba first, his soft black eyes never to see the harvests of his second year, his grave so small it could have been a cat's. As he lay dying, those eyes begged Ibrahim for understanding and help, accusing eyes that increased his guilt so that the baby's death was nothing but blessed relief.

Tani fell next, ten-year-old Tani of the laughing face, struck down and dead within a night, her passing such a sudden departure that it took him a week to realize she wasn't there anymore. Oh, God, your ways of pain are so rich and full!

The Koran says to live in the world as one already dead. Reena fell from grief, dead while alive, the body finally accepting what the heart had dictated. Ibrahim had dug her grave with his hands, but couldn't bear to hold her in his arms long enough to consign her to the ground. He couldn't. He just couldn't.

The darkness helped. It was invented to cloak dark deeds. Ibrahim returned to the table and sat, picking up the knife, its blade like dancing fire in the light of the candle. He had sharpened it on the wheel to a keen edge, an edge so sharp it was painless.

You can't do this thing.

Who are you to tell me that? Are you God?

No. Life is to be lived. The pain will pass.

Hu! No, you're not God. You're a fool.

I can take your body and stop you.

But not forever.

No.

Then my will be done.

David had a nose for death. He was drawn to it irresistibly, almost sexually. What pain had reached out its tentacle and drawn him to this unhappy man, he didn't know, and what to do now that he was here was even more of a problem. He could stop it, but did he have the right?

Won't you reconsider?

Allow me my final dignity, please. I can stand no more pain. I seek after the night.

David backed off, unhappily, watching through the man's eyes as he shoved up the sleeve of his robe and exposed the dark wrist, thick blue veins standing out. The man's mind was calm and serene as he picked up the blade. The cheek muscles pulled to a smile as he filled his mind with his family, with the happy times, with moments of love and passion, celestial moments worthy of any god. At the last second, David thought to intervene, but something stopped him. The pull that suctioned the man toward death was the strongest he had ever seen in a living person. It smacked of some happy inevitability.

He watched the wrist and the blade laid upon it. Ibrahim knew what he must do. He dug deep, pulling the blade longways up his arm. At first, for a few seconds, there was nothing. As if it were all some monstrous joke, and the man wasn't a man at all, the artery lay open and dry—that second of realization when you've hurt yourself and wait for the pain to strike the understanding.

Then the blood came. In thick, dark gobs it oozed out of the artery and washed over the arm, and something...something took hold of David, spinning him away. A memory, a realization, had control of him in his weakness and drove him to

to

to

Davy Wolf didn't like Herbert at all. Herbert came around when Daddy went to call business and he didn't call him Sport or play with him at all. He always wanted Momma to "get rid of the kid," or "shut him in the closet."

Davy didn't like to go in the closet. It was dark in there, so dark, and he thought that maybe something could be in there with him sometimes.

But Herbert liked Momma a lot, and she sat on his lap and giggled when he put his face in her neck. This time, though, he had a new ball that could bounce higher than anything and even old Herbert would like that.

He went up to him while he sat on the couch in his chocolate suit and Momma was in the bathroom "fixing her face." Davy bounced the ball near him a time or two to help him get the idea, but Herbert just sat there, looking at his watch and staring at the walls. So Davy ran up to him and climbed up on his lap like he did with Daddy.

"Throw the ball?" Davy said. "The ball?"

Herbert frowned and stared meanly at Davy, then reached into his pocket and pulled out a shiny quarter.

"Here, kid," he said. "Take this and go play. If you play nice and quiet, I'll give you another one when I leave."

Davy stared, unbelieving. He'd never had a quarter before. He turned it over in his hand, staring at the picture of the man with the funny hair that was stamped on it.

David sat at the back of his three-year-old mind, uncomprehending at first, even as to where he was. When he realized it was his own childhood, he decided to just sit and watch, especially since he wanted no child exposed to the sewer of his adult brain.

He didn't remember Herbert, or this incident. Why he was here was a total mystery.

"Well, see? That didn't take so long, did it?" Naomi said, coming into the living room. Davy didn't understand. Momma was dressed for bed, even though it was daytime, but her face was all painted up like she was going out.

"You look great, honey," Herbert said. "Just like a doll. Just like a little kewpie doll from the fair."

Herbert got off the couch, moving toward her with outstretched arms. He grabbed her and she giggled, then pushed him away when he tried to kiss her.

"Not with Davy here," she said.

"C'mon," he said, pulling her down the hallway. "Let's go to the room."

"Wait," she said, turning back to Davy.

He stood, staring up at them, so huge, like giants. "It's time to go play in the closet for a while, Little Bit."

The fear washed over him like a terrible, cold wave and it was all David could do to ride out that fright with the boy. "Not the closet, Momma!" he screamed. "No, Momma. . . . Momma . . . Momma!"

"It's all right, Naomi," Herbert said, moving up to Davy, diamonds glinting from several of his pudgy fingers. "He'll be all right. Me and him got an understanding, don't we, boy?"

Davy's face lit up, and he opened his sweaty palm to reveal the money. "He give me quarter, Momma."

Naomi laughed and slapped Herbert playfully on the chest. "You capitalist," she said.

"We call that greasin' the rod in the oil business, honey," Herbert said, and took Naomi by the hand and went once more down the hall.

He slipped into the bedroom, Naomi lagging behind at the

door. "Now you play nice, Davy. Stay out of trouble and be Momma's big boy."

"Yes, ma'am," Davy said as Naomi disappeared into the bedroom, closing the door behind her.

Davy moved through the house. It seemed so large and empty, so quiet, without anybody but him to play in it. But he was determined to play and be a Big Boy, like Momma asked, so he wouldn't have to go back in the closet.

The boy went to the couch, climbing on it, then jumping off the arm into Daddy's easy chair and back again. He played innocently, his mind clear, but David brooded over the man with his mother. His father was definitely around at this point, that was very clear in the boy's mind, but it was certainly not gin rummy that Naomi and Herbert were playing in the bedroom.

He moved through the small house with the boy, marveling at how tiny it seemed in contrast to his memory of it. Davy soon tired of doing all the things Momma would let him do any time, and began concentrating on the things he never got to do.

He pulled the cords out of the electric sockets. He got in the cabinet under the sink that he couldn't go in, and carefully lined up all the bottles that had strange strong smells that Momma used for cleaning. He melted a crayon on the floor furnace, then lost his new quarter down the furnace when he dropped it on the grating to see how it would sound, David sitting on the edge of panic the entire time that Davy bumbled innocently around.

Then the boy decided that he was hungry. David knew that the hunger, and perhaps everything that followed, was motivated by Davy's fear of being cut off from Naomi; Davy merely knew that he wanted what he called "serio."

He ran down the hall, tripping and falling once, then made it to his mother's bedroom door to ask for food.

"Momma?" he said softly, but no one answered. Instead, there were strange animal sounds coming from behind the door and Davy could tell that Momma and Herbert were jumping on the bed the way her and Daddy did sometimes, something that grownups got to do that kids didn't.

"Momma?" he called again to no avail.

Dejected, he returned to the living room, crying softly. He picked up his new ball and sat on the floor, holding it tight and feeling very alone. But then he remembered that he was supposed to be a Big Boy, and he knew that Big Boys could get their own food. So, off he went to the kitchen.

The serio was easy enough to get. A big box of Trix sat on the lowest shelf of the pantry, the familiar rabbit on the box smiling out at him, reassuring. The bowl was a little tougher. He had to climb up on a chair to reach the high wooden cabinets, and it was with a great sense of accomplishment that he got down the big bowl with the flowers painted around the edge.

He only spilled a little of the serio getting it into the bowl, David finally relaxing and enjoying his early culinary efforts, efforts that hadn't gotten much more sophisticated after he had grown. Then Davy went for the milk.

The bottle was glass and full. The milkman had just been there that morning, and the bottle was slick with condensation. Davy held it with both hands, but barely cleared the refrigerator shelf before losing it.

It hit the linoleum floor with a dull plop, milk going everywhere. Had there been warning, David might have intervened, but the mind of the child moved with agility and speed—at once sensing trouble, then hurrying to avoid it.

His little hand snaked out, grabbing for glass. When he brought it back, he was surprised that his arm was wet and red. He stared, uncomprehending for a moment, David frantic by this point, at a total loss as to what to do. His view was the same as in Egypt, an arm, oozing blood.

I remember! I've got a scar. I always heard that it happened when I was a baby.

The boy, squatting, fell to a sitting position, still staring at the pumping blood as it dripped from his arm to make little snaky swirls in the white milk. The surprise turned to comprehension, then to pain, finally to panic.

"Momma!" he screamed, all control gone—the death fear again, so strong, more so in children. "Momma!"

Then he let out a sound, a scream, something primal and atavistic. No human ears could hear it without reaction.

Naomi was there, a robe wrapped hastily around her. She grabbed him up in her warm embrace, his panic becoming hers as he relaxed in the grasp of someone who would make it all right.

"Oh, baby!" she wailed. "Oh, Davy, I'm so sorry, so . . ."

The blood was all over both of them now, Naomi realizing

she had to do something. She pulled the arm out straight, knowing immediately it was more than she could handle.

Herbert was there, dressed only in his chocolate pants, his large belly overhanging the belt. "Aw shit!" he said, angry. "Shit!"

Naomi pulled the boy to her. "Call a doctor, please!" she told Herbert. "We'll get him to the office."

"Don't know the number," Herbert said. "You do it."

She stared at the man, shocked, but passive. "I'll be right back, Davy," she said, putting him back on the floor. Then she jumped up, shoving her way past Herbert.

"Get dressed," she called over her shoulder, then ran for the phone.

The man glared down at Davy, a tiny ball of pain and fear on the floor, tears dripping thick, like castor oil. He reached out to the man in his fright, a tiny hand imploring. "Quarter?"

"You little bastard!" Herbert whispered loudly. "I ought to whip your ass for what you did."

David couldn't stand it. He took the child, just for a second. "You lay one finger on me, you fucking son of a bitch," the boy said, "and I'll kill you."

The man backed away then, eyes wide, an unspoken question on his lips.

Eternity is a terrible thought. I mean, where's it going to end?

—Tom Stoppard

David had been losing himself in mind skimming when Hersh announced he had planned an outing to Alexandria for some purpose meant to remain mysterious. Unwilling to take time out for the journey, he told the general he would meet his party for dinner on the evening of 12 August 1799, at which time Hersh promised he would have something of tremendous import to tell both him and Silv.

Since the march back from Syria in June, Silv had been making some attempt at breaking out of her shell, and had turned out to be something of a comfort not only to David, but to Hersh as well. She had begun to realize that she, herself, was a valuable link in the chain of Bonaparte's psyche in that she could talk to Hersh about his own time in ways that David never could. Once sunk into the realization, she took to it, showing a remarkable surfeit of energy in attempting to aid in the general's rehabilitation.

So, David found that he had an amount of time on his hands, that working in tandem with Silv, he was able to take time away from Hersh to pursue his own adventures in timelessness, or in what he had begun to call "the weightless mind." He had sent a body ahead with the party, in the form of Jon Valance, who for all the wrong reasons had turned out to be his most compatible host, and did some exploring. His exploration had turned into an odyssey that was to last for several years.

The dilation, he had found, had its own internal sense of consistency. If he left whatever host body he was inhabiting, and traveled anywhere else during the same time frame, then time passed normally. In other words, if he left Valance and traveled, say, to America in the form of a Sioux Indian for two hours, then two of Jon Valance's hours would have passed when he returned. But if he traveled back in time and lived, for a minute, a day, a year, whatever, he could return to the exact minute that he'd left the host.

David was careful, as Silv trusted him to be, in not interacting enough with the hosts he inhabited to cause any changes in historical perspective. This actually added a dimension to the skimming, since he couldn't feel responsible for any of the actions of the host body, and felt a moral obligation, in fact, *not* to interfere. So, when he dwelt for a month in the brain of the vicious emperor Caligula, he was able to be morally outraged by the man's excessive behavior while at the same time vicariously enjoying it. There are those who could call him perverted for that and other similar choices of hosts, but he felt that what he was doing was beyond morality of any kind. He was put in mind of Mo Frankel's fears about the demon that resided within himself. If feeling the proper moral justification, he began to feel that any human being was capable of morally unjustifiable behavior of the most debased kind—all of it laughter in the face of death. Such realizations had begun to harden him to what he considered the hopelessness of life.

Likewise, he never had traveled forward from Napoleon's time, until the accidental visit to his three-year-old self. He liked to tell himself he'd not made the trip because Silv had asked him not to, but he knew that wasn't the case. He was afraid, afraid she had been right and that he could be jumping into a deep, bottomless blackness, never to return. It was a frightening thought. His repellence/fascination for death was close to all-consuming, but he wasn't ready to test its dark waters himself.

But all that was cancelled now. He had traveled forward unwittingly, and there was a future there, and it seemed unchanged, at least on basic levels. He was anxious to share the revelation with Silv.

One of the most interesting discoveries he had made in his travels was that he could visit and affect a different time frame only once. If he'd lived something in his memory, he could always return to it, but he would get caught up in his own thoughts from the previous visit, like a current memory, and he could do nothing but ride it out, like watching a movie. The choices were unlimited, but the options weren't.

And always he searched—for meaning, for happiness, for whatever that spark was that he lacked. He could share it in others, or disdain it as he chose, but he could never grasp it for himself. The world was a kaleidoscope, ever spinning, ever changing, and he was merely the eye that watched it from a distance. In his worst moments, he hated himself; in his best moments, he hated everyone else. He knew one thing: mere experience wasn't the answer. Experience could fill his hours, but not his heart, and timelessness could be nothing more than a long sentence in hell.

Other rivers run north to south, but not the Nile. It runs northward from Lake Victoria in the Ugandan highlands, through the Sudan, bisecting Egypt to empty into the Mediterranean. When David took the mind of Jon Valance, the first sight he had was of the mouth of the mighty river where it flowed into the sea.

It was, perhaps, eleven at night. He was standing on a wooden barge tied up close to shore and knew, from Jon's mind, that they were somewhere between Alexandria and Aboukir, where Hersh had fought a wildly successful battle against the Turks, driving them into the sea and managing to salvage an amount of self-respect from the Egyptian campaign. He was leaning against a rough rail, staring back toward shore. A small fire defined the parameters of the camp, and David was surprised at how small the party was—six tents, pitched on the sand dunes. He could make out Berthier standing near the fire. There were very few others. Roustam, Napoleon's Mameluke servant, tended the fire.

This part of the land was dangerous with Bedouin. It made no sense to be out there, exposed like this without an escort.

Hello, Jon.

They've been waiting dinner for you, and I'm hungry.

He turned Jon's body and saw Napoleon and Gerard Cuvier sharing a glass of wine at a small table. Beyond them, at anchor a hundred yards distant, the silhouettes of two frigates swayed gently in the warm, lapping waters—the remnants of Hersh's fleet.

David sank comfortably into Jon and moved to stand at the table, the man's bad stomach complaining bitterly.

Napoleon looked up at him with dancing eyes. "You've come," he said simply. "Sit. Join us."

David complied, shoving aside an ornate, covered vase that sat before him. He shared a look with Silv.

"You've been skimming," she said. "I can tell the look."

"I've been doing some traveling," David said, "several years' worth. I almost forgot about our dinner."

"Ah, my friend," Napoleon said, "but you didn't." The general turned toward shore and cupped his hands over his mouth. "Roustam! Monsieur Roustam! Bring the supper!"

The young Turk jumped from the fire and charged around, gathering things for the barge.

"Did you learn anything on your travels?" Silv asked, then she drank half her wine in one swallow. "Anything...valuable?"

"Only that we can all be depended upon to live down to our baser impulses," David answered, and got angry at himself for his negativity. He hadn't seen Hersh and Silv for a long time and realized that he had missed them.

Napoleon poured David a glass of wine from the European bottle on the table. "A present from Sidney Smith," he said. "But don't drink it yet. I have a surprise for you and Sergeant Valance first. Monsieur Roustam. Hurry!"

Roustam had gathered a large tray full of food and put it atop his head. He then waded into the gently lapping water and walked through it, waist high, to the barge.

"Berthier doesn't seem too happy left on shore," David said. "Should we invite him aboard?"

"No," Hersh said quickly. "This is a night for us alone."

Roustam had reached the barge, and pushed the tray onto its floor. Then he hoisted himself on deck and proceeded, dripping wet in blue pantaloons and red turban, to serve them a dinner of roast chicken, rice, and watermelon. David's surprise was then set before him, a large glass of goat's milk.

"That is to coat Valance's stomach," Hersh said, "to make your night a little easier."

"Thank you, sir," Jon said, Napoleon waving him off.

"I, also, suffer from an occasional bad stomach. This will help you at least tonight."

David didn't like milk, to say nothing of goat's milk, so he abstracted while Valance gratefully drank it down, then came back after to a far better disposition. He then reached for the wine.

To Bonaparte, eating was an unpleasant necessity of life, something to be done with quickly, like a tooth extraction, so that it could be gotten out of the way and life returned to normal. As was his habit, they ate in five or six minutes, and silently, so as to concentrate on the task at hand. Napoleon finished first, instructing Roustam to take away the plates, even though Cuvier and Valance were still eating.

"What's the vase for?" David asked, licking chicken grease off his fingers.

"It's a reliquary," Silv said.

David narrowed his eyes. "What's in it?"

"Max Cafferilli's heart," Hersh said sadly. "I had it embalmed and it will always travel with me."

David thought about General Cafferilli. An absolutely fearless and loyal soldier, his was a friendship Napoleon had valued highly, more so since his disenchantment with Josephine had soured him on love. Killed at the siege of Acre, Cafferilli had hobbled through many battles with the general, despite his wooden leg, a handicap that had prompted the homesick troops to say, "No need to worry about old Cafferilli. He's got one foot in France."

"On his deathbed," Hersh said, "he had asked to have read to him Voltaire's preface to Montesquieu's *L'Esprit des lois*." The man shook his head. "He was so keen to hear that preface, but he never lived through it."

"It gets to you, too, doesn't it?" David asked quietly, sipping his wine.

"The fragility?" Hersh said. "Fleeting, transitory life. Loyalties lie. They ebb and flow like the tides, not real, not like rocks. Max was a rock. I could tie down to him and believe in something solid and real."

Somewhere aboard one of the distant frigates, a sailor had

begun to play a concertina, its hollow, pleading sound drifting to them on the gentle winds and the water's sounding board.

"In the quad," Silv said, Cuvier's voice slurred somewhat from the wine, "we worshipped the river, its freedom, its purity."

"Fragile life seeks the swiftness of movement," Hersh said, his eyes fixed on the reliquary. "It's escape. It's a way of not dwelling on the truth of the matter. But we've lost that, haven't we? We can see the truth whether we want to or not. We sit here, tied up on the waters as they flow past. We're not a part of this anymore."

"Being permanent ourselves," David said, "we seek permanence around us, but it's not to be found."

"We're only permanent while we wish to be, David," Silv reminded him. "We could always go back to what we were."

"Would it be the same, though," David replied, realizing how much like Hersh he was beginning to sound, "now that we know?"

"Know what?" Hersh asked.

"How useless it all is," David said. "How briefly and mindlessly the flames burn, and how quickly they wink out forever."

"Forever?" Silv said. "The genes live on, don't they? We're proof of that. In itself, that's permanence of a sort. We have our duty. That gives us stability and strength."

"Just words," David said. "I just spent several years traveling with the army of Alexander of Macedonia while he conquered much of the same territory we're standing on tonight, all under the guise of pacifying the 'barbarians' on the frontier. It was an excuse for massacre after massacre, while Alexander had himself declared a god, only stopping his wild expansion when his army refused to follow him anymore."

"Maybe another skimmer," Hersh said, smiling.

"It's not funny," David replied, and he watched Silv down another glass of wine. He'd never seen her drink before. "I see nothing but pain and misery all around me, and I see no reason for it, no . . . point to it."

"Why must there be a point?" Hersh asked, standing. He moved away from the table, gazing out over the dark waters, almost as if he were searching for the source of the music. He spoke with his back to them. "The moments are what matter, within them lies the meaning. You spoke of Alexander and the pain he caused. Yet, his rule brought a renaissance of Hellenic culture to the ancient world that persists to this day. How much pain was later avoided by the larger, civilized studies of Aristotle and Plutarch that his 'massacres' ushered in. The Greeks brought mass education and, with it, that pain was avoided.''

He turned abruptly, pointing at David, and it was Bonaparte speaking. ''Am I so different than Alexander?'' he asked with a strange smile. ''Alexander donned Oriental garb, as I did, albeit briefly. He traveled with education and science, as I have done, trying to spread the more humane ideas as he went, ideas that may never have spread otherwise. He even conquered the same territory.''

He returned to his chair, his face alive with purpose. ''I have fought many campaigns, campaigns filled with glory and with infamy. I've known conquests and defeats, and have seen death so thick it seemed there was nothing else before me. And I'll tell you something: the true conquests, the only ones that leave no regret, are those that have been wrested from ignorance. Therein lies purpose and meaning. How dare you say there is no point. We move always toward our own nobility; that we fail to succeed doesn't make the quest worthless, it simply makes it a harder reach.''

''I don't buy that,'' David said.

''Then, I feel very sorry for you,'' Napoleon replied. ''You are among the dead already.''

''If each life is precious,'' David said, ''then none of us has the right to take it away from anyone, no matter how pure any of our motives are.''

''You must stop thinking in terms of life and death, and deal only with the moments,'' Hersh said, returning.

''Unless it's your life we're talling about,'' Silv said. ''You've just managed to justify your own murderous selfishness.''

''If, as David says, life is meaningless,'' Hersh said, ''then what does it matter if you live or die? You design drugs to make people do what you want them to do, Silv. Is that not death of a sort?''

Silv just stared across the table at him, not innocent and knowing it. Hersh's theories may not have been right, but they kept him going.

''I want a child,'' Hersh said. ''I want to see my life in a baby's face, and know I'm bringing him into the best world I can make. That's true immortality."

"I had a vasectomy," David said, "so I'd never bring children into this rotten world."

"You could do it now," Hersh said, "in another body."

"But not another world," David replied, and he looked to Silv. Gerard Cuvier was wiping tears from his eyes.

"I'm leaving you tonight," Hersh said to end the uneasy silence that had enveloped them. "Going away."

"What do you mean?" Silv said.

"The English blockade had kept all news away from us for a long time," Hersh said. "But when Sidney Smith and I negotiated a prisoner exchange after the battle with the Turks at Aboukir, he gave me many European newspapers, along with the wine we're drinking.

"France is in turmoil. England, Turkey, Naples, Austria, and Russia have all declared war on us. The English and Russians have landed in Holland; Switzerland is in danger of falling as Corfu has already fallen." He looked at them in anguish. "All my gains in Italy are undone by the damned Austrians. They've dismantled my Cisalpine Republic. The royalty hates us for bringing power to the working classes, and band against us on all sides. Even the Bourbons are planning to take power again in Paris. I cannot wait here any longer. I must go back and offer my aid."

"Have you been ordered back?" Silv asked.

Hersh made a throwaway gesture. "It's only a matter of time. I anticipate it, so I go now."

David and Silv shared a look. Life had settled down for a time in Egypt and they had felt free to work on Hersh there, far away from European politics. This changed things considerably. They had made small gains with the man, but circumstances could unwind the ball of string quickly.

"You should await orders," David said.

"The decision is made," Hersh said. "I leave tonight, within the hour. We will run the blockades by night. I left a letter for Kleber. He's in charge now."

"It will look like you're running away from your defeats," Silv said. "And stranding your army at the same time."

"I've been criticized before," Hersh said.

"We'll, of course, go with you," Silv said.

The man shook his head. "Not this time. I've handpicked

my crew of my own lineage. It's taken me a month to find them, but you cannot travel with me this time.''

David didn't like this at all. He knew what the man was getting at. ''Why go to that kind of trouble? We can jump ahead to Paris and find people close to you there. So you can't escape us.''

There was no candle on the table, just the light of the moon and the stars, and they couldn't see Hersh's eyes as he stared at them there. He was a child, of course, barely thirty years old, his face boyish but inspired. He wore his uniform as one born to it. His hat, sporting the tricolors, sat poised upon his lap.

''I can get away from you for a while,'' he said. ''A couple of months by sea. I've enjoyed the association and the advice, but I must concentrate on my place in the scheme of things without interference.''

''But what of our talks,'' Silv said, ''our contact with you?''

''He goes to seek power, Silv,'' David said. ''He's afraid we might stop him.''

The boyish smile played on the general's lips. ''But you have said that you can catch up to me in Paris.''

''Which one of you came up with this?'' David asked. ''Listen to me, Hersh. If it was the general's idea, it's because he thinks he can absorb you into his personality on the trip back.''

''Go to hell, David,'' Napoleon said.

''General, listen to me,'' David persisted. ''This won't work. He can control you whenever he wants. You're far too intelligent to want a crazy man running your life.''

''You have failed with your 'talks,' haven't you,'' Bonaparte said quietly. ''We'll try it on our own now for a time.''

''What of Josephine?'' Silv asked.

''The chessboard sits before her, old woman,'' Napoleon said. ''It is up to her to move the pieces now.''

''And Talleyrand?'' David asked.

''He is my bridge to the power of the outlawed Church and the aristocracy. I'll find a way to control him.''

The general stood, putting on his hat. It was apparently some sort of signal, for a small boat was pushed down off the beach into the surf, Bonaparte's entourage boarding and rowing toward the barge.

''I'd like to propose a toast,'' Hersh said, raising his glass.

David and Silv stood also, picking up their glasses.

"To the profusion of moments," Hersh said, "and to their clarity."

"To pain," David said.

"And duty," Silv added.

They drank, the three sides of the triangle, all desperately wanting to rectify the angles of their intersection.

Hersh set his glass down and picked up the reliquary. "Don't be so foolish as to try and stop me," he said. "It would be worse than useless. Come along, Max."

"If you must do this, Hersh," David said, "remember that you, yourself, are a worthwhile human being. Retain your individuality and self-respect. We'll meet you in Paris."

"You already have knowledge of my future, David Wolf," Napoleon said. "I hope that your knowledge matches up to my expectations."

"I fear that it does," David replied.

Napoleon saluted them quickly, then climbed over the side of the barge and into the rowboat, Cafferilli's heart held close to his own. Silv and David walked to the rail and watched them slide quietly into the darkness.

"Now what?" Silv said.

"For the time being, he's beaten us," David replied, putting a hand on Cuvier's shoulder. "All we can do is watch all our work come undone."

"You've changed, David," Silv said. "Your skin has thickened."

"I've been skimming for several years," he said. "I've seen a lot of things."

"Perhaps the wrong things, eh?"

He turned to Cuvier, using the hand on his shoulder to turn his face around. "I accidentally went to the future," he said, then shrugged. "It's there."

Silv nodded, it seemed, sadly. "And the future survives?"

"Maybe it's time that we go there together and see what we've wrought."

With an air of resignation, Silv returned to the table, filling their glasses with the last bit of wine in the bottle. She sat and picked up her glass. "We've lived in the future. It's not all it's made out to be."

He came and sat at the table with her. "Our answers lie there," he said.

"So they do."

David picked up his wine, sipping, wondering what was happening to Silv. And soon, Bonaparte's skiff had disappeared in the shadow of the frigates and they were left with only the sad music of the concertina to interrupt their thoughts. And soon enough, that too, was gone.

You too must not count overmuch on your reality as you feel it today, since, like that of yesterday, it may prove an illusion for you tomorrow.

—Luigi Pirandello

David sat behind the wheel of his '57 Chevy under the glare of the harsh neon lights at the Sonic Drive-in and watched Mary Ann Boyd skate past to retrieve the tray hooked on the window of the pickup truck next to him. He marveled at the fullness of her hips under the tight short uniform skirt she wore, at how her ass seemed to wiggle on oiled ball bearings with each move she made, his stomach feeling light and fluttery, like when the flu was getting ready to set in.

If only . . .

No. This isn't it. Keep going.

The big, open front seat of the Chevy melted away all around him, coalescing within seconds, reforming and tightening into the white Porsche from which he had left this world so long ago.

He turned slightly, Liz staring at him from the seat beside, her face once melting into that of Linda Griggs, a high school girlfriend, before solidifying again into that of his sister.

"Liz!" he said, reaching out to touch her. "God, it's good to see you." He took her in his arms, holding tight. After the years he'd spent skimming, Liz was the only person he truly regretted being away from. She looked great. The years hadn't changed her.

She pulled away from him, looking frightened. "What is it?" she asked loudly. "What's wrong?"

He laughed, realizing that no time had passed for her at all. The years he had spent worrying about her problems, and hoping she was doing all right, simply hadn't happened for her.

"Nothing," he said, and kissed her quickly on the cheek. "Didn't mean to startle you."

He couldn't hold her face. It alternately became the faces

of many women in his life; the trees behind her, outside the window in the distance, kept growing and shrinking, leafing and dying, even as he watched, even as the cars parked near them kept melting and reforming—Studebakers and big Plymouths with huge fins and '65 Chevys with she's-real-fine-my-409s under the hood and glass packs on the exhaust.

He slapped his pockets, looking for the syringes, and realized that Silv had taken them. "The needles, Liz. I need the syringes."

She narrowed her gaze, pulling her purse up on her lap. Present reality was nearly impossible to hold when on the drug. Being ongoing and not an induced memory, the reality kept wanting to slip somewhere else, to dwell in the traces of the past and done.

Liz was just reaching into her bag when she grimaced in pain, throwing her head back on the seat, only to stare at him seconds later in practiced reserve.

"Silv, is that you?" he asked.

"You were expecting someone else?" she replied, and he laughed at that, more from surprise that Silv had made a joke than from the joke itself.

"Quick," he said. "Inject me before I lose it."

"Why waste it?" she asked. "We're not staying here anyway. There's no reason to come all the way back."

"Stop kidding around," he said. "I'm having a difficult time here."

Liz's face hiding Silv had turned into the face of Jeanne Maxwell, the first girl he had ever made love to, and his mind kept wanting to relive the night, the Sonic trying to change into the choppy waters of Lake Hefner where in the backseat she had slowly unbuttoned her sweater, the smell of her perfume a shock that would haunt him for years afterward, the old stirrings arising whenever he smelled the same perfume in the store or . . .

No. Back . . . back.

"There's no reason," Silv said. "Let's just do our business and move on."

He tried to reach for the bag himself, but when his hand touched his sister's leg, he hurtled immediately back to that night at the lake in 1966, sweating in the backseat, every second that passed bringing secret and forbidden revelations, the opening of a new and incredible world of sensation.

He forced himself back, incredibly horny now, the teenaged

sex drive like fire pulsing through his veins, the need itself nearly strong enough to force him back. With a tremendous effort of will, he concentrated his wandering mind to a single point and recaptured his present.

". . . and move on," Silv was saying. "No reason to dwell here now."

"This is a memory for you," he said. "You're not going through what I am."

"I'm not going to do it, David," she said. "Let's just do some checking and go someplace else to talk about it."

"Why?"

"Because."

"That's no answer."

Liz/Silv had become his mother, telling him he had to eat his entire hamburger before he could have the piece of peppermint laying on the tray.

Why?

Because, that's why.

"I'm not going to be able to drive this way," he said.

She had already opened the door on her side. "We'll switch," she said, walking around the car to open his door for him.

He got out, shakily, and she helped him around to the passenger side, the carhop running up to them.

"Is something wrong?" she asked, and turned into Mary Ann Boyd as he watched.

"No," Silv said. "My . . . brother just got a little sleepy, that's all."

"You want me to take the tray?"

"Please."

It was 1968 and Dave Wolf was drunk on his college-aged butt, his friend Georgie helping him around to the passenger side, so he could try and drive Dave back to the dorm, while keeping him from grabbing at the carhops as he passed them.

Silv got him into the car and hooked him up with the seat belt. "We'll try a library," she said. "Your sister knows where one is."

"Fine," he said, the nausea of the 1968 drunk still lingering even though the memory had passed.

Silv climbed behind the wheel. "I'm not totally sure how to do this," she said.

"Back off and let Liz do it," David replied.

"Promise you won't try for the syringes," Silv said.

"Why is that so damned important?"

"Promise."

"All right . . . all right."

Liz started the car and backed onto Meridian Avenue. "Are you okay?" she asked, voice concerned.

"Yes," he replied, and found that he could hold a semblance of the present by staring at the Porsche logo on the gearshift, a new image to his mental lexicon. "I'm under influence of the drug and it's hard to hold the present."

"It all works, then?"

"Oh, darlin', does it ever."

She turned onto Northwest Highway from Meridian, moving toward the Warr Acres branch library. Whenever he brought his gaze up from the gearshift, he watched buildings rise out of wooded fields, only to crumble back to nothingness, like flowers opening and closing with the sun. He could observe the vast patchwork quilt of progress filling in a square at a time, never better, simply different, all closing up the chapters of the book of his youth, smoothing over his life as if it had never existed. The unending nature of change was never so apparent to him.

"You've been traveling for a long time," she said. "I get that much from Silv's mind. I find it almost impossible to believe."

"It's true," he said. "You know what we're looking for?"

"Information on Bonaparte," Liz said. "How important is that?"

"To me, it's plenty important. To you . . . who knows?"

"Almost there," she said. "Hang on."

He thought about Liz, and about the last conversation they had had many years previously. "I want you to know," he said, "that I'm sorry I couldn't talk to you about Momma. It's a difficult subject for me."

She stared at him in surprise. "Quite an admission from you," she said.

"I've been doing some thinking," he replied, and his reality tripped back to his first lover, to the time she had sat with him in his car when he had told her he didn't want to see her anymore.

I've been doing some thinking . . .

He forced back the logo. "I've also . . . seen some things."

"What things?"

"Not now," he said, too quickly. "I'm not . . . I just want

you to know that I think you're doing the right thing in seeing the shrink, that's all. He can help you."

She reached over and touched his arm, her hand becoming Jeanne's when she begged him not to dump her, saying she was now ruined for life. He fought off the anguish, hers and his both.

"Here we are," Liz said, wheeling into the parking lot of the small branch library. "By the way, I'll drive this heap anytime."

He turned to her and could physically feel Silv sinking back into his sister, taking her body. "Good-bye, Liz," he said, and before he got the words out, she was gone.

Silv got out of the car and came around to help him, and she became his mother, bringing him to the library when he was small to work on his first geography report for D. D. Kirkland school.

He allowed Naomi to open his door and put an arm around his shoulder, leading him through the entrance and into the cool recesses of the quiet building.

They moved toward the card catalog area, but it was set with computers now and kicked him back to the present. He had no idea how to work the computers, it had been that long since he'd seen the inside of a library, but Silv used it easily and he knew it was her knowledge, not Liz's, that was at work here.

She pulled out a number of headings on the screen listed under BONAPARTE, N., and led him to the shelves.

"This is incredible," she whispered to him. "I've never seen so many books in my whole life."

"This is just a small branch," he replied, feeling himself grow and shrink as they walked the aisles. "The main library and the college libraries have a lot more."

She shook her head. "So many trees," she said.

She stopped in front of a section and quickly scanned the Dewey decimal numbers with Liz's eyes, pulling a volume out that had a picture of Hersh on the cover.

The library had a small alcove of reading tables set in the center of the building. Silv led David to one of them and they sat, thumbing through Napoleon's life until they came to the Egypt section.

They read together, with increasing disbelief. David noticed small discrepancies between the detail in the book and the Napoleon he had come to know, but these seemed to fall mostly under the heading of historically passed-down inaccuracies, and were easily forgiven. But for the most part the history was crystal clear, the events so forceful that they kept tripping David back to the actual happenings.

It was there, every bit of it—the Syrian campaign, the civilian scientists, the execution of the prisoners, the loss at Acre—just the way he and Silv remembered.

She closed the book loudly and stared at him.

"What does it mean?" he asked.

"I don't know," she said. "Perhaps Hersh has less control over Napoleon than we thought. Perhaps a brand-new reality was created and has changed everything we remember."

"There's another possibility," David said, and it chilled him to think of it. "Perhaps we are, and have always been, a part of past history. Perhaps we've always gone back in time and always affected the events that shaped history. Perhaps the freedom of our . . . moments isn't free at all."

"Destiny?" Silv said quietly.

"With a capital *D*," David replied. "The future and the past, one and the same, a giant jigsaw puzzle where all the pieces fit."

David Wolf, inhabiting the mind of quick, young playwright Antoine Arnault stood in the courtyard garden at 6, rue de la Victoire, recently renamed from rue Chantereine, and listened to the flower vendors on the corner singing, "Five for a louis! Five for a louis!"

It was their little joke on the Directory of five and on the Bourbon movement to put Louis XVIII on the throne, but the roots of the story were deadly serious. Faced with troubles within and without, France was in terrible shape. The economy was in collapse. Seven eighths of the Parisian artisans were unemployed, and civil servants had been long unpaid, though inflation was so rampant that even those with money found it worthless. The roads were jammed with bandits, stealing from travelers and from one another. Government itself had turned into a bad joke, the Directory suspending the Constitution at will whenever they feared being overruled by the Council of Five Hundred.

The people sensed a change in the air, and David stood in awe of Napoleon's uncanny ability of being in the right place at the right time. He wanted the power, and history was making it available to him.

Hersh's house was small but quietly elegant, overlooking a placid cobbled street on the west end. It was fenced in dark iron, a narrow but lengthy garden running beside the fence, a garden that was now filled with generals who paced nervously, swords clanging against their sides as they walked up and down. It was never a question of duty itself to the soldiers; the only difficulty came in determining, in times of turmoil, just what that duty was.

General Lefèbvre was the prize. A big, gruff man, he stood quietly, staring at nothing. As military governor of Paris, he risked a great deal just being at Napoleon's address on this day. A former sergeant-major, his loyalty and sense of honor were his most valued traits—his honor something that he was even now trying to align with truth.

David didn't believe much in truth. He had come back to Paris because that's where Silv had wanted to meet and discuss their futures, or perhaps their pasts. He had picked Arnault's body as the host because he appreciated the man's intelligence and artistic sensibilities. Though he missed the casual acceptance he had received from Jon Valance, it was a blessing to be out of the bodies of soldiers. Arnault accepted him philosophically, and he responded by giving the man his head in exchange for cooperation. Actually, he truly enjoyed the young man. It was the first time he had dwelled for any length of time within a brain that was wittier and quicker than his own.

He had been in Paris for two days, having met Hersh upon his arrival. In that time he hadn't, as yet, come upon Silv and was really beginning to wonder where she had gotten off to. He wouldn't wait forever for her, but time, he had come to appreciate, is the most plastic of all realities and consequently the most malleable. And perhaps she was leaving him alone on purpose, giving him some time to think, to plan his life from this point.

He wasn't sure about Hersh's condition, though he was absolutely convinced that the long ocean voyage without medical help could be nothing but harmful. He sensed a war going on inside of the body of Napoleon, and wasn't sure whether interference on his part was warranted at this point. The general was a strong personality—perhaps he could handle Hersh on his own. Though David worried for his patient's life should Napoleon be able to oust him.

Josephine had not met Hersh upon his arrival back in France, a fact which seemed to pour fuel on the psychological fire raging within Napoleon's body, almost as if the war being fought within came to a matrix over the woman. Napoleon would alternately scream for divorce and good riddance, or cry over the lost love of his "dearest Josephine," who, up until the time of her marriage, had been known to all as Rose. Napoleon had thought the name too tawdry and changed it to Josephine while at the same time trying to change the questionable image of the woman's past. More of Hersh's delusions playing themselves out?

Josephine had finally come home an hour before, with a small entourage, saying that she had gone to meet her husband, but that they had passed in transit. Napoleon had refused to see her, instead locking her out of his study, so beginning a feminine campaign of tears and pleading that had ultimately driven David out of the house.

The screaming and petty arguing of the distaff lovers only made David more irritable. The job of being Hersh's shrink was an impossible undertaking, just another sign of David's failure as a doctor and a human being. He had no idea of where he wanted to go from here. When he had thought he could be saving history, his exploits had a heroic stature in his own mind, but once he realized that it didn't matter what he did, that history would be served anyway, he had once again become faced with the uselessness of his own life.

Should he forget all the foolishness and go home? The thought still frightened him. Not only did he have nothing there, but the idea of being trapped in one body, in one lifetime, was nearly impossible to accept after seeing the possibilities. But where would he go?

He had neither the courage to embrace his own death nor the stupidity to think his life had meaning. He was a thinking, feeling animal at odds with itself. He felt he had the unfortunate curse of seeing clearly the fact that human beings led brief, meaningless, pain-filled lives under the illusion of freedom and purpose. If only he had the guts to simply end it once and for all.

Please, monsieur. Not in my body!

Don't worry, Antoine. I'll hurt no one but myself.

Like always, eh?

Mind your own business.

He thought about the Egyptian in Cairo, about the suicide he had witnessed. He remembered that happy suction that drew Ibrahim toward death, and the *rightness* of it all. Though he had felt that same pull himself from time to time, it had never been enough to take hold of him completely. It still wasn't. Perhaps Fate wasn't through making a fool of him yet.

"Monsieur Arnault," came a voice behind him.

Startled, he turned to see Thérèsia Tallien standing beside him. A close friend of Josephine's, Madame Tallien had returned with her that morning from parts unknown and had tried, unsuccessfully, to intercede between the general and his penitent wife.

He nodded to the woman. "Madame," he said, bowing slightly.

"I seem to have disturbed your reverie," she said.

He shook his head. "No, not at all. You merely rescued me from the dark poet's soul."

"Then, I have done a good deed for certain," she replied, smiling with her eyes and with her red mouth.

She was a beautiful woman with jet-black hair who had survived prison under the Terror to marry the man who had done more than anyone to topple Robespierre and end the ghastly reign. She was famous in Paris for her transparent clothing and her scandalous streak. Today she wore a coiffure a la guillotine, with her hair cropped short and lifted off her neck, a narrow red satin ribbon encircling her throat. Her bosom, barely concealed in the scooped-neck, popular Grecian style, gave both Arnault and David pause for reflection.

"You look truly lovely today," Arnault said, bending to kiss her hand.

She tapped his hand lightly with her fan when he failed to release hers, and he straightened, her eyes staring boldly at him. "I saw your play, *Oscar,* Monsieur."

"Antoine, please."

"I found it quite good . . . Antoine. I hear it's made you a millionaire."

David smiled. "After only twelve performances," he replied. "A measure at how poor Parisians really are."

"Will the general relent, Antoine, and forgive his suffering wife?"

Arnault bowed again. "Only Destiny can answer that question, Madame," he said.

The woman narrowed her eyes. "David?" she said.

He smiled broadly. "Silv? I've been wondering where you were."

Her demeanor relaxed, all defense systems dropped. "I've been traveling with Josephine," she said, "working myself into the household that way."

He regarded her with trepidation, unused to the wrapping that now housed the package of Silv. The fact that he was attracted to her physically only made matters worse. "You chose a strange host to come back in," he said, though it didn't express what he was really feeling.

"How so?" she asked, unable to accept his words on their face value. "Thérèsia is intelligent, honest, healthy—an altogether first-rate choice as a host."

He didn't know what to say to her. "You were . . . before, you came as a man. I suppose I assumed you could get closer to the situation that way."

"It was convenient to be a man before," she said. "Now it is convenient not to be."

He began to realize that Silv was either lying to him or to herself. "Not just a woman, though, Silv. One of the most beautiful, desirable women in Paris."

"I suppose I should thank you for the compliment," she said.

He pointed at her, smiling, finally using his medical brain to figure her out. "You're beginning to loosen up," he said, letting his eyes take in her beauty without embarrassment. "You're a woman, and you want to be a woman now, and it has nothing to do with Napoleon. You want to have some fun."

"I beg your pardon!" she said coldly. "And I'll thank you not to look at me that way."

"You overcome David Wolf *and* Antoine Arnault, madame," he said, bowing. "Our infatuation causes us to lose control."

She slapped him hard, her eyebrows pulling tight. "Stop it!" she said. "It's me in here, David. Nothing's different, just the host. You'll kindly treat me as you always have."

"I can't," he said. "You chose a host that you knew was desirable and I am responding. If you want me to treat you as

I did when you looked like Gerard Cuvier, then transfer into a soldier again."

"I don't have to," she said, and opened her fan, bringing it up to cover her heaving bosom. "I deserve respect for the essence of myself; the package has nothing to do with it."

"Despite what Marie Antoinette said, you can't have your cake and eat it, too." He took her fan away and closed it up, sticking it down the front of her dress. "Admit it," he said. "You enjoy the attention. You enjoy being a woman again. There's nothing wrong with that."

She grabbed the fan out of her bosom, looking around to make sure no one else saw. "I've got a job to do here."

He turned from her, looking out the bars toward the street, at the beggars and rag salesmen passing by. "You have no job here anymore. Neither one of us has."

She came up beside him, leaning against the bars to stare into his face. "I saw nothing that changed my sense of duty," she said.

He turned to her angrily. "Stop lying to me," he said through clenched teeth. "Nothing we do makes any difference. If I put a gun to your head and pulled the trigger, it would be because it was supposed to be that way."

No, monsieur. Not such a lovely head!

I'm only speaking figuratively, Antoine.

"I don't relate to that," she said. "I had my duty, and still have it. When I can make Hersh return, then all will be as it was."

"What about me?" he said. "I'm not going back."

"Perhaps your duty, then, is to stay here?"

She smiled at him, and in the smile lay a promise. This was totally out of hand. It was almost as if she were seducing him!

He reached out and took her by the arms, shaking slightly. "What are you trying to do?" he asked.

"People are watching," she whispered harshly. "Let go of me."

He released her arms, turning to stare down the generals who had stopped pacing to look at the altercation.

"I'm sorry," he said. "I'm just very confused."

"All right," she said quietly. "Let's be honest. Perhaps things have changed somewhat. I'm not sure what's happening right now, but I feel more comfortable here, doing this, than I do anywhere. I've done some traveling myself since

I've last seen you, and right now I feel more . . . at home with my duty while I sort things out. Maybe you will too.''

"Why is that important to you?''

"Why do you say it is?''

"Because you wouldn't bring me all the way in, back home, as if you were afraid I'd stay back there.''

"I just didn't want to waste a good dose when I figured we'd be returning to talk about it anyway,'' she said, then tried unsuccessfully to be subtle in changing the topic. "How is our patient?''

Something was up. David was convinced of it now. He decided to play along and see what he could learn on his own. A cement bench was set by the garden path. He moved to it and sat, patting the place beside him for Silv. "It's hard to know,'' he said, feeling Arnault's body stir when she sat beside him, their hips touching. "He's fighting some real internal battles with Napoleon that have driven him inward even farther. I wouldn't suggest telling him about our discoveries, though. It may confuse the issue even more.''

"I disagree,'' she said quickly, Arnault moving his leg slightly against Madame Tallien's, hers responding in kind. "The sooner he knows the truth, the better. Maybe it will shock him back to sanity.''

"Emotional illness isn't some sort of headache you can cure with an aspirin,'' he replied, Arnault's hand coming to rest on his thigh, two fingers touching Thérèsia's thigh. "Revelations need to be accompanied by corresponding acceptance of responsibility. Hersh is in no condition to deal with anything like that in his present state. We're not cheap magicians with cheap tricks, Silv.''

She looked down, startled, at how Arnault's hand had come to rest on her leg and she pulled away, scooting farther down the bench. David laughed inside. He couldn't blame the poor guy for trying.

"I've come to respect your profession in the last several months,'' she said, the fan coming open again, fluttering nervously. "I understand the meticulous character rebuilding that goes along with success in rehabilitation. But in this case I think you're wrong. Perhaps a dose of absolute truth will shake him awake. After all, his believing the reality of his dream is what helped kick him into his delusions to begin with.''

"Don't believe it," David said. "Hersh's problems are deeply rooted, and—"

She tapped him quickly on the leg to warn him that Hersh had come into the garden. He looked drawn, worn out from his emotional battles. He was in full dress uniform: white breeches, blue frockcoat with wide gold-embroidered lapels, at his waist a red, white, and blue sash and the sword he had worn during the Syrian campaigns and at the battle of Aboukir.

He walked immediately to General Lefèbvre who stood beside a trellis full of blooming red roses. The two men appraised one another, Lefèbvre large and imposing, Napoleon like a tightened mainspring ready to burst.

David and Silv strained to hear the words.

"I had misgivings about coming here, General," Lefèbvre said in his thick Alsatian accent.

"And why would that be?" Hersh asked, the two men locked in deadly eye contact.

"It occurred to me that intrigues could be happening at this place," the man replied forthrightly, "that conspiracies could be hatched in such an atmosphere."

"Conspiracy is a word of many shadings and gradations," Hersh replied.

Lefèbvre snorted and pulled on his long chin. "What in hell is going on here?" he asked.

"The salvation of France," Hersh answered. "Your loyalty and your sword arm are needed more now than in any battle you've ever fought in. I seek to preserve the Republic that we fought so hard to found. You came from the ranks, my friend. Will you return to them? The Bourbons want the throne, and if we, loyal soldiers, don't do anything to stop them, our country is lost, along with our heads."

"What of the Directory, and the Five Hundred in Council?"

Hersh looked at him, then unhooked his sword and handed it to the man. "We're soldiers," he said. "We will be doing our duty to our countrymen and ourselves. Here is the sword I carried at the Battle of the Pyramids. I give it to you as a token of my esteem and confidence."

The man looked at the weapon, respecting the value of so personal a gift, valuing more the trust of one soldier for another. "The Paris garrison is yours to command," he said after a moment. "I'm ready to throw those buggers of lawyers into the river."

"Good," Hersh said. "Return to your garrison. I will be in touch."

Lefèbvre saluted. "My general," he said, and walked past Silv and David to the gate, then into the streets.

David shook his head, in awe, as usual, of the man who so desperately needed his help, the man who could talk of revolution as others talked about the weather.

Hersh turned to them, at once taking in their companionship and knowing its reasons. He strode to stand before them, his arms folded across his chest.

"So," he said. "The chicks have returned to the roost."

"How are you, Hersh?" Silv asked sweetly.

"I was busily forgetting about the past until you two came along," Hersh said. "I feel wonderful. I've decided that I shall run this country before the year is out."

"Repressing the past is no way to prepare for the future, Hersh," David said. "Human beings are a collection of what's come before. Understanding is the key."

"Always sniffing around, aren't you, David?" Hersh asked. "Always trying to catch me being unwell. Well, I'm fine. I feel like a new man."

"Will you take Josephine back?" Silv asked.

His eyes flashed hard, then relaxed. "Don't speak to me of her," he said coldly.

David watched him carefully. His personality was torn, desperately trying to mend itself even as he pushed through his dreams of power, the dreams being the plane of intersection between the general's two halves.

"We have something important to tell you," Silv said, and David groaned beside her.

Hersh pulled a pocket watch out of his frock. "Inside, then," he said. "We'll have tea and talk while I wait for Talleyrand."

"He's coming here?" David asked.

"With a surprise." Hersh winked, then bent to tousle David's hair. "Don't look so glum. The world is ours."

They moved into the house and right to the den where Napoleon carried on all his business affairs. The room was large, the wall space taken up with bookcases from floor to ceiling. He had made a great deal of money while conquering Italy, most of it going into the house. A huge fire roared in the corner of the room to hold back the early fall chill.

High-backed chairs were set in a circle around the center of the room. Napoleon threw himself in one, hoisting a leg over the chair arm to slouch sideways. David moved to a small table set with food, taking a pastry and pouring a cup of tea for himself. Silv just sat, Thérèsia probably convincing her that it wouldn't be good for her figure.

Sugar, please, two spoons.

In tea? Please spare me!

I can't drink it without.

David grudgingly put two spoonfuls of sugar in the tea and stirred. He took a seat by Silv, Arnault wanting to be near Thérèsia Tallien.

Hersh stared at them, the sound of muffled crying drifting to them through a closed door. "You have something to tell me," he said to Silv, his face set hard.

She took a brief look at David, who shook his head no. She ignored him. "David and I went back to his time," she said.

"How nice for you," he replied.

"We looked at the history books and found that everything that has happened is just as it should be."

The man's face got quizzical and he straightened in his chair. "What do you mean?" he asked.

"I feared that you would change history," Silv replied, "but you didn't. You are a part of history, your traveling to this time was . . . meant to be."

His face darkened. "I—I don't understand."

"This is all happening because it's supposed to," David said, watching a look of pain cross the man's face.

"No, no," Hersh said, smiling. "It's not going to work. This is my dream. I control it as I choose."

Silv shook her head. "You're wrong. You're a part of it all, not a free entity."

"No!" he screamed. "I don't hear you!"

Silv looked at David, her face frightened.

"Don't worry about it now, Hersh," he said. "This is nothing to be concerned about at the moment."

Hersh stood, hands behind his back. He paced nervously. "My actions are free, I know that," he said, his body jerking wildly. "If that weren't true, I—I wouldn't be real. Of course I'm real. I *choose* to be real."

There was a knocking on the door to the outside, servants hurrying to open it. At that moment, a teenaged boy dressed in a velvet suit strode in—Eugene, Josephine's son from a previous marriage.

Napoleon saw him, pulling him close and tugging on his ears before shaking hands with him. "There's my lad," he said. "Did you miss me while I was off fighting the heathens?"

Eugene smiled. "I'm here on a mission that I fear won't be to your liking," he said, tugging at his collar. "Forgive Mother, she promises not to see Uncle Charles again."

"Uncle Charles!" Hersh screamed loudly. "Is that what they called your young hussar?"

Josephine's voice screamed from behind the door, "What about Madame Fourès, your Cleopatra in Egypt?"

"My revenge, you bitch!" Hersh threw himself in the chair again. "The warriors of Egypt are like those of Troy. Their wives have been equally faithful."

"She really was going to meet you," Silv said. "She took the Burgundy route . . ."

"And I the Nevers," he finished, his face softening somewhat. Then it hardened again, and he leaned toward Eugene. "Tell your mother to get herself a lawyer."

The boy nodded knowingly and walked with dignity out of the room, passing three men coming in. Talleyrand led the way, David knowing him immediately. He was tall and handsome, his airs those of a dandy. Yet he commanded a certain presence that drew all eyes, including Napoleon's, to him. Next came faces familiar to Arnault: Emmanuel Sieyès and Pierre-Roger Ducos, both members of the Directory.

"Sit, gentlemen," Hersh said, standing and bowing. "Please, accept my hospitality. Have something to eat."

All three men went to the food table, Talleyrand stealing glances at Silv. Something akin to jealousy flashed through David's mind.

This is crazy!

Sieyès was a strange little man with a domed head and hunched, sharply defined features. Ducos, on the other hand, was totally nondescript, a quiet man in drab clothes, who was known for a deep, probing mind.

"So!" Hersh said, too loudly. "I see you've left your hats at home. The ones with the three-foot plumes!"

"Those are for official times only," Sieyès said, frowning deeply at the insult.

"And is it true that now the Five Hundred wears Grecian robes?"

"That is so," Talleyrand said, moving to sit on the other side of Silv.

"Foolishness!" Hersh screamed, then inclined his head toward the door that closed Josephine off from the proceedings. "Foolishness!"

David quickly finished his pastry and stood, anxious to get Silv away from Talleyrand, toward whom he had already taken a strong dislike. "Perhaps we should leave you honored sirs to discuss your business," he said. "Madame Tallien and I will withdraw until later."

"Nonsense," Hersh said, and he was still too loud, too on edge. "Stay. Perhaps my colleagues in the government can help us in our discussion."

"Indeed," Talleyrand said, looking at Silv the whole time. "The presence of Madame Tallien certainly brightens our discussions." He kissed her hand, his eyes locked with hers.

"No, we couldn't . . ." David began.

"Of course you can," Hersh said, then looked at the others. "Arnault and Madame Tallien and I were discussing Destiny, gentlemen. Certainly a good topic for today."

"We have delicate matters to discuss here," Sieyès said, his dislike of Napoleon obvious.

"They shall stay," Hersh said, then to Talleyrand, "Barras is working to bring back Louis. He offered me a place in his coup d'état yesterday."

"All the lines shuffle," Talleyrand said. "Barras goes with the money."

"And you, gentlemen," Hersh said to the two Directors. "What motivates your lives?"

"We seek the stability of France," Sieyès says. "We seek its salvation in a new order."

"In other words, you want the power," Hersh said, "and you need a sword arm to back you up."

"There's no reason to be indelicate," Ducos said.

"My friend Arnault and the lady Tallien tell me that our lives are guided purely by Destiny," Hersh said, standing again, agitated. "That we have no Free Will per se."

"The hand of God, then?" Talleyrand said directly to Silv. "A philosophy uncommon in these modern times. In fact, a philosophy officially frowned upon."

David really disliked this man. He never seemed to say what he was really thinking.

"I mentioned nothing of God," Silv said. "That suggests order."

"What is Destiny besides order?" Talleyrand asked.

Sieyès drank nearly his whole cup of tea in one swallow, then spoke to Napoleon. "Your return to France at such an unexpected and opportune time would certainly suggest the intrusion of Destiny or of tremendous luck."

"Is it by luck that men became great?" Napoleon asked.

"No, but being great, they were able to master luck."

"Grandeur of that nature is what put the Bourbons out of power," Sieyès said, staring.

Napoleon returned the stare. "Then, perhaps I misunderstand your reasons for being here, monsieur."

Silv spoke to Talleyrand. "Destiny could simply be the acceptance of Time as an existent reality. Times existing, as rocks, for good and all."

"I didn't give you enough credit," the man replied. "Your metaphysics are deeply thought out."

Tallien blushed. "Thank you," she said sweetly.

"Predestined chaos?" David said. "That doesn't make sense."

' Chaos and order are just words, David," Silv said. "We invented them to try and explain our lives."

"But time is the proof of order, is it not?" Talleyrand asked. "The universe, like the clocks of our Swiss allies, each second, each moment, laid in linear symmetry, moving the world gloriously forward."

"That's not right either," David said. "Time is also an invention. The speed of light is the only constant."

"The speed of light!" Ducos exclaimed. "Oh dear, I fear our young poet speaks in metaphors beyond my comprehension."

"It's no metaphor . . ." David began.

"What *exactly* are you doing here today?" Hersh interrupted, moving to stand before Sieyès.

The Director answered without hesitation. "We are here seeking a man not afraid to face change."

"Ha!" Hersh said loudly. "Face change? I *am* change. My dreams go far beyond the petty bickering of nearsighted hypocrites. And I'll tell you something else: I act not from love of power but because I am better educated, more perceptive—plus *clairvoyant*—and better qualified than anyone else."

"What are you saying, General?" Ducos said.

"I am unused to the games of politicians," Hersh said. "I speak my mind. You are looking for a sword, and I am your instrument—but I am also more than that."

Sieyès frowned around a mouthful of cake. "Bold words from a man who faces arrest as a traitor for deserting his troops without orders."

"On the roads to Paris I was greeted by crowds everywhere," Hersh said, hands on hips, staring down at Sieyès. "They cheered the hero of Aboukir, the router of Turks. The Directory wouldn't dare arrest me and you know it. Besides, I was abandoned in Egypt . . . wasn't I, Charles?"

Napoleon had turned to Talleyrand and was pointing at him. "Why didn't you make peace with the Turks?" he said loudly. "Where were you when I needed you?"

Talleyrand smiled, putting a hand to his chest, unruffled. "My dear general," he said. "Just because I worked for the Foreign Office doesn't mean I made all the decisions. I wanted desperately to come, but I was held back, unable to. I've been dismissed from that post since. Is that not proof enough of my sincerity and my lack of control over matters? Had I been guilty of what you accused me of, would I come here today and help bring this alliance to fruition?"

David was beginning to understand the fatal attraction that Napoleon had for Talleyrand. The man was like a precocious child, naughty but infinitely lovable. Napoleon, who appreciated intelligence and foresight above all, was absolutely drawn to Talleyrand despite the man's opportunism and faithlessness.

A teenaged girl entered the room dressed in gingham, a shawl wrapped around her shoulders. Hortense, Josephine's daughter.

Hersh flared around at her entry, rushing to take her in his arms. "Little flower," he cried. "Let your stepfather embrace you."

The girl stayed rigid in his grasp, her dislike of her stepfather obvious to all except Napoleon himself, Hersh still living the fantasy.

"Please, sir," she said in a small voice when they had parted. "Please end my mother's anguish and forgive her. She is truly penitent."

"The bitch sends children to plead her cause!" he shouted. "The woman who left me with less than a hundred louis in my bank account!"

"Oh, sir," Hortense pleaded. "Mother only wanted the house to be beautiful for your return. Redecoration takes money."

"So does high living!" Hersh shouted.

The crying got louder on the other side of the door.

"Oh, please," Hortense sobbed. "We fear she will take ill from all her emotional suffering!"

"And I fear, as the cuckold of Europe, that I will never be taken seriously again!"

"I'm sorry!" Josephine cried from behind the door. "If you don't take me back, I will kill myself from grief!"

Napoleon's eyes softened for a second, then solidified again. "Well, don't be messy about it. We'd hate to ruin the redecoration!"

Her cries turned into wails.

"Perhaps we should go," Ducos said, standing, setting his cake plate on the floor beside his chair.

"No!" Hersh shouted, walking up to glare him back to his chair. "We haven't concluded our business yet."

"You have domestic problems," Sieyès said, his jaw muscles tight. "Perhaps the affairs of state take less precedence than affairs of the heart."

"It's Destiny we talk about here, remember?" Hersh said coldly. "And I see Destiny as an expression of Free Will." He raised a clenched fist. "As men of Free Will, we hold the Destiny of France in our grasp, if only you gentlemen have the courage to face up to your own choices."

Sieyès stood and faced Bonaparte. "Courage is not only for the soldier," he said. "We propose a bold plan. Perhaps it is *your* mettle we test."

"Your plan, then," Hersh said in a near whisper, and suddenly the room got very quiet, except for Josephine's sobs from the next room.

"The Directory can be easily ours," Sieyès said.

"How?" Hersh asked.

Sieyès turned toward David and Silv, motioning with his hand.

"I would not have them here could they not be trusted, Monsieur Director," Hersh said, now nearly nose to nose with Sieyès. "If you have something to tell me, stop holding it in."

Talleyrand stood, walking over to place himself between the two men. "My general," he said. "Barras has proven that he can be purchased easily enough, so he is no problem. You have two Directors here before you. If we can convince the Five Hundred that a military coup threatens them, we can have the hero of Aboukir installed as commander of the Paris district . . .''

"Seven thousand men," Hersh said.

"Enough," Sieyès said.

"Then," Talleyrand continued, "we can convince them to hold the Council at Saint-Cloud for their own protection, thereby moving the government away from Paris. We will secure the resignation of the Directors, with the Council out of the way; then, using your troops as a lever, convince the Council to install Ducos and Sieyès as leaders, making any changes we need to properly run the country."

Hersh laughed. "And what is this supposed to do for me?"

"You will have several good reasons for backing us in this," Sieyès said. "First, you will be doing the Republic a great service. Second, a great deal of money will undoubtedly come your way. Third, you will be able to name whatever position in government you choose to fill."

"Good," Hersh said, "Then, I want to be a Director, along with you good gentlemen."

Ducos also stood, the four men forming a circle. "But that is impossible," he said. "The Constitution clearly states that one must be at least forty years old to be a Director."

Hersh smiled broadly. "Then we must have a new constitution," he said. "Think of it. We have no government because we have no Constitution, at least not the kind we need. It is for your genius to produce one. Once that is done, nothing will be easier than to govern. So, I propose that we follow your plan with minor exceptions. At Saint-Cloud we will, indeed, secure the resignations of the Directors, all of them, including yourselves. Then we will appoint a committee of three to be about the business of writing a new Constitution. We, gentlemen, will be the three. Our new Constitution will leave us, of course, in charge when we are finished. Equal risks, equal rewards."

"Preposterous," Ducos said.

"But not so preposterous as you wanting me to risk my commission and my neck for no rewards at all, eh?" Hersh said.

Sieyès shook his head and spoke slowly. "Of all the

military men I have ever known," he said, "you are most like a civilian."

Hersh bowed deeply. "I will accept that as a compliment."

"We will think over your proposition, General Buonaparte," Sieyès said.

"That's Bonaparte," Hersh said.

"Of course."

There was a dull banging on Josephine's door, darkness crossing Hersh's face. "What!" he screamed, then ran to the door, knocking over two chairs in his haste. He stood before the door, fists clenched. "What!"

"I am banging my head on your door," Josephine said. "I will destroy my stupid, stupid brain."

"Don't harm yourself," Hersh said, softening.

"I don't deserve to live," the woman sobbed, and began banging again.

David made to stand, worried, but Silv put a hand on his arm, smiling. "Rose has a flair for the dramatic," she whispered.

Talleyrand walked up to Silv, bending to take her hand, his frilly shirt smelling of perfume. "We will take our leave now," he said low. "It is my fondest hope that you and I will meet again soon under more . . . relaxed circumstances."

"But, my lord," Silv said sweetly. "Are you not a clergyman?"

"I am a republican," Talleyrand said, his eyes telling a story. "And I am taken by you."

Thérèsia fluttered her eyes. "I blush under your attention," she said, David feeling sick to his stomach.

"Please!" Hersh screamed. "Please stop!"

"The grave calls to me!" Josephine moaned.

"No!"

"I will send a footman around to your house with a message, madame," Talleyrand said.

"Discretion, my lord. I'm a married woman."

"Will you stay away from that bastard Charles?" Hersh yelled.

"Yes, my love, yes! Anything!"

"I go now, then," Talleyrand said, kissing her hand. "You will be in my dreams tonight."

"I hope they are . . . pleasant dreams," Silv said, fluttering her fan in the man's direction.

Talleyrand blew her a kiss and left with the Directors.

"Why did you play up to that asshole?" David asked.

"He was very nice," Silv said.

"Will you try to not spend my money too freely?" Hersh called.

"I'll wear sackcloth to be near you!"

Hersh backed away from the door, his face a war of conflicting emotions. It looked as if he were going to turn and walk off, when he literally sprang at the door, throwing it open.

Josephine stood in the doorway, tears streaking her homely face, her new gown ripped in several places where she had chastised herself. She and Hersh fell into each other's arms, both of them crying, holding one another for dear life.

"Hersh has won," David said.

"But at what cost?" Silv replied. "I'm sorry I told him our news. He seems so . . ."

"Out of control?" David finished, and nodded, shrugging. "You're right. He is. A full-blown paranoid psychotic is about to take control of the French government."

I have discovered that we may be in some degree whatever character we choose. Besides, practice forms a man to anything.

—James Boswell

It was gray and overcast as David, in the body of Antoine Arnault, stepped out of the coach in front of 6, rue de la Victoire, on the morning of November 10, 1799—the day the Revolutionary Council called 19 Brumaire.

In the chill air he bundled his greatcoat around him as he climbed down, the body only slightly hungover, and paid the driver in government consuls which had increased in value only the day before when Bonaparte was placed in charge of the Paris garrison.

For once, the drinking of the night before had been more of a celebration than a vent to depression. David Wolf had made up his mind, and it seemed to ease him somewhat.

He crossed the cobbled street and entered the gate to Bonaparte's house, the garden now jammed with military personnel. This was it, the day Hersh intended to begin his singular reign over France, though Directors Sieyès and Ducos had no idea that they weren't running the show. Today,

Napoleon faced the Council of Five Hundred to demand a new Constitution.

There was little David could do for Hersh except try and maintain the rapport. The man was as eaten up by his delusions as at any time during the Syrian campaign, and reaching him on a meaningful level was nearly impossible. Not that David worried overmuch about it. He knew that Napoleon would take power, though he wasn't sure how, and that, perhaps, it was a madman who would rule.

Maybe madmen always rule. Maybe that's all there are.

David made his way through the crowds in the garden and moved up to the great door, using the gold knocker in the shape of a bee to announce his presence.

He had spent the last month in the body of Arnault, a truly compatible body, one that he had enjoyed talking and drinking with. In fact it was Arnault who had been the catalyst for David's having at last reached his decision, though he secretly knew that Antoine had ulterior motives for his advice.

Arnault had fallen in love with Thérèsia Tallien and, David suspected, she had with him. The natural attraction had been too much for the both of them, since they were forced together time and again because of Silv and David. David didn't know what to think of the arrangement, and certainly didn't know of his own feelings in the matter. Was he a person or a nonentity, a spirit?

The feelings were strong in Antoine, and in David when he allowed himself to sink into the young man's body too far. The love affair, because of Silv's prudishness, had remained unconsummated, and because of it, Arnault had vowed personal chastity until he could consumate his relationship with Thérèsia. It was all too confusing for David, who kept whatever personal feelings he had bottled up, not thinking himself "real" enough to have feelings.

And that's what formed the crux of his decision. He and Arnault had talked the entire night before, mind to mind, David baring his soul to the young man, who responded that the only way David could ever find any personal happiness would be to return to his own life and try and straighten it out. That had made sense to David. If he was real at all, he was real in his own world, the one he had been born to. Perhaps, if he could go back and untangle the mess of his own life, he'd be free to explore other possibilities. But, as it was, he'd never have any peace as long as his own reality was in a shambles.

It was worth a try, and, in fact, the idea and daring of inhabiting a fragile shell again, always a mistake away from death, was exciting. The idea of having to live with the decisions he was making gave the idea of life a tense immediacy that he had been missing for a long time.

There was another reason, too. Somewhere, in some dark, frightening corner of his mind, he feared he was falling in love also. Was it Thérèsia, though, who attracted him, or the woman who pulled the strings, his own descendant, at least the descendant of his blood? Did he have a right to partake in the biological reactions of Arnault's body, or was Arnault simply picking up on his feelings? At any rate, it was Arnault's body that thrilled to the presence of Thérèsia Tallien, and David felt dirty, somehow, for encroaching. Sex in the mind of others had never bothered him at all before, but this was different, this involved him in a very personal way.

How do you separate the body from the soul that inhabits it? What incredible combination of natural and biochemical urges plus mental and emotional emergence adds up to the reaction we call love?

Thérèsia had certainly been good for Silv, and David had realized that Silv had chosen her as the host for a variety of good reasons. The woman's outlandishness covered a shrewd political mind that had played a great behind-the-scenes part in the formation and direction of France under the Directory. Silv was responding in kind, opening up herself a bit, loosening the tight reins that had constrained her attitudes so. David found he enjoyed her company tremendously, though would he have had she still been in the body of Gerard Cuvier? He couldn't straighten it out, so he chose to forcibly ignore it.

David was going to go home. There was meaning there, a sense of straightening out unfinished business, a sense of place and, yes, time. He needed that right now. When and if he left it again, he would start from scratch, approaching skimming in a new light. But not quite yet. He had watched the general's political and military maneuvers at work for the last month. He had to be there for the payoff, just to see.

Josephine's daughter, Hortense, opened the door, smiling, and then blushing as she led Arnault into the study.

"So, how long will you keep me waiting for you, my sweetness?" Arnault said, knowing the girl had a crush on him. "When will you marry me and run away with me?"

"Please, sir," she said, covering her scarlet cheeks with her hands. "My stepfather would never allow it."

"Ha! I'll duel with him myself for your hand," he said gallantly. "I'll run him through for love!"

She looked at him, her head somewhat inclined. "I've always heard that the pen is mightier," she said in a small voice.

"A poem, then," Arnault said, smiling and hugging her warmly. "Would you like me to write you a poem?"

"Oh, yes!" she said happily. "No one has ever written me a poem before."

They had arrived at the study. Arnault bowed with a flourish. "Then it will be my honor to be the first," he said, then straightened, removing his coat. "How is it today, eh?"

Hortense took his greatcoat and shrugged. "They've been arguing all morning," she whispered.

David nodded knowingly, then winked at her and walked into the large room. Napoleon stood, frowning deeply, with his hands behind his back. A circle of men cordoned him from the rest of the room, which was, literally, filled with military and civilian conspirators. In the circle were Murat and Berthier, loyal marshals from the Egyptian wars; his brother Lucien, President of the Deputies' Council of the Five Hundred; Sieyès and Ducos, ready to play their part; and General Lefèbvre, who, like an impeccably honest old colonel lending his picture to a spurious note-heading, was always close at hand to give the appearance of legitimacy to Hersh's delusions.

"The Deputies will not be swayed by your rhetoric," Sieyès said, waving his arms in exasperation. "Even now, the Jacobin members are uniting against us. They sense something in the air."

"I've fought many battles," Hersh said, shaking his head, the frown deepening. "I will use words as I use my sword and cut them down."

"This isn't the battlefield," Ducos said.

"But it could be," the dashing Murat said, his wild, long hair hanging almost down to his heavily braided uniform. "We are soldiers, my general. We must handle this thing as soldiers. We take the troops right into Saint-Cloud and force them to listen to reason on the edge of the blade.''

''No!'' Hersh yelled, his face reddening. ''No, no, no! This is my dream, and it will go as I order it. I will be swept into power constitutionally, by acclamation. I need not raise my sword-arm to my countrymen. I will explain to them and they will understand.''

''Well said,'' Lefèbvre replied. ''It is still our government. We must respect it.''

''We're overthrowing the government,'' Sieyès said, ''and the words and thoughts of soldiers hold very little sway over men whose lives it is to bandy and twist words to their own ends. Please, be ready with your troops, but leave the talking to the professionals. We'll handle this smoothly enough.''

Hersh reached out and took the man by the lapel. ''You wanted my sword, and now you've got it. And along with it comes my heart and my brain. You invited me in and now I'm here, and if *you* don't like it, I'll let you speak to the sword you coveted so much.''

''Gentlemen,'' Lucien, the novelist, said, subtly extricating his brother's hand from Monsieur Director's coat. ''Let me ease this through. I will be in charge of the meeting and can direct it carefully toward our ends.''

''I will speak, Lucien,'' Hersh said. ''None of you think I can handle a few civilians. You speak of my leadership, my heroism, my luck, yet think I won't be able to make a roomful of men in togas bow to my will. I governed Italy, gentlemen. I governed Egypt. I will do this thing! I have no idea what breach of faith has brought you to this point, but understand that I will do what I say!''

''This is different . . .'' Sieyès began.

''Silence!'' Hersh screamed, shaking his fists in the air. ''I will listen to no more!''

David wandered into the room, seeing Silv sitting off by herself in the corner, near the fire. She was dressed modestly in heavy wools, her face serious as she listened to the continuing discussions.

He moved through the crowd to her, pulling up a straight-backed chair to sit beside her. ''You look cold,'' he said.

She smiled. ''Underground it's always the same temperature,'' she said. ''I'm not used to cold.''

"Pull back from the host a little," he replied.

"Can't," she said. "This host is too interested in your host. We don't need that today."

"Let's at least let them say hello," he said.

She smiled at him with her eyes, nodding gently, as David pulled back a touch. Arnault took Thérèsia's hands in his, bringing them to his lips.

"My love," he said hoarsely.

"Sweet Antoine," she whispered in return, and brushed a hand across his face. "Your eyes seem so melancholy."

"Curse the Fates that keep us apart," Arnault said. "Would that I were struck blind rather than being able to see you and not have you near me."

"Soon . . ." the woman said, then her eyes hardened.

David came back. "Soon?" he said.

"I've told her I won't hold her forever," Silv said.

"Sporting of you," David replied.

Silv began to get angry, thought better of it. "He's been terrible all morning," she said, nodding toward a sulking Bonaparte.

David watched the man, his erratic movements. "He's seriously in the throes of it. I wonder how Napoleon is dealing with all this."

"He's doing all right," she replied. "He's a man smart enough to take it as it comes."

"When do they go to Saint-Cloud?"

"Soon," she replied. "We're waiting for word from Talleyrand on the handling of the other Directors."

At just that moment, Talleyrand, magnificent in a doeskin jacket and gold ascot, came into the room, his arms outstretched. "Success!" he cried.

All movement stopped, everyone turning to the man. "The news!" Hersh called. "Let's have the news!"

Talleyrand practically glowed, and David, not for the first time, wondered how instrumental he had been in the conception of this whole idea. "I met Director Barras coming out of his bath," he said, smiling broadly. "And I convinced him that his resignation was worth half a million francs to us, but that his Bourbon plotting was worth only his head."

"He took the money!" Berthier called.

"Quicker than I could get it out of my pocket!" Talleyrand laughed.

"And what of the others," Hersh asked, "Gohier and General Moulins?"

"A little harder to convince," Talleyrand said. "They are being held under guard at the Luxembourg. They will succumb, one way or the other."

"Which way makes no difference to me!" Murat called, drawing his sword, and the whole room laughed and applauded.

"Where's Roederer?" Hersh called. "Where's my journalist?"

"I passed him on the way in," Talleyrand said. "He has gone to distribute your handbills."

Hersh walked to the center of the room, holding his hands up for silence. "Then, all is in readiness," he said softly. "The time has come for action. Wine, everyone!"

Glasses of wine were hurriedly passed around, David taking his with a feeling of tense excitement. Despite the knowledge that this scene was being played out in his own brain, despite his fears for his patient, despite his obvious reasons for feeling removed from the entire procedure, he was caught up in the movements of history. He was watching a major life-change in the offing.

"To dreams!" Hersh said, his stock toast, raising his glass high. Then he looked around the room until he saw David and Silv and held his glass out to them. "And to dreamers."

"To dreams!" everyone shouted back, and cheered.

David downed his glass in one swallow, cheering with the rest of them. He found himself wanting Hersh to succeed.

"Everyone knows his part," Hersh said, still commanding the floor. "We leave now for Saint-Cloud. We will return, victorious, on the evening."

Everyone moved at once, a confusion of men and coats and shouted directions as people left the house of conspiracy to pluck the ripe apple of their desires. The excitement was a physical thing, hanging in the air like swirling cigar smoke. Power. It's liberation. It's laughter in the face of their own fears—of death.

David and Silv pushed through the confusion to find Hersh saying good-bye to Josephine, who, at least for the last month, had been as good as her word of fidelity given when the general took her back.

Hersh embraced his wife warmly, yet from the parting it was obvious that not all was as it should be. Josephine, seeing Thérèsia, broke the embrace and stared at her.

"You go to Saint-Cloud?"

"I have need of her counsel," Hersh said, then looked at David. "You two will ride in my coach."

"I was hoping you'd ask," David said.

"Her husband is one of the Five Hundred," Josephine said, her auburn hair hanging in ringlets around her aging face.

Hersh turned, perfunctorily pecking his wife on the cheek. "Her husband is still with my troops in Egypt. This will hardly affect him on any level."

"I observe," Thérèsia said. "I'll tell you all about it tonight."

Josephine smiled, but only halfway. She nodded. "Be careful," she said, then laid her hand on Bonaparte's braided sleeve for just a second before turning and walking from the room.

"What's wrong with her?" Silv asked.

"Nothing," Hersh snapped. "Let's go."

The carriage waited for them out front, Napoleon putting a heavy coat on over his uniform. David found himself wishing for a heater since he was sunk completely into the host, and Silv, for her part, had cuddled up close to him for warmth.

Ah, this is heaven. Should the cold but stay with us forever!

Not now, Antoine.

They started off, surrounded by a military escort of Murat's regiment. Lefèbvre rode atop the coach, continually barking driving orders to the coachman, who needed none.

"It will all be mine after today," Hersh said.

"Someone had better tell that to Sieyès," Silv said, David enjoying the close proximity to her himself.

"I'll brush him off like dust on my coat," Hersh replied. "He has no sense of Destiny."

"Not a word you were willing to use last week," David said.

"Yes, but I *know* my Destiny," Hersh said. "I'm God, I control it. Mark me. I will not fail in this."

"Just don't forget what brought you this far," Silv said.

"You're just like the rest of them," Hersh said, angry. "And you *know* who I am."

"And I know you don't control this like you think you do."

Hersh fixed her with eyes colder than the day. "Don't push me, old woman. Your presence can be done without."

"I have an announcement to make," David said to break the tension.

They both looked at him. Silv leaning away slightly to stare.

"After today," David said. "I'll be leaving."

"What!" Silv said.

"To where?" Hersh asked.

"Back home," David said. "To my own time."

"You can't," Silv said.

"Why not?"

She looked at him, fear in her eyes. "There's nothing there for you. Why torture yourself? Stay here with us. Make a new life."

"In someone else's body?" David asked. "How could I do that? This isn't my time or place. Aren't you going home sometime, Silv?"

The woman moved away from him, turning her head to stare out at the gray morning city reluctantly coming awake.

"Silv?"

"Don't do it, David," she said quietly.

"Why?" he asked loudly. "Ever since I've known you, you've tried to keep me from going back, while trying to get me to help you take Hersh back. Won't I be as dangerous as Hersh to leave in the wrong time and place?"

"She's trying to save you, David," Hersh said contemptuously. "You're so damned smart, but you can't figure out a thing."

"Save me from what?"

"Tell him, old woman," Hersh taunted. "Tell him what this is really all about."

Silv didn't answer. She kept staring out the window.

David shook her. "Tell me!" he demanded, but she ignored him. He looked at Hersh. "Somebody tell me."

Hersh smiled slightly, his face intense. "It's simple," he said. "It hardly took any time at all for me to figure it out."

"Figure out what?"

"You're dead, David. You're not alive anymore and you

can't escape it. If you go back, you'll have to go through with it.''

David sighed, sitting back. ''You figured it all out, you say?'' He smiled. ''And how did you reach that conclusion?''

''Well, to begin with,'' Hersh said, ''Silv is dead. I should know. I killed her myself.''

David felt a knife blade go into his brain as Arnault's body stiffened involuntarily. He sat on the edge of the seat. ''Go on,'' he said.

''I killed her back at the quad when I realized that she'd never let me stay in my dreams if I didn't. She's escaped the end through the drug, but can never go back or it will catch up to her. I figure that the same is true for you.''

David stared at Hersh, watched his eyes until he was sure the man was telling the truth. He grabbed Silv by the shoulders and spun her around.

''Is it true?'' he asked, voice cracking.

She looked at him in confusion for several seconds, then closed her eyes, nodding her head slightly.

''How?'' He demanded.

''I don't know all the details,'' she said. ''I found out as I was drifting through your sister's future. Your wife shoots you with your own gun, then gets out of the country before they can stop her.''

''B-Bailey?'' he said, his mouth going dry. ''I don't be-lieve it.''

She shrugged, then turned back to the window. ''Probably better that way,'' she said.

''No!'' He spun her around again. ''Why should I believe you? This is insane!''

She looked at him then, and her eyes reflected a pain so deep, a blackness so unfathomable, that he knew her sorrow and sadness were not just for him, but for both of them—and he believed.

''A dead man,'' he whispered. ''When?...''

She took his hands in hers, squeezing. Arnault, independent of David's will, took the woman in his arms and held her fiercely in sadness and consolation.

''No more than two or three days from our trip to the library,'' he said into his ear.

He sobbed loudly, hardly able to comprehend the revelation on any level. It was like going to the doctor and having him say that a terminal cancer was eating him away. His life in his own time hadn't been much, granted, but it was the only *real* life he had. How had he thought about it before—a mistake away from death? He had, apparently, made the mistake.

He broke the embrace, taking Thérèsia's face in his hands. "You kept it to yourself all this time."

She nodded, tears filling her eyes. "I was hoping to spare you the pain that I've lived with on this account, hoping, I guess, that you'd stay of your own will."

"My own will," he repeated softly, and kissed the woman on the mouth. "Thank you for trying. Then, you've always known how the dilation worked?"

She moved away from him slightly, Thérèsia's pale face grown paler. "I wasn't sure until we went to the library," she said, "but I think I suspected from the beginning."

"Why?" he asked. "Why did you do this for me?"

She just looked at him, while Napoleon chuckled lightly from his seat across from them. Her eyes were like the thinnest stem of pristine crystal, delicate and breakable, ready at a glance to shatter into a million pieces. He let the question rest.

They made the rest of the seven-mile ride mostly in silence, David and Silv lost in their own thoughts while Napoleon sang snatches of his current favorite song, *"Ecoutez, honorable assistance."*

David contemplated his own end in sorrow, and the sorrow wasn't for himself, but for the waste he had made of his days and the pain he had caused those closest to him. It had been nothing to be proud of, his life. As lives go, it had been worse than useless in that it had caused more pain than it had alleviated. He found it interesting that the subject of pain caused should be so high on his list of priorities; yet, he realized it wasn't so strange. He had traveled the timelines and the centuries and the face of the globe, and had found pain—pain caused through ignorance and premeditation, pain caused stupidly because people strike out rather than face the death that lives within them all. And when all is said and done, when all is finished—death awaits anyway.

After a while, they heard Lefèbvre's voice from the top of the coach. "Saint-Cloud ahead!"

Murat, on a magnificent Arabian stallion rode up to the coach and leaned down to speak inside. "We will be ready to assist you when you need us," he said, while holding his hat on.

"I'll not be needing you," Hersh said confidently, and David knew at that moment, that the man was going to be facing a personal crisis very soon. His overconfidence in the face of reason was going to hurt him badly.

David looked out the window as they pulled up to the Orangery. Saint-Cloud was a tall, heavy palace with pilasters on the main facade and an awkward curb roof. Bonaparte's men were already there, tents pitched in the driveway. He could see a few fiery grenadiers, but the vast majority of soldiers were placid veterans whose job it was to act as a parliamentary guard. They stood in small groups, talking and smoking. A single pipe was being passed around, the final indignity to men unpaid for months.

The coach stopped, Sieyès moving up to look into the cutout at Napoleon.

"Is everything ready?" Hersh asked.

Sieyès's eyes were frightened. "Nothing is ready," he said. "The workmen are still preparing for council."

"How long?" Hersh asked.

The man shrugged sadly and walked away.

"No matter," Hersh muttered to himself. "No matter."

They moved out of the coach and waited, David watching the preparations and the arrival of the Elders and the Five Hundred with only half an eye, his mind dwelling in the overstuffed attic of his own confusion.

The hours dragged on, Hersh becoming more and more frantic as time passed. As a general, he was used to totally controlling the fantasy. As a politician, he was having to learn the humility of waiting.

David and Silv passed the time, walking through the palace, at first watching the construction of the council— benches, chairs, hangings, daises and rostrums decorated with Minerva—realizing just how inbred the Five Hundred had become. By this time, Napoleon had joined Sieyès in a study on the first floor, preparing, despite himself, for a long wait.

David walked the great halls, admiring the rich frescoes by Mignard celebrating the Sun God and, indirectly, the Sun King. The council's orchestra arrived, striking up *"La Marseillaise"* as its first number. And David watched Silv in her strength and her sadness, and still the question of why she brought him with her to the past hung over him. And another question had begun to intrude itself into his psyche. It had to do with the mutability of Destiny and the possibility of saving himself.

By late afternoon, the tension had begun to steadily mount. When the Council of Elders finally called their meeting to order at half past three, David and Silv hurried to join Hersh in the study. There he waited with those he could trust: Murat, Berthier, and Lefèbvre. Sieyès had gone to the Council meeting.

"I've heard of fifty different plots in the last hour," Hersh told them as they walked in. "It's the damned workmen. Why did they take so long? These idiots in their togas could hatch any scheme if given enough time."

"Consolidate your losses," Lefèbvre said. "Pledge your support of the Constitution. It's not too late to save yourself."

"No," Hersh said quickly. "I can outtalk anyone."

"My men are still ready," Murat said low. "It's time for bold deeds."

The study door burst open, Sieyès storming into the high-ceilinged room. "All is lost!" he cried.

"What are you saying?" Hersh replied, running to the man and taking him by the shoulders.

Sieyès was sweating profusely, wiping it on a laced handkerchief. "The Elders, upon hearing that the Directors had resigned, simply brushed aside the issue of a new Constitution and voted to appoint all new Directors."

"And then what?"

"Then nothing," Sieyès said loudly. "They voted, then suspended the rest of the session."

"Were they told of a plot?"

"They suspect a plot all right," the Director said, pulling away from Napoleon and walked to lean his stiff arms on a table. He took deep breaths, trying to calm himself. "They suspect us! This will not come to a good end."

"Politicians!" Hersh screamed. "I don't intend politicians to jerk the strings of my life. I told you I wanted to speak!"

"It's too late," Sieyès said, wiping his brow. "It's too late."

"The devil you say!" Hersh snapped. "I'm going to straighten this out now."

"Give it up!" Lefèbvre called to him, but the words were wasted.

He charged from the room, David and Silv hurrying to keep up. David, divorced from his own sense of life, found himself caught up in Hersh's struggle.

They hurried down the gilded halls, running into General Augereau, one of Hersh's allies, as they went.

"Are they still in the great hall?" Hersh asked the man.

"Yes," the general said, his eyes hard as he sought his own salvation in this disaster. "And you're in a fine pickle."

"Rubbish," Hersh said, hurrying past him. "It was much worse at Arcole."

Berthier caught up to them, determined to share Hersh's fate, while Murat hurried outside to his troops. They reached the tall doors, pushing them open to march inside the Council of Elders, David and Silv hanging back a pace to listen.

The large room was filled with men in red togas and scarlet toques. Hersh put his hands on his hips and strode resolutely into their midst, desperately trying to hold onto his fantasy.

"Representatives of the people!" he shouted. "This is no normal situation. You are on the edge of a volcano. Allow me to speak with the frankness of a soldier. I swear that the *patrie* has no more zealous defender than I . . . I am entirely at your orders . . ."

The Elders were murmuring loudly, their faces hard. Hersh was fumbling, David realizing that the speeches that moved soldiers hungry for loot would do nothing among these fornicators of language.

Hersh pushed ahead blindly. "Let us save at all costs the two things for which we have sacrificed so much, liberty and equality!"

"And the Constitution?" someone shouted.

Hersh waved his arms. "The Constitution is no longer respected . . . no longer a guarantee for the people!"

The Elders began talking loudly, yelling at Hersh. David got up close to him, touching for support.

"Conspiracies are being hatched in the name of the Constitution!" Hersh shouted.

"What dangers?"

"Name the conspirators!"

"Barras and Moulins!" Hersh said, reaching. "They want

to overthrow the people, they want to overthrow this august body!''

He could barely be heard now, so loud were the objections of the Elders, who were moving closer to him, threateningly. Hersh hated closed-in places, David had determined that long ago. It brought him too close to the reality of his own past.

''I shall preserve you from dangers,'' he said, glancing back at the open door and safety, ''surrounded by my comrades in arms.''

The grenadiers, on hearing the commotion, had come into the hall. No one could be sure of their loyalties.

''Grenadiers!'' Hersh yelled. ''I see your bearskins and bayonets . . . with them I have founded republics!''

That was enough for the Elders. They began closing in on Hersh, shoving, the man totally out of control.

''If some orator in the pay of a foreign power should propose to outlaw me, may the lightning of war instantly crush him! If he proposed to outlaw me, I should call on you, my brave companions in arms! Remember that I march accompanied by the god of victory and the god of fortune!''

The Elders were shouting then, yelling for Napoleon to remove himself from the hall. They had turned angry.

David grabbed Hersh by the arm and began pulling him from the room, the man still babbling about ''forming committees'' as he was dragged away.

They got out of the hall, the grenadiers following out of habit, as angry shouts followed Hersh down the long hallway.

''Why did you take me away?'' he asked David. ''I wasn't finished yet. I still had things . . . to say . . . to explain.''

David put an arm around him. ''Not now. Not yet.'' His sorrow was with Hersh. Some dreams should be allowed to come true.

''The Council of Deputies,'' Hersh said. ''I have another chance with them. They'll have to vote, too. I'll talk to them.''

''I think you've talked enough for one day,'' Berthier said.

''No! The Council of Deputies waits!''

He broke from David and ran back to the study. When they

reached him, he was writing furiously on a sheet of paper.

"See that this gets to Josephine," he said, handing the paper to Lefèbvre. "She'll be worried why I'm not home yet."

Lefèbvre looked quizzically at the paper, then gave it to one of the grenadiers.

"I'm going into the Orangery," Hersh said, tucking a silver-tipped riding stick under his arm. "I'll speak with the Deputies. Lucien is their president. He'll stand for me."

With that, he marched out of the room, back down the hall again toward the room where the second consular body was meeting. David stood at one arm with Silv at the other, the military trailing behind.

"This can do you no good, Hersh," he said. "This isn't your dream and you're not controlling it. Please stop before you hurt yourself."

"You're a fool!" Hersh said. "Of course it will go my way. It must! It's my dream!"

"It's no dream, dammit!" David said. "It's a delusion. Please, save yourself."

Hersh stopped walking, staring fire at David. "Sometimes," he said, "you must believe in something no matter what the Fates have in store. You were dead inside, David, long before your physical body died." He pointed down the hall. "I go to Glory. By tonight, I'll either run this country or have been murdered by it."

He moved down the hall, David unwilling to let him go alone, entered an Orangery already in turmoil. Word had spread quickly.

Rough hands grabbed the general no sooner than he had made the hall. "How dare you!" a Jacobin member shouted. "You're violating the sanctuary of law!"

They descended on him in force, David being jostled right along with him, Arnault's body quivering with fright.

"Outlaw the dictator!"

The shouts were overpowering as men punched and grabbed the hero of Italy and Egypt. They covered him, fright heavy in his eyes as they closed in while Lucien shouted from the dais to let his brother speak.

David shoved through the angry mob, pulling on his friend, trying to get through the crowd. But it was impossible. Hersh, small and frightened, had gone to the floor, whining softly as blows rained down on him and David.

David fell upon him, covering him with his own body, determined to save his patient at the cost of his own life. Then a hand was pulling him up. Berthier was there, surrounded by soldiers who had pushed back the Deputies.

"Get out . . . now!" he whispered urgently as David helped up Hersh, the man shaken badly, his face streaming blood from cuts and scratches.

Screaming followed them to the door, civilians, pumped up, ready to show the soldier their mettle.

Silv was waiting for them in the hall as Napoleon was whisked out of the building. "The sons of bitches," David said to her, his voice shaking with emotion. "The sons of bitches, I'll kill them!"

They made it outside, Hersh a pitiful figure bloodied and frightened, while the Deputies still screamed at him through the windows, pointing. "Outlaw! Outlaw!"

"It's over," a broken Hersh muttered. "I'm finished."

"I'll be damned," David told him through clenched teeth as the soldiers gathered round, unsure of what was happening.

"Outlaw! Outlaw!"

Hersh stood, taking David by the lapels, pleading. "What do I do?" he said, pale eyes searching David's face. "Please, what do I do?"

"Get Murat," David said, the anger still flushing through him. "Call out the troops."

Hersh stared at him for a moment, as if letting the concept sink in. Then his face hardened. "The troops," he said.

"No," Lefèbvre said. "This isn't right. This isn't the way."

"The troops!" Hersh shouted loudly.

Lucien came running out of the building, screaming at the troops. "Loyal soldiers!" he called. "The Five Hundred are being terrorized within by armed members. Look at my brother! Look what they've done to him!"

The soldiers were talking among themselves, several hundred of them, while the Deputies still shouted from inside.

"You must go into the hall and restore the majority!" Lucien shouted, as Murat rode up on his magnificent horse, his face set in a deadly grin.

Hersh drew himself up, letting the blood flow down his face. "Soldiers!" he called. "I led you to victory, can I count on you? Four times I risked my life for the Republic—at Toulon...in Italy...in Egypt...and on the treacherous voyage home—only to find worse danger in an assembly of assassins. Will you stand with me?"

There were shouts of "Long live Bonaparte," but still they hesitated, and David watched the support disintegrating around him. Finally Lucien drew his sword and pointed it at his brother's breast.

"I swear," he called, "to run my own brother through if ever he interferes with the freedom of Frenchmen!"

The emotional gesture turned the men, who cheered as a unit, shaking their rifles above their heads. Murat rode up to Napoleon, bending low. "Orders?" he said, smiling.

"Clear them out," Hersh said, the fear in his face supplanted by a wave of darkness.

"Yes, sir!" Murat said, then straightened on his horse. "Sound the drums!"

The drums began, a steady roll, as the grenadiers mustered and fell into formation, marching slowly into the palace.

David turned, looking for Silv. She stood on the periphery. "I'm going in," he said. "Care to join me?"

She looked at him for a moment, then smiled. "Why not?"

They took the bodies of grenadiers, took them fully and quickly as they marched down the long hallways. Within the Orangery they could hear the cries of the Deputies—"Let us die for freedom!" But as the doors banged open, no one thought of death, as members began to flee, discarding their red robes and jumping from the windows. But many remained, determined to hold their ground.

"Citizens!" Murat called. "You are dismissed."

The remaining Deputies moved on the grenadiers. Lefèbvre, who had steadfastly spoken against intervention, became livid when he saw one of the Deputies tear the sleeve of a grenadier.

"Chuck the rabble out!" he screamed, and jumped into the fray.

David moved into the crowds, all thoughts lost except the playing-out of his frustrations. He pushed them back, using the butt of his rifle to keep them away. The Deputies began crumbling under the assault, jumping from the windows and rushing into the November dusk.

And it was over in minutes, the hall cleared forcibly, the edge of the bayonet tearing the parchment of the Constitution. David found Silv, putting an arm around his, once again, male comrade.

"How'd you like that?" he laughed, still caught up in the excitement.

"I loved it!" she replied. "I've been trying to get my nerve up for something like this for a long time."

He looked at her quizzically, then let the remark pass as they returned to the bodies of Arnault and Tallien.

The next stage went painlessly, David and Silv waiting in the large study while the troops rounded up a majority of the Deputies to vote, favorably, for Napoleon's proposals. All pretense of legality was mercifully put aside by now, Murat having been right all along.

As the evening wore on, the study cleared, all the conspirators moving to the hall to hear the vote. When they were alone, David walked up to Silv who stood, as always, near the fire.

"What did you mean before," he asked, "when you said you'd been trying to get up the nerve to live someone else's life for a long time?"

She looked at him, smiling slightly. "I'm dead, David," she said. "My body died and I'm locked in the dilation somewhere before the onslaught of brain death. I've been living as a shadow, really, unable to take real control over the hosts I've been in."

"Why?"

"Because our pasts are very difficult things to overcome." She reached up and touched his face. "None of this makes sense. I think I can see you, David Wolf, no matter what body you inhabit. There's a way you look . . . a cast to your eyes . . ."

He took her hand, kissing the fingers. "What are you trying to say?"

"Simply that I'm afraid. Where I come from, I'm a little, frightened old lady who lives in a wheelchair because her body won't support her at all anymore."

He laughed. "It's hard to picture you as an old lady."

"One hundred forty-seven years old," she said.

He pulled her close, holding her tightly in his arms. "You

don't feel like an old lady," he said, then kissed her fiercely on the lips. "You don't kiss like an old lady. At this point, you can be what you want to be. Isn't that what you've wanted to tell me?"

"Yes," she said huskily. "I've just been so . . . afraid for so many years . . . it's been a hard habit to break."

He held her again. "Why did you want to save me?" he asked.

She moved away from him to watch the fire, so magnificent in its own singular destruction. "I've watched you your whole life," she said, "watched you try and gallantly deal with the pain you had to live with. I've felt responsibility for you, and I've . . . cared for you. I couldn't let you die without trying."

"You've cared for me?" he asked, joining her to feel the liberated heat as the wood consumed itself.

She stared at him again. "More than I've ever cared for anything."

The door opened, Hersh stepping in, his face slack, Napoleon's charisma nowhere to be felt.

"It's done," he said. "The government is mine."

"Congratulations!" David said, moving to shake his hand.

"Bah!" Hersh said, refusing the handshake. "I was saved by momentum, nothing more. I was no more than a child in their hands today."

"Welcome to the real world," David said.

The man looked at him, his eyes sad pools reflecting eternity.

"Before the others come," David said, "I want to tell you both something."

"I was afraid of this," Silv said, moving away from the fire to walk near him.

"I'm going back anyway," he said quickly. "I think . . . no, I want to try and stop what's supposed to happen to me."

"It's impossible," Silv said. "You know that."

"But I've got to try," David replied. "Can you understand that? I just can't have my life, my real life, slip away without trying to do something about it."

"If you get caught, you're dead," Hersh said.

"I know. I've got to try anyway. Please don't do anything to try and stop me."

Silv shook her head sadly, the tears coming again. "No one

will stop you, David. This is a decision that is totally yours to make.''

David nodded. "I don't know if I'll ever see either of you again," he said, then hesitated for a moment. "But if I don't . . ."

Silv cried loudly, running from the room with her hands covering her face.

"Women," Napoleon said.

David nodded sadly. Leaving Silv was the hardest thing he'd ever do. "I've got to try," he explained.

This time Hersh shook his hand. "I know," he said. "And David, if you ever do come back . . . I want . . . I want . . . to work with you about my . . . problem with reality. I can't ignore it any longer. Today proved that."

David hugged him close, the tears blinding his own eyes. "That admission is the hardest part of the problem," he said. "Work with Silv. She can help."

He moved away, both men appraising one another, David suddenly wondering what Hersh really looked like. He started to say something else, thought better of it, then jumped into the timestream.

David concentrated on the library and the Porsche emblem and found himself dizzily leaning against the hood of the car on stiff arms, Liz standing beside him with a hand on his shoulder.

"David?" she asked.

He straightened and turned to her, reality fading and bending, like a comics page transferred onto Silly Putty. "Liz . . . is it . . . is it just you?"

"So far."

"Quickly, the antidote."

"In the car," she said, helping him around to the passenger side and getting him in.

He sat there, muscles tense, concentration centered on the emblem as she hurried around to the driver's side.

"All right," she said, fumbling in her purse. "The red one?"

"Yes, please hurry."

He turned and stared as she readied the needle, his mind skimming back to childhood and the first needle he ever took. He was just a baby, head lolling, mind full of trust. Then there was this gleaming instrument, so pretty, the doctor's face intent, not responding to his love vibrations. Then pain! Pain for love . . . pain for love. . . .

He struggled back to see Liz hovering over him.

"Hurry!"

"Where do I . . . put it?"

He reached out a trembling hand, feeling for the pulse on his neck, his mind racing to the first time he had taken pulses in medical school.

"Here . . . where my finger is . . . hurry!"

She stuck him amateurishly, the pain becoming all pain as the hot fluid washed his system and he could feel himself unwinding slowly, dreams melting away, leaving him suddenly alone, like a family house after all the furniture has been moved to another place. He felt stupid, unable to grasp even the simplest notions of memory.

He sat back, letting the reality slide in, and realizing he didn't really want it to.

"Are you all right?" Liz asked.

He turned to her, smiling. "Relative terms, Sis," he said, and hugged her. He felt isolated, a roving spirit locked up in a single cell, appreciating firsthand the loneliness and aloneness that all humans must live with all the time. It had been a long time.

"Where have you been since I last saw you?" she asked.

"Overthrowing the Directors," he replied casually. "What have you been doing?"

She returned his smile somewhat skeptically. "Well, a half minute back, I was in the library with you. Not much has happened since then. I did notice a run in my hose back there a few seconds ago."

They both laughed, David glad to be with family, although, in a very real sense, he had never been away from family.

"What do we do now?" she asked. "Are you finished with traveling?"

"I need to go home," he said. "There are things I need to do. And no, I don't think I'm finished with traveling. I may never finish with traveling."

"Are you well enough to drive?"

He looked around him, at surroundings that seemed odd and distant. "You drive," he said. "I'm not even sure I could find my way. It's been years."

She started the car and nosed them toward the new money. "This is all so bizarre," she said, after a few embarrassing minutes of silence from David. "Time traveling . . . what's Napoleon like?"

"Strong," David said. "Frail. Capable of grandeur and pettiness. A totally unique individual with a grand vision and the gall to make it reality . . . at least, when he's not fighting the psychotic who lives within him." He rubbed his eyes, realizing that his body was tired and that he couldn't escape the feeling. "I don't know. Sometimes I feel like Hersh's psychosis is the spark plug that makes the greatness within cut loose."

"You mean that if Hersh wasn't in him that Napoleon wouldn't have been great?"

"Idle speculation at this point, isn't it?" David watched the car in front of them slam on its brakes. "Watch out!" he screamed, grabbing the dash with both hands.

Liz slowed easily, turning to him with narrowed brows. "What's wrong?"

He sat back, breathing out. "Whoa. I guess being in my own body scares me a little. Anything could happen . . . any moment. A car doesn't slow down and—bam!" He clapped his hands together. "We're gone."

"Well, don't lose any sleep over it," she said lightly, and he wished he were with Silv and Hersh. Only they could understand the fear of the blackness the way he could.

He looked at her for a minute, watched her involved in the driving as if it were the only thing on earth. "Do you know about me?" he asked quietly. "About . . . what happens to me?"

She swallowed hard, but didn't turn to him. "Some," she said, almost a whisper. "I couldn't help but glimpse a little, though Silv tried to keep as much as possible closed to me. I'm just as glad, really."

"I had a host go crazy on me once," David replied. "He desperately wanted to know, so I showed him his death. He went nuts worrying about it."

"How awful!"

"Yeah," he said, the guilt no less now than when it had happened. "You know about my death?"

She nodded, but didn't speak.

"Tell me everything you know."

Liz took a deep breath, tears coming to her eyes. She'd

been walling herself off from the memories, but now they came unbidden. "It happens soon," she said. "I think the day after tomorrow."

"What time of day?"

"Late, I think, in the evening. In your living room."

"What else?"

"Bailey shoots you with Momma's gun, you know the one . . . the one . . ."

"All right," David said. "So, it was Bailey."

"Maybe her and that writing teacher we saw her with in the kitchen last night."

"Last night," David repeated, and tried to remember what it was she was talking about. "Oh, that party. I remember. Bailey fucked the guy in the garage."

She stared oddly at him. "That's the one, all right," she replied, shaking her head.

They had reached the neighborhood. Liz eased them off the main drag and began the winding climb to the top of the hill, redbud and cottonwood trees lining the streets with intertwining branches.

"She shot you," Liz continued, her lips quivering slightly. "Then she left the country the same night for . . . some South American country where they don't extradite." She looked at him then, her cheeks wet. "Oh, David, isn't there something we can do?"

He reached across the console and patted her leg. "I'm going to try," he said. "I've got a few ideas on that subject."

She reached the house and pulled into the big circular drive, bringing him right to the door. "I don't believe that you'll die, David," she said after she stopped the car. "I can't believe . . . won't believe that we don't make our own futures. I don't want you to go. You're all I've got left."

He smiled, reaching across the seat for her hand. It felt so small in his, so wispy. "I love you, Liz," he said, the words choking with emotion.

The floodgates opened full and Liz fell into his arms. "Oh, David," she cried loudly. "Please don't die . . . please!"

And he was crying with her, both of them purging their fear with salty tears. "You've been a good sister—" he began, but she silenced him with a hand on his mouth.

"Don't talk like that," she said harshly, moving away from him. "Take action, hide out, do something!"

He got out of the car. "I intend to," he said, moving around to the driver's side and leaning down as she opened the window. "I've got a lot of preparations to make. But after I do, when I'm absolutely sure it's safe, I'll call you and we'll celebrate and laugh at our foolishness."

She smiled again, wiping her eyes. "I just thought of something stupid," she said. "Now that I've brought you home, how do I get back to my car?"

He straightened, grinning. "You like this one, don't you?"

"Sure, but . . ."

"It's yours, take it. I'll have my secretary notarize the title over to you."

"What?"

"Money," he said, "possessions. They don't mean anything. I can live in rich men and poor men, whichever I choose. When I'm skimming, nothing material really matters. I don't even think of things like that anymore. So, I want you to have the car. I hope you enjoy it."

"What'll you drive?"

"I'm sure there's something in the garage," he smiled, straightening. "Don't worry about it."

She shrugged, her face brightening like a burning candle. "Thanks," she said.

"It's nothing," he replied, and meant it. "It's nothing at all. Now you'd better get out of here. I've got a lot to accomplish and a very short time to do it."

She started the car, smiling as she looked at the interior. Then she turned back to him, holding a hand out the window space. "Please be careful. I kinda like having you around."

He took her hand, squeezing hard. "I'll call you," he said, then deliberately turned away and walked to the house. He wasn't as sure as Liz that he could control this thing. Hersh thought he was controlling it, and seemed to be controlling it—but he wasn't. Yet, somehow, this seemed different. This wasn't the past; it was his future. Of course he had the freedom to control his own destiny.

He bent and retrieved the spare house key from under the welcome mat, and stuck it in the lock. He had accidentally given Liz his house key with the car keys.

The crimp in his argument about control was that his death

wasn't a part of his past, but it *was* a part of Silv's. It existed for her just as solidly as Bonaparte did for him.

He got inside the door, the house looking eerie, like a landscape in a recurring nightmare. It should be different, but it wasn't. He didn't belong here. It was a part of his existence that had relegated itself to the status of a bad memory. But here it was, still solid, still beckoning him . . .

to his death.

He supposed he could try and forget this part of himself and survive in the timestreams for his part of eternity—but he just couldn't. He had been human for thirty-six years. Giving over his corporeal form was not a thought he could comprehend objectively. He was a living, breathing entity and intended to stay that way, even though it was becoming clearer all the time that he would return to the past. Someday, he hoped, he could learn to live with himself, and perhaps come back to his present and finish out his allotted time span in a natural way. Silv was the living dead. He didn't want to be.

But, in so deciding, he found himself embarking on a dangerous journey. He had arrived at this point in his life, days away from his own demise, bringing himself, as it were, to the scene of the crime. He was in danger every moment now, coming here like this. The fact wasn't lost on him. He was scared to death.

The stakes were high, for he knew death as nothing but perpetual darkness. He was trading, perhaps, an infinity of moments for the blackness of a moonless night. A desperate gamble to save his life.

The gun.

He ran through the living room, taking the stairs up two at a time. The house was exactly as he remembered it, yet it seemed odd, a place where he didn't belong. Not until he arrived at his office did he begin to feel comfortable at all.

He moved inside, going right for the big desk, its top still in disarray after his night of sleep there. He opened the drawer, the gun still where he had left it.

He didn't realize how relieved he was until after he had found it. A key piece in the puzzle of his life was now in his possession. If he was shot with this gun, then simply rendering the gun unshootable would take care of the murder weapon.

He released the clip containing the bullets from the butt of the thing and it dropped into his hand. It was as simple as that. He stuck the clip in his pocket, then walked to the couch and stuck the gun itself under a cushion.

Could this be it? He was free. He patted his pocket. "You're going to stay with me," he said to the clip.

Now what?

He moved to the small bar by the door, frowning at the empty Scotch bottle that he had finished the previous night, so long ago. Rather than hunt up another, he poured himself a straight shot of bourbon and moved behind his desk to sit down and think.

There could be some mistake about the gun, he supposed. Maybe Liz just thought it was Naomi's gun. Most small guns looked about the same. To think he had saved himself at this point was a fool's paradise.

He thought about Bailey. She wasn't here. Where was she? He tried to conjure up her face, but not very successfully. At this stage, he had no feelings about her one way or the other. After years of skimming, she seemed just another lousy part of his lousy past. There was no love lost between them, just emotion.

What would she want—freedom to marry Jeffery? Money? He could give her both easily, but he was going to have to find her first.

His telephone answering machine sat across the desk from him. The red "Message" light was blinking. He smiled, pulling it over nearer himself, studying its contours. He had forgotten how it worked.

After several bogus attempts, he finally got it going, playing back a whole tape full of messages—all but one of them from Mo Frankel, his voice sounding frightened and desperate. He wasn't sure what to do about Mo. He had foolishly sent the man into the past, and now he was paying the freight on it.

He hit the jackpot on the one call that wasn't from Mo, however. It was from Bailey, and she gave him a beeper number to get her back. A beeper, for God's sake. What possible use could Bailey have for a beeper?

He pulled the phone over near him and took a deep breath. He had to handle this just right. He punched up the number and listened for the tone on the other end. It was difficult for him to keep his voice under control as he spoke.

"Bailey," he said, husky. "I'm home. Call."

When he hung up, his hand was shaking. He laughed nervously. "This is stupid. It doesn't happen until day after tomorrow."

The rationalization didn't help. He drained the bourbon, then got up and poured another, old habit patterns coming back easily, old memories.

He walked to the bookcase, staring at his fascination with death. Volume after volume on the processes of death and dying. Elisabeth Kübler-Ross never had a problem like his, though. He toasted the bookcase, and wondered if his lifelong obsessions could have been some manner of precognitive understanding of his later problems.

The phone rang.

He walked over and stared at it. Something cold about this invention. Better in person, or through a letter you can think about. But phones—power in being something you're not; the ability to later deny what you swear to—a bad invention. He drained the second glass and picked up the phone.

"Bailey?"

"Now, don't start in."

"I'm not going to start in. Please, let's just talk."

"There's nothing to talk about."

"There's a great deal to talk about."

"It's over. I'm not coming back to you anymore . . ."

"Bailey . . ."

"Let me finish dammit!"

"I'm not trying to—"

"You asshole! Let me finish!"

He closed his eyes, his heart pounding frantically. "Finish," he said softly, walking the phone back over to the bar and another drink.

"We're through," she said, her voice choked with anger. "I'm going to live with Jeffery and there's nothing you can do about it. You'll probably want to use Charles for your divorce lawyer, but I'll tell you straight out I'm going to try and get back what you've stolen from me. I've got my own lawyer and he says I've got a really good case."

"Good," he said softly.

"What?"

"I don't blame you," he said. "In fact, I agree with you."

"What sort of game is this?"

"No game. I want to talk to you and Jeffery."

"Sure you do."

"I promise, no scenes. In fact, I guarantee that you'll be happy with the discussion."

"I don't trust you, David."

"Please." He kept his voice calm and steady, though his insides were on fire. "Ten minutes of your time in a public place. No scenes, all public."

"Why?"

"We have important business to discuss, it will—"

"Un huh."

"It will be worth a lot of money to you and Jeffery."

"This is some kind of setup."

"I promise you. I'm not the same man as I was . . . yesterday."

"Hold on."

He stood, drinking, listening to a quiet phone, wondering if death schemes were being plotted on the quiet end. All at once Jeffery's voice was on the line.

"How stupid do you think we are, Wolf?"

"Ten minutes of your time," David said calmly. "In a public place. Guaranteed, no trouble."

After a brief silence, Jeffery said, "We're at the university, in the liberal arts building. Come to my office. But if this is some kind of trick, I promise I'll tear you to pieces."

"No tricks. I'll be there in twenty minutes."

It took almost forty minutes for David to get to Central University. He took the old Cadillac from the garage and drove at barely half the speed limit, he was so frightened of the possibility of a wreck.

Once at school, he found Jeffery's niche easily in the small suite of English department offices. The door was open, several adoring students grouped around the writer's desk fawning over the pearls of wisdom he dispensed as easily as most people pass gas. Bailey sat in the corner, her purse clutched against her stomach, her face drawn in concern. David did his best to stifle his own fears. He reassured himself by patting the syringes in his back pocket and walked into the maelstrom.

Bailey saw him first, and she stiffened in her chair. He smiled in what he hoped was a nonthreatening manner, surprised at his reactions to seeing her. Even in the same room, it was as if she were a stranger he had met once long ago. Their marriage was nothing but a blur to him. There were no tugs, no bonds left intact.

Jeffery caught Bailey's reaction, his eyes turning to fix on David. He held him in a deadly stare. David had been around soldiers enough to know that this man could be dangerous when pushed to it.

While Jeffery's eyes stayed angry, a smile lit up his face. "Ladies and gentlemen," he said to the students, "I have an appointment." He stood, moving around the desk. "You'll all have to excuse me."

David watched them troop out, all the children who thought they were grown-up, and he realized what a time machine teaching must be. The teacher's world was always populated by faces the same age while he got older—the same ages, the same lectures—the fixed point in an ever-changing universe. No wonder college seemed a world to itself and teachers had such a difficult time acclimating to the reality of the outside world.

The office was small, enough room for a desk and a couple of chairs. The walls were bookcases, Jeffery's detective stigmata book displayed prominently.

Without taking his eyes from David, Jeffery moved past him to close the door.

"Leave it open," David said.

"What?"

"Why don't you leave it open. That way there'll be no temptation for things to get . . . out of hand."

Jeffery shared a look with Bailey, then moved back to sit behind his desk. The only other chair in the office was right beside Bailey. David dragged it across the floor and set it next to the open doorway so he could escape quickly if he needed to.

"Well, you're the one who wanted to talk," Bailey said. "Let's get it over with."

He looked at her. She was beautiful, her blond hair, slightly teased, hanging almost to her shoulders. She looked as young as the students. No match for Thérèsia Tallien, though. No match at all.

"This won't take long," he said, and had to clear his throat twice before continuing. "First off, I'm truly sorry for what I did to you two. It was unforgivable."

"Get on with it," Jeffery said. "Don't bullshit us."

David was perplexed. Sincerity didn't seem to have much

sway. "Okay. I've been wrong. I've taken all of Bailey's money during the years we were together and hidden it every place I could. I want to make up for that."

"Why?" Jeffery said, and lit a cigarette.

"It's the right thing to do," David said.

Both Bailey and Jeffery laughed loudly. Jeffery let out a long streamer of gray-white smoke and leaned back in his chair, putting his feet up on the desk. He was wearing tennis shoes. "And just how do you intend to make it up?"

"Any way you say," David replied.

"Okay," Jeffery countered, "I'll play. Make public disclosure of all your holdings and open your books for our perusal."

"I can do better than that," David said. "I can liquidate my holdings and give them to you in cash."

"Why?" Jeffery asked again.

"I don't want it anymore," David said. "I know this sounds strange, but I've taken a close look at myself and don't like what I've seen. I want to clear it all out, right the wrongs and start from scratch."

"You're drunk," Bailey said, then turned to Jeffery. "He's drunk."

Jeffery stood, walking around the desk to stare down at David. The cigarette hung out of the side of his mouth, bobbing as he spoke, just the way David always pictured James Dean smoking.

"Diane and I are going to live together, Wolf," he said, eyes hard. "We're going to share a house . . . and a bed. I'm going to be fucking her all the time—doesn't that bother you?"

David shook his head. "Not especially. People pair-bond for a variety of reasons, the most important being that they share similar outlooks of life and want to emotionally support one another. If that situation exists between the two of you, I wish you well and give you every blessing in the world."

Jeffery blew smoke in David's face. "You're sure as hell playing some weird kind of game, mister."

"Does fifteen million dollars deposited in a Swiss bank in your name sound straightforward enough to you?"

Jeffery turned to Bailey. Her face had grown pale. She shook her head and shrugged. Jeffery turned back. "What's the catch?" he asked.

"I do have a stipulation or two," David replied. "First off, I want to keep the house I live in now. Second, this needs to happen quickly, within the next day or so. Thirdly, I want to give Liz a million of it. Fourth, I think you guys should take a little trip together, a cruise or something, that leaves within the next two days."

Bailey jumped to her feet, her purse falling at her feet. "How did you know!" she asked loudly.

"Know what?" David asked, glancing at the door. Jeffery was awfully close. Could he get away if he needed to?

"About the trip," Bailey said, nervous.

"Enough," Jeffery told her.

"You already have a trip planned?" David asked, mouth dry.

Jeffery tightened his lips, then spoke reluctantly. "I've been offered a position at the American diplomat's university in Rio de Janeiro. I'm going down to check it out and Diane's going with me."

"When do you leave?"

"Day after tomorrow."

David took a long breath. They could murder him and fly away, scot-free, to Rio. He forced himself calm. "I think I can have the money put away for you by then," he said.

"Exactly how much are we talking about?" Jeffery asked, and David wondered if Bailey were getting ready to make her own history repeat itself.

"Can't be sure," David said. "Liquidating quickly will cost us. But it will be in the millions, clean, and in cash. What more do you want? If I fought you in court, believe me, you'd lose. I have two other ex-wives who could testify to that."

"Why are you doing this?" Jeffery asked for the third time.

"I've already told you."

"He's drunk," Bailey said.

David stood. "I'm sober enough to know a couple of idiots when I see them," he said, exasperated.

"Make us believe you," Jeffery said.

David met his gaze, then pulled the cigarette out of the man's mouth, dropping it on the floor. "I'll tell you how to open the Swiss account," he said. "I'll have the liquidation wired into it. There's no way I can touch your money once it's in there. You'll see it with your own eyes."

Jeffery turned and walked back to Bailey, bending down to whisper in her ear. He stood. "Are you willing to sign a paper that verifies all this, something we can show around to lawyers and whatever?"

It was David's turn to laugh. "You mean something along the lines of admitting my guilt and giving everything to you?"

"Something like that."

"Sure," David said easily. "In fact, I'll sign almost anything you put in front of me."

Bailey's expression never wavered. She didn't believe him for a moment. But it was good old Jeffery that he had been counting on from the first. The man was obviously cursed with the stigmata of worldly avarice, and willing to take a chance.

"We'll think it over tonight," Jeffery said, "and let you know in the morning."

"Good," David said. "If you can think of anything I can do to help your decision, let me know."

"Obliging of you," Jeffery said.

David shrugged. "I want you two to be happy together."

Bailey rolled her eyes. She hadn't been so cynical when David first met her. "I'll need to come by the house and pick up a few things," she said.

"Sure," he said, "anything. I'm going to spend the next couple of days at a hotel, so feel free to come by anytime."

"Why a hotel?" Jeffery said.

"New life," David said. "New surroundings."

David sat, naked, on the flowered couch in the Marriott suite and put his feet up on the coffee table, the telephone resting on his shoulder. The furnishings were, interestingly, French Provincial, and knickknacks on the polished tables phony antiques that were bolted down to avoid theft. Progress. Every light in the suite was turned on.

"I don't have time, Charlie," he said into the receiver. "If I had time to meet with you in your office tomorrow, I wouldn't need you for what I need you for."

"That doesn't make sense, David," Charles Kornfeld said.

"And what are you doing in a hotel? Did Diane kick you out? Are we going to be looking at another divorce?"

"Yeah, but that's not the important thing . . ."

"Not the important thing! Of course it's the important thing. You pile up enough of these lopsided divorces and the judges are going to start believing the fraud allegations the women in your life are so fond of filing against you."

"That's all behind me now, Charlie."

"Right."

"Honest to God. I don't care about the material things anymore. They mean nothing to me."

Kornfeld laughed. "Talk like that will get you put away," he said. "Come to think of it, that might be a good defense."

"Poverty of spirit?"

"No. Insanity, when they catch you on the fraud charges."

"Meet me tomorrow morning in the coffee shop, will you?"

"What time?"

"How about six A.M.?"

"Lawyers have to swear when they take the bar that they'll never get up that early."

"Make an exception," David said softly. "This is really important."

"Okay," he said. "Just so long as the ethical review panel doesn't get wind of it."

"Maybe you should come in disguise. Bye, Charlie."

"Yeah . . . and David? As your lawyer, I advise you to give up women—they make you crazy."

David hung up the phone and stared down at the table. Two prized possessions sat on its shiny walnut top, two incongruencies that right now were controlling the direction of his life—the case containing the syringes, and the magazine holding the bullets that would bring the endless darkness.

He stood and walked to the double suite doors, making sure, for the third time, that the locks were secured. He had registered under the name Arpi Lamell, an old high-school friend, in case Jeffery came looking for him. He believed that the writer was the one with the real killer instinct and it was the writer he most feared. He had been a fool to mention that he was going to stay at a hotel. Even if Bailey were to drop the hammer, it would be because Jeffery moved her to it.

A wet bar sat in the far corner of the room, an array of liquors lined up on the cabinet behind. He walked to it and poured a Scotch over rocks and walked to the balcony.

The sliding door opened easily, and he walked out onto the cement porch, the night world stretching out sixteen stories below. The Oklahoma wind was up high, whipping his hair around his face, as he stared out at the pool-table-flat landscape easing off to the horizon. He could make out Moore township, then, farther on, the lights of Norman, Oklahoma. That was seventeen miles away and he could still see it.

He felt like God, and sometimes he *was* God. But now he was just fragility and loneliness—and fear. He thought again of the man in Egypt, of his suicide call to the darkness that David feared and rejoiced in all at once.

David had always been an atheist, a nonbeliever in almost anything. It wasn't an intellectual choice, something he had any control over. It was just the opposite, just totally the opposite. Belief came hard to him. Belief in an orderly universe and a being that controlled it was simply beyond his ken. No theistic argument he had ever heard made sense to him. He didn't actively try to make it that way. It just was, and long ago he had come to accept himself as someone who would never share in the vast emotional benefits that religion brought. His discoveries about history simply confused him even more.

If there was order to the framework of history—intelligent order—then what kind of mind conceived the horror that life on Plant Earth was for most people? He had seen it repeated again and again, cycles of repression and violence and degradation, over and over and over. God must be a sadist.

Or a comedian.

The host body was exhausted, and this time there wasn't anything he could do about it. He walked back into the suite, stopping to pick up the syringes and the clip, then went to the bedroom where his clothes lay scattered on the floor. His wallet lay among the clothes, credit cards, and money scattered around the room.

He was like a junkie in his reverence for the objects he carried, like a zealot with his relics. He looked at them, felt their contours, then slipped them beneath the pillows on the king-sized bed. Only then, when they were safe and close at hand, could he throw himself, dead tired, on the mattress.

Sleep frightened him most of all. Sleep was vulnerability and its own kind of darkness. He had given up residing in sleeping hosts years before, preferring to move through the conscious brains of active humans instead. That he would have to give himself over to the inevitability of unconsciousness was a horrible thought.

David was riveted to the menu. It was filled with ice creams and cold, sweet drinks and french fries and hamburgers with everything—all the things he hadn't eaten for years. His body, his host, was ravenous. He was so accustomed to not thinking about food that he had forgotten to feed it. His stomach felt as if it had been excavated with a backhoe and needed to be filled in. Several times he had forgotten and had tried unsuccessfully to remove himself from the host to avoid the hunger pangs.

He knew he would acclimate again eventually to being human. The problem was, he didn't really want to.

"This better be good," came a voice beside him.

He turned to see Charles, complete with fake nose and glasses with attached moustache. He was in disguise.

"Charlie," David said warmly, standing to shake the man's hand. "You've never looked better."

"Yeah?" Charlie said, taking a seat. "This is what I wear when I prowl the neighborhood at night stealing ladies' panties off the clotheslines."

David reached across the table and pulled his nose off, everything else coming with it. "You've got an Oedipal complex, buddy. Make an appointment to come see me."

"Can't afford you. Besides, in my neighborhood, if you hung wash on a line you'd be breaking the association covenants. I ought to know. I wrote them."

It was good to see Charles. Though their relationship was simply a business one, it was warm and honest and had survived through a great many years. Charlie Kornfeld was a smallish man with piercing brown eyes and a close-cropped salt-and-pepper beard. He was loyal and straightforward, relaxed in a way people can afford when they don't feel they have to prove anything.

"Hungry?" David asked.

Charles looked at his watch. "My stomach doesn't even

wake up for another three hours," he said. "Now come on, give me a hint as to why you wanted me down here so early."

But David had already caught the waitress's eye and she was walking toward them through the fake greenery and bright yellow walls meant to resemble a springtime garden.

"David . . ." Charles said.

"In a minute."

The waitress wore a brown uniform dress with red-and-white-checked apron and hat. Neither old nor young, she was simply tired and alive. She held a pot of coffee in her hand and asked them the obvious question.

"Coffee?"

"Please," Charles said, turning his cup over.

"I want a milk shake," David said.

She stared at him for a second, but didn't write anything down on her pad. "Do you need a few minutes to—"

"We're ready to order," David said.

She took a breath of resignation and set the coffeepot on the table, preparing to write.

"Charles?" David said.

"I'll have an English muffin and some cantaloupe," Charles said.

"And you, sir?" the waitress asked.

"Okay," David said excitedly. "I'll start off with a double cheeseburger . . ."

"I'm sorry, sir, but we're only serving from the breakfast menu."

David smiled up at her and reached into his pocket, drawing out a wad of cash. He peeled off two hundred-dollar bills and gave them to the wide-eyed woman. "One for you and one for the cook," he said.

She tucked the money in her apron pouch. "One double cheeseburger," she said, writing it down. "And a milk shake. What flavor?"

"Strawberry," David said. "And I want fries and onion rings, and a piece of cherry cheesecake, and a chocolate sundae, and . . . clam chowder. And put a rush on it."

"Is that all?" the woman asked with a straight face.

David looked at her, then back at the menu. "And bring me some ketchup for the fries."

"Yes, sir," she said brightly and hurried off.

David looked over at Charles, who was staring at him open-mouthed. "You're on drugs," he said.

"Bailey thinks it's booze," David replied. "You know, money is the most amazing thing. I've never really appreciated it before. You just give it to people and they'll do all sorts of things for you."

"Maybe you *have* gone crazy," Charles said. "Has something happened?"

David considered telling him, but he didn't think it would help. "I have a big job for you," he said.

"You've just spent two hundred dollars on breakfast," Charles said.

"It's only money."

"I'm going to make an appointment for you with my doctor," Charles said.

"I'm a doctor," David replied. "Now, do you want me to tell you why you're here or not?"

Charles leaned back in the chair and shook his head. "Go ahead," he said, folding his arms across his chest. "I've got a feeling I won't be prepared for it."

"I want you to liquidate all my holdings," David said.

"Why?"

"I want to get rid of it," David replied. "I want to give it to Bailey."

Charles stood and walked to David, putting a hand on his forehead. "What are you taking, David? Have you been on any medication, valium or something? I'm no expert, but—"

"Sit down, Charlie," David laughed. "I'm perfectly fine."

Charles returned to his seat, genuinely concerned. "How can I believe that when you're talking the craziest shit I've ever heard?"

"Look," David said. "I'm not sick and I'm not crazy. I've got my own reasons for doing this and I don't want to talk about it. I just need it done. Will you liquidate the holdings for me?"

"If you really want me to, I will," Charles said. "But you're hardly being rational."

"Bear with me. I need to dump it all quickly...by tomorrow."

Charles sprang to his feet. "Tomorrow! That's insane, I—"

"Charles," David said sternly. "Sit down and hear me

out." Charles sat. "I know it won't be easy, but what I'm trying to do is liquidate and put all the proceeds in a numbered account in Switzerland in Bailey's name."

"If you're serious," Charles said, tasting his coffee, then sugaring it, "we're going to have some problems. We might be able to turn some of it to cash, but lots of it is tied up in real estate, municipal bonds and securities and the money market, for God's sake. Hell, you own a fleet of shrimp boats operating out of Galveston. And what about the Arabian horse ranch in Tishomingo?"

"I'm not talking dollar value here," David said, as the waitress set a chocolate sundae in front of him. "I'm talking dumping this shit. I'm talking about taking what I can get. If you can't move it at any other price, I'll take ten cents on the dollar. I want to liquidate at any price."

"You'll lose millions, David, millions!"

"I don't care about that," David said, and took a spoonful of the sundae. It was incredible, the sweet chocolate cutting through him like a warm breeze through a country garden. He thought about Hersh and the licorice he always carried.

"Are you listening to me, David?" Charles asked.

David watched the waitress set the clam chowder and the cheesecake on the table. "My mind's made up," he said. "You tell me it's impossible, but I know better. If the price is right, anything's possible. You like the horse ranch? I'll give it to you for ten thousand dollars cash."

"It's worth—"

"I know what it's worth," David replied. "I'm just proving my point to you."

"You've got a thirty-million-dollar fortune," Charles said. "If I do what you say, you'll be lucky to make a third of that back. I can't do that to you."

"Let me put it to you another way," David said, dipping into the clam chowder. "If you take care of this for me, and I certainly hope you will, on top of your regular fee, I'll give you a bonus of, say, a hundred thousand, in cash, under the table if you want. On the other hand, if you still don't want to help me, I'll have to fire you right now and get somebody else to do it."

The fries and cheeseburger showed up, Charles watching, astounded, as David tore into the burger, eating as if he had been waiting years for one.

"Well," Charles said after a minute. "My mother always told me that lawyers were second best, but this is ridiculous."

"You'll do it?" David asked, then drank from the newly arrived milk shake, a pale moustache staying on his lip when he pulled the glass away.

"Only because I can probably get more for you than anybody else." Charles looked down at his sliver of melon and dried muffin, pushed them away, and finished his coffee. "You know, if you're later found to be incompetent, some of this could come back on me."

"There won't be any problem," David said, putting a hand to his stomach, "except maybe indigestion."

They sat in silence for a few minutes after that, Charles watching David eat. Then the man got up and left, David suddenly worrying that he might do something, call someone, to take him away. He patted his sports jacket pocket, reassuring himself with the feel of the syringes. Then he feared that they might get to him before he could use the drug.

He left a fifty on the table to pay for the food and left the restaurant, moving toward the registration desk across the big, wide-open lobby. Charles knew where he was and that was dangerous. He checked out then, walking straight out the door to the parking lot. The Hilton was right down the street. He'd check in there. This time he'd keep his whereabouts a secret from everyone.

He had to do it quickly, before he changed his mind. The remaining four syringes full of the drug and its antidote had become the most important things David had ever possessed. As he walked into State, he was continually touching them in his coat pocket. He thought of them all the time, occasionally jerking his hand to the breast pocket where they resided if he had gone too long without thinking about them. He feared muggers. Each thought of pickpockets would send him into a cold sweat. He found himself giving everyone he met a wide berth, lest they bump into him and take his syringes, or, worse yet, accidentally break them.

The surroundings were the same as he remembered them, the sterile, alcohol smell comfortable and reassuring. As he worked his way through the cold, dirty hallway toward the elevator, he had to work to remember what floor the psych unit was on.

He took the lift up, watching the walls pass in front of him through the accordion gate. He tapped his syringe pocket twice on the ride up.

Christine, the head nurse, was at the station as he walked toward it. She was talking with Mo Frankel. He had hoped not to run into Mo while he was here, but obviously Fate was working against him in this regard. Perhaps it was better to confront the man and get it out of the way.

"Good morning, everybody," he said, trying to keep his voice at a level they would consider normal.

"Thank God," Mo said. "I've been trying to get hold of you since yesterday afternoon."

David shrugged. "Here I am," he said, then felt stupid for saying it. Mo looked terrible. It was obvious the man hadn't slept the night before. He looked at Christine. "Where's Sara?"

"They moved her to med-surg," she said coldly, "to die."

"What room?" he asked.

"We've got to talk," Mo said. "I've been up thinking all night. It's absolutely imperative that you send me back."

The man grabbed David's sleeve with a white-gloved hand, holding tight.

"Not now, Mo," David said. "Please? I've got a lot on my own mind. What room, Chris?"

The woman looked at him, wrinkles standing out around her tightly clamped lips. "Four seventeen," she said. "But there's nothing else you can do . . . for her."

He returned her glare. "Let me be the judge of that, Nurse Beckman."

"What do you want Sara for?" Mo asked, the hand tightening on David's sleeve. "What do you think you're going to do?"

"I'm going to set things right," David said, pulling Mo's hand from his sleeve. "Please. We'll talk later."

He turned and hurried from the nurses' station, moving quickly toward the elevator.

"David! Wait!" Mo called, hurrying to catch him, his old, withered body no match for the younger man's stride. David turned once and looked behind him. Christine was following, too, limping to catch Frankel. The two made a strange pair chasing him down the hall. Christine had been a nurse for the Nazis during the war, her limp the product of a Russian bullet when the Red army poured into Germany.

David reached the elevator well ahead of them and closed the gate.

"David, wait!" Mo called, but the door closed and drowned out anything else.

David rode to four, then hurried quickly to 417. He pushed open the heavy wooden door to near darkness. The only sound was the hiss of oxygen, the only illumination the pale green glow of the life-support equipment's running lights.

He moved to the bed. Sara lay, unmoving, on her back. Her face was drawn hard, troubled, and he knew that terror filled her dreams. He couldn't leave her this way. He just couldn't.

He reached gingerly into his breast pocket and drew out the zipper case.

"Don't worry," he said to the sleeping form. "We'll get you out of there in a minute."

He unzipped the case, bringing out two syringes, one red, one clear, leaving one of each in the case, which he put back in his jacket pocket.

The syringes practically burned his hand, and he had to turn his head from them to go on with his scheme. He felt it was his own lifeblood he was preparing to give away.

He pulled the stopper off the clear needle and squirted a little out to make sure it was free of air bubbles.

The door swung open, Mo hitting the switch that bathed the room in harsh light. Christine was right behind him, her own face drawn in confused concern.

David ignored their presence and moved to the woman's neck.

"I beg you, don't," Mo pleaded. "It's too precious to be used this way."

"More precious than this woman's life?" David said. "I can't live with that responsibility. I made her this way. I've got to get her back."

"There's more at stake than her life," Mo said, moving closer to David.

"What's going on?" Christine asked. "What medication are you giving her?"

"It doesn't have a name," David said, and injected Sara in the carotid.

"No!" Frankel screamed loudly, a mourning wail. *"Ribbono Shel Olom!"* The man folded up like paper withering under fire and collapsed on the floor.

"Dr. Frankel!" the nurse screamed, stooping to the man.

David ignored them and pulled the stopper off the red liquid.

"What are you doing?" Christine yelled at David. "Help me!"

David moved to the woman's neck, pinching up the skin.

"Dr. Wolf!" Beckman said, her accent thick with German authority. "You must help me now. I don't know what kind of experimentation you're doing here, but I'll see to it that you never practice medicine in this state again."

David slid the needle in, squeezing the fluid into the woman, hoping that the memory trip could restore some semblance of her mind. As soon as he had finished, he threw the syringe away and bent to help Mo.

The man was syncopal. He bent his ear to Mo's mouth, hearing a slight, raspy breath, the frail chest rising and falling lightly. The air passage was clear. "Smelling salts," David said to Christine as he placed an index finger on Mo's throat, feeling the steady pulse.

Without a word, Christine jumped up and ran from the room, David pulling Mo's tie loose and ripping his shirt open, buttons chattering across the linoleum floor.

"Mo!" he yelled, shaking the man slightly. "Come on! Mo!"

Christine came back into the room. "I've got . . ." she began, then screamed, dropping the smelling salts to the floor.

David looked up at her, meeting a drained face and open mouth. She was staring past him.

He turned to see Sara sitting up in bed, a slight, all-knowing smile touching her lips.

"Where in the world am I?" she asked.

The door banged open full, a nurse pushing a gurney into the cramped room. David picked Mo up, cradling him like a child, and laid him, semiconscious now, on the portable stretcher.

"Take him upstairs to my office," he said, then bent to the old man's ear. "You'll be all right. I'll be up in a few minutes and we'll talk."

The man tried to speak, his words jumbling unintelligibly. David straightened and nodded to the nurse, who pushed the gurney out of the room.

Christine had walked to stand before Sara, her eyes filled with tears. David moved to the woman, taking the IVs out of her arm. "How do you feel?" he asked her.

"I feel all right," Sara said. "I've been traveling, visiting with my family."

"I know," David said, pulling a folded stethoscope out of his pocket and slipping it around his neck. "Well, this is State Hospital in Oklahoma City, Oklahoma, in the United States of America."

"What year?" Sara asked.

"What is all this?" Christine asked, taking her glasses off to wipe at her eyes.

"Well," David said, smiling and patting Sara on the leg. "Our patient has been away for a long time, but she's here now, back to stay, I think." He listened to her heart, had her breathe and cough.

"Do you know your name?" he asked Sara.

She nodded, smiling wide. "I'm Molly Barlow," she said. "I think I remember this place. I was put in here by my mother. She thought I was too rebellious. Will she make me stay?"

"No," David said. "In fact, I'll bet that once we get you used to things, you'll be able to get out on your own and live however you want. Would you like that?"

"Oh, yes, Doctor!"

David put the stethoscope away and reached out to smooth the woman's hair. He felt good, clean. "I have to go now," he said, "but we'll get you moved to another room and see how we can prepare you for a strange world."

"Thank you, Doctor," the woman said in a small voice.

He started to walk away, then turned back and hugged her for all he was worth. "No," he said, his own eyes misting. "Thank *you*, Molly Barlow."

He left then, Christine following him into the hall. He stopped walking and turned to her. "I think she'll be okay now," he said. "Let's test her, and if it looks positive, see what kinds of rehab we can get her into. A lot of her life is gone, but maybe she can live the rest of it free."

"What did you do to her back there?" Christine asked. "What in the name of God did you do?"

"God had nothing to do with it," David said, then turned and walked toward the elevators and a confrontation with Mo that he wasn't looking forward to.

The man was sitting up on the gurney when David reached the office, looking like a character out of a sitcom with his torn-open white shirt, his loosened tie still wound, in a wide loop, around his neck. His thin, fine hair was disheveled and sticking out from his head in crazy angles.

When he saw David enter the office, he climbed down off the stretcher and hobbled toward him. "Do you understand?" he said, taking David by the arms, his eyes alarmed. "We make it happen. It's us!"

"Calm down," David said, frightened of Mo's proximity to the syringes and his intentions. He pulled away, putting some distance between the two of them. "Now explain to me what you're talking about."

Frankel looked hollowly at David for several seconds, then moved to stand at the window, watching out. "I've been thinking since I've come back, researching." He spoke to the window, his back to David. "I feel like such a fool."

Mo turned around then, his hands, balled into fists, held out in front of him. "Jews are born to scholarship," he said. "To have the time to study the holy books at leisure is our highest aspiration. So, when I went back, I studied, I observed." He walked back, shoving the gurney aside so he could sit on David's couch. "I accepted my condition and rejoiced in the opportunities . . . but I never thought, never thought what trouble my presence in those climes could mean."

"I think I know what—"

"Let me finish," Mo said. "I can only hope to talk to expiate the guilt of two thousand years." He leaned forward, burying his face in his gloved hands and crying softly. "How could I know? How could I know?"

He looked up, red-eyed, and David was watching a broken man, a man terrified, a man undignified. "When I gave Simon Peter the dream," he said, a rasp, "I destroyed my people."

"You mean at the house of Simon the tanner?"

"Yesss," he hissed. "I've been studying Christian history and the books of what you call the New Testament. I've been putting things together. Listen. When Jesus died, his followers, all Jews, busied themselves with trying to convince the rest of the Jewish world that the messiah they were waiting for had already come. The success of such an enterprise was doomed from the start: Jesus hadn't done any of the things the messiah was supposed to do. Jews would never accept him. His movement probably would have floundered and died on its own in those early years, if only . . .''

The man got up, choking back his words, and paced the room nervously, as if his own personal Harpies chased him up and down. David looked at his watch. He wanted to get away from here as soon as he could. He still needed to shut down his office. He continued to stand, torn between Mo's desperate need for him and his own priorities.

Mo, working hard to hold onto rationality, formed his words carefully. ''When Peter went to the house of Simon the tanner, he was going through a crisis of conscience. He could see his movement failing, could feel it like the hunger in his own stomach. But the dream . . . it was a vision to him. In order to accept the dream of shellfish, to act innocently upon his own hunger and still eat that which was forbidden, his mind forced him to accept the dream as divinely inspired. It was telling him something. It was telling him to stop trying to convert Jews, and take his religion to the Gentile.

''The next part's incredible. Peter and the others, most notably John, began to reform their religious cult along Roman lines. They tailored it for the large Roman poor classes, offering eternal rewards for the meek, for the poor. Since they were approaching the Romans directly now, it became important to change the story of Jesus in some fundamental ways; namely, the Roman government, which was responsible for his death, had to be shown innocent of the charge. So, the blame was symbolically shifted, through the washing of the hands of Pontius Pilate, to the Jews themselves, the Pharisees. And so began a long history of the hatred and persecution of Jews by Christians, for the crime of 'killing Jesus,' which is in reality only a way of masking the fact that Christians are trying to prove themselves right and the Jews wrong in the time-honored way—by killing them.''

''The fear of death,'' David said.

Mo was wringing his hands, the horror in his dark-rimmed eyes a pain far deeper than anything physical. ''It all started that night, David, with that stupid dream—my egocentric psychiatrist's idea that I could fix everything up subconsciously. It led to the pain of ages . . . to the countless pogroms, and the crusades, and the inquisitions that have filled Jewish history, culminating in the death of millions in the Holocaust and tens of millions in Stalin's cultural revolution. And it's all my fault.''

The man whimpered slightly and returned to the couch, throwing himself down as if his admission had carved his insides out and left an empty shell.

"It's not your fault, Mo," David said. "Each human being makes decisions for himself. We daily choose between right and wrong."

"If I hadn't given Peter the dream, the Christian movement would have died there in Jaffa. I caused it. *Me!* For the love of God, David, don't you see what I've done?"

David started to go to him, to put his arms around the man, but he feared getting too close with the syringes. "I've found in my travels," he said, "that the moments are structured this way. What happened with you *had* to happen. It was destined to happen."

"Are you trying to tell me that God has *wanted* so many Jews to suffer, and that he chose me as the instrument of such suffering?"

"I don't know from God," David said. "I only know that things are the way they are, and we can't change them."

"I refuse to believe that!" he said loudly, his voice suddenly strong. "You can tell me that all day long and I won't believe it. Neither would you, if you were me."

David thought of his own attempts at controlling a predestined future. "What do you want from me, Mo?"

"What kind of a question is that?" Mo said, his body becoming animated. He stood, walking toward David, who moved away from him and sat behind the desk. Mo leaned across the desk to speak. "I want you to send me back. I want another crack at this business with Peter. I won't give him the dream this time."

"Won't work," David said. "You can go back a second time, but you'll just run into yourself back there and be unable to change anything. I've already tried that."

Mo pulled at his hair. "Then, send me back for Hitler. I'll get him and save only six million lives!"

"It's already happened. It won't change."

"I don't believe you!"

David was shaking inside. He kept looking for the door, ready to bolt if Mo got too weird. There was no talking to the man.

"Just calm down a bit, and we'll talk about this . . ."

"How many?" Mo asked.

"What?"

"How many syringes have you got left?"

"I don't know what—"

"How many!"

"One of each," David said.

"And you want it for yourself, don't you?"

David didn't answer him. He just sat.

"That's what this is really all about," Mo said, moving away from the desk, pacing again. "You want that last syringe to help you escape this world and you don't want to hear anything different from anybody."

"I think you should leave now," David said, standing and moving toward the door.

The man turned and stared at him from across the room, so small and childlike. When David had picked him up, it was like picking up a sack full of old bones. The torment reached across the space between them, electricity that fed from one to the other, back and forth, alternating current.

"Let's analyze it," Mo said softly. "We'll send it to the lab, break it down, and make some for each of us. That's simple enough."

David swallowed hard. "I—I can't," he said.

"Why not?"

David opened the door and stood beside it. Mo Frankel made no move to leave.

"Think about it," David said. "If what you say is true, then making more of this stuff would simply cause more problems."

"But if what *you* believe is true," Mo countered, "then it doesn't matter what we do."

"It's caused nothing but unhappiness," David said uneasily. "It doesn't need to exist anymore."

"Then, destroy the last vial of it right now, right here in front of me."

David's hand went reflexively to his chest in a protective gesture.

"You've got it right there," Mo said, taking a step toward him. "And you want it for yourself."

David put his hands out in front of him as Mo walked closer. "Don't try anything," he said.

The old man pulled his tie off, wadding it up to stick in the pocket of his lab coat. "I feel sorry for you," he said, running hands through his hair to try and straighten it back into place. "So caught up in yourself, so addicted."

"And you're not?" David asked. "Don't you desperately want to get out of the old, broken prison you call a body and be free again? How badly do you really want to help your people?"

"How dare you," Mo whispered, pulling his shirt and his dignity together as much as he could. "I will bear my sorrow, my responsibility, because I know I've done what I can. But you, my friend, how will you live with yourself for what you're doing?"

"I'm entitled to a life," David said.

"At what cost?" Mo asked, walking past David and out the door. "How much self-respect are you willing to give away?"

"I'm dying," David said as the old man hobbled to the waiting-room door.

Mo pushed against the swinging doors and walked partway through before turning back. "Who isn't?" he asked, then left, the doors swinging back and forth in dampening oscillation before whispering closed.

David hurried to the door, opening it just enough to peek through and watch Mo, so small, shuffling toward the elevators. As soon as he had disappeared into one, David ran to the stairs at the other end of the hall.

He raced down the stairs, his out-of-shape lungs near bursting by the time he reached ground level and peeked into the lobby. It was deserted. Breathing heavily, he moved out of the stairwell and into the lobby, crossing it quickly, not relaxing until he was in his car and driving back out of Thirteenth Street.

How much truth was to be found in Mo's words, he didn't know. The drug was an awesome responsibility and its creation, he had already decided, was something beyond the ken of human beings. It was a monster made to destroy life, in retrospect. No way would he ever make any more of it. Like Mo's horror over his creation of Christianity, David feared the continued existence of the drug. So, then, why didn't he destroy the last syringe?

He clutched the zipper case closer to his chest through the jacket. He *was* hooked, that was why, on the most powerful mind-altering substance ever conceived of. Mo was hooked, too. He was as convinced of that as anything. Mo was so hooked he didn't even know he was hooked.

David drove to his office where Nancy, his secretary, was still trying to contact all of his patients and tell them he was out sick. He gave the woman a ten-thousand-dollar bonus in cash and told her to call the patients and tell them he was shutting down operations for good. He didn't worry for his patients' lack of care. They could all find some other hack to alleviate their guilt for the right price.

Then he went to the Hilton on Northwest Highway. He had checked in there during the morning under the name of Sid Howard. Now came the worst part—the waiting.

What was wrong with him? Why was it closets, always closets?

David Wolf stood quietly in the closet in his office, listening to Bailey and her writer moving carelessly through the house. Skimming was the ultimate form of innocent voyeurism, and it came so naturally to him now that he had to force himself to stop and realize how silly his position was.

But what else could he do?

He stood perfectly still, feeling the sweat roll thickly down his neck to wet the collar of his knit shirt. It pooled under his arms and on his sternum and the hollow of his back. His left hand was on his pants pocket, tightly grasping the cold rectangle of steel that represented the darkness. His right hand felt the sports jacket breast pocket and the syringes that resided there. Eternity in one hand, Death in the other.

This was to be the night of his fabled demise, and here he was, where he was supposed to be, the instruments of his destruction all close at hand. He hadn't intended it to be that way.

After shutting down his office the day before, he had gone directly to the Hilton and locked himself in his room, taking food with him. He had blocked the door with a tilted chair and simply waited.

He had waited, wide awake, through the entire night. The phone never rang, though he wouldn't have answered it if it had. When the maids had come the next morning to clean the room, he'd sent them away, telling them the bed hadn't been slept in and the towels remained unused. He had realized he was dirty after that and had taken a shower, getting the floor wet because he'd left the shower curtain open so he could keep an eye on the door.

He'd called Charles in the late afternoon and the man had,

not surprisingly, been able to do as he had asked. The liquidation had come to nearly ten million in hard cash, which had already been deposited in the Swiss bank under Bailey's name. This amount had included the cheap price David had offered Charles on the horse ranch.

After that came the problems. He had managed to reach Bailey on her beeper and had given her the good news. He had been forced to call her back on the beeper a little later after she had verified everything, both of them afraid to give out any details as to where they could be reached.

When they talked the second time, Bailey expressed small gratitude and a bit of surprise. Beyond that she had been no help. Were they leaving today as planned? Yes. What time? I won't tell you. Could he take them to the airport? No. Just leave it at that, at that, at that. Then she had hung up, telling him that she was disconnecting the beeper.

David hadn't liked it. He had done everything for them, and now they were avoiding him completely. He had called the overseas airlines without turning up any listing of their names. Were they registering under assumed names? Why?

He heard them coming down the hallway, giggling, probably feeling each other up. Their voices moved up and down the hallway as they carried things out of the house, things that Bailey wanted for herself. David couldn't have cared less. The glue of life had little to do with its material substance.

The talking got louder. He felt himself tense. They were right in front of his office door!

He had come to the house just to check. He had determined that he would spend this night anywhere but at the house. But when it came right to it, he had to check. He had to look through the place and see if Bailey had really cleaned out her stuff. It was the only way he could know if she really was leaving.

The house had drawn him like a rat to the cheese-trap. The great dichotomy of life—the one place where answers lay; the one place he shouldn't go. His fear had propelled him here to see the final results of that fear in action.

He had parked down the street, entering the house by the back door so he could check and make sure her car wasn't in the garage. Not five minutes later, as he glanced through the upstairs bedroom, he heard her fiddling with the lock on the front door.

He nearly froze, his mind twisting through the dark labyrinth where clear action got jumbled with a million other concepts and died on the vine. He was able to get his legs moving just enough to run blindly to his office and the closet that sat waiting for him there. Old habit patterns never die.

They stood right beside the closet door. His muscles were tensed, quivering from overuse. Sweat was running down into his eyes and mouth now, and he could taste the warm salt on his lips and tongue.

"So, this is his office?" Jeffery said.

"His drinking room, is more like it."

"He's quite well-read, your husband."

"He's a jerk, Jeffery. Even jerks read sometime."

"But *what* reading. Look, here's the Tibetan Book of the Dead."

"He's depressed most of the time. What else should he read?"

"What are we doing in here, anyway?"

"I'm looking for something."

His eyes burned from the sweat. He blinked them, but it didn't help. He could hear her going through his desk. Her voice showed irritation.

"He used to keep a . . . gun in here somewhere."

"What difference—"

"He's gone nuts, Jeffery, if you haven't noticed. I'd rather have that gun in my possession instead of his, right now. Damn! I can't find it!"

"Let's just go," he said. "The plane leaves in a hour and a half."

"Yeah . . . still."

"Come on."

They left the office, moving back down the hall to the stairs. He breathed heavily, wiping his forehead and face with his own shirt. She had tried for the gun and failed. What did it mean?

He heard the front door shut loudly. He carefully opened his closet door and listened. The house was silent. He ran into the hall and into the guest bathroom, stepping into the tub to peer out the window. They were just pulling out of the driveway, its gravel crunching loudly beneath the tires of Bailey's Cadillac. They were gone!

His heart leapt. He jumped out of the tub and ran back to the office, throwing the cushions off the couch. The small gun was still there, right where he'd put it.

The thoughts were jumbling giddily in his head. Calm down, what next? What next? He had to know that they'd really leave; that meant going to the airport.

He hurried downstairs, running out the front door and across the lawn. He ran, laughing, like a child, skipping and jumping over hedges. He climbed into the car.

It started easily and he hurried off, his sheer exuberance pushing the speedometer up close to the speed limit. He laughed. Tonight he threw caution to the wind!

The traffic was early evening sparse and he reached the airport in minutes. It was called the Will Rogers World airport, but the only places in the world its planes seemed to go without connections were Dallas, Chicago, and St. Louis.

He pulled up to the automatic gate and took a ticket from the machine, parking in the lower-level covered area. He left his ticket on the dash and went across the street and into the airport proper.

He walked into the baggage-claim area, then took the escalator up to the ticket counters just in time to see Bailey and Jeffery check their bags into a local, Oklahoma-to-Dallas shuttle. No wonder he hadn't been able to trace them. Maybe they were connecting with something larger in Dallas. It made sense.

From across the wide-open room he watched them get their tickets and wander down to where the loading lobbies were, himself following within moments after checking the gate number on the big board.

They were easy to find, being right where they were supposed to be. David couldn't get too close, however. Bailey looked around continually, her eyes hawkish, searching—for him? Why? He didn't know for sure. All he knew was that they were there when they were supposed to be killing him. They were at the airport without the murder weapon, getting ready to leave the country.

He found a small, stand-up cocktail lounge not too far from their waiting area. He had time for three drinks before he heard over the loudspeakers that their flight was boarding.

He snuck down near the gate and watched his wife board the plane with Jeffery. There was no remorse at her passing, no sense of loss or hurt. There was only the relief inherent in taking care of a difficult problem, like paying off back taxes.

The job wasn't complete until the plane took off, though. He waited it out patiently, his heart pounding with the expectation. The plane got off a few minutes late, but it did get off, and unless they had figured out some new way to exit an aircraft, Bailey and Jeffery got off, too.

"I did it!" he yelled, everyone nearby turning to stare at him. He waved to them and practically danced out of the airport.

The ride home slid by in a blur. Like the passing of a sudden illness, he was wrung out but well again, and was able to dwell on all he had accomplished in two days. He had moved those who would hurt him out of the country, liquidated an entire lifetime of work and struggle, mended many fences, saved a woman's life and her future, *and* beaten Destiny at its own game.

He pulled into the driveway of the only possession he had left and went inside. This would be it, his base of operations for his time skimming. He could come back here when he needed a breather, or when he was ready to live out his life. It was his "safe" house.

Stopping at the bar in the living room, he fixed himself a Scotch to go along with the other Scotches he'd had at the airport. Then he went up and retrieved the gun from the couch.

He carried the gun and the drink to set them on his desk and picked up the phone, dialing Liz's number. Her voice came on, tense and high-pitched.

"Sis . . ."

"Oh, thank God," she said. "You're all right?"

"I've just broken the jinx," he said.

"All right!"

"What are you doing right now?"

"I've been waiting to hear from you."

"Well, jump in that little sports car of yours and hightail it over here. We're going out to do some celebrating!"

"Sounds great. I want you to know that if you want the Porsche back now that—"

"Fuck the Porsche! Get over here!"

He hung up, drinking deeply. He knew now how people on death row at the penitentiary felt, and he knew how a reprieve felt and he knew how a pardon felt.

He grabbed the gun and the drink and hurried downstairs to the living room. He could feel his mind working on other channels now. He thought about Silv and Hersh, wondered how they were doing. Now that he had saved his own future, he was anxious to go back and help them with theirs. And the sooner the better.

He finished the drink and fixed another. He thought of Bailey and how she was making herself crazy not trusting him. She hadn't let up her vigilance for a minute at the airport. Hell, he hadn't treated her that badly. He'd been a lot worse on Jeri, his first wife.

Before becoming a nearly famous writer, Bailey had been a nearly famous sculptor; the fruits of her labors, in abstract forms and curves, were set on pedestals all around the room. He was suddenly struck by an idea.

He took off his sports jacket and laid it across the orange corduroy couch. Then he sat himself down and scooted the coffee table a bit closer to him. Then he drank some Scotch, and laid the gun and the clip on the table.

He shoved the clip into the butt of the weapon and pushed it up to lock. An abstract Madonna and Child, done in black, was set up near the bar. David took careful aim and pulled the trigger, but nothing happened. He looked at the gun and saw the safety was still engaged. He thumbed at the safety and fired at the statue, the gun kicking slightly in his hand, its noise a loud crack.

The statue broke in half, the formless woman's head and shoulders falling to the floor and breaking again. David laughed. This was fun!

He picked out a Prometheus Chained to a Rock and blasted away, missing the first time, but shattering it with the next shot.

Then he saw it, tucked in a quiet corner behind the bar. Bailey had been unhappy with the way it had turned out but, with the vanity of the amateur artist, had not been able to destroy it. So, she simply put it in an out-of-the-way place. A bust of Napoleon.

He took aim at the slightly pudgy face that captured none of the looks and charisma of the man he knew. It was simply a block of hardened clay waiting for a donor, a life-force, to animate it. He would go back to Hersh, perhaps tonight. He would go where he was needed.

He pulled the trigger, the sound loud in his head, the bullet entering the face of Napoleon but not breaking it.

The doorbell rang, twice quickly, again before he could even get up from the couch. Liz.

He jumped up and started for the door, then realized he still had the gun in his hands. He set it on the bar and ran to the door, the bell still ringing. He threw the door open.

"Liz, I . . ."

He was looking into the twisted face of Mo Frankel.

"I knew you'd come back here eventually," Mo said, and pushed past him to stand in the living room, looking around contemptuously. "Nice house."

"I have an appointment," David said. "My sister Liz. You remember Liz."

"This won't take long."

"Let's talk tomorrow," David said. "I've got things to do tonight, but tomorrow would be great. What do you think?"

"I think you're so understanding about tomorrow that you intend to leave tonight."

The old man walked farther into the house.

"I really have nothing to say to you."

"But I have a great deal to say to you, David Wolf," he said, his voice heavy with pain. "Look at me, my remorse is tearing me to pieces."

David had heard the term "walking death" before. You didn't work around hospitals without knowing it when you saw it. Looking at Mo's sunken eyes and bloodless lips made him realize that he'd never really appreciated the concept before. He looked as he must have looked in the concentration camps.

What to say? "I'm sorry for what happened, Mo, but—"

"You're sorry!" the man screamed. "The horror, the pain . . . the suffering of ages is on my hands and you tell me you're sorry!"

"What else do you want from me?"

"You're going to give me that last syringe, David," he said low. "The evil in you that keeps it from me will not stop me this time. I come to save a people. Where is it? Where? It was in your jacket, before . . ."

The man started looking around the room, David glancing quickly at the jacket that lay ten feet from him on the couch.

"There!" Mo said, pointing at the jacket, but David was already moving toward it. He snatched it up, then turned triumphantly to Mo.

But the old man wasn't looking at him. He was moving toward the bar and the gun that lay atop it.

"What are you doing?" David said, following after.

Mo turned to him, the gun in his hand. David stopped, backing away slowly.

"Stop right there," Mo said, the gun shaking wildly. "Please . . . give me the syringe."

"No," David said, slipping the case out of the breast pocket and unzipping it as the jacket fell to the floor. "Put the gun down. It's not your style."

"Don't push me, David," Mo said, tears blinding his eyes. "I'll shoot you with this, God help me. I must save my people . . . the suffering . . . the suffering . . ."

David feared Mo's lack of balance. Anything could happen with the gun in his hands. He also realized he had a vial full of the antidote left that anyone could use to bring him back once he had gone.

"Here," he said, slipping the antidote out of the pouch. "Here it is." As Mo walked toward him, relaxing, David whirled and threw the syringe against the wall, where it broke, the liquid running down to wet the carpet.

He had hoped to make a grab for the old man then, but Mo backed away too quickly, leaving David up short.

"Give me the real syringe," Mo said.

They were no more than five feet apart. They looked into one another's eyes and David saw the look of madness in the eyes of his old mentor. He saw pain so deep that the deepest well could not hold that pain. He saw the absolute determination that guided the man's actions.

"My anguish and pain run deep, Son-I-Never-had," Mo said. "Please give me the syringe."

"No," David said, slowly bringing the needle up to his neck. He couldn't give it up. No matter what the consequences, he couldn't give it up.

"David . . . don't!"

"I won't," he said as he drew the syringe closer.

"Stop! David, stop!"

The old man was crying loudly, shaking, his whole frame vibrating, and still David brought the needle to his neck.

"This is crazy," David said. "We're friends, coworkers. We're healers, not murderers."

"People have killed for a lot worse reasons," Mo replied, his lips twitching. "If you only knew . . ."

"I've seen death, Mo," David said. "Put down the gun. We'll talk."

"We can't talk," Mo said, leveling the gun with two

hands. "I have no choice in this. You're evil. Give me the syringe now."

Push had come to shove and David didn't have the where-withal to deny himself. He stuck the needle in, hearing the shot one second, then realizing he was on the floor the next. Blood was pumping from a chest wound and Mo was walking toward him. He kept plunging the liquid into his neck as he watched the blood gurgling from his chest like the water that had continually gurgled out of the drinking fountain at Memorial Park when he was a kid.

Mo was beside him, pulling the needle out of his neck and throwing it away. There was no gun in his hands now as he bent, wailing, over David, his tears falling into the ever-growing puddle of blood.

"This is . . . so stupid," David said, choking on his own blood. "You've killed me, Mo."

Mo just stared at him, his face no longer a human face. He had done the one thing in his life that he could never live with himself for doing. And though he still moved around, still cried, still drew breath, he was every bit as dead as David, who felt himself whirling into the blackness at that very moment, only to be pried out of it again by the memory of the only time in his life he had ever gone hunting and how he had cried over the rabbit he had killed so uselessly.

Maurice Frankel moved slowly away from the body of David Wolf, the man he had just killed. His mind was very sharp at this moment, very intensely concentrated, though it was moving along the rocky shoals of consciousness that most people avoided at all costs.

His immaculate white gloves were now dyed red with innocent blood, his sin in the Death camp now complete, his own capacity for evil a self-fulfilling prophecy. He pulled the gloves off, exposing his sin, exposing the hideously scarred hand. He wandered around David's house until he found the stationery he was searching for.

He sat at the kitchen table and wrote a brief letter to himself, addressed an envelope, put a stamp on. Then he got up and left the house, climbing into his old beat-up Ford and driving away.

He stopped at the corner to put his letter in the box there. As he leaned out the window to drop it in the elongated slot, he saw a white Porsche drive past that reminded him of David's car.

Then he drove away, drove to Lake Hefner that supplied the drinking and recreational water to Oklahoma City. He drove up on the high road that defined the dam and started around the dark waters that swirled wildly in a stiff wind.

It was just getting good and dark, and from somewhere across the lake a loud siren blared out small-craft warnings. Mo floated off on a cloud of boyhood memories in Warsaw, of the common ovens in which the whole neighborhood baked challah for Shabbos, of the smells, of his mother's laughing eyes and his father's great beard and payos shaking as he sang zemiros at the Shabbos table.

And then he simply didn't make the curve when the road turned. He flew for a second, never losing the memories, and plunged into the dark waters, sliding quietly, as was his nature, beneath the churning wind-made waves.

No one saw him.

No one found him.

He was to rest there, for several generations, until some engineers, draining the lake to build houses on its dry bed would find his skeleton still behind the wheel, still remembering.

> *The grave's a fine and private place,*
> *But none, I fear, do there embrace.*
> —Andrew Marvell

The ceremony would be brief, as all ceremonies were. There was always work to do as the last generations of human beings fought desperately to deny the second law of thermodynamics—the unstoppable flow toward total decay.

Silv was up somewhere near the front of the processions, the white-robed crowds jamming up all around her, she in her brand-new purple robes of the Chemists' Guild. She had been awake all through sleep period, excited, her mind racing as she heard the other girls in her co-op giggling in the dark and whispering out their own excitement.

The processions were moving into the agri-tunnels, glowing white fingers of light branching out into a maze of tunnels that only those who had worked the fields their entire lives could navigate without fear of getting lost.

She breathed pure oxygen through an airtight mask to avoid the overpowering smells of the decomposing bodies that were carried above the heads of the celebrants on reusable, metal pallets. The common workers had no oxygen. Instead, they wore traditional masks stuffed with perfumed rags: sunfaces, animal heads, smiling cloud puffs. They hummed, a low, steady, toneless melody that filled the caverns with echoed resonance. The mood was festive, spirits high without chemical alteration. It was the first of the month—Renewal Day.

It was also the day chosen to induct Silv's class into the ranks of the professional guild. She looked beside her. Mar, her bunkmate, was staring around in wonder, her eyes wide and glassy above her oxygen feed. She saw Silv watching her and reached out, hugging the girl. She tried to speak, but it didn't get out of her oxygen mask.

The tunnel they were walking through suddenly widened into a large chamber of many small rooms divided by rock pillars and wall-like protuberances. Huge electric bulbs with platinum filaments hung from the ceilings, bathing the area in harsh, hot light. The ground was gray dirt, tired from centuries of giving up its chemicals to feed the plants that fed the humans. This was field #4. There were six major fields, each one renewed twice a year, fulfilling the planting-harvest cycle.

The rock floor had turned into a rusted metal walkway that stretched across and above the field for two hundred yards. At the end of the walkway were stairs that led up to a platform overlooking the fields; behind that, the miniature waterfall of diverted river that provided irrigation to #4. Silv could squint and see Mother Sharin' standing on the platform, supported by the exoskeleton that held her old, withered body together. She couldn't imagine ever being that old.

In the fields themselves, men in black were walking between the rows of mounded earth, raking up bones and putting them into large sacks they carried on their backs. They were cleaning up from the last renewal of field #4, a renewal that could take place in only one fashion in such a closed society. The bones themselves would be ground into mulch and used as fertilizer.

There was a sound intruding now, a harsh sound that Silv could barely make out above the humming voices. Mar tapped her on the shoulder and pointed to a corner behind and to the left of Mother Sharin'. It was the huge furnace that provided the heat energy to light the growth bulbs.

As they neared the end of the platform, only the Guilders

and the Olds continued walking, the rest of the procession stopping on the catwalk to await the blessing.

It was all Silv could do to keep from running up the stairs two at a time when they got there. This was and would be the biggest day of her life—a Guilder at age fourteen. She was the youngest in her group, some said the youngest since Mother Sharin's induction. She had taken to it naturally when she had been picked out of Trades Training at age ten. She had designed her first recreational psychotropic drug at age eleven, her first ataractic and beta blocker at age twelve. She was an idealist who saw, with the clarity of someone much older, the importance of what she was doing. To her fell the responsibility of keeping civilization alive by keeping the population on an even keel emotionally by keeping them balanced chemically. Skinner's conditioned response was never enough—the mind, the mind had always to be contended with. And sometimes, the radicalists said, the genes.

She moved up the stairs, Mother Sharin's eyes following her, a slight smile touching her maskless lips. Mother Sharin' had told Silv once that Guild leadership could be hers if she kept her mind, body, and spirit pure and her chemicals creative. In a world absolutely bound together by routine, chemistry allowed the only freedom of creation, as the mix was never wholly satisfactory and was constantly looking toward improvement. Silv liked that part a great deal. But there was something else she liked about the Guild even better. It was something never spoken of by any of them, but understood by all. It was something no one was officially allowed to desire, but that everyone secretly coveted above all else. It was the thing such a close-knit society could offer to only a few—privacy.

The wide-eyed girls in their new purple robes lined up behind Mother Sharin' on the metal platform, occasional water sprays from the falls drifting to wrap them in cool fingers. The Olds, ten of them, trooped dutifully past Mother Sharin', their eyes shining under the influence of massive doses of what everyone called Heaven, the recreational invented by Mother herself to be used only by those volunteering to help with the renewal. As they shuffled past her, Mother Sharin' said the words and poured water from a small pitcher over each of their heads. They then walked past her to move down the steps behind the platform toward the catwalk that led to the furnace.

When she was finished with the Olds, she raised her hands in the air, the humming stopping immediately, the only sounds now the rush of the falls and the roar of the fire—opposite extremes of the same lifeline. Silv felt her mouth grow dry. This was it.

"Civilization is a body!" Mother Sharin' called to the crowd, her unamplified voice bounding and rebounding through the great caverns. "Its people are the limbs and fingers of the body of civilization; its government, the brain; its religion, the throbbing heart; its dead, the sustenance!"

"The sustenance," the crowd repeated, Silv hearing her own voice loud within the confines of her mask.

Mother Sharin's hands were still upraised. A simple gesture—she turned the palms down. With a cheer, the fieldhands threw a month's worth of bodies off the catwalk to land, amidst clouds of dust, in the fields, the black-robed men hurrying to drag the carcasses through the dirt, spacing them evenly in the fields to be plowed under later.

"Renewable resources!" Mother Sharin' called.

"Renewable resources!" the crowd responded.

"And what do we need to bring forth the fruits of the earth?"

"Light!"

Mother Sharin' turned and pointed to the Olds on the catwalk. "Let there be light!" she called.

Someone used a long pole to open a trapdoor in the top of the huge, rumbling furnace. One by one, the Olds, waving and smiling, walked to the end of the catwalk and jumped through the trapdoor and into the fire. The crowds cheered each one.

"Our energy is never lost!" Mother Sharin' told the fieldhands. "It is renewable!"

"Renewable!"

"And the energy of age?"

"Renewable! Renewable!"

"Yes!" Mother Sharin' called loudly. She stepped aside, making a wide gesture toward the platform full of young girls. "Ladies and Gentlemen . . . I give you the next generation of Chemists!"

The fieldhands cheered and applauded, Mother Sharin' joining with them. All the girls' pale, pockmarked skin turned crimson, flushing with embarrassment and excitement.

Silv's heart was pounding with the majesty and rightness of

it all. Through control they survived. Through control their civilization and government had survived intact longer than any other ever to occupy the planet. Because of her position, Silv was giving up all things human for the good of her world. She would know not family, nor lovers, nor children from her womb. Her world was the microscopic land of carbons and enzymes. Her life was being dedicated to the survival of the human race.

She would be as a god to her people.

"As I call each of your names," Mother Sharin' said, turning to look at the girls, "please come forward to be acknowledged by your people, and to receive the symbol of your high office and lofty purposes . . ."

She held it in the air, gold and shiny. It sparkled in the overhead lights, Silv's own heart soaring higher than those lights.

"The key!" Mother Sharin' called. "The key to your own, *private* room!"

"The key," the fieldhands said reverently, their heads bowed.

David Wolf sided the second-floor curtain and looked out at the City of Death. Though it was September daytime in London in the year of our Lord 1665, it was nearly as black as night. It was the year of the great London plague, the rebirth of the buboes. The streets below were dark and twisted, the ornate gables of his banker's house stretching across the narrow street, nearly touching those of Mr. Morrison's house across Wilby Lane. The smoke and soot from thousands of factory smokestacks and chimneys left an oily black cloud roiling through the city like a fog out of hell.

He watched Mr. Morrison's window open across the lane, both men seeing one another, neither acknowledging. He watched Mr. Morrison struggling to get a bundle up on the large casement adorned with bright wooden flowers. When the man began tying the rope to his large package, he knew the death cart must be down the street. Judging from the size of the bundle, it would be one of his children. David and his host watched without feeling as portly Mr. Morrison began lowering the body to the street below.

David had performed the same task six times himself. After the first time, the constables came and painted the red cross on his door and locked him and the rest of the family in for a forty-day quarantine. They didn't need forty days; they had all died within a fortnight.

Death was everywhere. A thousand a day were dying right now. They had to come and get them all the time, not just at night anymore. He heard a scream below and watched a woman running naked through the streets, shrieking. A minute later he heard the bell tolling on the death cart, and pushed open the window to watch.

The air had its own peculiar odor. The rakers from the lay stalls didn't come anymore, so garbage and bodily waste lay uncollected all over the streets, the sickly sweet odor of offal tinged with the permeating reek of death, the most distinctive smell of all.

And still David was an outsider. Not dead, not alive, he had wandered these streets of the damned, watching dogs and cats killed by the thousands while the rats, the real villains, were allowed to propagate and multiply. He had gone to the bawdy houses where those who could still afford it wallowed in rented flesh, thinking that venereal disease rendered one immune to the plague. He searched for Truth among the dead, the truth of his life, the truth of all life. He had watched that peculiar pull toward death time after time, almost allowing himself into that enchantment on more than one occasion. But he wasn't ready somehow. That peace eluded him. He saw it in children of tender years and in lovers full of the flower of life; but to him, to David Wolf, late of Oklahoma City now citizen of the timestream, it would not come.

He was a zombie. He stood outside life watching it like a bug under a magnifying glass, and the more he looked the less he understood.

It was maddening.

The bell of the death cart tolled close-by now. He leaned out the window and watched it stop in front of Mr. Morrison's house. The man in black who drove the horse cart waved up to Mr. Morrison and cut the rope away from the body of his child. He gathered it up like a bundle of wood and dropped it in the cart. Perhaps fifteen bodies already occupied the floor of the wagon, very few of them bundled the way Mr. Morrison's was. They lay peacefully, like new kittens sleeping in a pile. Their next resting place would be a mass grave in Aldgate churchyard, outside the city gates.

The death-cart man's name was Hendrick. David had

walked with him many times before the red *X* was painted on his own door. And in all the wanderings he'd never found out how it was that Hendrick had come to the job he now occupied. There were some things best not known.

Mr. Morrison solemnly watched the wagon with his child move on down the street, watching until it was out of sight and the bell's music had drifted away on fickle winds. Then he looked up to meet David's eye. The men watched one another, drained beyond hope, then Mr. Morrison quietly shut his window and pulled the curtain closed.

David likewise closed his and moved into the house proper. For three weeks he had stayed there thus, walking aimlessly through the now-lifeless rooms waiting for something, anything, to happen that would make some sense of this. The host was named Jack Huggins, a large, red-faced, fun-loving man who now lived himself with the dead. And every day, a little more each day, David could feel that pull toward the darkness in Jack. And every day he longed to understand it, to no avail.

Citizen of the timestream, dweller in the netherworld. He had hoped that immersing himself in death would make a difference. It didn't. It explained nothing and gave him no comfort.

He would live, he supposed, if what he was doing could be described as living. He walked to the bedroom he had shared with his wife, Sarah, and threw himself on the big four-poster, a lingering touch of her perfume alive in him despite the smells of death there. The room was crowded with shelves and knickknacks, small portraits hung from the papered walls (the best a banker could afford), and hundreds of small curios that Sarah was so fond of collecting. It all had spelled permanence to her.

Failing in life, David had also failed at death. He could feel the restlessness in him. It was time to return to the stream. It was time to find others of his kind, for there was no peace to be found in the City of Death.

David was looking into the face of an owl, or rather, at the reflection of his own owl's face.

David, you're back!

Sadder but wiser, Antoine. How are you?

If adversity is good for the soul, then I am well. Silv pines for you.

What makes you say that?

She sulks. Thérèsia tells me she spends most of her time sulking.

Thérèsia. Have you . . . will you . . . ?

Our love remains unexpressed. Sometimes Silv gets so angry she won't even let me come around. Can't you talk with her, David? Get her to leave us alone for a while?

Silv has a mind of her own.

But so does Thérèsia . . .

I understand.

David looked closely at the figure in the mirror. Arnault was dressed as a bird, in a black leotard layered with feathers. His mask fit gently over his head, the owl's face keen and alert.

Why are we dressed up like this?

There is a masque tonight. We celebrate impending victory in Italy. The First Consul will be leaving in several days.

Italy?

The Austrians again . . . a nasty business.

You called him First Consul.

Yes. Sieyès and Ducos have been pensioned off. They were bores anyway.

So, Bonaparte rules alone?

Not alone, David. There are many of us to help him.

You live here, at the Tuileries?

Napoleon has invited me for an indefinite time . . . I think he has hoped for your return.

And what about you, writer of words? Have you feared or hoped for my return to you?

Hoped, monsieur. Only you can intercede for me to Silv.

They moved from the mirror, David pleased that his return seemed to have put Monsieur Arnault in a pleasant enough mood. A touch of it even passed to him despite himself.

He found it strange to think that Silv had missed him. A woman of remarkable self-reliance, she more than anyone he had ever known seemed independent of the need for companionship. Perhaps Antoine had built it up to explain his unrequited love for Thérèsia Tallien.

Arnault sat on the large feather bed to put on his shoes, light slippers with attached claws. The room was large and well appointed, actually consisting of a sitting room, toilet, and the bed chamber. It was spotlessly clean and free of odors of any kind, in keeping with Bonaparte's wishes. He had an aversion to unpleasant smells, and wouldn't suffer them in his surroundings if at all possible.

Did Talleyrand take his leave with the Directors?

A joke, eh? The bishop is bound to the First Consul as if by rope.

I don't trust him.

No one does. Except Napoleon.

There was a knock on the door, then a high, musical voice. "Antoine . . . Antoine."

"Thérèsia," Arnault whispered, and practically ran to the door, throwing it open. The woman stood there, dressed like a water nymph in diaphanous robes and twinkling, fragile wings. Her hair was done up like a bouquet of flowers. She carried a gold-colored mask on a stick, and white gloves rode her arms all the way to the elbows.

Both David and Antoine stood frozen in place. She was beautiful, her barely concealed body lithe and fluid as she brushed past him to enter the sitting room.

"Put your tongue back in and tell me what you think," she said, turning a circle. "Is the lipstick too dark? I feel pale as a ghost today."

"You're incredible," David said. "It is to die for, Silv."

She froze in midturn, her eyes going wide. "David?" she said quietly.

"In the flesh," he replied. "At least, in Antoine's flesh."

"David!" She ran to him, throwing herself in his arms, Antoine's gladly folding her to him. "I've been so worried. I was afraid . . . afraid . . ."

David stroked her hair. "I'm here now," he said, and felt Antoine's body reacting to her closeness. "I don't think I'm real anymore, but I'm here anyway."

Thérèsia felt Antoine's erection, pushing herself against him until Silv realized what was happening. She backed away, staring at the unmistakable bulge in his leotards, then fixed David with accusing eyes.

"It's not my fault," David said defensively. "The kid has taken a vow of chastity until he can have you. He's probably going crazy with this."

That's it! That's right!

A look of pain crossed her face, then fled. "I—I can't react to such a statement,'' she said, folding her arms across her chest. ''I'm not here for that.''

You see? A rock. The woman's heart was cast in bronze!

David took Arnault completely and walked to Silv. He took her shoulders and stared into the endless pool of her eyes. ''I've died, Silv,'' he said. ''My mind is on the edge. I don't know how I can go on.''

She held his eyes, forging the pain that passed between them as if on a bellows. ''We continue,'' she said softly, and put her arms around him again, speaking into his shoulder. ''I don't know how else to say it. What is it that makes us human? What is it that makes us real? Like you, my body has died . . . yet, I continue.''

''As what, though?'' David asked, anguish choking his words. ''We take bodies that don't belong to us. We change their lives to suit ourselves. But it's not us. We're not real anymore.''

She pulled away from him and walked to the fireplace. No wood sat in the grate. It was a cold, dead thing, an air hole to the outside. She turned back, her fairy wings rustling with the movement. ''I'm not ready to . . . fade yet,'' she said. ''Thérèsia allows me within her. I'm not sure if I'd stay otherwise. I've tried to accept Fate and let myself go . . . but I can't. I'm not ready. Are you?''

He looked at the floor, at the ridiculous claws on his feet. ''No,'' he said.

''Then, what is there for us?''

''How long will our hosts tolerate us?''

''Not forever.''

''I suppose . . . we continue, at least for now.''

She nodded sad agreement. ''I don't know what else to do. Are we cowards for not embracing death?''

''We're acting human, is all. Perhaps one day we'll stop doing that. Besides, what does cowardice or heroics mean to us now? Nothing matters.''

''My self-respect matters to me, David,'' she said, her voice stronger now. ''Something, even now, has to make sense. If it doesn't, we're worse than the worst mind we've ever been in. I can't accept that our essence isn't noble.''

A decanter of the common burgundy that Napoleon favored was sitting on the washstand in the corner. David moved to it and poured himself a drink. He lifted the glass in Silv's direction, but she declined with a shake of the head. David drank, the warmth reassuring. "I guess I'm not as evolved as you are," he said. "As far as I'm concerned right now, it's all up for grabs."

"That route leads to madness, David," she said.

He drained the glass and poured another. "Oh, come on, Silv. Have you seen anything in your travels that *wasn't* insane?"

The sadness leaked out of her eyes again and she walked to him and put a hand on his arm. "Don't stop being strong for me," she said, her voice small. "I can't tell you how I've depended on you."

He pulled his arm from her grasp and finished the second glass. "Let's go party," he said. "I want to see Hersh."

She smiled. "He'll be glad to see you," she said. "He talks about you all the time."

They left the apartment, moving casually through the opulence of Louis XVI's grand palace. The walls were hung with Persian tapestries, the cornices painted in gold leaf. And everywhere the grenadiers stood solemn watch over the possessions of the master.

David walked through it all with supreme detachment. The departure of his physical existence had left him in a state of advanced solipsism. He couldn't help but think of everything as a dream, and, as Silv had said, on that road lay madness, the same delusional state that controlled Hersh.

They walked down the wide, twisting staircase to the ground floor, where guests were arriving in great numbers. The military was well represented, as were the trades; even a few of the old aristocracy that had found favor were mixing with the commoners in republican harmony, for Bonaparte fancied himself First Consul of all Frenchmen. The costumes heavily favored the Middle East, a style popularized by Napoleon's adventures in Egypt and Syria, but there were also clowns in motley, forest animals, chess pieces, headless aristocrats, knights in armor, masked monks, American Indians, and more than a goodly portion of joke red togas, official uniform of the late, unlamented Council of Five Hundred.

Silv took David's hand and squeezed tightly, whispering to him, "Stay close to me tonight. I'm here to help you. I know what you're going through."

I wish she knew what I was going through!

Not now, Antoine.

They walked to the ballroom with a crowd that included a

man with a donkey head. The ballroom at the Tuileries was a huge masterpiece of glass and cornice that held thousands. Dazzling chandeliers hung from the ceilings, reflecting their candlelight through multiple prisms of delicate crystal. Large mirrors and paintings by Napoleon's personal artist, David, hung on the walls, covering the religious frescoes ordered by Marie Antoinette.

Many hundreds already jammed up the room, sweating in their generated heat. David reached under his mask and wiped a line of perspiration from Arnault's upper lip and wished for air-conditioning.

Despite the heat, a huge fire fed by entire tree trunks blazed at the far end of the room, another of Hersh's preoccupations. David had seen Silv's detestation of the cold, and understood it when he saw it in Hersh. The walls were ringed with tables full of good, common fare and an orchestra played *"Ah! c'en est fait, je me marie,"* a sentimental favorite of the day.

Silv spotted Josephine receiving guests at the head table near the fireplace and they moved in that direction, David stopping for more wine at the bar. Napoleon kept no wine cellar, preferring to simply have sent in what he needed. The cheap burgundy seemed to be the mainstay at the palace, and even that Napoleon ordered cut with water. No matter, David would just drink more, faster.

Will you give me a headache tomorrow, David?

I tender my apologies in advance, dear friend.

Shall you then stay with me as I suffer through it?

Perhaps. Perhaps this time I will.

I will remind you of that tomorrow when my insides are witnessing the light of day.

You poets!

Josephine was not in costume, but rather was wearing the new style of clothing that she, herself, had commissioned as part of the deal Napoleon had made when he came back to her after Hippolyte Charles. Hersh had demanded an end to the low-cut, transparent clothing, and was rewarded with classicism: high waist, short puffed sleeves, tunic falling straight, molding her figure without stressing it. Her hair was cut short and adorned with ribbons. She looked elegant and satisfied. Marriage was agreeing with her, though David doubted that her infidelity would ever be forgotten by the man she married.

"Dearest Rose," Silv said, embracing Josephine. "You look every bit the queen tonight."

Josephine rolled her eyes. "I was mad," she said, "to be the wife of a plowman. I've come to despise these parties and long only for decade's end and my gardens at Malmaison."

"I fear you are getting old," Silv said. "Is this my friend from the days of the Pompeian cottage and all-night parties?"

Josephine put a finger to her lips and looked around, smiling. "Why, dear Madame Tallien. I don't know what you're talking about."

Arnault kissed Josephine's hand and smiled into her eyes. "And where is the mighty gardener of Malmaison?"

"Playing his little games," she said. "Tonight, he's decided to fool everyone at the masque, to disguise well so that no one will know who he is."

At that moment, the orchestra struck up the chords of *"La Marseillaise"* and everyone in the room applauded loudly. In the middle of the ballroom stood Napoleon, dressed as a domino, his famous buckled shoes still securely on his feet. He had been discovered immediately by nearly the entire company.

He put up his hands for silence, then strode out of the room.

"He had ten costumes brought in today," Josephine said. "He will try until he fools everyone."

David had finished his wine. Silv and Josephine had lapsed off into a private conversation, so he wandered off in search of something else to drink. The orchestra was now playing a favorite of Napoleon's, *"Non, non, cela est impossible/ D'avoir un plus aimable enfant."* Except that when Napoleon sang it in his loud, off-key way, he substituted the word *z'il* for *cela*, an Italianism he simply couldn't resist.

The heroes of Brumaire were all present, the military to a man dressed in formal uniform. Brothers Lucien and Joseph were there; Murat attended with Napoleon's sister Caroline in tow. Berthier talked with Lefèbvre and Lannes. Augereau drank and argued with Bourrienne, after their usual fashion.

After a few minutes, the orchestra struck up *"La Marseillaise"* once again. Napoleon had already been rediscovered, this time dressed as a stag in full antlers. Angry, he once again strode out of the hall.

David stayed well sunk into Arnault to better experience the alcohol. Somewhere along the line he'd lost his mask, and staggered around, half man, half bird. He drank heavily, somehow trying to numb himself to his burden. It never worked completely or for long, but it did provide some consolation.

"Your eyes seem so sad," came a voice beside him.

He turned to see Napoleon's stepdaughter, Hortense, standing beside him wearing an extremely low-cut gown, with a black mask covering her eyes.

"The poet must be sad, don't you see?" he replied, and found his voice slurring somewhat. "We must, after all, write from our pain."

"Is there nothing then left for pleasure?"

She put a hand on his arm, her body brushing against him. What was she doing? She could be no older than fifteen years. He looked at her eyes, boldly encased in the mask, and saw she was as old as sin.

"Dear child," he answered. "I am a voice only. I cry out at civilization from beyond it. In the place where I reside, there is only pain, only frustration."

She took his hand in both of hers and pulled it to her bosom. "Feel my heart beating, Antoine. It flutters like an injured bird in your hand."

Through the curtain of wine, he could feel Arnault's dependable body stirring again.

Antoine, she's just a baby.

Tell that to my John Thomas!

David pulled his hand from hers and looked her in the eyes. "You bring me your innocence," he said, "and I can offer you only corruption." He took her hand and placed it firmly on Antoine's erection, holding it there, her eyes growing wide in horror. "Fly away, little bird. Forget your fantasies and protect yourself. The world is a cruel and hateful place."

He released her hand, her face reddening, her eyes welling up with tears.

"Enjoy your tender years," he said sadly, the wine bringing melancholy. "You will awaken to the grotesqueries soon enough. Find a simple man, one whose eyes see joy and wonder. I am nothing but a voice."

She stared at the ground for a moment, then, unable to hold back the tears, she hurried from him, losing herself in the crowd.

And the band played *"La Marseillaise"* for the third time. Napoleon had been discovered again, dressed as one of his own servants in pale blue livery with silver lace. This time he stayed, explaining to the crowd that greatness could not be hidden no matter how clever the costume. "I am a prisoner of myself!" he declared, and only David understood exactly what he meant by that.

He poured another glass of wine and wandered over near the small crowd that had gathered around the First Consul. Napoleon was standing by a tableful of food, eating and talking quickly at the same time with two large, heavyset men who were not in costume.

Who are those men with him?

The older one with the pigeon wings on his wig is Charles Lebrun, a writer of some note and a financial wizard who helped set up the Bank of France. He's Third Consul. The other, prissy one, is Jean Cambacérès, a lawyer and legislator. He's Second Consul.

Puppets?

But talented.

David pushed past a woman in a topless gown, averting Antoine's head to avoid any more embarrassing moments, and stood near Hersh, studying him with professional interest, noting almost immediately that it seemed Hersh had sublimated himself to Bonaparte.

"What kind of food is this for the ruler of France?" Cambacérès asked, picking up a potato and staring at it in distaste. "Lentils, white beans, bouchée à la reine, vol-au-vent. You have the greatest chef in France in your employ and you insult him by having him cook peasant food!"

"Common food," Napoleon corrected, "for a man of the people." He patted the Consul's generous stomach. "And what have all your rich sauces gotten you, Jean, your truffle pâtés and vanilla soufflés and roasted and grilled partridges? From looking at your stomach, I fear that power is beginning to corrupt."

Everyone laughed, including Arnault. David simply listened as if it were a radio playing. He felt in the middle of some strange nightmare where everyone talked nonsense while the world fell in around them. The booze wasn't helping tonight; it was making him edgy and bitter. Perhaps he shouldn't have come here. But where else would he go?

"I went to one of Monsieur Cambacérès's dinners before," Lebrun said. "Everyone ate in deadly silence. When I endeavored to break the mood with conversation, Jean said, 'Ssh. We can't concentrate.' A serious business.''

"At least his food is edible," Napoleon said, unable to let anyone have the last word. "I've always said, to eat quickly, dine with me. To eat well, with the Second Consul, and to eat badly, with the Third.''

Everyone laughed again, David using Arnault to laugh too loudly and too derisively, drawing attention to himself.

"Something disturbs our young poet?" Cambacérès asked.

David looked at the First Consul. "Does something disturb me, Monsieur Hersh?''

The smile crept into Napoleon's face when he realized that David had returned. "Perhaps our friend has had too much wine, eh?''

"It's the cheap burgundy," Cambacérès said with conviction. "Such wine does the disposition no good when drunk in quantity.''

The military men were beginning to drift over, never too far from their commander. David knew that he should keep his mouth shut. He had been beaten up more than once in his younger years because he couldn't control his mouth when he'd been drinking. But it just didn't seem to matter very much anymore.

"Aren't we a bunch of fine, jolly, noble fellows," David said, moving up to put an arm around Hersh. "Here is your First Consul, the hero of Egypt. But he's not what you think he is . . .''

"David," a voice whispered from the edge of the crowd, and he turned to see Silv watching him sadly.

He pointed to her. "Neither is she. Neither am I. We're all imposters.''

Monsieur!

Shut up.

Everyone laughed.

"A poem!" Murat yelled. "We'll have a poem from the sotted sage!''

"A poem about France," David said, nearly falling over. He raised his glass high. "The French, they are a funny race. They fight with their feet and they fuck with their face.''

There was nervous laughter and a few murmurs. David was totally out of control.

"Tell them about us," Hersh said in his hateful way. "Tell them all the truth.''

David walked away from him, Antoine's body responding poorly, weaving. He'd gone much too far this time and knew it. But still he went on.

"We're spirits," he said, staring slowly at the circle of people in costume that had gathered around him. "We're the broken, godless spirits of useless, godless people. We're the takers of the Earth who give nothing back to it. We're you, all of you. We're the future of your petty, grasping hands and your slimy pricks and your lying words. We're the children you brought into the world to help you destroy it and yourselves along with it. We're the pain you inflict in the name of France, in the name of God, in the name of greed, in the name of holiness, in the name of expediency . . . in the name of fucking carnal lust.

"We're parasites who have invaded your bodies with the eyes of eternity. We can see the lust and the fears that rule your insignificant lives."

His brain was on fire, his words tumbling out without thought. All the frustration, all the waste, all the blindness, was forcing itself through poor Arnault's mouth. He felt Silv's hand on his sleeve and shook it off. He had to speak.

"We can see the waste of your lives and feel the futile grasping of your greedy hands and know—*know*—that it's all for naught. For we're spirits cursed, cursed with the knowledge of death, the knowledge that you spend your lives hiding from. We see you prance around and wear your fine clothes and build your lives and your buildings from stone.

"And we know you, because we're just like you. We practice our 'sciences' and use them to wall us off from the lessons of nature. We speak in fancy words that mean nothing. We call on our gods to save us and to help us and protect us. But nothing can protect us from ourselves. I have seen the enemy and he is us! Oh, my fine friends, how we can hurt each other. We live, all of us, to cause suffering. If not to ourselves, then to the other creatures that inhabit this planet, and finally to the planet itself."

His glass slipped from his hand. He heard it crash from a long way away. He balled his hands into fists, shaking them out in front of him, feathers jiggling. "Let me tell you a secret. Let me tell you the secret of life. It's pointless—no, worse than pointless, it's evil. Words, words, words! Who invented them? They're nothing but lies!"

His hands went to his face as the tears came, unbidden.

"It's all so sad. Why can't you understand how sad it is? My words are so hollow. No words can touch the sadness that I feel. Why was I cursed with this vision? Why!?"

The tears flowed unhampered down Arnault's cheeks. "If only I could see what you see," he whispered. "If only my world was fine buildings and new uniforms instead of horrors and decay."

He broke down then, head hanging, feathered hands tugging at his hair. "God, that they could lobotomize my brain and . . . end this . . . nightmare." He stumbled once against the table, feeling nauseated, then fell, the room spinning. He crashed through a tableful of food, getting a close-up look at Louis XVI's parquet floor, then Antoine's vision went black.

True to the curse, David's didn't.

Through the lightless cave of Arnault's mind, he could hear Hersh laughing, then applauding. "That's from Antoine's new play," he said, and everyone began laughing and applauding.

"The best blind-drunk actor I've ever seen," Berthier said loudly, and the applause grew in intensity.

And all of David's words, all of his feelings, were as dead leaves whirling in a fall wind.

He heard voices around him, then sensed that the host body was moving. He heard Hersh's voice saying to take him to his chambers, and then the sounds from the masque were fading away.

He could have fled to another body, but he didn't, preferring to stay for a while in Antoine's darkness and abide there.

"Oh, David," came Silv's sad voice, and he was glad that she was going with him.

"David," Hersh said into the darkness. "I know you can hear me. What a show! What a performance! Everyone loved it . . . you *could* make it a play, you know . . . charge admission to your feelings. It's so wonderful that you're back to stay. With your help we'll make a go of it, I know we will. But you've got to help me, you've—"

"Maybe this isn't the best time," Silv's voice said.

"Nonsense. It's the perfect time. Listen." His lips came close to Arnault's ear and he whispered loudly. "I'm a soldier. That's all I know. You've got to help me get my mind away from thinking I can only make war. Ever since Brumaire, I've been afraid to turn around. I know that something's wrong with me. Only you can help."

Then he heard Hersh's voice from a distance. "This will work out. I know it will. Between the two of us we'll show this whole world what a good, republican government is. You sleep, and we'll talk later."

Then he was gone.

There was a moment of silence, David thinking he was alone. Then he felt soft fingers on Antoine's face.

"Poor David," Silv said low. "Even in his misery, he's expected to be professional."

He felt soft lips brush Arnault's cheek, and even Antoine, out cold, stirred a little under the touch.

"The reality's only as ugly as you make it," she said. "Seeing something and seeing through something are two different things. Is it the heart of the world you condemn or your own heart? You're a man torn apart. You must reconcile with yourself. I don't know what our life here is . . . but I know that it *is* life, and I want it."

He could hear her crying softly then, sobbing as quietly as she could. Then he felt her tears on Arnault's face.

"And I want you to share it with me," she said quietly. Then her hands touched his face once and she was gone.

He stayed there in a darkness for a long time, trying to figure out exactly what she had meant. Reconcile with yourself, she had said. Physician, heal thyself. Viewpoint is everything. He thought about his mother and about the life he had led. He thought of her death and his death, and then his thoughts became crowded out as Antoine entered the dream state.

David found himself standing in the middle of a room in the Tuileries that smelled musty with age and reeking of sweat. It was a dusty room, one not used, and heavy purple drapes hung from tall windows, blocking out the light. A large candle burned on a stand in the corner.

Suddenly, the room was filled with people with indistinct faces, though David, through Antoine, knew exactly who all of them were.

Talleyrand lay naked on the bed with a huge erection. It had to be three feet long and stood up straight as a telephone pole. A number of women danced around the huge penis as if it were a maypole. The women were also naked and indistinct, their forms sometimes male, sometimes female, though David knew they were all girls.

He recognized Arnault's mother and his mother's sister.

There was a third cousin named Jeanette, and two girls he had taken schooling with. There was a Parisian streetwalker whose name neither one of them knew, and, finally, Thérèsia Tallien. Thérèsia was the most distinct, and the most enamored by Talleyrand's genitals.

David walked to the dream door and pulled it open, only to be confronted by Antoine himself. The man was in an incredible state of sexual excitement, and the feeling transferred over to David.

Antoine brushed past him, dressed as a ballerina, and David tried to leave the room, but the halls were filled with demons eating live dogs, so he went back in the room.

Antoine was attempting to pull Thérèsia away from Talleyrand's monstrous penis while at the same time struggling to remove his tutu. They fell to the floor together while Talleyrand laughed. Thérèsia began moaning on the floor, reaching out to Antoine.

David walked past them to the window, siding the curtain. He was looking out at a landscape that stretched flat and unbroken to the horizon. The land was barren except for mammoth letters and words chiselled from rock that were set here and there. David dropped the curtain.

The other women all pulled Antoine's clothes off and he grabbed Thérèsia, rolling on top of her. But then she began laughing. They were all laughing. Arnault had no genitals at all. He was totally blank down there.

And the woman turned into the same dogs the demons were eating in the hallway. But their teeth were big and razor sharp. Drooling heavily, they began nipping at Antoine.

David couldn't stand any more of it. . . .

David maneuvered his own three-year-old body as he chose, using the innocence of his own youth as a springboard to deeper understanding of himself. He didn't mind taking the child full now, because he had discovered, the last time, that children live in a world of total fantasy anyway. The fantasy of David's knowledge was just another wonderful mystery to Davy Wolf, and the boy's obsession with death may have sprung from that mystery, making David Wolf the ultimate in self-made men.

"Hungry," he said, staring up into the deep blue eyes of his mother as she moved around the kitchen, cleaning it.

"Would you like an apple, Davy?" she asked sweetly, bending slightly to the child to touch his face.

"You . . . cut it for me?"

"Okay."

He watched her take an apple from the windowsill and wash it in the sink. Something was wrong with her today. Her eyes seemed deeper, her face less relaxed, less pretty. David knew that something was up. She had made a couple of trips to the family doctor, leaving him in the waiting room to stare at the blank faces of those who sat in the chairs that ringed the cinder-block walls.

She had cried yesterday, and had argued with his father that evening. Today she had been strangely silent, her mind laboriously working through some sort of thinking process. He sensed something getting ready to happen.

"An apple for Davy," she said, holding the two halves in the palm of her hand.

He reached for the apple and she pulled it away. The usual game. He reached again, and again she took it back. She went down on a knee and got at eye level with him.

"Momma loves Davy very much," she said.

"Hungry, Momma," Davy said.

"Does Davy know where his food comes from?"

"From you, Momma."

"That's right. Without me to give you this food, you'd starve and die. I'm the one who does this for you. Do you love me?"

He put his little arms around her neck. "I love you," he said.

She kissed him on the cheek and hugged him to her. "I love you, too, sweetheart."

He released her and she gave him the apple. "Don't ever forget," she said, and stood.

They both turned toward the living room, at the rustling of the door being unlocked. His mother stiffened, her facial muscles tightening.

"Naomi!" came his father's voice from the doorway. "Honey!"

"I need to talk to Daddy," she said, almost mechanically. "You play like a good boy."

With that she moved out of the small kitchen and into the living room. David hurried to the refrigerator and put the apple in there.

Hungry!

In a minute, Davy.

He scurried down the hall toward the bedroom. His parents discussed everything important in the bedroom, the one place in which Naomi felt superior. He fell once near the doorway, but was able to scramble up and get into the bedroom before they started down the hall.

The sliding closet door was partway open. He got to the crack and slipped inside, sliding back into the corner. It smelled human in there, partly perfume, partly sweat. It was comfortable, like a cocoon or an isolation tank. David Wolf sat more still than any three-year-old ever could and waited.

He had waited two months for this moment. He had felt it building quietly and intensely for quite a while. The Destiny of it was nearly overpowering. He had gotten to where he could literally experience Fate in action and know when it was dealing out the hands. This one had built for months.

During the two months spent in the child's body, he had come to understand a great deal about himself and the source of his problems. He had come to know his father as a fine and gentle man, willing to do anything for the woman he loved, but a prisoner of her sex. Naomi used sex to manipulate everyone and everything around her, constantly making a fool out of Sonny by screwing his friends and then telling him about it. He was helpless in her hands, the anger he would sometimes feel easily transferred by Naomi into sexual frenzy whenever she chose. It was a sad thing to watch.

Naomi, for her part, was having the time of her life. Her sexual freedom was, for her, a liberating and special gift, one that set her apart from those around her. She was no different than anyone else on the planet because she fucked, but *she* didn't know that. To herself she was the siren of all time, the repository not only of men's seed, but of their value and self-worth, too. She fucked often and well, trying at all times to find the rich man who would take care of her better than Sonny could. The only reason Sonny was still around was the nature of his slavish devotion. She hadn't found anybody yet who would put up with her the way her husband did.

He had watched her in the course of the last weeks bringing her relationship with the oilman, Herbert, to some kind of peak. She had something on her mind, all right, and David was convinced that today was the day for revelations.

He heard them coming into the bedroom, Sonny's voice

relaxed and casual, totally unprepared. "Where's Davy?" he asked. "I come home for lunch . . . thought I'd see him, too."

"I told him to play," Naomi said, voice tight. "You and I have to talk."

He heard the bedroom door shut and lock.

"What is it?" Sonny asked, and David heard the bedsprings creak when he sat down. "What's wrong?"

"I've got something to tell you."

David slid over a bit so he could peek around the sliding door and see them. Sonny was sitting on the edge of the bed, his blue jeans and white T-shirt filthy from his construction job. He was lean and gaunt, his face still boyish, though it had become harder, more angular with age. He looked at Naomi like an adoring puppy. David felt sorry for him.

"What is it, hon?" he asked, and began handrolling a cigarette from a drawstring bag of Bull Durham.

"I'm pregnant," she said without fanfare.

The half-rolled cigarette snapped in his hands, tobacco going everywhere as he jumped up, wrapping his arms around her. "That's great!" he said, but she stood stiffly in his arms, unresponsive. He pulled back slightly. "What's wrong?"

"It's not yours," she lied.

He backed away, bumping against the bed and sitting again. "What do you mean?" he asked, and his eyes showed he understood more than he pretended.

"I mean that it's somebody else's baby."

"W-well you don't know that, you—"

"I know it, Sonny. I know whose baby it is and whose baby it's going to be."

"You're my wife," he said sternly, and David could see his pitiful mind racing through the possibilities to try and figure out what she was getting at.

She moved away from him slightly and stood near the closet door. "I'm in love with somebody else," she said, "and I intend to live with him and raise his child."

"You're puttin' the cart before the horse, ain't you?" he said, standing. He began methodically trying to brush the spilled tobacco into a pile on the bed. "You're my wife and you live here with me."

"You dumb fuck," she spat. "Don't you know when you're getting shoved out? I don't *want* to be around you anymore. I don't want to see you or talk to you, and I certainly won't ever share a bed with you again."

He scooped the tobacco into the hand and tried to put it back in the pouch. "Naomi, I—"

"Would you stop that!" she grabbed his hand, the tobacco going everywhere again. She spun him around to face her. "Listen to me! I want you out of here, Sonny. You make me sick. When you touch me, it makes my skin crawl. And the thought of your scrawny dick inside me makes me want to vomit."

She came back to the closet, reaching inside. Davy had to scoot to the side quickly to avoid her. She pulled a small suitcase off the floor and carried it to the bed.

"I've packed some things for you," she said. "Get out! I'll send the rest of your stuff to you."

"You've got this all figured out, haven't you?"

"Yeah, that's right," she said. "I don't need you anymore. I've got somebody better. Get out."

"This is my house, too. I don't have to leave."

"Well, then, Davy and I will go. We'll live in the car and eat out of garbage cans while you have the nice house."

"No," Sonny said, "no. Y-you can't do that. I'll go, but . . . I'll tell you where, so you won't worry . . ."

"I don't give a damn if you jump off the Brooklyn Bridge, just do it now."

They moved out of the bedroom, still talking. Davy crawled out of the closet and followed them down the hall.

"I still have some rights to Davy," Sonny said from the doorway.

"Why?" Naomi replied. "He's not yours either."

He slapped her. "You bitch!"

She laughed loudly. "In fact, I think he might just be your brother!"

David peeked up over the arm of Sonny's weathered chair and watched his father's face go white. She had done it that time. He could tell that Sonny didn't totally believe her about Davy's parentage, but the fact that he had to consider it was too much even for him.

"All right," he said low. "I'm goin'. I came home to lunch to tell you I had an offer to go to work in the oil fields. Think I'll take it starting right now. You're gonna get what you want, Naomi. You always think that I'm the dumb one, but maybe I'm finally smart enough to see that I need to get away from you to save myself. You live with your dreams, girl. See what they get you."

He turned then and walked out of the house, David knew, for the last time.

"Dumb fuck," Naomi said again, and slammed the door behind him. It wasn't until she heard him start the car that she realized he was taking it. She ran outside, but he was already way down the street.

She marched back in, her face red. David had come out from behind the chair. "Did you see that?" she said to him. "That lousy son of a bitch took my car. Imagine, leaving a pregnant woman with a small child to fend for themselves. That asshole! He'll pay for this, he surely will."

She brushed past Davy, heading for the old black telephone in its own wall alcove, a modern shrine. "That motherfucker ran out on me and took the car," she said angrily as she dialed the phone. "I'll fix it so—"

She stopped talking for a second, her voice calming and taking on a sweet teenaged quality. "Good morning. Herbert Jasper please."

Davy moved down the hall and sat on the floor beside her. He happily munched the apple and listened.

"Me? This is . . . uh . . . Naomi . . . uh, Stevens. With a 'V.' That's right. Yes . . . I'll hold."

Her foot tapped angrily on the wood floor of the hall. David was amazed at the tension that crackled like electricity from her.

"Herbert, darling, I . . . yes, I know I promised not to call you there, but . . . yes, I'm sorry, but it's an emergency. Yes, with Sonny. I told him, I . . . yes, I kept your name out of it, but . . . Herbert, listen! He's gone. I've gotten rid of him completely. Yes! Isn't that exciting? Well . . . I told him that I was going to have your baby . . . Herbert? But, it's not supposed to be funny . . . I *am* going to be the mother of your child. And, darling, I couldn't be happier, I . . . Please stop talking so loud. Didn't you hear me? I've gotten rid of Sonny so you and I can live together and . . . you'll get a divorce, I suppose. You've always said that she didn't . . . I *know* this is sudden, but . . . You're going to have to lower your voice. Everyone can probably hear you . . . What do you mean how do I know? Of course it's yours, who . . . You've got no call to say that, Herbert. You have responsibilities to me, too, you know. No! You listen to me, you son of a bitch, I won't . . . Herbert . . . Herbert?"

David watched his mother stare dumbly at the phone for a

long time before quietly hanging it up. She couldn't understand what had just happened to her, and never would. She walked slowly to the bedroom and went in, throwing herself on the bed, sobbing loudly, then cursing Herbert, her curses finally centering on Sonny, the man who had deserted her.

After a few minutes Davy went into the bedroom. David had stopped the child from doing it for a time because he was angry with Naomi for her manipulation and her stupidity. Davy didn't relate to any of that. He saw a fellow traveler in pain and wanted to try and ease the burden.

"Momma cry," the boy said.

He climbed up onto the bed, sliding over quietly to put a hand on his mother's back. The woman, red-eyed, pulled the boy to her fiercely, hugging him while crying into his tiny shoulder.

"It's just you and me now, Davy," she said. "It's just you and me against all of them."

For David Wolf, it was time to leave.

> *We are not free to use today, or to promise tomorrow,*
> *because we are already mortgaged to yesterday.*
> > —Emerson

"What are we doing here?" Silv asked, a hand on her head, holding on her new bonnet as Antoine Arnault dragged her along by her free arm. They were moving rapidly through the acre-wide rose nursery at the botanical gardens toward the huge greenhouses that occupied the west end of the grounds, opposite Geoffroy Saint-Hilaire's zoo on the east side.

"I think there's something here that will aid us," David said through Arnault. "Just wait."

The sky above was bright blue, the early spring air still slighty chilled. Roses of red and white, neatly trimmed and blooming in fragrant elegance, stood taller than David and, like walls, defined the pathway to the greenhouses. It reminded him of Josephine's gardens at Malmaison, where magnificent stands of roses were laid out in the ancient fashion to form mazes.

David was in decent spirits today. His time spent as a three-year-old had begun to fill in a great many blank spaces in the story of his life. Silv had told him that reality was what he would make of it, and today he was making it a good

thing. Understanding his childhood was helping him understand his adulthood, and in that, he found hope. If he couldn't
find answers for the reasons for things, at least he was
making progress in understanding himself.

The greenhouses were large buildings with high roofs of
glass, and a pristine, technocratic feel to them. A physical
manifestation of eighteenth-century thought. David pulled her
through the door of the building marked EXOTIC TREASURES,
the temperature inside making them sweat immediately.

The smells were overpowering. Sweet odors, almost too
sweet, seemed to waft through the enclosed chamber in
invisible layers, blooming plants set in large pots jammed
together in apparently random confusion. But there was a
method. The plants were placed together geographically, then
cross-indexed with more familiar plants of the same general
family.

"What are we looking for?" Thérèsia asked. "I can't help
unless I know."

"A plant," David said, frowning at Silv's laughing face.
"I think Savigny had it sent back from Egypt. I'll bet it's in
here somewhere."

Silv pointed to a small man in a white smock on the other
side of the hothouse. "Maybe he can help us."

"No," David said, moving rapidly down the large center
aisle, his head turning back and forth as he walked. Silv
hurried to catch up, her face already flushed, a thin film of
perspiration slicking her nearly bare, heaving bosom. "For
what we're going to do, we don't want any help. Ah . . . here
we are."

He pointed down an aisle that branched off from the main
fork and pushed deeply into a tropical jungle of rubber plants
with huge leaves that overhung the path.

The Egyptian section was deep in the rubber-plant jungle,
totally hidden from the rest of the building. David scanned it
rapidly, while Silv watched him in perplexity. He smiled at
the blue water-lily that Savigny had been so excited about in
Cairo, then he stopped, with a short intake of breath.

"Here it is," he said low, and bent slightly to study a
small, scrawny-looking herb that was growing in profusion
amidst beautiful, flowering plants.

Silv bent to study it with him. "What is it?" she asked.
He smiled at her. "This should be of interest to a chemist

like yourself," he said. "This is a prime example of what we call *Rauwolfia serpentina*."

Her face lit up. "The ataractic derivative."

"It originally came from India, but the expedition found it in Egypt," David said. "The people over there chew it to calm themselves down."

"Do you realize that this is the original source material for all tranquilizers?" Silv asked.

"You bet," David said, then pulled a handful of it out of its clay pot. "In fact, the French invented Thorazine because of this little plant. To Savigny, though, this was nothing compared to his water lily. He only included it because I talked him into it."

David pulled some more of the herb out of the black soil and stuck it in the pocket of his frock. He dusted off his hands. "Let's get out of here."

He walked off, Silv right behind him. "I don't understand. You want to give this to Hersh?"

"Nonsense," he said over his shoulder. "Hersh is in your laboratory in the future. I want to give this to Napoleon so he'll leave Hersh alone long enough to let me get the man into therapy."

They hurried through the hothouse, then out into the spring chill again. The abrupt change in temperature made Thérèsia shiver, and she pulled close to Antoine for warmth. He removed his frock and placed it around her shoulders, then pulled her close, holding her as they walked.

And David was beginning to have a difficult time separating his feelings about Silv from Antoine's about Thérèsia. He knew two things: he felt comfortably close to the woman who huddled against him, and he had been anxious to return from his travels to be with her.

He leaned down, kissing her just behind the ear.

"Don't," she whispered, her body physically tightening in his grasp. He could feel her rejection and her excitement at the same time, and despaired that it would be ever thus.

"I just—"

"Please, David," she said, eyes glistening. "Let's don't talk about it now."

"Okay."

She pulled away from him, warmer now, and in a moment she returned his purple velvet frock. They walked through the roses in embarrassed silence, David finally breaking the mood because he wasn't ready to get depressed again.

"I think I can make quick progress with Hersh now," he said, and she brightened, not wanting the mood to stay dark either.

"You've changed since we put you to bed last night," she said. "What happened?"

"I went back as you suggested," he told her, a slight smile creasing her lips. "I saw some pivotal moments of my youth, and my psychiatrists's training filled in the blanks. Considering the double binds my mother put me in, it's little wonder that I treated women the way I did. It just struck me that if we could do the same sort of thing with Hersh, we might be able to overcome the negative conditioning of his unbringing."

She bristled a bit at the term "negative conditioning," but let it go quickly enough. Instead she said, "Today, this is important to you."

It was a term that said much more than it implied.

They had reached the zoo, the sounds from the huge aviary cage loud and raucous. The smells changed, too, animal excrement sitting heavy on the still air. David wondered if they used the animal waste as fertilizer in the gardens.

They walked into the zoo pathways, large crowds of unemployed moving slowly, talking slowly, observing slowly— killing time. Time.

"I can help Hersh," David said, as they stopped to look at the African lions. "That's my job, my life. I can help myself; that's my crusade. I can continue to exist; that's my curse." He turned and looked hard at her. "I can search for peace of mind—that's my necessity."

There was pain on her face as she tried to share her eyes as deeply as was possible. "I understand," she said simply, then struggled out the next words. "I received a letter from Jean."

He started. "Your husband . . . er, Thérèsia's husband?"

She nodded.

"Mail is getting through from Egypt, then?"

"A lot more is getting through, a lot more."

Her voice caught and she turned and began walking very fast. David watched her in confusion for a second, then felt Antoine's fear build inside. He hurried after her, pushing his way through the large crowds.

He caught her as she was boarding the coach they had hired to bring them there. It was set in a long line of coaches that stretched across the cobbles of the rue de Madeline. People picnicked on the grounds all around them, war veterans waiting nearby for handouts. In the distance, the skyline of Paris imposed itself upon the rustic beauty of the gardens.

He climbed in after her, sitting on the facing leather bench. "What's going on?" he asked, then lurched toward her as the coach jerked and started on its way.

"He's coming back," she said, daubing at her eyes with a perfumed lace handkerchief. "Probably within the next two months."

No, this isn't fair!

Antoine, I . . .

No! You people have no right to keep us apart.

"What are you going to do?"

"I don't know what I'm going to do," she said, her voice heavy with frustration. "I don't think I can hide my presence from him. He's going to want closeness. He's going to want . . . sex. And to complicate matters, I don't think Thérèsia is any happier than I am about all this."

"There are worse things in the world than sex, Silv," David said, and felt stupid immediately.

"My bodily functions are none of your business," she said, trying to sound harsh but still sounding frightened.

"And Thérèsia's are none of your business!" he heard Antoine say, the man's anger allowing him to grab control away from David momentarily.

"That's right!" Thérèsia said, then her hand went to her mouth, her eyes wide and frightened. The woman bent her head, a hand going to her temple. A moment later, she stared at David.

"Thérèsia wants to talk," Silv said.

"So does Antoine," David replied. "They have rights, you know."

Silv nodded. "I'm used to things being in their place. This sort of thing . . ."

"They have rights," David said. "You told me that you were living inside Thérèsia with her permission."

"She is," Thérèsia said. "I feel close to Silv. Being with her, I understand a great many things . . . but she must stop controlling my body."

Her face blanked for a second, then Silv spoke. "This isn't right," she said. "How much of the feelings that flow between Antoine and Thérèsia are caused by our presence?"

"Are you saying," David asked, "that the feelings exist between you and I, and that the other two are bystanders?"

"I didn't say anything like that," Silv said.

"I love Thérèsia," Antoine said, David drifting off slightly to let him speak freely. "You two have no right to keep us apart. If it bothers you so much, leave us alone. Then you'll see if we care for one another or not."

"It's not that easy," Silv said. "You don't know what forces are at work on you. Can't you just leave things as they are for now? We'll leave soon enough."

"When?" Antoine asked.

Do you mean that?

Don't push me, David.

"Well, I know what forces are at work on me," Thérèsia said. "You've kept me celibate for many months and it's driving me crazy. My body's on fire. You heard Antoine. He loves me, and I love him. We want to consummate our love and it's none of your business."

"It'll just complicate things even more," Silv said.

"We don't care about complications," Antoine said. "*We're* human. We thrive on complications."

The remark stung David, the implications cutting deeply.

"This is madness," Silv said, shaking Thérèsia's head. "David. Talk some sense into them."

"There is no sense, Silv, and you know it," David replied. "We have no right to control their bodies against their will."

"But can't you explain to them what a horrible mistake this is?"

David just stared at her, marveling at the fear that rimmed her features. "What's so horrible?" he asked. "I'll be perfectly honest. My feelings are involved, too."

"The body chemistry affects you," she said.

"No," he replied. "My body isn't even here. I have feelings, Silv. I think they're for you. My mind, your mind. I want to make love with you, whichever of you I'm really talking to. The feelings are overpowering."

"Not true," Silv said. "You can control them."

"Why should I want to?"

"Because it's not right, it's . . ."

"It's what, Silv?" David stared at her. The coach was making its way through the outskirts of Paris. The hovels and makeshift houses for the poor an outward reflection of the real reasons for the Revolution. "I know that in your time you've grown old. Perhaps you've let your mind grow old, too. Remember when you were young and the world was nothing but love for you. Your mind can still be as young. Only the body has to grow old. Remember what it's like to make love, the last time you . . ."

"There was no last time," Silv said in a low voice.

"What?" David said.

She stared at the floor, unable to look up and meet his eyes. "I was chosen as special by my people at a young age. I've never . . . never . . ."

"You're a virgin," Antoine said, his voice a whisper.

"Oh, Silv," David said, reaching out to take her hands in his. "You're so fragile." He reached out a hand and took her under the chin, forcing her eyes to his. "You're afraid, that's all."

"Of course I'm afraid."

"You don't need to be. I would never hurt you."

"You've said that to others."

He nodded, moving over to sit beside her. "I deserved that," he said. "But I'm changing. I can feel it. I'm not the same person you met at the hospital that night."

"What right have we to ask for love, David? We're dead."

He put an arm around her. "You're the one who told me that we were alive," he said. "If we live, we have a right to love. Do you love me?"

"There's never been anything but duty before. I don't know what I feel. I only know I want to be with you."

He turned her to face him on the seat, the fear in her eyes siphoning the protectiveness out of him. He took her face in his hands, brought her trembling lips close to his. "You've been teaching me not to be afraid. Let me teach you."

"Oh, David. I'm an old woman. I feel so foolish, I—"

He brought her lips to his, holding back the urgency that both Antoine and Thérèsia tried to put into it. She shook in his hands, quaking, and the kiss became more intense as her lips parted to accept his exploring tongue. Through the sensations of Antoine's young body, he let his own mind drift with the feelings. He let go even more, allowing Antoine to take control of the situation while he simply enjoyed.

His arms went around her, pulling her close, closer, their bodies as one. Antoine's hand drifted down her back, taking in the fullness of her buttocks, and Thérèsia moaned, pushing herself even tighter against him and opening her legs slightly.

His hand moved down her leg, tugging at her skirts, then under them to her stockinged thighs.

"No!" Silv stiffened, pushing away from him, jerking Thérèsia's hand from the belt buckle she was so desperately trying to undo.

David reluctantly took control of Antoine and pulled away from the woman, moving across to the other seat.

Her hands were shaking as she brought them to her face and cried. "I—I'm sorry," she sobbed. "I wanted to let go . . . but I j-just couldn't." She cried loudly. "I'll never be free, never!"

"Your conditioning has been just as strong as Hersh's," David said, his voice forced to a calm that Antoine's body didn't share. "Don't worry about it." He leaned over and pulled her hands from her face, kissing each tear-damp palm in turn. "We've got all the time in the world."

"But our hosts don't."

"It's all right," David heard Antoine say, his voice choked with emotion. "We'll just live a day at a time."

"Until Jean gets back," Thérèsia said, and sighed loudly.

Napoleon Bonaparte studied the herb that David had placed into his hand. "I don't believe much in medicines," he said. "The body is its own healer, fresh air the curative."

The First Consul was dressed for work in cashmere breeches and linen shirt, muslin cravat and the simple frock of a colonel in the Chasseurs—dark green with gilt buttons and scarlet collar.

"This isn't a medicine," David replied. "It's a psychiatric experiment designed to help with Hersh's therapy."

"Bah, you babble like Pinel, the brain doctor at Charenton."

Napoleon and Antoine stood in the First Consul's study at the Tuileries, windows open wide, the curtains fluttering in the breeze that had lost its morning chill. Napoleon was pacing, giving dictation to one of his secretaries.

"Pinel treats the insane as patients rather than as curios," David said. "He's regarded as Freud's forerunner."

Napoleon frowned and walked to his desk, picking up a copy of a book that lay there. He walked back to David, who stood in the center of the eight-room suite of offices and living space, and handed him the book.

"Ever seen this before?" he asked.

Antoine glanced at the title: *On Literature Considered in Its*

Relationship to Social Institutions. He smiled. "Madame de Staël's treatise," he said, "talking about the evolution of the human spirit. I read and enjoyed it."

"Cult of the individual," Bonaparte spat. "Useless nonsense, just like your friend Pinel, and Burke and the rest of the ideologues. I'm having it banned."

"But why?" David asked.

Bonaparte took the book from David and threw it at his secretary, Fain, who ducked, then sheepishly retrieved it as if he should have taken the blow.

"Take that to Fontanes," Napoleon said. "Tell him to damn it." He turned his attention back to David as the secretary fled with the fat volume. "Why, you ask? Because people are the same, have always been the same, and will always be the same. These social theories are futile polemics that simply interfere with my policies. People need to be controlled, governed. The art of government is to keep the people reasonably happy by giving them what they want and getting from them what you can."

"What of liberty?" David asked, drawing him out.

"Just a word. Men are like ciphers: they acquire their value from their position. My job is to give everyone a chance to attain that position to insure their docility. Men are moved by two levers only—fear and self-interest."

"Who's talking?" David asked. "Who's influencing whom? Hersh has known nothing but the kind of Skinneresque control you're talking about, yet it hasn't kept him 'reasonably happy.'"

Napoleon stared at him darkly. "Hersh waits in the background," he said. "I'm capable of my own thoughts. I'm trying to build a country from scratch, and he keeps forcing me back to war in Italy."

"Why?"

"He fears this part of it," Bonaparte said. "He knows nothing of building, only in tearing down. My control makes him edgy."

"Maybe I can help," David said, and walked to a small divan set in a square of furniture for meetings. He sat. "Talk to me, Hersh."

Napoleon walked to sit in a high-backed chair near David, his eyes losing none of their dark power. "I feel lost," Hersh said, the voice weaker, a hand to his temple. "I came for the power, but now I'm only confused. This is my dream, but I can't control it. What's wrong with me?"

"You've lost sight, Hersh, of who and what you are," David said. "I'm here to help you if you want it."

"How will you do it?"

David pointed to the herb that Napoleon still held in his fist. "With the help of your host and this herb, you're going to go back to some of your earlier experiences and then we'll talk about them together. It's called naming your demons. When we can understand why we do things, we've gone a long way toward understanding and handling our problems. Are you willing to take a chance with me?"

The man rubbed his face, staring at the plant in his hand.

"This will be good for the both of you," David said for Napoleon's benefit.

"I don't like eating things if I don't know what they are," Napoleon said. "Will you guarantee results if I take this?"

"There're no guarantees in anything," David replied. "In my business, just like in war, we make it up as we go along. Some things work, others don't. There are no hard and fast rules. We're writing the book on this as we go along."

Napoleon studied the plant closely, then sniffed it. "This won't hurt me?"

David shook his head. "What do you two think?"

In response, Napoleon grimaced and closed his eyes, sticking the plant into his mouth, chewing tentatively. "It's bitter," he said.

"It's supposed to be; just eat."

David watched the man. The idea of the drug had occurred to him because it had gotten so difficult to separate the two personalities. Hersh was living a fantasy, so whenever he relinquished control to the stronger personality, he tended to pull inward and lose himself in Bonaparte, who used that knowledge to control Hersh in a thousand different ways. He fed false information to Hersh, or thought in absurd directions in critical times. If Hersh was to survive, he had to know his own mind, his own identity. And the survival of those lost in the timestream had become very important to David. Since he had nothing else, he clung to his new life.

"How do you feel?" David asked.

Napoleon, eyes still closed, had put his head back on the chair. He still chewed, but slowly, thoughtfully. "My mouth is somewhat numb," he said dreamily, "and I'm experiencing a kind of floating sensation . . . not unpleasant, actually."

"Good," David said, soothing. "Just relax and let yourself go with the feelings. If you should feel any anxiety, tell me and we'll talk about it, all right?"

"Can I trust you, David Wolf?"

"You know me by now," David said.

"I know many men, and they would have to be exceptional rascals to be as bad as I assume them to be."

"You're projecting," David said. "Trust me."

"To a point, I will."

They sat in silence for a moment, the only sound that of papers rustling on the desk in the warm breeze.

"Hersh?" David said quietly.

"Yes," the man said.

"You and I have never worked well together because you have never accepted the fact that you have a problem," David said, sitting on the edge of the sofa and leaning forward. "Now that you want help, you and I will try and untangle this mess together. I'm going to tell you what I'm going to do and why.

"The cornerstone of all psychiatry lies in the understanding of adolescent behavior and its projection upon later events. The usual way of attaining this knowledge is tedious and painstaking, and is achieved after long hours of associative thought, if at all.

"I think we have a way of circumventing those long hours. With Silv's drug, you can return to your childhood anytime you want and study its content within the perspective of total reality. With me to help interpret these events, we may arrive at truth in relatively short order. That achieved, we can then hope to figure out what it is you're hiding from."

"Is that what I'm doing . . . hiding?"

"In a manner of speaking," David said, and it looked as if Napoleon was almost asleep. "I believe that something dramatic in your life has caused your violent behavior *and* your escape into another reality."

"You're here, too."

"I'm dead. I've got nowhere else to go."

"Where do you want to send me?"

"Back to before you were born, Hersh. I want you to concentrate on your mother . . . your mother's relationship with your father."

"But, I—"

"It's the only way."

"Yes."

There was only a second of silence before Hersh moaned loudly, then sat up, eyes wide and staring.. He looked at David, and there was something otherworldly etched on his face.

"What happened?" David asked.

Hersh took a breath, his face strained, and he began talking. . . .

Bert'a stood at the long steel counter and tried to listen attentively to the questions the man in the green robes was asking her.

"...aware that any issue emanating from this congress shall be property of the quad?"

"I—I don't understand," Bert'a said.

The man sighed loudly, and just flicked her with dark eyes before typing something into the computer before him. "I'm simply telling you that if you have a baby, you don't get to keep it. Now. Do you understand and agree?"

"Yes," Bert'a said.

"Good. Now. Job classification?"

"Brown-4," Bert'a said.

"Current status?"

"Excuse me?"

"Where do you work now."

"Clerical . . . food services."

The man nodded, his eyes fixed on his screen. His hood was down, exposing the thatchy clumps of his reddish hair. "I need your Life Class card and your basal chart."

Bert'a brought her ditty up on the counter and fished out the steel Class card, handing it to him proudly. Even though she was just a Brown, she was a high-achieving Brown, and besides, any Brown was still a level above any Purple.

The man took the card and typed something else. "Basal chart," he said.

She fumbled through the ditty, finally coming out with the small computer graphic whose connecting lines somehow told them that she was fertile.

The man in green took the information, then handed her

back the graphic. "You should come in here today and the next four days in a row. Do you understand?"

"Yes," Bert'a said anxiously, sensing the interview was almost over.

The man grunted, slid a template over near her hand, and recited from memory. "In exchange for your cooperation in this endeavor, the quad will accept all responsibility for your maintenance should you become pregnant. You will not have to work during the term of your pregnancy, and afterward, for a period of three hundred days, you will receive a monthly stipend not to exceed your current monthly allowance to be used however you wish. If you agree to the above-stated terms and conditions, fix your thumb on the plate."

Bert'a reached out without hesitation and sealed the bargain with her thumbprint.

"Done," the man said, and raised a section of the counter, allowing her to pass within. She did so, looking triumphantly at the other women who sat in the waiting room for their turns.

The man gestured to the door behind him. "Go through that door," he said, "and walk past the open cubicles. Choose whomever you wish. On the successive days, you may choose others. Or you may choose as many as you want today." He handed her a small red ring. "Put this on and I'll pass you the rest of the week."

"Thank you," Bert'a said, and the man shrugged.

Excitement was building within her as she moved to put her hand on the doorknob.

"And, miss," the man said.

She turned to him. "Yes?"

"Don't lose the ring."

"Yes, sir."

Bert'a moved through the door with an air of supremacy. Her whole life, people had paid no attention to her because she was a Brown. But here . . . here she was special. Here she was doing something important for the quad that very few others could do. She wasn't sure why they chose Browns for this work and she didn't care. She was going to be pampered, cared for, as if she were a White, or even a Blue. And all she had to do was enjoy herself.

She had entered a dark hallway carved right from the rock, the air heavy with perfumed smoke. Small grottos seemed to be carved from the rockface on both sides of the hallway, flickering light from within them making its way into the unlit hall.

She walked slowly, letting her eyes accustom themselves to the darkness. The first grotto she passed had a small curtain covering the opening. From within, she could hear soft wailing.

Moving on, she saw the grotto on the other side. Within the featureless room was a single bed with a small table for the candle. A naked man lay on the bed, making a cat's cradle with a piece of string, staring at it intently.

Bert'a started when she saw him. He was beautiful, his face soft and innocent, his body trim, the muscles taut. Maylor had told her about the men, but somehow she had never expected them to be this exceptional.

The man realized she was staring at him and turned his brown eyes to hers. He smiled, then took his penis in his hand and began to masturbate, his eyes never leaving hers. She would have gone in, but it seemed foolish. The hallway was so long, the possibilities so endless. She'd be foolish to walk into the first bed she saw. Besides, she could always come back.

She turned and walked on, passing another ten cubicles before slowing her pace. Each of the men was as pretty as the first had been, each as developed and muscular—logical choice was a near impossibility. She would have taken any of them. The next room she reached held a blond man of about twenty. His eyes were blue, his biceps a solid as the rock walls that surrounded him.

When he saw her, he spoke. "You come to me?"

"Yes," she said, and walked into the room.

"Pretty girl," he said, standing. He closed the curtain and turned to her.

She walked to him and shrugged. "What now?"

He looked perplexed. "Fuck," he said, and reached out to pull her brown robes up over her head. He smiled at her, then looked at her body, masturbating himself to erection.

Taking her by the hand, he led her to the bed. His body was smooth and unmarked, except for a crescent-shaped birthmark on the outside of his left thigh.

He climbed into bed, pulling her down beside him. He tried immediatcly to climb on top of her.

"Wait a minute," she said, pushing away. "I don't even know your name."

Her face took on a childlike hurt, and she realized he was probably a Purple and at least partially retarded. Well, no matter.

"I'm Bert'a," she said.

He pointed to himself. "Mac." Then he made an expansive gesture. "Everybody Mac."

"H-how did you end up here?"

Mac just shrugged, shaking his head.

Oh, well, she hadn't come here for small talk anyway. She let her eyes travel the length of his body, her hand moving with her eyes. His muscles were astounding. He surely had to spend hours a day just to keep himself in such physical condition.

She stared at his erection, his penis large, the purplish head throbbing. She reached out a hand, peeling it up and down the hard stalk. He jerked to a sitting position, slapping her hand away.

"Not outside . . . must be in you."

With that, he rolled her over, pulled her legs up over his shoulders and forced himself into her. She was dry, and his entry hurt, but she tried to get a rhythm going with him. He was without understanding of sexual ways. Immediately upon entering her he began pumping like a machine, very quickly, and within thirty seconds had spent himself. He rolled off her and turned on his side, falling asleep, his breathing even and innocent.

Bert'a stood and put her robes back on, somehow knowing that she was even then impregnated. So that was it. No wonder Maylor hadn't made a big thing out of it. Well, anyway, she still had the next nine months to look forward to.

". . . never saw my father again," Hersh said, Napoleon's classical features strained to sadness. "She never saw me when I was born. The quad took me and put me in the isolation tunnels."

"So," David said. "You were being groomed for the military."

"Groomed," Hersh said. "What fancy words you use. I was bred, David, bred. Like a packmule, I was the product of idiots, meant to be an idiot myself."

"They wanted people who would follow orders without questioning."

Hersh sat up stiffly, grinding a fist into an open palm. "You don't know what war is like in the quads," he said. "They wanted meat—meat that could kill and meat that could be killed without any loss to the quad."

David sat back, thinking. "I wonder about your father, I—"

"No!" Hersh said, standing abruptly, his eyes still heavy from the herb. "No more of this. I won't think about this any more." His fists were clenched in rage. "I can't go on with this thing . . . I can't . . ."

Hersh kicked a small table out of his way and strode toward the door.

"Where are you going?" David called after him.

"Italy!" the man yelled, and was gone.

David stood slowly, walking to the window. Outside, carriages came and went across the wide, nondescript courtyard; messengers ran or rode horses while military men, all young, walked in small groups discussing the formation of a new country. All this in reaction to the power plays of the most troubled man David had ever known.

He had lost Hersh for now. It was a matter of some sadness to him that he might not get him back.

Though a man excels in everything, unless he has been a lover his life is lonely, and he may be likened to a jewelled cup which can contain no wine.
—Yoshida Kenko

We are not the same person this year as last; nor are those we love. It is a happy chance if we, changing, continue to love a changed person.
—W. Somerset Maugham

The candles glowed warmly, lighting the wine, as the sun dipped outside of Malmaison. It was a time of evening David had always enjoyed—the darkness encroaching, the light not yet able to dispel that darkness—and even though the sunset was missing the beautiful pollution-filtered colors of late twentieth-century America, it was still spectacular, and the warm, melancholy feeling of this time of night was ever strong in him.

David still lingered over Josephine's table, the food not yet cleared away, and thoughtfully ran a finger around the rim of his glass of burgundy.

Will we get drunk tonight?
No, Antoine, I think not.
Good. You've made me old before my time.

Everyone else had moved off into the small palace, leaving him alone at table. Josephine was packing for a trip to the salt baths at Plombières in the hopes that they would make her fertile enough to bear the First Consul an heir. Hortense was off with Napoleon's brother Louis, her yearning for Antoine converting itself quickly enough. Bonaparte's sister Caroline strolled in Josephine's rose maze, pining for Murat who was with her brother in Italy. And Silv . . . he wasn't sure where Silv was.

Hersh had forced Napoleon off to Italy, David more convinced than ever that the man was running away from something greater than the conditioning of the quad. David had opted not to go to the Italian campaign. He had spent so much time immersing himself in mankind's baser fears and conceits that he felt dangerously close to the edge of madness hiself. He had to breathe fresh air for a while, had to adjust the realities for his own peace of mind. It had been three weeks since Hersh's departure, and David missed the campaign not at all.

He had spent the days leisurely. Antoine was working on a new play in which David took no interest. He simply floated, his mind working on its own sort of restructuring as he visited his childhood more and more often. Perhaps it was the comfort of being in a body that had actually been his that drew him there, but more likely it was the ability to view his life from a detached plane that captivated his analytical mind.

"You've been skimming again," came Thérèsia's voice from beside him.

He turned and smiled at her. She had changed from the simple shift that she had been wearing earlier into a white lace gown with an extremely low bodice. She looked beautiful in the half-light, her face glowing angelically in the warmth of the candles.

"What makes you say that?" he replied.

She sat across the table from him, pouring herself a half glass of wine. "You get that look on your face," she said. "You've been in thought for a long time. Usually that means you've been skimming."

He turned sideways in his seat, putting his feet up on the

empty chair beside and unbuttoning his plain vest. "I've been in my childhood," he said, "learning from myself."

"Learning what?" she asked, sipping the wine, a drop hanging on the burgundy of her own lips.

"About the way my mother messed me up," he said. "About how she used every resource available to tie me to her and justify her destructive life-style."

"She sounds like a terribly frightened woman."

"She ruined my life, Silv."

"You're angry."

"You bet I am!" he said, and finished his own glass. "I died the way I lived, alone and unloved. I was an emotional retard bludgeoning my way through relationships and responsibilities."

"And you blame her."

He took a breath, calming himself. "I'm sorry," he said. "I still think too much about myself, don't I?"

"Do you?"

"You sound like a shrink," he laughed. "By the way, you look lovely tonight."

"Thank you, sir," she said, bowing slightly. "I've been dealing with Rose's problems so much lately, that I decided to dress up, have a drink, and take care of myself for a change."

"What's wrong with her?"

"The usual," Silv said, drinking again. "Ever since Hersh returned from Egypt, he's cooled off on their relationship. She's afraid that if she can't provide him with an heir, he'll find someone who can."

"Bonaparte never liked her," he said. "She was always more Hersh's type. And now that there's a kingdom to run, Hersh is hiding and Napoleon is handling things."

"Has Napoleon taken complete control, then?"

David shrugged. "What can I say? Napoleon has been Hersh's host for many years now. The separation gets more and more difficult. Freud once said that paranoic delusion is a caricature of a philosophic system. Napoleon's philosophy of government is barely discernible from the behavioral control practiced by the quad."

"Now, David . . ."

He put up a hand. "Wait, truce!" He laughed. "I'm not condemning your system. I'm simply saying that Napoleon is picking up, probably subconsciously, Hersh's conditioning. On another front, I wonder how much of Napoleon's prowess in battle is directly attributable to Hersh. People in the dream state are capable of tremendous feats of daring and heroism, and Hersh lives in the dream state.''

She stood, moving around to David's side of the table. She slid his feet off the chair and sat on it herself, the two of them facing one another, knees nearly touching.

''So,'' she said, placing her hands primly on her knees, ''does it turn out that the reason for our existences is to make historical personages what they are?''

''I don't think it has a purpose,'' he said, ''just a circularity. But you're right. Hersh is as much Napoleon as Napoleon himself is. Maybe everyone travels in his dreams. Maybe everyone exerts influence on everything. I'd certainly rather believe that than rest on the shambles I made of my own life.''

''You regret much of it, don't you?''

''My life? I regret all of it. I regret the wasted, crazy years. I regret all the pain I caused to so many. How about you? Are there any regrets in your life?''

She reached across the table and picked up her glass. ''I have my regrets,'' she said, ''but for reasons opposite yours.'' She held the glass before her face, swirling the liquid in a circular motion, watching the whirlpool intently. ''My life was spent in service to others. I was a god to them, and, so, above them and untouchable. I don't know if I ever performed a selfish act in my life.''

''What's wrong with that?''

''Because the reason is, I never had the opportunity to be selfish. In the quad, everything's structured. So it was with my life. For a hundred forty-seven years, I did what I was supposed to do.''

''Sounds miserable.''

She drank, finishing the glass. ''I was more numb than miserable. I think my greatest regret was in never being able to have a child. I really believe people need children to feel total and alive. I see that in Hersh, too, that longing.''

He lowered his eyes. ''I—I feel the same way,'' he said, tears coming despite him. ''I kept myself from having them. I hated the world. I hated myself. And so now I'm gone, to live only as a shadow. Do you wonder why I'm so angry at my mother?''

''You didn't have to give in to it.''

''I have a talent for melancholy.'' He wiped his eyes, the

tears gone already, pulled from an empty cistern. "I just wish this all made sense somehow."

She put down her empty glass, and took his hands in hers. "Why?"

He kissed her hands. "I don't know. Maybe if I could understand why . . . I don't know, maybe I'd be . . . happier somehow."

"What would a psychiatrist say about that?"

He smiled again. "He'd say that happiness comes from within."

Silv cleared her throat nervously, lowering her eyes. "I've got something to say, and I just want to get it out as best I can, all right?"

"Sure."

"I've been . . . talking with Thérèsia," she said, then cleared her throat again. "I don't think that it's fair for me to deny her bodily needs any longer."

David felt her hands grow clammy in his. "What do you mean?"

"She . . . wants you, er, Antoine. Wants to have sex with . . . Antoine. And I'm going to let her. Who am I to stand in her way?"

Praise the heavens! Praise the muse of poetry and all things bright and wonderful. Praise my celibacy and my enduring love and respect. Praise the loose buttons on my breeches!

David released her hands and forced her face to look at his. "And you, Silv. What will you be doing while Thérèsia is making love to Antoine?"

Her face flushed crimson. "I will . . . remove myself, of course. Won't you?"

It was David's turn to clear his throat. "Well . . . yes, of course."

She let out a deep breath, her body obviously relaxing. "Oh, good. I've gotten that out of the way. When shall they do it?"

Now, now, now, now, now, now, now.

Anxious?

Who . . . me?

"Well, there's a saying where I come from," David said. "There's no time like the present."

Thérèsia's eyes were hot wax. Silv made her nod courteously. "That will be acceptable. Where shall they go?"

"So formal," David said.

Will you really withdraw?

I don't know. Will you be jealous?

I'm liberal-minded. She likes the both of us.

"Well, how about Antoine's room," David said in mock seriousness. "I hear that's how the Parisians do it."

"Don't make fun, I'm nervous."

David leaned forward, bracing his hands on her knees, and kissed her deeply on the lips. "It's *supposed* to be fun," he said. "Don't be embarrassed."

Her face had flushed again, David smiling, knowing that Silv hadn't been able to escape his kiss in time. She stood, smoothing her white floor-length skirt. He could almost feel the sexuality oozing from her.

"Shall we go?" she said, her voice husky.

He stood immediately, picking up the bottle of wine. "In case they get thirsty," he said.

"Does sex make one thirsty?" Silv asked in a small voice.

"Sometimes."

He put an arm around her waist and led her from the dining room. Servants hurried through the house, lighting candles and closing drapes, the bulging, tent-draped ceiling casting ominous shadows on the papered walls.

They passed the magnificent library, one of Napoleon's obsessions, and turned up the stairs. Caroline Bonaparte came in the front door as they ascended the stairs, and stood, watching them silently as they made their way up.

"Do you think she knows?" Silv whispered as they reached the top of the stairs.

"Know what?"

"What we're going to do?"

David laughed. "What difference?"

Her face flushed. "It's . . . I don't know . . . embarrassing. I mean . . . I'm not so sure, I . . ."

"It's springtime," David said, hugging her close. "We're in Paris, young and in love, just like everyone else here. People *expect* us to do this."

"I'm not young, I—"

He put a hand over her mouth. "Tonight, you are anything you want to be. Silv is dead, remember? She doesn't exist physically anymore. You are whatever you think yourself to be."

She pulled his hand from her mouth as he led her into his

room and closed the door after them. "You're right," she said. "If only I could convince my brain of that."

She stopped walking when she reached the canopied bed, her eyes widening fearfully. "David . . ." she said, reaching for him, clutching.

He set the bottle on the floor and put his arms around her. "Just go with it," he said, "or just go. It's going to happen this time regardless."

"Are . . . are *you* going to go?" she asked in a tiny voice.

"What do you *want* me to do?"

She held him fiercely. "Oh, David, I'm so frightened."

"Don't be," he whispered. "I won't hurt you. I promise."

She looked into his eyes, hers brimming with fear and need. "I trust you," she said.

"Oh, Silv," he said, picking her up and spinning her around. "That's the nicest thing anyone's ever said to me."

She laughed as she spun, her old woman's fear of falling gone completely. She *was* what she wanted to be, and she loved it.

He set her down, both of them laughing. She put a hand on her head. "Oh . . . I'm dizzy."

"Me, too," David said. "But it's got nothing to do with spinning around."

He leaned down and kissed her then, hungrily, and he wanted this woman more than he had ever wanted a woman in his life.

She returned the kiss without hesitation, letting Thérèsia's experience lead her into uncharted territory. All thought of leaving swept away, she reveled in the feel of his lower body pushing against hers and in the dampness between her own thighs.

David shared with Antoine, each of them bringing his own sense of spirituality to the act. David was amazed at his own feelings. Sex was always a taking to him, a contest with clearly defined winners and losers. All he wanted to do now was share. And more than anything, much more than anything, he wanted to keep from hurting Silv in any way. Her gentle nature, her trust—he wanted them protected at any price. And he nearly laughed when he realized he was thinking of someone besides himself.

He ran strong hands down her back, cupping her buttocks and pulling her closer. She responded by opening her legs slightly and straddling him, rocking against his erection.

Oh, Gods, I don't know if I can keep this up without . . .
Courage, Antoine. Think of other things!
I'm doubling numbers, but it's not helping.
Then, think about her husband catching you!

David brought his hands up to her shoulders, gently sliding aside the straps of her gown and pushing downward. The dress fell to her waist, her milky breasts firm and high, hard-pointed nipples straining upward. He cupped her breasts, then kissed them, her moaning loud in his ears.

He fell to his knees, his tongue working its way down her stomach as she helped him slide the white lace over her hips and to the floor. And he buried his face in her crotch, her hands coming to the back of his head to pull him against her.

"David!" Silv cried. "It feels wonderful!"

Oh, Silv. It was my name you called.

She pulled him to his feet, devilment lighting her eyes. "There's something else I'm interested in," she said, and pushed him backward to fall on the bed.

Laughing, she climbed up with him and began undoing the buttons on his breeches. As she tugged on his pants, he sat up slightly and got rid of his shirt and vest.

She pulled his boots off, then his pants, then crawled up his body, grabbing Antoine's ample erection with both hands.

Oh, I know I can't hold it!

Keep counting, keep counting!

Twice sixty-four is one twenty-eight . . . twice one twenty-eight is two fifty-six . . .

David pulled her up to kiss her, her body smooth and exquisite against him. This was life in all its complexity and simplicity. Love and sharing—selfishness be damned! There is hope!

They kissed deeply, Thérèsia's hands still pulling insistently on his penis. "Come inside me," she rasped. "I can't wait, I can't . . ."

He rolled on top of her, and she fondled him lovingly before pulling him into her.

Twice two thousand forty-eight is four thousand ninety-six . . .

He moved slowly in her at first, then faster, her face changing form even as he watched her, moving between the well-practiced quiet passion of Thérèsia Tallien and the excited discoveries of Silv.

And within minutes, spurred on by Thérèsia's excitement and Antoine's lack of control, David felt the passions surging

wildly through him. He let his mind go, hearing Silv screaming out her pleasure from inside, not outside. They climaxed
with a thrashing of hips, Thérèsia jerking off the bed to wrap
clutching arms around Antoine's neck, her breath coming in
tiny gasps as he collapsed atop her.

They lay there panting, David's brain, tied to Antoine's
system, feeling like it had exploded into shards, David having
to wind himself back from nearly real visions of primordial
sex experiences that weren't all human. It was a long climb
back, so totally had he given of himself.

Antoine rolled off Thérèsia and lay on his back, still trying
to catch his breath. David made him roll over on his side to
stare at her.

"Wow," he said low.

"I never realized," Thérèsia said, but he knew it was Silv
talking. She smiled wide, showing white teeth. "A whole
world they kept from me."

David reached out a hand, touching a budding nipple. "A
whole world just waiting for you," he said.

"Yes!" She threw her arms exuberantly around him. "A
whole world for us. David, I love you so!"

He started, watching her innocence. He had accepted this
fragile woman's faith and was now its trustee. A bolt of fear
passed through him, then subsided. She had said that she
trusted him. And now he had to be worthy of that trust. He
could do it. He *would* do it.

"I love you, too," he said, and in those words were the
key to his bondage. Free to love, he was free to feel.

Silv sat up, her hands going to her hair, pulling it wildly
out from her head. "I'm free!" she shouted, and David
realized they had both been chained by the same fears. Was it
as simple as this? Was salvation this easy?

She turned to him, her face alight. "That was so much
fun!" she said loudly. "No wonder they kept me from sex in
the quad. I'd have never gotten anything else done."

He stifled a grin. "So, I guess you liked it okay, then,
huh?"

"Like it? I can't *believe* it!" She stared down the length of
his body, frowning when she saw how his penis had shrunk.
"Can we do it again soon? I'd really like to try that again."

David put his hands behind his head and yawned. "You
might need to let me rest a little first," he said sheepishly.
"These things take time."

She turned to smile at him, then a wicked look flashed across her face. "Really?" she said to no one. "Why not?"

"What . . . ?" David began, but Silv had already turned back around, lowering her lips to his penis. She took it in, David watching in fascination as Antoine's young organ stiffened again immediately.

Ah, the exuberance of youth.

I'm just getting warmed up, David. This time I'll do it without counting.

Good, math was never one of my favorite subjects.

She fellated him for a moment, then moved away, staring at his erection in triumph. "I did it!" she squealed, and David began laughing, Silv's enthusiasm contagious. For the first time in her long, long life she had learned to do something that *she* wanted to do, and now there was no end to the possibilities.

Excited again, David reached for her, pulling her to him. This time they went slower, their preliminaries tender, their explorations sensually drawn out. And when he made to crawl on top of her, she gently but firmly rolled him over on his back.

"Let me on top," she said, straddling him.

"My pleasure," he said, watching as she held his penis steady and placed it within herself.

Silv pumped slowly, eyes closed, moaning low. David held Antoine back, letting Silv set the pace, enjoying as she savored the moment.

She opened her eyes and stared into his. "Switch places with me," she said.

"What?"

"Trade minds. I'm dying to know what it feels like for you."

"W-wait a minute," David said, feeling strange. "I'm not sure if—"

"Don't be so shy," she teased. "You can be anything you want to be."

"God, I've created a monster," he said, then warmed to the idea. "I can do it if you can."

She ground herself against him, purring deep in her throat. "All right," she said, opening her eyes wide. "Do it now!"

David let go, sliding through the pleasure to catch the timestream, images tumbling upon themselves. Every sexual encounter his genes had ever known flooded back in a confused jumble, and he sorted rapidly through them searching for Thérèsia. Somewhere in transit, he passed Silv going the other way, their minds merging as a unit for just an instant before hurrying on. This was existence as David had never comprehended it. Who needed life? They had intellect and sentience, humor and understanding. They were the essence of man without his detriments.

Suddenly, David was staring at himself. At least, he was staring at Antoine, who had been him at one time. He locked in, feeling Antoine's penis filling him up.

He was repulsed at first, a lifetime of conditioning rearing up to buck him like an angry horse. He nearly panicked and jumped back into the stream.

"David?" Antoine's voice said, and David stared at the man's smiling face.

"I'm here," David said, and tried to calm down. "This is very bizarre."

"Remember what you are," Antoine said. "Inhibitions have no part of you."

Hello, David.

Thérèsia. I can feel your mind. You're a good person.

So are you, but get rid of your fears; you're making me lose the feeling.

I'll try.

David made an effort, letting himself go the way he had done in Antoine's more familiar psyche earlier.

He began to accept, then cherish, the feelings. He was a creature of giving who had opened himself up in a literal way to take the measure of another's body. Antoine filled him up, the sweet surrender of his body to the man's penis a ritual of life as old as the species.

He had never understood what a woman feels before, the passivity to another body's intrusion the ultimate giving-over. As he moved his vagina up and down the length of that magnificent stalk, pausing to make clitoral contact on the downward thrust, he felt the emotional giving as something totally apart from the sexual feelings but just as strong. Where sex to a man was conquest and gratification, to a woman it was the emotional offering of herself to the domination of another, its pleasure not just physical, but also all tied up with the pristine act of surrender through trust. He understood in an instant why rape was such a horrid crime. That something so profound should be taken instead of given freely was a negation of all things human, a reaffirmation of the dark side of man's character.

He felt a glow spreading through him. As a man, everything centered on the penis as the exquisite pain built to a fever pitch. But as a woman, the feeling was total. His whole body was involved, his system flushing with excitement.

"Ohhh, David," Silv said through Antoine. "Now I understand why men like guns so much!"

Antoine was pumping hard now, matching Thérèsia's strokes, and every time their pubic bones touched, a shiver ran through David's inflamed mind. He was giving through love, and in the giving lay the taking.

It was perfect,
    more than perfect,
        it was total.

The orgasm wracked him in uncontrollable waves, Thérèsia's body shuddering wildly, grinding the spurting penis all the way into herself. He heard screaming, and realized it was coming from his mouth. And then, through flashes of white, he felt himself cast down upon Antoine's chest, breathing heavily, the man's penis shrinking slowly to slide out of him an inch at a time.

"Good God almighty," David said, a whisper. "I never knew it could be anything like that."

"Oh boy," was all Antoine could say. "When can we do it again?"

David moved away from Antoine, beginning to feel a little self-conscious again. "Well," he said. "You're the one with the erector set. You tell me."

Antoine rolled onto his side and braced himself with an elbow. "Which do you think is better, being a man or a woman?"

"Being alive is great," he said through Thérèsia. "All the rest is just commentary."

Naomi usually went for oil-field trash, shot-hole drillers or rig builders, wildcatters who suddenly had more money than they knew what to do with and who didn't mind dropping it on a pretty face who'd provide them with a few decent meals and the best sex they'd ever had until the cash ran out. They were always "Y" names: Sonny, Billy, Marty, Johnny, and they were always "friends" she had met at the "club," Naomi's fancy name for the Sipango Lounge, where she plied, in a civilized manner, a trade that those less astute were put in jail for.

It was one of her "friends," a man named Eddie, who sat across the dinner table from Dave Wolf and laughed at him.

"A doctor, huh?" Eddie snorted, his mouth full of Naomi's fried chicken. "What makes you think they'd ever let a poor boy like you be a doctor?"

David sat in the back of the high-school boy's mind, listening to the exchanges. At this age he was unable to dip any closer to the source, afraid of upsetting the boy's tender psyche.

"Oh, Eddie," Naomi said. "Let the boy dream. It don't mean nothin'."

"You stay out of this," Eddie said, mean. "It's time your boy learned the facts of life." The flabby man slammed his fork down on the table and leaned toward Dave. When he spoke, his voice contained hatreds so intense that David began wondering what sort of childhood traumas had ruined him. "Listen to me. You're trash, boy, and you'll always be trash. That's the way of it. Them rich bastards'll keep it all. They don't let nobody like you into their club. So, you just get out there and work the harvests or the oil patch like the rest of us, and keep your mouth shut."

"I can be a doctor if I want to," Dave said with intensity.

"You can shut my mouth, too," Eddie said, standing and kicking his chair out from under him. "That's if you're man enough."

"Stop it!" Naomi said. "The boy's just dreamin'."

"I'm not dreaming!" Dave shouted at her. "I'm going to college. I'm going to medical school, and I'm going to be a doctor. I *can* do it."

"Don't you shout at your mother, you little asshole!" Eddie said, coming around the table for him.

"Leave him alone!" Naomi shouted. Liz broke out crying and jumped up from the table, running into the back of the small house.

Eddie stopped short of Dave, flaring angrily to Naomi. "What did you say to me, bitch?"

"Eddie," she purred in a little-girl voice. "I'm sorry." She moved to him, taking him by the arm. "Why don't we just go back in the room and have a drink and relax."

"Yeah," Eddie said, turning to stare his superiority at Dave. "Let's go back in the room."

Eddie reached out a beefy hand and took Naomi's right breast, kneading it through the flower-printed shift she wore. He stared at Dave the whole time.

"Eddie!" Naomi said, trying to wriggle away from him. "Not here."

He held her firmly, squeezing harder. He smiled lewdly at Dave.

"Leave her alone," Dave said low, taking a step toward them.

"No!" Naomi said to him. "It's . . . all right. Eddie just plays this way."

"That's right," Eddie said, releasing her breast and putting his hand down the front of the dress. "I just like to play . . . *Doctor* Wolf."

He started laughing again. Dave's fists clenched involuntarily, and it took a major effort of will not to go after the man. Instead, he turned and charged from the house and peeled off in the '57 Chevy he had gotten from a junkyard and restored in the garage.

It was difficult for David to remain silent as he rode out the emotional rollercoaster his younger self was suffering. The boy's doubts were overpowering, the emotional equipment he used to cope with those doubts faulty and misguided. It was horrible. He wanted to tell the boy—but what? That he'd become a doctor but it wouldn't change anything? That he would live a life of selfishness and self-destructiveness because of his upbringing? He remained silent and in the background.

He went to the northside Y, where he worked as a lifeguard, and swam for thirty minutes trying to relieve the frustration in his usual way. But this time it didn't work. He changed back to street clothes and got in the car again.

Dave drove aimlessly for about thirty minutes, then stopped at Corsin's Grocery on Western Avenue and bought beer from a friend of his who worked there and who didn't check IDs. Then he drove out to the bowling alley on Villa and Northwest Highway and parked on the side, facing Villa. This way he could watch the screen of the Northwest Highway Drive-in across the street without paying to get in.

Dave turned on the radio since he had no movie speaker and listened to the Stones singing "Heart of Stone." He used the churchkey on his key chain to open the Coors, and methodically drank. Of all the problems in Dave Wolf's life that he couldn't solve, there were none he couldn't run away from for a little while. By the time he had finished the third beer, he had distanced them pretty well.

Dave needed a friend to talk to, but avoided close relationships because he feared them finding out about his home life. He needed a balanced viewpoint, but had nowhere to get out. He needed love desperately, but received only mixed signals and double binds.

It was May 23, 1967. The night of Naomi Wolf's suicide.

While Dave drank and watched the movie, *Riot on Sunset Strip*, David waited apprehensively. He had avoided coming to this night for a long time, but he knew that he eventually had to face up to it. So, here he was, suffering with his young self.

David had remembered very little of this night over the intervening years, though the Aldo Ray movie he was watching had stuck in his mind very clearly. There were answers here, he was convinced of that, but did he want to know those answers? Ultimately, it wasn't a question of what he wanted. He had been drawn to this night ever since he had begun skimming. Tonight, for good or ill, he would know *exactly* what had transpired. Tonight all the questions would be answered.

Dave finished his six-pack and started on another. His brain was a black, twisted thing, a writhing mass of hatreds and guilt that never synthesized the feelings, but simply compartmentalized them to be projected onto future actions. Young Dave was busy making himself neurotic.

He stopped drinking sometime before the number of cans reached his age. He was dizzy, having left the house before he had eaten much dinner, but he couldn't find anything open on the way home. The boy bumped into the drive, halfway up on the lawn, and nearly fell on the cement when he tried to get out of the car. Eddie was still there, his Ford Fairlane parked on the street.

He staggered, oblivious and unsuspecting, to the front door while David's apprehension grew. It was all he could do to keep from screaming out a warning to the boy. Something was happening. David's fears had grown all out of proportion to the timing. His deeper mind knew something his conscious brain didn't and it was trying to protect that knowledge at all costs.

His pocket seemed so deep as he tried to fish the house key out of it. He finally got the thing, then fumbled for five minutes trying to get it in the lock while David's mind swirled with fears.

Then, all at once, the door came open and the cord began to unwind.

Dave could hear the cries from the living room, his drunken brain working slowly, tying the sounds to a human being only after listening to them for several minutes.

"What the hell . . ."

He moved through the now-dark house, bumping into the coffee table as he passed it. The dinner dishes still sat on the table, the food untouched since his departure. He got into the hallway, the sounds of slapping mixed with the heart-wrenching pleadings of his sister.

"Liz?" he called, guiding himself along the wall in the dark hallway. "Liz!"

He nearly tripped over a dark form huddled on the floor by Liz's door. It was Naomi, crouching like an animal, staring up at him, the whites of her eyes glistening in the darkness.

"Momma . . . what . . . ?"

Naomi stood, blocking the closed door. On the other side, Dave could hear Eddie's perverted laughter mixing with Liz's screams of pain and humiliation.

"Go to bed," Naomi ordered in clipped tones. "You're drunk. Go to bed."

"What's going on in there? What's he doing to Liz?"

"Walk away, Davy," she said, in that same businesslike tone. "Go to bed. Just walk away."

Liz screamed loudly, painfully.

"No!" Dave said, pushing his mother aside. "Liz! What's happening?"

He tried the door. Something was pushed up against it, blocking it.

"Liz!"

Naomi threw herself on him, trying to pull him back. Dave pushed her off. She fell in a heap before the door.

"He's doing something to her, isn't he?"

"Dave, no . . ."

"Isn't he! That fucking Eddie is doing something to her! Liz!"

"Stop it!" Naomi hissed. "She's doing what she has to do. *You're* the one who wants to go to medical school. *You're* the one who wants all the advantages. Just how the hell do you think we'll get the money for it, Mr. Hotshot?"

"No," Dave said, backing away, banging drunkenly into the wall, his hands on the sides of his head. "No. Not like this. No. Momma!"

"It's for you, Davy. It's all for you."

He backed away, crying now, stumbling into things. Naomi stalked him relentlessly, moving through the living room with him.

"You want things, I get them," she said. "Because I love you, Davy. I love you."

The boy's mind was reeling crazily as he somehow got out of the house and wandered around the front lawn in a daze. What was happening? What?

He tried to get back in the house, but Naomi had locked the front door, keeping him out. He could hear muffled screaming coming from inside the house, but he no longer remembered what it was all about.

His car. He walked, falling down several times, to the Chevy. The driver's door was still open from when he had fallen out earlier. He crawled into the front seat, fumbling for his keys. He either couldn't find them or couldn't get them out, for after several futile minutes of searching his pockets, he simply gave out and fell asleep there in the car, his feet hanging out the open door-space.

David stayed in the darkness of his mind, trying to calm himself down. She had done it to him, had tied him inexorably to her own perversity by laying every bit of her guilt on his responsibility. She might just as well have stuck a knife in him.

So, he had lived that way. Locked subconsciously into her formula, he had followed it blindly, his mind resisting any attempt to ferret out his own self-destructive tendencies. He hated her. God, how he hated her. So much more because he was just like her.

He stayed in the black mind a little longer, for there was something else he wanted to be sure of. He lay there, waiting. After a time of darkness, he heard the sounds of someone leaving the house. It had to be Eddie. He was muttering under his breath.

David heard his car start, then screech away. He remained,

listening. A while later, he heard it. A loud pop, muffled by layers of house, disturbed the night for only a second. David thought of the gun that so fittingly ended his life, and how it brought full circle Naomi's perversion.

Damn her.

He left then, traveled back to Malmaison and Silv. He needed no new memories of the next part. He remembered with crystal clarity what Dave Wolf would find the next morning upon awakening and what effect it would have on the rest of his life.

Napoleon Bonaparte rode like a passenger in his own body as the spiritual presence of Hersh commanded the movement of the cannons over the Great Saint Bernard pass in the Swiss Alps. He could use his eyes, but only in the direction that Hersh wanted to look. He could use his mind, but only as an adviser to the force in charge of his body. He hated the presence, and sometimes he loved it. Hersh had been a part of his life on and off since childhood, and he ofttimes found that when the man was busy running his body, *he* was free to think, to plan, to scheme. And since so much of anyone's life is caught up in the everyday pursuits of simply living, the freedom of physical sharing gave him much more time to think and reason abstractly. It was in large part due to his dual nature that he had been so successful at so young an age.

He and Hersh sat a mule, bundled to the eyes, at the summit of the pass, the swirling, snowy landscape whipping frenzy as it met the boiling clouds that locked them all in a never-ending chamber of white. It was bitter cold, the bite alleviated somewhat by the sharing, though both he and Hersh had to be vigilant lest their body suffer without their brains knowing about it.

"Just like Hannibal," Hersh said.

Just like Hannibal, Napoleon repeated dutifully, amazed at how his reading about the famous general had stirred Hersh to such a dreamlike intensity that he wanted to duplicate the feat.

The pass stretched for many miles in both directions. It was May 20, and they were bringing the cannons across to try and cut off General Melas's supply and communication lines at Ivrea, while the Austrian futilely laid siege to the French forces at Genoa who were under the able command of

General Masséna. The line of one hundred men trooped dutifully past Napoleon's position, dragging the long rope attached to the hollowed tree trunks that cradled the eight-pounders and the mortars. It took two days to get the cannons through the pass this way, but it worked. The idea had been Hersh's. Napoleon never thought for a minute that they could make a go of it.

Once the procession passed Napoleon's vantage point, it started down the slope on the other side, toward the hospice that nestled quietly in the valley far below, trickles of bright smoke rising indolently from its gray stone stacks. Troops were camped all around the monastery, the monks who lived there scurrying through the encampments doing their best to see to the needs of the army. Saint Bernard dogs sat on the hillside with their heads cocked, watching the strange procession that snaked its way past them.

"The monks have been helpful," Hersh said. "We should properly reward them."

Their helpfulness is not generated by choice, but reward is in order nonetheless.

"That's how we do it in the quad."

Indeed. I've noticed that you've been thinking a great deal about Rose's boy the last several days.

"Eugene? So what?"

You feel he's ready for power?

"He's an intelligent and motivated lad. I think Italy would be an excellent place to test his mettle."

Isn't he a bit young to rule a country?

"You're no old man yourself."

Well, perhaps we'd better conquer it first.

"We will."

Napoleon felt a jumble of confused thoughts swirl like the snow through Hersh's brain. Then Hersh said, "You don't like my relationship with David, do you?"

You're the one who ran away from it.

"But, I can't run away forever."

We're doing fine. We don't need him.

"You mean, you don't need him. You've got me under control pretty well. I believe you fear his making me well."

Napoleon immediately turned his thoughts elsewhere to avoid Hersh's knowing that he was right on that score. He had discovered over the years how to control Hersh by giving in to him in small ways and manipulating him in large. He used the

man's weaknesses against him, turning them to his advantage.
A well Hersh would be a less controllable Hersh.

"You're not going to answer me?"

You're the one who wanted to come to Italy, not me.

"You gave in when you saw David was making progress.
You let my fears drive us away."

*We rule an entire country, Hersh. We control our own
destiny. Why dilute a perfect mix?*

"Because I'm losing myself in you, that's way. I have no
sense of self, of time and place. Inside, I feel that whatever
belongs to me is disappearing, and me along with it. I know
that doesn't matter to you."

*Why should it? I never invited you into my mind. If you
don't like it, go somewhere else.*

One of the men pulling the rope lost his balance, slipping
to the ground and taking several other men with him. Others
lost their grips, the weight of the cannons threatening to take
them all back down the pass again.

Napoleon jumped from the mule, running to the men who
were on the ground, still holding the rope that was dragging
them back the way they had come.

"Up men, up!" Hersh shouted, grabbing the rope himself
and planting his feet. "Heave on three. Ready? One . . .
two . . . three!"

The men pulled together, stopping the backward slide while
their fellows regained their feet and got back in position.
Within a minute, their laborious trek continued.

Hersh stood, dusting packed snow from his gray campaign
coat. He walked away from the procession, moving to the
summit again to stare down the long sloping hillside into the
valley below. He smiled.

"When we're through in Italy," Hersh said, "I'm going
back into therapy with David. I know he can help me to find
myself."

*I'll fight you every step. If you must stay within me, I want
the relationship to stay as it is.*

"Nothing ever stays the same."

*I'll talk you into pouring wine on your head at state
functions. I'll have you drop your pants in the Council
chambers. I can't get rid of you, but I know how to make your
life hell.*

"I can't let you push me around anymore. I'm going under
David's care."

I'll make you do things like this . . .

Napoleon surged his control quickly, before Hersh could hold it solid. He jumped suddenly from the summit, hitting the hillside and sliding.

The wind rushed in their ears as they began the four-hundred-foot slide to the valley, spinning and rolling, the excitement so invigorating that both of them began laughing as they fell, visions of Napoleon's youth strong in both of them. In some ways they were just alike, just exactly alike. They were moving fast, landscape rushing past them in blurry white lines.

"We've got to work something out!" Hersh screamed into the wind.

Yes. You do what I say.

"Never! We must compromise!"

Napoleon had gotten his legs in the air and was sliding on his back, holding his feet. *How do we compromise?*

"There must be something that you want that I can give."

They continued to tumble, the trip to the bottom taking several minutes. They crashed down into a snowdrift, completely buried, and emerged seconds later on hands and knees, laughing and covered with white. Napoleon stood and walked on shaky legs toward the hospice.

There is something I want.

"What is it?" Hersh asked. "If it doesn't entail my leaving . . ."

It doesn't exactly do that. I'll make a deal with you. I'll help you with your therapy if you do something for me.

"What?"

What indeed, my friend, What indeed.

David and Silv sat in Napoleon's private box at the Comédie Français, drinking wine and laughing along with the crowd at Mlle. George, one of Napoleon's mistresses, who was playing Emilie to perfection.

David was happy, genuinely happy, for the first time in his life. He seemed free from his past, and at ease with someone who understood life the way he did. He'd always dreamed of this kind of a life, and love was the key. He was like a teenager, flush with the passions of first love.

It was hot in the theater, the heat making everyone sweat, as a thousand hands fluttered a thousand fans all at once.

David's cheeks were hot, his shirt damp, but it was invigorating. The orchestra filled his ears; the footlights seeped dirty gray smoke as Mlle. George strutted around the stage. They had interrupted the performance earlier to report that Napoleon had beaten the Austrians at Marengo and secured Italy once more. The news had pumped the crowd even more. The jokes became funnier, the wine tastier, the moment more crystalline and memorable, as if the crowd were creating its own special narcosynthesis to harken back to in later days. They were all making memories.

"What have you done with the wine!" Silv yelled above the orchestra.

David reached beside him and picked up the bottle, taking a quick drink before passing it to Silv. David felt himself getting tipsy and didn't know if it was the wine or the reality making him that way. He rarely got drunk anymore. It wasn't a conscious thing. He simply didn't need it now. For the first time, he was running toward things, not away from them.

Silv drank right from the bottle, turning to look at him with a huge smile on her face. "I love the theater!" she said, and threw her arms around him, kissing him full on the lips.

"I can tell," he replied, hugging her again before letting her go. "Don't they have things like this in the quad?"

She shook her head. "Not enough space," she said. "Drugs were the only recreation the com allowed—a pill for everything."

Her eyes twinkled. David took a great deal of his happiness from watching Silv's happiness. It seemed to him that both Thérèsia and Silv were living an altered existence, totally apart from the mainstream of life. Not being intimately connected to their time and place, both David and Silv were able to appreciate what they had removed from the usual slings and arrows of existence. It was perfect and pristine, and infectious. Antoine and Thérèsia both were caught up in it too.

Silv was like a child. Removed from the restrictions that had programmed her life, she simply cut loose, grabbing at every experience that came her way. Even the return of Thérèsia's husband from Egypt hadn't daunted her. She quietly and efficiently announced that they were no longer man and wife, then used Napoleon's new streamlined divorce laws to make it a legal reality. David had wondered if there might have been an emotional price to pay for such laissez-faire attitudes about life, but if there was, he didn't see it mirrored in her behavior.

"I want something to eat when we leave," Silv said. "Something sweet with whipped cream."

The orchestra reached a crescendo, drowning out conversation, then the curtain closed on Act I.

"You'd better watch out for Thérèsia's figure," David replied as he applauded with the rest of the audience.

Silv narrowed her gaze. "Will you still love me if I'm fat?"

David touched her face. "If you're fat, thin, pretty, ugly, man or woman," he said. "I love what you are, Silv."

"Of course you do. I'm just like you."

"What do you mean?"

"Haven't you noticed?" she asked. "Every day our minds become more and more alike. It's just the genetics of the situation, I guess."

"Whatever it is," David said, picking up the wine bottle and drinking again, "it's made my life complete."

"Do you ever feel guilty?" she asked.

Below them, the crowds were moving into the lobby, stretching their legs, waiting for the next act. Napoleon loved the theater, too, but this was his usual cue to leave. He rarely sat through more than one act. He simply couldn't sit still that long.

"Guilty, how?"

She took the wine from him, staring at the bottle. "Everyone else suffers, while we're happy."

"Should we, then, suffer too? Haven't we suffered a great deal ourselves? Are you saying we don't deserve happiness?"

"No . . . not that. I don't know." She shrugged. "I'm sitting here, faced with unlimited possibilities while everyone else struggles. I sometimes wonder . . ."

"About the downside," David finished. He stood, leaning over the box railing to look at the heads straight down from him. When he was a kid, he used to sit in the balcony at the Will Rogers Theater and drop popcorn or Coke on the heads of those below.

A bald man was just getting back into his seat directly below, his head a target just screaming to be used. "Give me the wine," David whispered.

She handed it to him, face puzzled. David leaned back over the rail and poured just a splash of burgundy on the shiny, bald head below. He watched, fixated by the target, until the man jumped up with the splash.

"Back!" David yelled, and went to the floor, hiding low, Silv crouching beside him.

"Ever make love in a theater box?" she asked him.

"Only thirty or forty times," David lied.

She slapped him. "Then we'll wait for someplace more original."

He pulled her close, and the two of them sat there, body to body, on the floor of the First Consul's box. "I love you so much," she said, clinging tightly.

"I love you," he said, kissing her on the top of the head. "I'm so glad I stayed here instead of going with Hersh to Italy."

"Is the time away from therapy going to hurt him?"

"Potentially. There aren't any rules here. Our situation is totally unique."

"But you'd rather have him close at hand."

"I feel . . . responsible for him," David said. "He needs me. But I didn't ask him to do this. Though, I think that his leaving had as much to do with Bonaparte as with Hersh."

She cuddled close, resting her head on his chest. Someone was knocking on the door to the box, but it was locked and they soon enough left it alone.

"I thought Napoleon wanted him out."

"Only until the talk of destiny came up," David said. "As soon as he realized that Hersh was supposed to be inside of him, Napoleon began working on controlling the man."

"Why don't we go pay Hersh a visit?" Silv said.

"What?"

"You heard me. Let's skim over to Hersh, congratulate him, and see how he's doing. We can be back in time for my snack."

He kissed her full on the mouth, always amazed at the passion that lurked under her surface just waiting to spring to the fore. "So impetuous," he said.

"Come on," she urged. "The world is ours. Marengo's even in the same time zone."

"Why not?" He kissed her again quickly. "I'll meet you at Marengo."

"Beat you there," she said, and Thérèsia put a hand to her head.

David dove into the timestream, centering his attention on

his old friend from Egypt, Sergeant Jon Valance. Many troops
had come back on the same ship as Jean Tallien and had
immediately joined the reserves that crossed the Alps with
Hersh. David had missed Jon's simple affection for him and
hoped to find the man in Italy.

He opened his eyes to frosty breath in torchlit darkness.
Valance was standing outside a highland chalet, overseeing
the chopping of wood for the fireplaces that Hersh liked
stoked to the fullest. Though there was a nighttime chill in the
air, spring had definitely come to northern Italy. The snows
covering the ground were melting patches covering spongy
ground. The treetops reflected no white back to the full moon
that shone that night. They were a dark carpet spreading to
the black valley below.

Hello, Jon.

*You again? I thought I'd left you behind with the heathen.
Welcome to my bad stomach.*

Still having problems?

*Oh, goodness, David. Sometimes it takes me to my knees
and makes me cry like a baby.*

I've told you to leave the spicy foods alone.

They're my only pleasure in life.

Then, stop complaining!

Hello all!

Silv? You too?

Lord, there's two of them now. No wonder I'm a sick man.

Ooh, what's wrong with his stomach?

*Gastritis. He won't take doctor's orders. What are you
doing here?*

I told you we have the same mind. I knew where you'd go.

You devil! Kind of cozy in here together, though.

Snug.

I think I'm going to be sick.

Take it easy, Jon. We'll only stay for a while. I promise.

Is one of you a female?

Little me!

*Oh, Lord, Lord. Almighty are your ways and mysterious
are your means. Though I know not why you have chosen me
as your vessel, I—*

Save it for Sunday, Jon.

What's he saying?

He thinks we're messengers from God.

Maybe in a sense we are. Is Napoleon in the chalet?

*Him and his marshals. They're setting up a government.
Let's go pay him a visit.*

Silv let David take control of Valance and walk him into
the sturdy wooden house that the First Consul had commandeered
for his purposes. Grenadiers were posted lightly within the
two-story building, but the atmosphere was loose. Melas had
surrendered quietly and withdrew. There was really no
danger in any sense.

They found Napoleon in a large family room, woodfire
blazing, along with Berthier—now minister of war—Murat,
Bourrienne, Marmont, Kellermann, Lannes, and Andre Masséna,
who had made much of the victory possible by his dogged
defense in tying down the Austrians at Genoa, then surrendering
when the time was ripe, withdrawing from that beleaguered
city with his troops intact.

The men were pacing and smoking, a few bottles of wine
in evidence. But this was no celebration, it was a serious
business meant to quickly solidify their gains while the
Austrians were in collapse. So, the marshals paced, young
men, excitable, restructuring life in Europe the way that
David and Silv were restructuring the ideas of human life
itself. The atmosphere crackled with life. It felt good to be in
that room.

But Bonaparte. Bonaparte looked troubled. He sat alone at
a desk, the rest of the room filled with smoke and voices. The
reliquary containing the heart of his old friend, Max Cafferilli,
sat before him.

David walked through the room to face the man, surprised,
when Bonaparte looked up, to see that his face was drawn, a
great sadness evident in the eyes.

"Yes?" he said.

"I bring you greetings from your fellow republicans in
Paris, Monsieur Hersh."

Napoleon's face flushed with color. "David? Is it really
you?"

"And Silv, too," Valance said.

Hersh stood, taking the man in his arms, hugging him
fiercely. "I am glad and relieved to see you," he said.

"Relieved? It was you who left me, remember?"

He nodded curtly. "How does Paris take the news?"

"The capital honors its first citizen. Silv and I also wanted
to honor you personally. Congratulations."

"Thank you. Will you talk with me?"

"At your command."

"Good." Hersh picked up the reliquary and turned to the marshals. "We will sleep on our ideas," he announced. "It is time for bed."

With that he marched from the room—David, Silv, and Jon Valance right behind him, a chorus of well-wishes following them from the smoky chamber.

Valance dutifully followed Hersh up the stairs and into a large bedroom that had obviously been vacated in haste. Family pictures still hung on the wall; personal items still sat in disarray on the dressers. It was the human equivalent of skimming.

Roustam, the Mameluke servant, was busily piling more logs on an already roaring fire. Hersh sent him away and lay down on the already turned bed, cradling the reliquary in the crook of his arm.

"Old Max has become my closest companion," he said, then held a booted foot in the air. "Do you mind?"

David moved to the bed, bracing himself solidly to begin pulling the knee-high boot. "Something is bothering you," he said, fighting the boot. "What is it?"

The boot held, then suddenly jerked off, almost knocking David down. He dropped it on the floor and started in on the other.

"I see the glimmer of Empire," Hersh said. "The men downstairs see it too. We will rule Europe together."

David grunted, the boot not wanting to give way.

"That's what you wanted, isn't it?"

"My dream, yes," Hersh said quietly, and the other boot slipped off.

David sat at the foot of the bed. "You're learning the curse of getting what you want."

"Yes. The dream will come, but I fear it won't make me happy. It hasn't yet."

"And it won't," David said flatly. "The only peace anyone ever finds is peace with himself."

Hersh sat up, holding the urn out in front of him. "We grasp, we want, we make ourselves crazy with desire for things that aren't worth having once we get them. Here is the only permanence."

"But you're immortal," Silv said, taking control for a moment.

Hersh looked at Valance in confusion. "But do I want to

be? I'm changing the world, but am unable to bear the truth of my own life. This is all just a dream—and not even my dream, at that. Did you know that Desaix is dead?''

David shook his head.

''I'd made a mistake,'' Hersh said. ''I assumed that Melas would divide his forces like the Austrians always do. So, I dispersed my troops for a great distance around Marengo. But General Melas had other ideas. He kept them in a body and caught me undermanned and without guns. We were nearly routed. Desaix saved me at the last moment with his cavalry, but he was caught in the first wave and killed immediately. If it hadn't have been for him, the dream would have ended right there. He died for my unfulfilling vision.''

''The dispatches we received in Paris never mentioned any of this,'' David said.

Hersh shook his head. ''Desaix has found his peace, just as Max has. He doesn't need to purchase it with glory.''

''But you do.''

''Something like that.'' Hersh set the reliquary on the night table. ''He knew he was going to die. He came to me and said, 'The bullets forget who I am.' The next day he was gone. He might have been the best among us.''

''And you blame yourself, your . . . unhappiness. Don't forget that this was predestined.''

''Is my misery also predestined?''

''You may still have peace, Hersh, but you've got to continue to face yourself and your past. I feel there may be tremendous pain attached to that, but what choice do you have?''

''I'm scared, David.''

''So is every human being who was ever born.''

''I—I want to go back again,'' he said, a hand tugging nervously on his chin. ''But I want you here with me, in case I see something I can't handle.''

''Like what?''

''I don't know,'' he said, too quickly, and stood, pacing to the fire. ''I believe there's something back there that I'm afraid to look at. I need a hand to hold.''

''What about your host?''

Hersh stood with his back to the fire, soaking up its warmth like a sponge. ''We've discussed this, and he's agreed to cooperate if . . .''

"If what?"

"Nothing," Hersh snapped, then walked away from the fireplace to stand before David. "I think I'd like to go back now, if you'll stay with me and help me." He stuck out a small hand.

David got off the bed and shook hands with the man. "All right. But I'd rather have you in Paris where everything's not so immediate."

"I'll travel back within the week. There's no longer any need for me here."

"Lay down," David said. "Relax. Should we give wine or something to the host?"

"There will be no problems," Hersh said, and took off his jacket and vest. He lay on the bed, crossing his legs.

"When you return to Paris, you'll have to train yourself to better understand the workings of government there and the social aspects of the job. You'll flounder for a time, but it's the only way."

"I understand," Hersh said.

"Okay," David said, and pulled up a chair that was near the fire. He sat beside Napoleon as if he were going to read to him.

David found himself slipping easily into his professional mode, Silv hanging in the background determined not to interfere.

"There's something I need to tell you," David said. "What we're going to do is explore the deepest areas of fear and motivation in your life. Reaching these levels, because of Silv's drug, will not be difficult. We'll see clearly . . . but seeing and understanding and accepting are different things. The pain will come in the acceptance of yourself. Do you understand that?"

"I think so."

"There are things that only you can do. You have my full support, but the strength must come from you, the answers, all from you. Are you ready?"

"Yes."

"I want you to go to your earliest days, to days before you remember days. I want to see how you were trained—to eat, to control your bladder and bowels. I want to see how the quad chose to raise a soldier, all right?"

But Hersh didn't hear him. He was already moving through the timestream. . . .

Hersh had never felt more helpless. The weakness in his legs, the poor control over his own motor functions, made him feel crippled somehow, retarded. He stared through bars, watching the woman in the brown robes coming toward him. The fear was unbelievable, physical apprehension sending his body into uncontrollable shakes at her approach.

He watched her walking closer. She towered over him, and as he bent farther back to look up at her stoic face, he fell on his rump and sat there, shaking.

"Good morning, Hersh," she said in clipped tones. "How was our control last night?"

She leaned over and picked him up, his fear near panic now as she held him over her shoulder and felt his bottom.

"Congratulations!" she said, squeezing him tightly. "I think you made it."

Her words were soothing, not nasty, and Hersh felt his child's body relaxing somewhat in the woman's arms. He even snuggled in closer, desperately taking even the barest affection in any measure he could get it.

The woman carried him down the center of the double row of cribs that filled Ward C of Function Training. Head on her shoulder, he watched behind him as other women moved to other cribs and checked the occupants in the same manner.

He was carried into a small room and laid upon a scale, the metal as cold as ice on his bare back. He squealed, trying to curse, but his vocal cords weren't sufficiently developed to do much more than croak pitifully. The woman dutifully wrote down his weight in a notebook, then moved to take his diaper off.

He became aware of the need to urinate, his younger mind totally panic-stricken over the thought. He held it in, though it wasn't easy, those muscles not yet fully developed by use.

He was picked up again, then laid, naked, on a cold white table. The woman began washing him with a small sponge. He looked past her toward a table against the other wall. Another brown-robed woman was laying another child upon it.

"Hersh crossed over today," his woman told the other women.

"Congratulations," the other woman said, then groaned as

she took off the other child's diaper. "It looks like old Jason, here, may never get the hang of it."

"Too bad."

"Yeah."

He watched, his child's self a bundle of nerves, as the woman at the other table unhooked the black wand from the rack, its shiny black tail attached to the stainless-steel box set in the wall.

"If you want this to stop, Jason," the other woman said, "you'll just have to get it right."

She then hooked her right hand in Jason's ankles and lifted him, upside down, off the table. Then she placed the wand on his young testicles and pressed a small stud, the electric charge jarring the child with a loud arcing sound.

The upside-down baby screamed savagely, a primal sound that chilled Hersh's blood. As he watched, the wand was taken from the boy's testicles and pushed into his rectum, the electrifying process repeated with the same results.

Hersh felt himself lifted into his woman's arms. "Okay," she said, carrying him out of the room and back through the ward. "Now we're going to go do it like the big boys do. You want to be a big boy, don't you?"

The question seemed to require no aswer, and Hersh offered none.

He was carried from the ward and into a room of many doors. The doors lined a wall, side by side. The woman took Hersh through one of the doors and set him on the floor, leaving immediately. He sat on the cold floor, the need to urinate very strong. He was inside another room, a tiny, narrow room. Besides the door he had been brought in, there was another door on the wall, facing him. Neither door had a knob. On the floor lay a small hammer. His young self pounced upon the hammer, grabbing it with two hands.

He looked back at the door he had been brought in, saw the eye staring at him through the peephole. Then a small grate at the bottom of the door was forced open, a white mouse shoved through. The mouse, squeaking loudly, began charging around the perimeter of the small room, seeking exit. Hersh and his young self watched it, Hersh surprised to find their feelings exactly the same, precisely the same, at this point.

He began walking at it, forcing it to keep running. He felt the intense need to release his bladder, but held it off for a while longer.

The mouse charged around the room until it fell from exhaustion, Hersh immediately jumping upon it. He held it down, then stood on its tail, the rodent struggling for freedom to no avail. It was time.

Hersh brought up the hammer and hit the mouse with it. His small arms held no strength and did no damage. He raised the hammer and hit it again, then again. He hit it many times until the mouse, eventually giving up the struggle, lay still, its tiny lungs wheezing in and out. He removed his foot and knelt in front of it, aiming his blows at the little head, finally crushing it until it wouldn't run anymore.

As soon as the mouse was dead, the door across from him sprang open with a loud click. The year-old boy dropped the bloody hammer and toddled through the doorway to the small toilets that lay beyond.

There were many children in the room, and several brown-robed women to help them with the toilets. A woman came and picked him up, setting him on a small, stainless-steel potty.

"You're a new one, aren't you?" she asked as she settled him down. "Congratulations."

He had made it. He had run the gamut and won the game. With a relieved breath, his other self let go of the bladder and urinated in the small pot. The woman made him sit there until he defecated, then sent him back out to the woman who had brought him there.

She spoke to him kindly as she took him back to his crib. And when he was safely tucked away, she gave him a sweet that not only tasted good, but left him floating in a euphoric, numbed sea of bliss and serenity.

The first thing Hersh saw when he opened his eyes was Silv's body laying on the floor. Broken and twisted, she looked more like a pile of old garbage carelessly left strewn around than a human being. Her dead eyes stared blindly at the ceiling of her lab, one of them nearly submerged in a pool of the drug she had invented, as it had dripped off the edge of the table to collect to her left socket.

There was a pain in his right shoulder. As he tried to keep his head clear, he reached up and felt the syringe still poking him in the neck. He pulled it out and stood, trying to desperately hold onto the reality he had rejected so many years before.

The syringe slipped from his fingers, shattering on the floor. He shuffled toward Silv's body, Paris trying to fade into the quad. He hated being here. It was a dream he didn't want to know about, a nightmare he couldn't seem to avoid.

He knelt to Silv, her old, withered body suddenly changing to Thérèsia Tallien's, and the hard floor becoming the lawn at Malmaison. The lab tables changed into a rosebush maze even as he watched.

"I'm sorry," he told the body, reaching out to close her eyes. "I had no right to do this to you. Please forgive me."

He stood then, closing his eyes, trying to bring back the nightmare. Instead, he opened his eyes to Marengo. He stood amidst French reserves, banging his riding crop against an open palm as his forces, nearly in rout, were retreating in total disarray. "Courage!" he called. "The reinforcements are on their way!"

"No!" He put his hands to the sides of his head, trying to bring back Silv, trying to bring back the lab. Marengo faded before him, the trees and river reforming themselves. He stood upon an island, high atop a rocky cliff. It was cold and gray. Far below, the winter ocean pounded the shore.

He felt sick at heart, his sadness at being in this place nearly overwhelming. He turned around to stare at the house he somehow knew would be there. It was. But between Hersh and that house stood troops, English troops.

They were watching him.

He turned and ran, but before he got far, a cinder-block wall materialized before him. He just barely got his hands up in front of him before colliding with it. He hit hard, falling backward to land on his rump on the floor. He sat for a minute, shaking, before standing and walking back to Silv.

With every ounce of determination, he forced himself to stay in this place of sadness. He stepped over Silv's body and began to methodically go through everything in the lab. If what he sought was in there, he'd find it.

> *It takes so many years*
> *To learn that one is dead.*
> —T. S. Eliot

David Wolf stood with Talleyrand and watched Napoleon cavorting on the Malmaison lawn with the visiting children and his pet gazelle that had come back from Egypt. Stockings down around his ankles, he ran, laughing as the children squealed and the antelope charged, head down, into their midst.

"What a spectacle," Talleyrand sighed, fluttering a hand in Napoleon's direction. "And with the English ambassador here, too."

"Everyone has to relax sometime," David said.

Prissy bastard.

Not now, Antoine.

I just can't stand it. He makes me sick.

Sick with jealousy, you mean.

"Relaxation should come out of public view," Talleyrand explained. "The eyes of the world are on our First Consul right now. What impression we make on our English neighbors is being decided at this moment. Oh, Lord. What is he doing now?"

David smiled. "He's giving the gazelle snuff, my lord," he said.

"Snuff?"

"Watch."

The gazelle was snorting, shaking his head. Then, bucking his hind quarters into the air several times, he put his head down and charged the group of visitors who stood on the outskirts of the lawn, drinking wine.

The screams of the women seemed to infuriate the animal, who picked out the wife of one of the papal representatives who were there to hammer out a concordat with Napoleon, and chased the poor woman mercilessly across the lawn, her ample buttocks bouncing with each leap she made to elude the horns of the precocious beast.

It finally hooked its horns under her taffeta dress and jerked backward, ripping her skirt totally from her body and exposing her bloomers which were colored the insipid green of the Italian flag. She ran from the lawn, her husband now chasing the gazelle and trying to retrieve the dress from its horns.

Napoleon had fallen to the ground, laughing, Talleyrand shaking his head sadly. "The man is a ruffian. He hasn't the breeding for such as this."

"Those with the breeding fell under Robespierre's blade, my lord," Antoine said of his own volition.

Talleyrand turned and smiled his condescending smile. "Not all, my young poet. Blood, like water, will ultimately seek its own level. Ah, here comes the lovely Madame

Tallien. A woman herself of true breeding, wouldn't you agree?''

''Madame Tallien is a great many things,'' David replied, watching Silv moving toward them from the house. ''All of them stunning.''

Talleyrand held a walking stick in his hand. He brought it up, using it to tap David's arm. ''Breeding,'' he said, ''will always seek itself out.'' The man tipped his cane to the brim of his high hat. ''Good luck to you, young man, in whatever endeavors you undertake.''

He turned then, and walked toward Silv, intercepting her twenty paces from Antoine. The two stood talking, Thérèsia laughing graciously, her face alight. Talleyrand was a difficult man to resist.

What was that exchange all about, Antoine?

Talleyrand intends to take Thérèsia away from us.

Hardly possible, given the circumstances.

So it is, as long as you and Silv are here.

I don't understand.

The times when you and Silv are . . . skimming elsewhere, Thérèsia and I have very little in common. We find ourselves making excuses not to be together.

But you love one another.

The fire goes out of it when your remove the embers of need that drive you and Silv together. Thérèsia is one of the most highly sought-after women in Paris. She seeks the excitement of power, something I'll never have to give. Talleyrand is much more her type than I am.

I don't believe this!

Look in my mind and see that it's true.

David looked, and he knew the sorrow of a love not meant to be. After the initial flush of conquest and the rush of hot blood, Thérèsia had begun cooling toward the young poet. With the infusion of David's and Silv's minds, the love remained real and fulfilling, but without it, there was nothing to hold Antoine and Thérèsia together.

''Solving the world's problems?'' came a gentle voice.

David broke his reverie to see Silv grinning up at him. ''Spaced out, I guess,'' he said. ''What did our minister of finance want?''

''The same thing all men want,'' she replied, ''—my irresistible body.'' She gestured toward the lawn. ''I see that Hersh is having a fine time.''

"I'm really worried about him," David said. "His behavior's gotten stranger every day since the therapy began in earnest."

She looped an arm through his, leaning against him. Despite what Antoine had told him, he couldn't help but feel that this woman would be with him always. The love flowed back and forth between them like an alternating current. He put his arm around her shoulder and pulled her close, protective.

"What do you think is wrong?" she asked.

"You've heard the expression, 'The truth shall set you free'? Well, I have this awful feeling that Hersh is having to deal with too much truth, too fast, and that he can't handle it."

"Are you trying to say you've been too successful?"

"Not me so much as your drug. It's unrelenting. Anything you want to see will be shown to you in pure, undiluted doses of reality. It seemed like a great tool at first, the psychiatrist's helper, but now I'm not so sure. We all, for the sake of our own sanity, spend an amount of time protecting ourselves by bending reality to suit our egos. To strip away all our veils in one fell swoop can be a totally devastating experience.

"To view Hersh's life experience in a completely objective light is to see the rearing of an animal, a pit bull trained to fight. The sentient, sensitive soul that has begun to peek out of his shell is horrified to undersand what he really is. I don't know if he can adjust to that. I'm not sure that anyone could. I've tried to cut back his therapies in order to give him time to adjust to each new revelation, but he won't work with me. He's drawn magnetically, self-destructively, to the answers."

"Look," she pointed. "He's coming back in."

The gazelle had lain down, exhausted, panting on the lawn. Hersh had bent to pet it, then gotten up and moved toward the crowd.

David watched him, fearful. The quad had raised Hersh to be something other than human, and he knew it—and it hurt. Raised to live with his military squad like a wolf in a pack, he had spent his uneducated years being rewarded for directed violence—and being punished when the violence was self-generated. He had had no feelings of individuality, relating only to the pack and his place in it. The pack had eaten together, slept together, taken drugs together, relieved sexual tensions together.

It was difficult for David to conceive of. He understood the imperatives that a self-contained society would institute, but the absolute denial of the individual seemed counterproductive. He also couldn't figure, given the options, what type of event could rattle Hersh out of his conditioned lethargy and into a pattern of nonprogrammed violence.

One thing he did know with absolute certainty was that given Hersh's life in the quad, the total freedom of the dream state could lead to nothing save delusions. Despite everything, Hersh wasn't really crazy in a psychiatric sense. He was troubled, deeply, but the root of his problems seemed environmental and, perhaps, fixable if the man could learn to live with himself and his former lifestyle. Questioning the imperative, he had come up with answers that he would now have to live with. It was at this juncture that David's own apprehensions resided.

Napoleon, sweating, had taken a seat at a table in the shade and was toweling off his thinning hair. A small group, including Talleyrand, had gathered around him as he poured himself a glass of burgundy.

"Shall we go and say hello?" Silv asked.

"Yeah," David said, and started walking toward the group on the far side of the flagstone veranda. "I want to hear how he's doing."

David was as worried about Hersh in the present as he was about Hersh in the future. When he had suggested that Hersh take over more of the responsibilities of state, he had had no idea what directions it would take. The man was direct and rude, ofttimes bungling until Napoleon was able to get back in and wrest control of the situation. Hersh wanted to do the right thing. He simply had no idea of what that was.

They reached the First Consul's table to find Hersh busily whittling the arm of his chair and giving the assembled ambassadors a lecture of the virtues of the feminine sex.

"Women are more obliging than men, it is true," he said. "And in that, I commend them, and owe them, in fact, a rare debt of gratitude. But in all other things, they are useless and should be ruled with an iron hand as one trains a dog."

"I beg your pardon," said the English ambassador, who was sitting right beside his wife, as were the papal emissaries, "but where I come from, we treat our wives with proper respect and value their opinions highly."

"Do you now?" Hersh said, fixing him with a sidelong glance that David knew meant trouble. "Well, that doesn't surprise me. Given that you are a nation of shopkeepers and drunks, you probably need a mother to look after you.''

"Are we interrupting?" David asked before the Englishman could make response.

"Ah, David," Hersh said, offering him an empty chair and ignoring Silv. "I will have need of your services in a few minutes."

"I'm sorry," David said. "I have an appointment."

The First Consul smiled slightly. "*I* am your appointment, the only one that matters. You will listen to me."

David sat, Thérèsia pulling up a chair right beside. Talleyrand winked at her from across the table, and David was appalled to find her winking back.

"Englishwomen always look like such frumps!" Hersh explained loudly. "Why do they always leave their hair so dirty and unbrushed?"

"I assure you, First Consul," the ambassador's wife said, "that English women are just as clean—"

Hersh, ignoring her, spoke to one of the Italian men. "Signóre Compini," he said. "Italian men know how to handle a woman, do they not?"

Compini, a middle bureaucrat with shiny, slick black hair and thin moustache, said, "We do . . . thanks to the auspices of Holy Mother Church, we—"

"Enough of that!" Hersh said. "Your Church robbed our people blind, and we're well off without it. So are you, Signóre. So are you."

"Our peasants don't feel that way," Talleyrand said, and everyone looked at him. It never ceased to amaze David how Talleyrand had the complete freedom of speech around Napoleon, the only person he'd ever seen who did.

"Go on, Finance Minister," Hersh said.

"We run an enlightened government, and rightly so," Talleyrand said, "but the majority of our people live on the farms . . ."

"The farms we gave them after confiscating Church lands," Hersh said.

". . . and are overwhelmingly Catholic."

"What are you getting at?" Hersh asked.

"Do you agree that religion is a great motivator of people?" Talleyrand asked.

"Yes, go on."

"The reverse doesn't have to be the case. The people want

the Church back into their lives. Our citizens in Italy certainly want Pius VII back in Rome. Why not give the people the Church without giving the Church the people and all they possess? I'm sure these learned gentlemen are here at your service and are more than willing to speak of compromise with the Holy See."

"And what of all those Jacobin bishops who rule their dioceses like feudal barons?" Napoleon asked, jumping in. "They'd preach against us soon enough."

"There are more bishops, First Consul, where those came from," Talleyrand said quietly.

"Fire the bishops," Hersh said, nodding. "And who would control the new ones coming in?"

Talleyrand sat back in his chair and smiled contentedly. "Even as we sow, so shall we reap."

Hersh pursed his lips and stuck the knife in the chair arm. He stood. "I like the way you think, Monsieur," he told Talleyrand. "Continue to work with these gentlemen and let me know what sort of agreements you come to. And now, I have some dictation to do, if you'll excuse me."

"First Consul," the English ambassador said. "We've been awaiting audience with you for two weeks in order to discuss the reopening of the free-trade agreements between our two countries."

Hersh looked down at him. "And flood my country with cheap, worthless English goods while my own people starve? No, thank you, sir. But when you're willing to discuss the English evacuation of Malta, perhaps we'll find grounds for common communication. Good day. David?"

We walked off immediately, David standing with Silv and following.

"He wants another session," David told her. "I'm not sure how long it will take."

"And after?" she said, touching his arm. "Will you come and visit me?"

He looked at her face and saw the pixie that was Silv gleaming out through the eyes. God, he loved her. Her love for him was open and without guile or manipulation—freed from the confines of want or need, it existed as an unblemished entity, wholly perfect and complete. He could not consider life without her.

"Just try and keep me away," he said, and pulled her close, knowing that the world was theirs for eternity.

"David!" Hersh called from the doorway.

He kissed Silv quickly, breaking the embrace before he forgot about everything else. "I'll see you soon."

She smiled sadly, and he wondered if she, also, had knowledge about the trouble between Antoine and Thérèsia. He followed Hersh into the house, forcing from his mind any thoughts of an imminent breakup. These things would happen. As long as he and Silv were still together, in whatever form, there was nothing to stand in the way of their happiness.

Hersh led him into the library, which was fixed up to resemble a tent, closing and locking the double doors behind them. He walked to the desk and sat on its top.

"I don't think this is a good idea," David said, moving to scan the shelves for something to read later.

"I feel on the edge of a breakthrough," Hersh said. "Why stop now?"

"Because you're not synthesizing your revelations," David said. "Because you're keeping everything inside and simply moving fast to keep from looking at it. Can you accept yourself as what you are?"

Hersh hiked a leg up on the desk and straightened the stocking, pulling it up snug against his breeches. "I'm not that person anymore," he said. "I can accept it without suffering with it."

David pulled a copy of Burke's *Reflections on the French Revolution* from the shelf and tucked it under his arm. He turned and stared hard at Hersh. "You *are* that person. You've simply been living a dream. But you are that man in the quad, and whatever you discover about him will be a discovery about yourself. I think we should slow down the therapy and let you digest everything you've learned up until this point."

Hersh pulled his other leg up on the desk and repeated the procedure with the stocking. "No," he said. "My personality has been defective because of something that happened back in the quad. You told me yourself that naming my demons would go a long way toward conquering them."

"But this is all moving so . . . fast."

"I don't care," Hersh said, putting his feet back on the floor. "I'm going to do this now. We're so close, I'm not going to back down."

David sighed and pulled up a chair. Arguing with Hersh or

Napoleon did absolutely no good. The man wasn't geared to take no for an answer. "Where did we leave off?" he asked.

Hersh hopped off the desk and took the chair behind it, almost as if he were the psychiatrist and David the patient. "We were going to war," he said.

The smoke always came first.

Hersh the First Consul stood inside the body of Hersh the soldier and watched thin gray smoke trickling into the holding area where his platoon was gathered. The holding area was a gouged-out section of rock attached to a never-ending, dark hallway that stretched out in both directions.

"Point man!" the platoon leader called.

Hersh moved to the hallway opening and saluted the man in the camouflage robes with the lieutenant's sword strapped on his back. "Yes, sir!"

"How far away do you make them?"

Hersh was the point man. It was his job to know these things. He walked several feet into the total darkness of the tunnel and sniffed the thin whiffs of smoke. Then he knelt on the hard rock floor and put his ear to the cold ground. They were coming. A lot of them.

He stood and hurried back to the lieutenant. "They're less than two miles off, sir," he said, "and comin' on fast. They'll be here'n twenty, thirty minutes tops."

"Good," the lieutenant said. "Have the Skins been brought up yet?"

"Be here any time."

"Break out the weapons," the man said, taking a long breath.

Hersh stared at the lieutenant for a second. His name was Dodge, and he had once been a grunt just like Hersh. He had moved up by being meaner than everybody else. The skimming Hersh recognized him more intimately. He had done something to this man. There was something . . . something . . .

"I said, break out the weapons!" Dodge demanded.

"Yes, sir!" Hersh said, and moved back into the holding area. "Weapons! Stop draggin' your butts!"

The smoke was getting thicker in the holding area, the atmosphere more claustrophobic. As his once-and-future body ran through its routines, Hersh tried to tie everything together. He knew, actually *knew*, that something important was getting ready to happen. It hung in the air like the ever-thickening smoke. He could literally feel the moment.

The crates were broken open, the spiked clubs passed out. War was simple and direct in the quad—you went into the halls swinging and took out everything that lived.

The quads had all been governed by a central authority at some time in the dim past, but now they simply fought one another. They fought for control in the ancient, deserted connecting tunnels that had once joined them. This one was called L–23, and it was exactly like every other tunnel Hersh had ever fought in. There were fifty men crammed in here, twice that many at the next holding area back. He had no idea how many men would be charging toward them with their smoke and their screams; he didn't like to think about that part—only the killing, only the thrill of the action, meant anything to him. It was the reason he lived.

His purpose.

"Goggles!" Lieutenant Dodge called, and everyone donned the goggles with the attached rebreathers against the smoke, which was turning the holding area into a fogbound dream.

Hersh watched those around him, figures wraithlike in the mist, with growing apprehension. He felt fear, dark panic, welling up inside him. It was going to happen. It was going to happen soon. He fought down the desire to hit the timestream on a dead run. He had to see this through.

"The Skins!" someone called, voice muted by the rebreather, and Hersh turned to watch their arrival.

There were about fifteen of them, middle-aged to old men. They were pushed into the confusion of the holding area, stark naked, fear rimming their dull, retarded eyes.

The grunts all laughed and pointed; finally, someone *they* could look down upon. No one was sure who and why the Skins existed, but it was a persistent rumor in the compounds that these were the aged breeding stock who had given the soldiers life. From his previous skimming, Hersh knew that this was true. And now, too old to perform worthily as breeders, they were being put to another use.

Hersh was shaking, nearly out of control with panic.

"Point!" Dodge called, and Hersh ran through the confusion to greet him at the mouth of the rough-hewn tunnel. "Get up there and get a fix on them."

"Yes, sir!"

Hersh ran the tunnel, ran through the smoke toward the

dark-faces of Quad 23. And as he ran, his apprehension lessened. It made no sense. The closer he came to danger, the safer he felt.

He ran hard, and it was a good thing. It cleared his head and eased the tension in his body. He could see absolutely nothing now, not even the smoke. He ran in a true straight line, just as the tunnel had been carved. True and straight, he ran into nothing, and when he stopped to catch a breath, he heard them.

They were moving at forced-march pace: jogging a hundred yards, marching a hundred yards. They moved with tiny lights and smoke machines. In the timeless void of the tunnels, he couldn't quite make out the distance, but he could see the dark plates that completely covered their face, and the black skintight suits they wore.

He stood, mesmerized by their approach, his brain lost in the confusion of conflicting emotions. Hersh the skimmer found himself paralyzed. He couldn't make the body he controlled do anything. He had to pull back, had to become a mere spectator, or die on the spot.

He receded, his small, compact body taking control of itself and charging back to the platoon. It took a long time to get back, longer than he had realized it would.

"Ten minutes!" he called as he ran into the holding area, and everyone screamed for blood as they pumped themselves to battle-ready and tied their robes up tightly against their bodies.

The Skins had been brought up near the mouth of the tunnel where the grunts continued to taunt them. They huddled in a bunch, understanding nothing of what was happening to them. They were truly animals, and it was all Hersh could do to keep from crying for their plight. This was not the way to live. Not this.

"Hey, Hersh," Merk from his squad called. "Look at this one."

Hersh moved toward Merk and the frightened Skins. His breath was coming in gasps, and his body kept telling itself he was winded from the long run.

Two of his squad had grabbed hold of one of the Skins and were pulling his left leg out while the poor man begged, "No, please . . . don't hurt . . . don't hurt."

"Look here," Merk said, pointing to the leg. "See this?"

He was pointing to a very distinct, crescent-shaped birth-mark on the Skin's left thigh.

"It's just like yours," Tad, another of his squadmates said. "This could be your Da, hey, Hersh?"

Hersh stared in horror at the birthmark, his eyes traveling up to meet the eyes he had seen in another life. Older, sallower, but it was him. His father. He knew it. He had always known it.

The two men, father and son, stared at one another, his father's lips moving wordlessly, his eyes nothing but an outlet for his fear.

Hersh broke the contact, listened to the others laughing all around him. They were staring at him, singling him out. He couldn't stand the questions in their eyes. Hersh the skimmer pulled back in agony and heard his other self say, "No! This isn't a man to give birth. He's a Skin, just a Skin." With that, he pushed the man out of their grasp to fall heavily to the ground. The Skin whimpered, grabbing at his leg where he had cut it in the fall.

Hersh turned from him, a fire raging within. He had denied him, his own father, his own flesh, his . . . memories. What dark sewage ran through him, what tainted blood, that could deny itself so coldly?

"Light!" Dodge screamed. "I can hear 'em!"

They turned on the big, heavy lights that burned the smoke into a bright, boiling thing, but penetrated no farther than the edge of the tunnel.

"Get the Skins ready!" Dodge called, and the lieutenant drew his long sword.

And they were up for it. This was what they had trained for. This moment in time held the sum total of their life experience.

"Ready," Dodge called, his voice lower. Everyone had quieted now, listening. They could hear the dark-faces, growling low, after their fashion. "Ready."

Hersh couldn't stand it. He couldn't stand his denial, his cowardice. How could he live with himself after this? He knew what would happen to the Skins, what always happened to the Skins. The First Consul and the soldier had become confused, inseparable. He moved, moved toward his father.

Dodge was pushing the Skins out into the hallway, driving them before the troops, a cushion of flesh for a second's advantage. They were Quad 14's answer to Quad 23's smoke.

Hersh and Dodge reached the man on the ground at the same time. His father was still sitting, nursing his cut leg, and Hersh realized that he had always been here, had always done this, his present, past, and future all inked indelibly in the same book.

"Get up!" Dodge yelled, jerking the man's arm. "Hurry!"

"Leave him!" Hersh yelled, pulling Dodge away. "We don't need him."

"Fuck you!" Dodge yelled, jerking from Hersh's grasp and kicking the Skin in the head. "Get up!"

"Stop it! Would you stop it!"

Hersh watched the man's sword-arm come up in a flash, and he knew he could never reach him to stop it. Dodge slashed savagely at the old man, his blade nearly severing the head with one blow. Hersh watched his father sag, the confusion never leaving his dead eyes.

"Let's go!" Dodge called, and the men screamed, following him into the hallway, shoving the crying Skins in front of them.

They flowed past Hersh like a river past an island, and he could feel the separation again as his other self swirled into a strange vortex of confused thoughts and feelings. But Hersh the First Consul was deadly calm, his actions deliberate.

He went to the weapons case and pulled out a club, then hurried to join the fighting. He ran past his father's body to the mouth of the tunnel, a bright wall of smoke, the other side of which held screaming, dying men. He jumped in.

The tunnel was eight feet wide and eight feet high, and once in the middle of it, there was nowhere else to go. It was a snake pit of writhing, crawling humanity, clubs flashing, steel teeth dripping red blood. Hersh waded into the middle of it, his own bludgeon out in front of him, constantly moving, covering his face defensively.

Men jostled, always off balance, as those closest to the walls were continually pushing inward, forcing the fight to the center of the tunnel. Friend and foe alike fell under the aggression of the clubs.

A dark form loomed out of the smoke—black mask, black clothes—and Hersh automatically jammed his club in the midsection as the man rose to bear down on him. The form buckled, and Hersh came straight up, ripping mask and face off in one motion. Men were falling all around him as he continued his relentless push forward. It was Dodge he wanted, only Dodge he cared about.

He reached the front lines, the last ten yards of which were nothing but a carpet of bodies piled two deep. They were pushing the dark-faces back, but he didn't notice or care about that. He only hoped that Dodge had survived the fighting.

He saw him then, nearly bumped into him in the smoke. The man had gutted a dark-face and had planted a booted foot on the dead man's face in order to jerk his blade from the stomach.

Hersh didn't wait or think. He strode straight up to Dodge and swung hard at his head, knocking him against the wall. Dodge crumpled atop the man he had just killed and was undoubtedly dead on contact. That didn't matter to Hersh. He began to pound the body, over and over, paying back the centuries of pain, avenging his father, trying to avenge his own guilt—unsuccessfully.

By the time they were able to pull him away, the smoke had cleared and Dodge was no longer recognizable as a human being. They put him in irons and dragged him back to the compound, sick with grief and remorse, cursing his existence and the harsh glaring light of his own memory.

―――――――――――――――――――――

"And he just sat there," David said, "—staring at nothing. I could feel his heart breaking from across the desk, but I just couldn't reach him to comfort him."

"You can't help him live with himself," Silv said. "You know that."

"I'm a doctor," David said. "It's my job to help people."

They were sitting on the cold stone of the veranda outside Antoine's chambers, leaning against the wall, watching the magnificent summer starfield. The night was quiet at Malmaison, as if all life were holding its breath. Silv leaned her head on David's shoulder and he pulled her a little closer.

"Now that he knows," she asked, "what do you think he'll do?"

David shrugged. "I honestly don't know. I just know he's in as much pain as any human being I've ever seen, and there's nothing I can do about it."

"Napoleon's strong. Maybe he'll reason with Hersh."

David stood and walked to the rail, looking down at the

dark lawn, at Josephine's swans roosting near the small pond out front. "I have a feeling that our friend Bonaparte may hide and watch on this one. To him, it may look like an opportunity to get rid of his boarder."

She was there beside him, hugging his arm. "How old are you, David?" she asked.

He turned to her, surprised. "I died at age thirty-six," he said.

"No, no. I mean, counting all your travels. How many years have you spent skimming?"

He half sat on the rail, one foot still on the veranda. "I never thought about it," he said. "I guess my mind is probably about a hundred years old. How about you?"

"Going on two hundred," she said, "give or take."

She moved right up to him, fitting easily into his arms. "Why?" he asked.

"I don't know. It seems to me that with all our years of crystal-clear insight, we're no closer to understanding things than we've ever been. We've conquered death, but not folly."

"That's because skimming is a curse, Silv, not a blessing." He looked into her eyes, barely visible in the night. His hands went to the soft contours of her hair, fingers smoothing, caressing. "We'll see truth, but it's all a lie. People were meant to reinvent their realities, to blind themselves, to convince themselves everything's all right when it's not. The truth we see makes no sense because there is no truth. I'll take blindness any time."

"Deny reality, then?"

"Every chance you get. I wish Hersh would."

"He was unhappy when he lived in the dream, and you know it. So were you, until you saw the truth of your life. Your invented reality didn't make you happy, either."

"What's the answer, then?"

She moved away from him, folding her arms against the night breeze and looking up into the sky. "I never saw the stars when I lived in the quad," she said, "but I knew, in truth, they were up there. And are they ever up there." She looked at him. "In science, we simply accept empirical truth and deal with that; pain doesn't enter into the picture. In human relations, we deny reality in order to avoid pain, which really isn't avoidable anyway."

"Accept pain, then?"

"Just as we accept joy."

"Easier said than done."

"You did it yourself," she said. "For a time there, you accepted nothing but pain. Now you want to accept nothing but happiness. Why not both at once?"

He smiled. "Story of my life," he said.

All at once there was a commotion in the halls, with much excited yelling and the sounds of running feet.

"What in the world..." David said, and ran into the darkened room. He turned to Silv. "Light some candles."

He threw the door open. The hallway was filled with people, all running, the candles they held lighting small sections of the walls. David saw Roustam hurrying past and grabbed him, the Mameluke's eyes huge in the candlelight.

"What's wrong?"

The man was jerking excitedly. "Bonaparte, he take something... please I must go!"

"Wait... what do you mean?"

"He die! He die!"

Silv was standing beside him. They shared a look.

"Where?" David demanded.

"In his bed!" the Mameluke yelled, and broke away from David's grasp, disappearing into the candle-flickering darkness.

David ran toward the apartments, angry at himself for the inevitability and the fact that he had seen this coming but hadn't been able to think of anything to do about it. He thought about his patient who took the dive off the Marriott balcony.

He reached the apartments, many people jammed in the hallways, grenadiers keeping everyone out. Josephine stood weeping loudly by the door, her servant trying to comfort her.

He made the doorway, turning to Silv's hand on his arm. "I'm going to stay here with Rose," she said.

He nodded and looked at the grenadier. "I'm a doctor," he said, and pushed his way into the ample sitting room.

He made his way to the bedroom. Napoleon lay in his nightshirt on the bed, his face as red as the Union Jack. His physician, Corvisart, sat on the bed with him, while Roustam knelt at the foot of the bed, crying softly. Murat, also dressed for bed, stood silently off to the side, his long hair wild and tangled.

David sat on the bed next to Corvisart and took Napoleon's wrist in his hand. The pulse was rapid, fluttering weakly. The First Consul was still alive. He touched Hersh's face. The man was burning up with fever.

"David," he said weakly.

"What's happened?" he asked Corvisart.

The man was stammering, his face blanched pale. "I—I suppose it was my fault," he said. "I've learned o-over the years to just do as I'm told, and keep quiet, I—"

"What's happened?" David demanded loudly.

"He's taken belladonna," the man said. "I gave it to him. That's my job. I didn't think that he meant to—"

"How much?" David asked.

The man looked at the floor. "A lot."

"How much?"

"He said he needed enough to kill two men."

"Two men!" David said. "Has he thrown up?"

"Yes, many times."

"Good."

David brought the night-table candle closer and checked Hersh's eyes. The pupils were dilated, and a definite rash had developed on the face and neck.

"Damn!" David said. "What I'd give for some real medicines."

"What do you mean?" Corvisart asked.

Hersh was mumbling excitedly, his voice hoarse, his words unintelligible. David turned to Roustam. "Gather up as much wine as you can," he said. "Bring it all here."

"Wine?" the Mameluke aked.

"Do it!"

The servant hurried off. David saw a bottle of burgundy sitting on the nightstand. He grabbed it, pouring the whole bottle on Napoleon.

"What are you doing?" Corvisart asked.

"The alcohol will bring the fever down," David said.

"How do you know so much?"

"Oxygen," David said, trying to remember his pharmacology, "and CO_2. Mouth to mouth."

He bent and began to administer mouth to mouth on the First Consul to the horror of Corvisart and Murat. It seemed to calm Hersh a bit. After several minutes, David checked the man's pulse again. It had stablized somewhat.

He rose from the bed, the doctor staring at him quizzically as Roustam ran in with an armful of bottles.

"Bathe him in the wine," David said.

"I suppose I should ask *you*," Corvisart said. "How is he?"

"I think he'll live," David said. "In a way, he saved

himself by taking such a massive dose. His stomach simply refused to hold it in. He may be delirious for a while, but it will pass. We'll keep a close eye on him for a few days.''

''I still don't...'' Corvisart began, David shaking it off.

''Don't ask,'' he said. ''You don't want to know.''

There was a scream in the hallway.

''What now?'' David said, and ran toward the sound.

He reached the sitting-room door in time to see a strange and frightening sight. Thérèsia Tallien, her face like a cornered animal's, had backed against the wall. She had a wild look to her, and everyone had moved away from her, giving her room.

She saw David, her hands going to the sides of her head. ''No!'' she screamed loudly. ''Not now! Not yet!''

''Silv?'' David said, and moved toward her.

''No!'' She shrank from his touch, sliding along the wall.

''Silv,'' he said again, ''—it's me, David.''

She looked at him, her eyes large and alien. He took a step toward her and she ran, shoving past the crowd in the hallway.

David ran after her. ''Silv! Silv!''

She had twenty paces on him. She turned a corner, David losing her for several seconds. When he rounded the corner she was there, leaning against the wall, looking dazed.

''Silv?'' he said quietly, moving to touch her arm.

She shook her head, staring up at him. ''It's Thérèsia,'' she said. ''Silv is gone.''

''What do you mean, gone?''

''Something...something happened. Something frightened her so badly that it chased her away.''

He took her by the arms. ''Where?''

The woman shook her head. ''Away'' was all she could say. She looked at him again, and there was pity in her eyes. ''David...I don't think she's coming back.''

David Wolf felt the bottom drop out of his existence.

David, in Silv and Thérèsia's minds, followed Antoine down the hallway for the tenth time. He sat in the background watching patiently, looking for a sign, any sign.

He watched himself reach the door, then he walked up and put his hand on his arm. ''I'm going to stay here with Rose,'' he heard Silv say, and then he took the sobbing woman in his arms as Antoine's body disappeared into the apartments.

He sat listening to Silv's voice soothing Josephine while David Wolf ministered to Hersh in the bedroom. Everything seemed right. Nothing seemed threatening. Silv's mind was fluctuating between concern for Josephine and Hersh, while occasionally dipping back to her own life and an incident of suicide that had affected her very deeply at the time. It had been a girl named Suki she had roomed with who had made her own poison out of recreational drugs.

She suddenly had begun to dwell on the drug, thinking hard about it. She still held a quaking Josephine, but it was Thérèsia who was calming the woman down. Silv had removed herself and was thinking desperately about the drug Suki had taken.

It was then that she screamed.

He stayed with her as she backed against the wall, her head a jumble of million conflicting thoughts. It was impossible to sort through the panicked mind to reach the source of her dilemma. One thing he did know: Silv was more frightened than she had ever been in her life.

He watched Antoine walk out of the chambers and stare at her in concern.

The meeting only increased her sense of panic. "No!" he heard himself scream. "Not now! Not yet!"

He watched Antoine approach and reach out. "No!" he shouted again, and ran, and David was riding an out-of-control mind. As with a frightened animal, flight was all that mattered.

He rounded the corner and the next step of flight occurred—the timestream. Silv plunged blindly into the stream, and it was with such horror and such finality that he knew why Thérèsia had said that Silv was not coming back.

He plunged after her, but it was like trying to pick a particular spot on the ocean. She was skimming blindly without rhyme or reason, and he simply could not follow. She was gone.

He retraced his steps, and found himself staring at a somber Thérèsia Tallien.

"No luck?" she asked.

He shook his head. "Her fear cancels out any sense of reason or directed thoughts. The human brain is so complex in its patterns of symbols and connections that when it's operating on purely abstract levels, its actions are impossible to follow rationally."

"You're giving up?"

"I'm giving up this part of it."

She stared at him then. They were sitting on the bed in Antoine's room. For three days he had waited for her to return while trying to relive the moment through Silv's brain to figure out what had happened.

"Does that mean I'm free?" she asked.

David felt Antoine's apprehension. "What do you mean?"

She reached out and took his hands, bringing them to her lips, lingering for a second before letting him go. "It's time for me to go on with my life," she said quietly, not meeting his eyes.

"And that life doesn't include me," he said.

Or me.

She stood, walking away from the bed to sit in a chair near the door. "We were complete, with Silv," she said, and he could tell that none of this was easy for her. "Now it's just . . . strange. Nothing against you, David, or Antoine. This thing for me has been beautiful and liberating and daring and indescribable in human terms. I'll never forget it, any of it . . ."

"But . . ."

"But my life now needs to move in other directions."

She looked small and frail, but determined. This was the woman who had survived the Bastille by hiding a note in a cabbage directed toward her future husband saying, "If you love me, stop this insanity." She was dressed simply but elegantly in dark green velvet, and David thought that she had never looked more beautiful. She was a woman who wanted much out of life, and in the final analysis, neither David nor Antoine would have been enough for her.

"Is it Talleyrand?" he asked impulsively.

"It's freedom," she replied. "Feelings change and shift; their meanings become lost in duty and selfishness. A human being could waste his whole life tied to feelings that don't exist. I have no time for such things. I've never trapped myself by emotions."

"I love you," David said.

"You respect me," she replied. "Antoine loves me, and you know that's true without me saying it."

He smiled. ''Old defense mechanisms at work,'' he said. ''Sorry.''

She returned the smile. ''You're really very fragile, David. It may be your most appealing quality.''

He stood and moved to where she sat, offering his hands. She took them, standing, and they were in one another's arms. ''I'll probably never see you again,'' he said, hugging her tightly. ''I want you to know that I'll always remember.''

She returned the embrace, then stepped away from him, a smile just touching her lips. ''When you go, I want Antoine to come back, so we can talk privately.''

He nodded, feeling a deep sorrow and frustration emanating from Antoine's psyche. He found himself feeling guilty.

''When I find Silv,'' he said, ''I'll send your regards.''

She moved to the door, eyes glowing. ''She's a good and just woman,'' Thérèsia said, opening the door. ''She reminds me of me. Good-bye, David.''

''Good-bye, Thérèsia.''

She was gone.

Oh, God, David. What am I going to do?

You're going to go on with your life, and as the years go by, your memories of all this will provide you with much to dwell happily on.

I can't live without her!

You'll live, and you'll thrive, all the better poet for what's happened to you. Do you blame me for any of this?

Only for the good parts, David. Only for the good parts. What now?

Well, several things. First we're going to visit our patient.

David left the room, turning to look at it for the last time. He walked down the hall toward Napoleon's apartments.

You're leaving, aren't you?

For two reasons. I must find Silv, I'm worried about her. And I can't stay any longer in you after all that's happened. You're entitled to your freedom, too.

You don't have to—

No! I've interrupted your life long enough. But thanks for the invitation. It means a lot to me.

He reached the apartments, getting immediate passage from the grenadier on duty at the doorway. When he entered the bedroom, Hersh was sitting propped up with several pillows, Corvisart sitting with him.

"Ah, David," Hersh said. "How good to see you. I was just asking this quack how many people he's killed today."

The doctor raised his eyebrows to David. "As you can see, he's getting much better."

David sat on the bed, and checked Napoleon's pupils, then took his pulse. "While you've been out of it these last three days," he said, "Monsieur Corvisart has been staying with you around the clock in case you needed anything."

"What do you mean? I'm a dying man. I shall not live long."

Corvisart smiled. "Am I not here to prevent that?"

"You think that, physician? I shall bury you!"

"I'm sure," Corvisart said. "Me and plenty more!"

They all laughed.

"Well," David said, standing. "I think it is obvious that you've weathered the storm. Europe can stop holding its breath."

"And start holding its ass," Hersh said.

David shared a look with the physician. "Can the First Consul and I have a few minutes alone?" he asked.

"Certainly," the man said, and walked to the door.

"Don't forget that ugly walking stick of yours," Napoleon called, "—the one you stole from Jean-Jacques."

"First Consul," Corvisart said. "The cane is merely inscribed with Rousseau's likeness. I paid fifteen hundred francs for it."

"Bah! You and Jean Jacques deserve one another. You're both great quacks!"

Corvisart put his hands in the air and retreated from the room, leaving David and Hersh to face one another.

"You're going to go after Silv, aren't you?" Hersh asked.

David moved to sit beside him on the bed again. "I'm leaving now," he said.

A look of great sadness crossed the man's face and he swallowed hard. "Do you have any sort of plan?"

David shook his head. "None. I have no idea how or where to look. I can't wait around here, though. Waiting will drive me crazy."

"What if she comes back after you've gone?"

"I'll return from time to time and check."

Hersh reached out and took his arm. "I don't want you to go. I need you here."

David patted his hand. "This is your dream, Hersh, not mine. You have an empire to run. All I want is love."

The man put a finger to the side of his nose. "I think that running an empire might be easier. What about my therapy?"

David frowned. "You've seen everything there is to see. The answers now must all come from you. I can't give you a reason to stay alive. If I could, the other night would never have happened. I've helped you face yourself, but I can't help you live with yourself. Will you try suicide again?"

Hersh released his arm. "I don't think so," he said, face fixed in concentration. "It was a matter of grief at the moment. The moment shall never be that sharp again."

"You know," David said, "things are only as important as we make them. Hundreds of thousands have died in your wars, yet I hear no remorse over their loss. This thing with your father will be as important as you make it. Give yourself a break. Pretend he was a soldier in your army."

"That's not fair, David."

"Of course it is! You were a victim yourself in the quad, a drugged, highly conditioned killer. How could you have reacted any other way? Now you mete out the conditioning, and others do the killing."

"That's different."

"Only in your mind."

David stood and paced the room. "I'm not trying to be hard on you. I'm only telling you that it's not your fault, and as soon as you can be a little more objective about your own life, you'll see that. It would be easy to condemn you, on an ethical level, as a killer who brings nothing but pain to the world—but who can say how important a contribution to the well-being of the world your conquests have become? You're bringing Europe, kicking and screaming, into a democratic age that will usher in untold freedoms to many billions of people. Perhaps that cancels out the pain. I don't know. I wish to God I did know. All I can see is that you don't worry about what's happening here, yet you *do* worry about what you did to your father. Balance out the scales, accept your share of responsibility for both things, then realize that all the values are simply made up in your own mind."

"Are you saying there're no ethics?"

"I'm saying that on a pragmatic level we control how we feel about things. Beyond that, I don't have a clue."

"I'm going to miss you, David Wolf."

David walked over and reached out his hand. Hersh shook it. "I really think you're going to be all right. Any remorse, even a little, is good for the soul. It means you're human after all. It means you care about something besides yourself. It means your days of delusion are behind you. I'm going to miss you too, Mr. Hersh, probably more then either of us know."

"If I see Silv, what should I tell her?"

"Tell her I love her."

Hersh swallowed hard, his eyes misting up. "Come here," he said, and the two men embraced fiercely, binding themselves with the contact.

"Don't be a stranger, David."

David smiled. "All the time in the world, remember? Good-bye, my friend."

"Adieu, David. Adieu."

Good-bye, Antoine.

Will I see you again?

No. I have interfered with your life path enough.

Then, I know my best days are behind me.

The best is always ahead, Antoine. Always. Farewell.

And David Wolf closed his eyes, groping blindly into the infinity of the timestream.

> *Two souls, alas! reside within my breast,*
> *And each withdraws from and repels his brother.*
>
> —Goethe

> *There is one kind of robber whom the law does not strike at, and who steals what is most precious to men: time.*
>
> —Napoleon I

> *What we have never had, remains;*
> *It is the things we have that go.*
>
> —Sara Teasdale

It was twilight, the Mediterranean spring full-bodied and bursting hot, promising a summer of intense heat and more political unrest. David Wolf stood on the Hill of Skulls, watching the full flower of man's dogged denial of his own humanity. The Roman procurator, Pontius Pilate, had come to

Jerusalem for the Jewish festivals, and was celebrating by nailing up on crosses as many Jews as he could get his hands on.

It was called crucifixion, and was a rather graphic lesson designed to quiet the small pockets of rebellion that always occurred in Jerusalem during the festivals, when the city was crowded to twice its population with pilgrims eager to visit the Temple. Tonight was Pesach, the first night of Passover, and even then hundreds of thousands of Jews were descending from the Mount of the Temple and pouring into the streets, returning home with their sacrificial offerings of lamb on their shoulders, the slaughtered animals wrapped in their own skins, to begin the seder feast.

There were many men nailed on crosses, but it was not an event of major note on such a busy holiday. A carnival atmosphere surrounded the executions, with food and souvenir vendors moving through the onlooking crowd of ghouls that in another time and place would be pushing close for a good look at the scene of the major auto accident, or screaming for the man on the ledge to "Jump!"

David had been here many times before, always from different perspectives, many times suffering embarrassment that his own ancestors made up such a large portion of the attendant thrill-seekers. Today was a bit different. He was in the body of one Marcus Noti, Pilate's personal physician, who was going through his own crisis of conscience at that moment over the barbarism his charge was capable of. Pilate was the cruelest of the cruel, and Noti could no longer justify his continued service to one whose inhumanity caused such suffering to so many.

Noti was there to jar himself to activity. David Wolf was there to see Jesus Christ and, hopefully, Silv. The first time he had gone to the crucifixion, he hadn't been able to spot Jesus; after that, he had gone and done some study, coming back to find a man named Joshua who had been crucified that day.

Joshua had been a fiery and charismatic rabbi who had come to Jerusalem with his Essene followers in tow to celebrate Passover, just as dozens of other rabbinical sects were doing. Trouble had erupted during one of his speeches, a tirade against the corruption of the priesthood in charge of the Temple. A scuffle broke out in the large attending crowd, punches were thrown, and a minor incident was created. Unfortunately, Pilate was casting about at the time for "examples'' to show the Jews what would happen in a city swollen to twice its size by pilgrims if order was not maintained. Several of the crowd were arrested, along with Joshua as the ''instigator.'' The executions were carried out the next day, even as the sacrificial offerings of sheep and goats were being raised on the Temple Mount, and thus came an untimely end to the career of a man who might have been one of the great rabbis.

Whether or not Rabbi Joshua would have pleaded guilty to the crime of being God, David didn't know, and that particular question wasn't of great interest to him. He was there because it was a historical event, and David was reliving major historical events in hopes of finding his lost love in attendance. It was the structure of time that he was trying to crack, and if there was an author of such a structure, that would surely be discovered once the mystery of the structure itself were revealed.

David cupped his hands to his mouth and yelled, ''Silv! Silv! Are you here?''

He waited several moments and repeated the anthem, getting nothing but silence and sidelong glances for his trouble. She wasn't here. He had known that coming in. He had tried it again because he was simply running out of ideas.

With a sense of resignation, David turned from the moaning on the hill, and from the strikingly beautiful silhouettes that the crosses made against the pink-streamered sky, and headed back down the stairs of the Via Dolorosa toward the Cardo.

The streets were filled with people, the hillsides surrounding the city jammed with the tents of pilgrims. It was a raucous time, with herds of sheep for sale around the Temple by the thousands, and the smells of Mesopotamian spices turning the air heavy with alien perfume. And the people. Jews and Jewish converts from all over the world had descended upon Jerusalem. From Syria and Asia Minor they had come, from Babylonia and Medea, Cyprus, Greece, Egypt, and even Rome. They filled the air with Hebrew and Greek and hundreds of Aramaic dialects in an avalanche of cultural interaction and excitement.

It all passed by David like a wind in darkness. He was the walking dead, feeling neither joy nor pain at the variegated follies of the humans who came within his sphere. He was not of the flesh, and felt not of the flesh. In one form or another, in various-sized bites of the apple of time, he had spent a hundred years searching for Silv. For a hundred years he had walked the endless corridors with one thought, one hope, in his mind. He had to find her. Nothing else mattered.

If all his years and all his travels amounted to one fact of the universe, it was that nothing ever changed. The same life processes were doomed to endless repetition; the same mistakes, the same triumphs, leading to the same conclusions and ultimate failures, were carried on in infinite variations in a thousand different places all at the same time. The passions were the passions of the moment, the insights always the same insights expressed in different words that never really contributed anything to the general sum of knowledge. David, by not feeling a part of the process, found it nothing but boring.

So he searched, all the while realizing the selfishness of his journey. He once spent a real lifetime searching for the meaning of peace in his own existence. Then he had found it with Silv, only to have it snatched from him in a moment. He wanted it back at any price, and the insane merry-go-round of the living world held absolutely no fascination for him. At all junctures, the world and its failings failed to match up to one moment of understanding shared with the woman he loved.

And above it all, much more tantalizing and frightening than the search for the invisible needle in the moving haystack, was the *why* of it.

Why did she leave? Why? What frightened her so that she would run away from the only man who could ever understand her and share her life, her eternity of life? Why did she go, leaving them both incomplete? For the longest time he had hoped that he, too, would fall apart as she had, and then he'd know. But it didn't happen. His curse was a dandy: The man who was drawn to both life and death was doomed to walk forever between those poles.

When the Romans occupied a town, they always rebuilt it to their specifications, with one street called the Cardo, or heart, that ran through town from north to south, and another, called the Decumanus, that crossed it and ran from east to west. David turned onto the Cardo and plunged into the heart of a city that thrived on trade.

As darkness descended in earnest, the face of the pillar-lined avenue began to change. The shops, which filled every available space during these busy times, were shutting down for the holiday. The fishermen from Lake Kinnereth, and the

Mount Ephraim grain merchants, were bargaining away the last of the perishable wares as the silversmiths hawked their golden adornments, called *Jerusalems*, until the last possible moment of daylight. Everyone was retreating indoors, making the extra soldiers that were put on the streets since Pilate's arrival from Caesaria seem more conspicuous. David and Noti were heading back north, toward the procurator's residence at Herod's palace, and a night of reflection. The man would be leaving in the morning, returning to Rome and his family. He's had enough of the wide world. As with David, it seemed a cruel and unholy place to Marcus Noti.

As to his search, David had begun logically a hundred years before. He had considered Silv's personality and possible interests, then tried to track her down like a detective of the psyche. Unfortunately, he had found that he didn't know the woman he loved as well as he should. Most of her background and feelings were locked doors to him. She had never said much about her past, had been almost secretive about it, probably from a lifetime of habit. Unable to proceed beyond his own death without experiencing it, David wasn't able, then, to journey to her real life to find out more about her.

He had begun with chemistry. Since she had been a chemist, he had first walked through a detailed history of chemistry hoping to find her somewhere along the way. His first stop had been with pre-Christian–era Egyptians, Greeks, and Chinese and their early philosophies concerning the nature of matter. Then he had moved directly to the modern era, Napoleon's time, and the work of Joseph Priestley and Antoine Lavoisier. He had been overjoyed to find that Lavoisier was a direct ancestor, and David had been residing within the man when he had opined the law of the conservation of matter, which found its ultimate fruition in Einstein's theory of relativity. But Silv had never come there. She had missed chemistry's most famous moment.

He had been present in the nineteenth century for the bitter debates between Louis Proust and Hersh's friend, Claude Berthollet over the law of definite proportions, which gave structure and form to the chemist's art. During this time, he had spent many pleasant evenings with Hersh at the Tuileries, but had failed to find Silv.

He then had journeyed to England and watched in fascination as a schoolmaster, John Dalton, compiled his atomic theory on the combination of atoms by weight. Jöns Berzelius and his invention of modern chemical symbols came after Dalton, followed by the work of Ernest Rutherford and Niels Bohr pertinent to the structure of the atom. And nowhere did he find her.

He ravaged the twentieth century and its explosion of knowledge, following the lives of literally hundreds of minor chemists and their discoveries, working under the assumption that in Silv's time the aim of history had leveled upon men unheralded in his day. He had moved through the discovery of penicillin and the wonder drugs, and into the drug cult of the 1950s that gave birth to the drug culture of the 1960s and 1970s. He had viewed life in depth and as methodically as he knew how, and at no time did Silv's shadow fall upon the landscapes that he traversed.

When he was finished with chemistry, he had tried history, skimming in great detail all the events that had been judged by historians to be the most important to man's development, then going back and leaning heavily upon events that would seem to be of import to Silv's culture—the use of chemical and nuclear weapons, advances made by behaviorists, the use of waste "dumps." He had gone so far as to spend an entire month skimming the life of B. F. Skinner in the hopes that Silv had at some time come to pay the master homage. He had even keyed on suicides because of Silv's last thoughts on that subject, coming away with a renewal of his own interest in the pull of the darkness, but finding no trace of Silv.

For the last ten years or so he had been hitting things at random, walking into the stream and seeing where he would come out. And everywhere life's parade marched past an increasingly withdrawn David like a television turned on without the sound, until he finally became the thing that now walked the Cardo. He suffered neither depression nor its opposite, preferring to live in a haze of intellectual ennui not unlike a meditative detachment. He felt philosophically bankrupt and as old as time itself.

He had stopped visiting Hersh fifty years before. The man was aging through his host at a normal rate, his ideas the ideas of a human on a limited time frame. After an amount of extra travel, David felt he no longer had anything in common with the man and cut him from the list of things to do. Besides, it hurt too much to visit the old haunts.

And here he was, walking streets he had walked before,

searching in places he had already searched, for someone he knew wasn't there. He had seen everything it was possible for a human being to see, and had done everything a human being could do—and still there were no answers. He felt absolutely and completely alone—worse in that he had discovered happiness and lost it rather than having never found it at all. He loved Silv and hated her at the same time.

A hundred years can be a very, very long time.

"Watch it!" someone farther down the street called. Then there was a scream, and David saw a small boy caught in a minor stampede within a makeshift camel pen about a half block away.

David ran to the place and threw open the rickety gate. The animals were stamping wildly and snorting, the boy laying face down in the center of the pen. Apparently he had been trying to feed them when they had become frightened.

Ignoring his own safety, he moved into the pen, shoving the huge bleating beasts aside to reach the child. The boy was alive, but stunned, and appeared to be cut in several places. David lifted him gently and carried him out of the pen, a group of men surrounding him, suspicious of why a Roman would help a Jew.

A muscular young man with long, kinky hair moved out of the crowd, holding his arms out. "I will take him," he said, smiling. "I'm a physician."

He recognized the man's Galilean dialect and responded in kind. "I am also a physician."

And then something totally incongruous happened. The man laughed slightly, then said in perfect English, "I'll just bet you are."

David was stunned, caught off guard. He nearly responded in English himself, then blurted out in Aramaic, "W-what did you say? I'm sorry, I don't understand."

The young man had moved up beside him, and now began expertly checking the boy's body, first pulling up his eyelids and checking the pupils. This was no shaman or herbalist. This was a real doctor, a . . . Could it be? He remembered back. Mo Frankel had talked about Jesus. Of course he would be here for this Passover. He tried something.

"Do you think he has a concussion?" David asked in Aramaic.

"Maybe a minor one, I . . ." The young man stopped

talking, then stared at David in perplexity. He narrowed his brows. "Where did you learn that word . . . concussion?"

It was Mo! David felt gooseflesh rise on Noti's arms. A familiar mind, a good friend. David wanted to reach out and grab him in a bear hug, but he hesitated.

"I told you, I'm a physician," David replied, and people were beginning to press in all around them.

Mo Frankel was also the man who had killed him, though this was obviously in a time before that had happened. Best that he keep his mouth shut. Mo looked happy and contented. There was no reason to drag ugly reality into the man's dream.

"Look at his wrist," David said. "We may be dealing with a fracture."

The man looked at him with dark, questioning eyes, then bent to the wrist, the boy moaning lazily when he manipulated it.

"I think you broke it, Moshe," Mo said, tousling the boy's black hair. "You found the easiest way to get out of feeding the camels."

The boy smiled wanly, but large tears were rolling from his eyes.

"Come on," David said, smiling at him. "It'll mend quick. You won't even get the chance to lay around and get fat."

The boy smiled for real then, David reaching out to wipe the tears from his eyes. He then looked up at Mo, who was staring at him intently.

"They call me Joseph," he said. "Will the Roman say his name?"

"I'm Marcus Noti," David said, and he was shaking inside. He so needed to reach out to someone. He had been alone for so many years without companionship or understanding.

Joseph took the child from him, then transferred the boy to the arms of his father. "Well, Marcus Noti," he said. "We are all grateful for the way you ran into the pen and saved Moshe. As you can see, it's nearly sundown, the beginning of Passover. We must go to our houses. I will make a splint for the boy at home. Will you join us for the seder? It's a traditional time of closeness for my people. We would all like to share that with you."

"I wouldn't want to interrupt your lives, I . . ."

Mo put a hand on his arm, staring at him with intensity and

feeling. "We would rejoice at your acceptance. *I* would rejoice. Who knows . . . we could talk shop."

David smiled wide. "I couldn't turn down an invitation like that if I lived to be a hundred."

"Good," Mo said. "It's settled, then."

And so they repaired to the house of Isaac, Moshe's father, who was a well-to-do merchant. The man had bought the camels specifically for Passover, using them to bring in spices and herbs from Mesopotamia and brightly colored material from Babylonia.

David and Mo worked together in attending to the boy, David nearly crying to see Mo young and vital, working with two good hands. He had been removed from life for so long that he was sucking up the smallest emotions like a sponge. How good it felt to share, even for a little while, the company of an old friend. He had never blamed Mo for his death, had never felt the man responsible, and this meeting only reaffirmed that feeling. Mo was fresh air to him, a little breathing space. And if dying had to bring him to this spot, then the trip was worth the price of admission.

Actually, it had been providential that David had shown up when he did. Jewish law prescribed that groups of ten were to share seder, ten being the number of people it took to eat a lamb in one sitting, and David made the tenth member of the feast. He shared the matzo with them, and the bitter herbs, as Isaac relived the story of the flight from Egypt, just as Jews had done, and would continue to do, for thousands of years. He opened the door to welcome the specter of Elijah, the prophet, and helped hide the matzo for the children to find.

During the service he drank the four prescribed glasses of wine and got a bit tipsy, realizing that he hadn't really drunk for a hundred years. The conversation had been stimulating, and the sight of an energetic and loving Mo relating to everyone around him made David feel good in ways he thought had been lost to him. And he left the table excited at the human contact, but melancholy at heart over the hollowness of his own life. With so much at his disposal, he was denied the small things that most took for granted. His mood wasn't helped by Noti's melancholy, either. The man had gone gladly to the feast, but, once in the family setting, all he did was pine for his own wife and children who he had neglected far too long so that he could chase after a little adventure.

Somehow, when it was all over, David found himself upon

the roof of the dwelling with Mo, wine in hand, staring out over the patchwork city of Jerusalem, culminating with the great defensive wall and Herod's fortress spiring into the night sky.

"You may be the most tortured, unhappy man I've ever seen," Joseph said to him as they sat on the edge of the flat roof, dangling their feet.

"And you're one of the happiest," David replied. "How do you do it?"

Joseph shrugged. "There's been unhappiness in my life," he said, "incredible unhappiness that will never leave me. But right now, today, I choose to ignore it."

"How can you? Doesn't it just sit there and eat away at you?"

"I live simply," Mo replied, taking a drink from his ceramic crock. "I love my work. I love study. I love the smiles of children and the simple affection that people have for one another. I wasn't always this way, but I've . . . escaped my pain enough that I can put it aside, at least for now. Things like this can only be done one day at a time. What demons torture you, my Roman friend?"

"Are we?"

"What?"

"Friends."

Mo smiled at him, and even though the face was completely different, he recognized the smile and a tear came to his eyes.

"Yes," said Mo, "we are friends. No Roman would have run into that camel pen the way you did. I believe that we have made a connection that goes beyond this time and this place."

"You talk like a philosopher."

Mo shook his head. "I feel a kinship between us, that's all; I feel you reaching out desperately for help."

David had to put a hand up to cover his misting eyes. He felt so empty, so cold. "I can't make myself care about any of it," he said. "I'm a stranger among men."

"You're not a stranger to the Almighty."

"What Almighty?"

"What Almighty do you want?"

David shook his head, wiping his eyes with the back of his hand. "I don't know. Sometimes I think that God is time—time that levels our ideas and our ideals, time that lets us see only a part of the picture . . ."

"Time that heals," Mo said. "Time that distances us from our problems." The man stood, stretching. "I know what you mean, though. The Romans killed a man today, and because of that one death, that one seemingly insignificant act, a future that affects untold generations will be altered forever. Only time can show the importance of events."

"You're talking like a philosopher again," David said, and he stood also, staring out at the stars beyond the city walls. "Have you got a philosophy for me? Are there words that can end my suffering?"

Mo looked at him. Moving close in the darkness, he reached out and put strong hands on David's shoulders, turning him until they were face to face. "Why are you unhappy?" he asked.

"There's no love in my life."

"That's not a reason. Others don't make us happy. We make ourselves happy. Now tell me—why?"

"Everything seems useless and empty to me."

"Good."

Mo released his hold on David and paced the roof. He was like an agile cat, moving with grace and precision. He was so much younger than Noti, yet so much older.

Mo turned to him. "You're a doctor. Does that seem useless to you?"

"Sometimes—not always. I fix them up so they can live a little longer and then die."

Mo laughed loudly. "Dying is a part of the package. We'll have to accept that as the given. But what about the good we do when we're alive? Any pleasure in that?"

"Life is a violent process that cancels out any good. Even the body is constantly at war with itself, with cells and viruses vying for control."

Mo laughed again, this time clapping his hands together. "You remind me of a man I knew a long time ago. We were colleagues. He took no pleasure from the things around him, as if he kept expecting something better to come along. Let me tell you a story."

He sat on the rooftop and crossed his legs, patting the ground in front of him. David sat also. After several minutes of silence, Mo spoke. "I had a patient once, a woman who came to me because she ruined relationship after relationship by being highly argumentative. It wasn't within her character to be this way and, in fact, she rarely even knew why she was arguing. She just continually did it. I decided to examine her physically before trying to figure out why she was so destructive. What I found was interesting. She had a problem with her adrenal gland, a small organ right above the kidneys that secretes a substance that helps to keep the body chemistry in balance. Her body wasn't secreting enough adrenaline. With the problem, she was suffering physically from the out-of-balance chemistry, but her body was trying to adjust itself with the arguments. You see, the high tension of arguing causes the body to up its production of adrenaline, so, when she argued, it put her back in physical balance. With a strict regimen of the proper vitamins, she returned to normal living and normal arguing within six months. Do you understand anything that I've said?"

David smiled. "You're telling me I'm out of balance."

"Just like the body of man, the body of civilization has its own balances—right and wrong, good and ill, inane and meaningful. I don't know why, but all the opposites need to be present in order for the balance to work.

"What's happened to you is that you only seem to be willing to look at one side of the argument. If things seem to have no point to you, then they're useless. If things seem bad to you, then there can be no good. Everyone else seems to be able to take the most important considerations from the most minor things. Why can't you? You know, every day can't be a feast of lanterns. Take the minor setbacks, put them with the minor victories, and look for the balance. It doesn't need to be anything cosmic—we are, after all, animals. What the hell do you want?" Mo stood, dusting off his bottom.

"I guess you think I'm pretty silly," David said, and stood also.

"No, Marcus Noti," Mo Frankel said, "I think you're pretty selfish to think that the world should turn for you. I also think you're a better person than you know. You probably saved Moshe's life tonight. That may not mean much to you, but, believe me, it means the world to that boy . . . and to me."

He took David in his arms and held him close. "Come back down out of the clouds and love the simple things. Stop using your head so much. Give it a rest and get on the runaway camel of your heart." He broke the embrace and swept the whole city up in a gesture. "*This* is life, all you need of it, as much as you want. It's not always good, it's not always bad. But it's always here for you, singing to your heart if you'll only listen."

A voice came from below. "Joseph! Are you up there?"

"Yes!" Mo called back down to Isaac.

"When are you going to sing for us?"

He looked at David, then called, "I'm coming down now!" He embraced David again. "Will you come down?"

David shook his head. "They'll be expecting me at the palace."

"I understand. I hope you don't find my advice...presumptuous, coming from one so young...and a Jew."

"Tonight may have saved my life, Joseph," David said. "I've been away for a long time. Your Passover supper and your warmth and closeness have rekindled some embers I thought long extinguished. I can't promise anything except that I'll try to take your advice for my own good."

"For everyone's good," Mo said, then he walked to the side of the house to climb down the ladder. "Until we meet again, my friend."

"Until we meet again," David said quietly, and he watched Mo put a leg over the edge of the building and climb down, dropping from sight in seconds.

David stood watching the night for a while longer, the smells of lamb drifting with the night air like a sweet dream. Within minutes he heard singing from the house, Joseph's voice clear and strong, rising like sacrificial smoke to his God, a song of the joy of life. And David again thought that things never changed. Mo was destined to be his father figure no matter what place in time the two of them occupied, and that, as Mo would say, was a good thing.

He set down his cup and climbed off the roof, continuing his interrupted journey to the palace of Herod. His thoughts turned to Hersh. Maybe it was a time to visit old friends. Maybe it was time to think with his heart.

Time deals gently only with those who take it gently.

—Anatole France

On loans and alms I long supported life,
I fawned on Barras, took his drab to wife;
I strangled Pichegru, shot Enghien down,
And for so many crimes received a crown.

—anonymous

Louis de Caulaincourt was in the Kremlin stable having Napoleon's horse reshod for ice when David took him fully and allowed his mind to sink completely into the reality of an incredible situation.

Good evening, Louis.

David? It's been years! I'd begun to think I'd been insane in my younger days.

Everyone's insane, Louis. It's cold!

It will get colder . . . much colder.

Why David had chosen this moment in time to visit Hersh he wasn't sure. He had left a large gap—perhaps ten of Napoleon's years—in his visits, and the Russian winter was certainly not a place he would have chosen to visit under most circumstances. Caulaincourt had been his choice of a host in previous visits. He had never again approached Antoine after the breakup with Thérèsia Tallien, and had had his fill of military men. Caulaincourt was an ambassador, a man of high intelligence and esteem, and most importantly, he was absolutely fearless in his outspoken honesty when dealing with Napoleon.

What David had done was this: When he had decided to revisit Hersh after such a long absence, he let the emotion direct him through the timestream, a habit he had picked up while searching for Silv. A great emotional flux was going on here and he had let himself be drawn to it.

"How's this?" the smithy asked, and David found himself staring at a horseshoe riveted with sharp studs for traction on ice.

"Good," David replied. "Do all of the household this way, and prepare for the rest of the horses."

Is he here?

In the palace. We'll go in now.

The stables were ornate and Byzantine, tiled in blues and yellows with scalloped wooden eaves, leading David to think of the gingerbread cottage that lured children to their deaths in the fairytale of Hansel and Gretel. But it still smelled like a stable, and David was glad enough to walk out into the fresh, twilight air.

Caulaincourt was depressed, his mind overtaken with a grim inevitability that frightened David. And as he picked the carcass of the man's brain, he knew that there was much to be frightened about.

Hersh had invaded Russia with 800,000 men, picking Moscow as the prize he needed to bring Tsar Alexander to the negotiating table and solidify his empire. But he had reached the great city with less than a quarter of his Grand Army intact, only to find it deserted with no one to fight *or* negotiate with. The blank vastness of the huge country was doing to Napoleon what no mortal army had ever been able to do.

He walked into the courtyard, the last rays of the setting sun glinting off the towering spires and golden roofs of the city's churches in a dazzling farewell to the day. It *was* like a fairy tale, a magnificent, deserted dream city in the midst of an infinity of desolate country.

What happens now?

Alexander will never negotiate, and the worst of winter draws nearer daily.

Will he winter here, then?

He's an impatient man, David. I just don't know what he'll do.

The Kremlin was a palace of Italian design, heavy like pasta and garlic, made from stone blocks reminiscent of the glory of Rome. Napoleon's quarters were at the head of an incongruously designed marble staircase leading way up into the building.

Caulaincourt bundled his greatcoat tighter around himself and hurried up the stairs, passing Berthier and Murat coming down.

"Is he in there?" David asked.

Murat, looking more like a circus ringmaster than a general, rolled his eyes. "He's busy freeing the serfs," the man replied.

David was taken aback. Berthier, chief of staff, had no light in his eyes. He was drawn like a sleepwalker, confused like a small child at the death of someone close. Murat, once so dashing and wild, now seemed small and frightened, his once tangled mane of hair shortened and streaked with gray. King of Naples now, he seemed ill at ease in the trappings of war.

Louis, I . . .

Much has changed since your last visit, David.

They climbed the stairs and moved past the contingent of Imperial Guard who barred the way, more bodyguards than David had ever seen for Hersh.

The cold seemed to permeate everything, David sunk in enough to be highly uncomfortable. He couldn't imagine having to be there. He couldn't imagine not being able to leave. When he had thought of the simplicity of human life, he wasn't taking into account the complex emotional pulls that take that simplicity away.

David started when they walked in the Tsar's study and saw Hersh there. The man had aged horribly. Barely forty years old, he looked all used up. Deep physical pain and exhaustion screamed out of his face, and he had put on a great deal of weight. David was looking at a broken man.

Napoleon sat at the Tsar's massive desk, Max Cafferilli's reliquary near at hand. No secretary was present. He was taking notes in his own hand, always a mistake for a man with totally illegible handwriting.

He moved to stand before the desk, the roaring fire taking the chill from the air. Napoleon just flicked him with tired eyes.

"So, Louis," he said, "are you finished tying up my blacksmith's valuable time?"

"This is no trifle," Caulaincourt said. "We need to do this for all your horses before winter sets in."

"Caulaincourt imagines himself frozen already," Napoleon said. "We won't be here long enough to worry about ice. Now that we've taken his largest city, Alexander will have to come to terms."

"You could occupy all of his cities and he'd never sit at the table with you as long as you're in Russia. His mother thinks you're the Antichrist—and the real power resides in her."

"Just leave the strategy to me, Ambassador."

"And you leave the analysis to me, Mr. Hersh."

Napoleon looked up slowly from his work, a smile gradually spreading across his face. "I've thought of you a thousand times," Hersh said.

"Memories," David said, and walked around the desk to embrace his former patient. The man held onto him. When they parted, David looked into his eyes. "You don't look well."

Hersh nodded sadly and sank back to his chair, indicating another by the side of the desk for David. "My lifestyle ravishes me," he said. "Fifteen years of mobile warfare and continual work can take it out of one.'' He smiled. "I suppose that's one of the problems with having two people share the same body—it wears out twice as fast.''

"It's deeper than that," David replied.

"Of course it is," Hersh said. "I'm a victim of myself, of the forces I've set in motion. I never thought any farther than the accomplishment of my dream. What I didn't realize is that once I realized the dream, there was nothing left but to lose it. No one tells you about the horrors of getting what you want. Dreams die, just like everything else. Then what's left?''

"Other dreams?''

"I've ruled the world, David. Where does one go from there?''

"Other worlds, worlds of science, worlds of the mind, of contemplation.''

Hersh stood slowly, painfully, and walked to the fire, turning from it and putting his hands behind his back. "I'm tired, very tired. I didn't want this war with Alexander. I tried to make him my ally to keep the dogs from nipping me into millions of tiny pieces, and he turned his back on me. I've been at war for as long as I can remember. I don't want to fight anymore, but I don't know how to stop. I'm being pressured on a hundred different fronts. The English won't leave me alone because they fear a united continent that could challenge them on the high seas and end their trade empire.''

"It's called cause and effect," David said. "The world stops turning for nobody.''

"There are in me two distinct men: the man of head and the man of heart," Hersh said. "The man of the head throws nearly a million men into the Russian wasteland without thought and divorces his beloved in order to make a political marriage. The man of the heart yearns for affection and makes his relatives and in-laws kings and queens of Europe while exalting to lofty positions generals of inferior ability because of old friendships. The end result: brothers and sisters who run their thrones in opposition to France and marshals in Spain who hate each other to such an extent that they are desperate at the thought of carrying out a movement that might add to the glory of another. And Talleyrand, a man I loved like no other, is merely a devil who beguiles me while selling my secrets to foreign powers. It was he who insisted that I seize Enghien, the royalist, on German soil and execute him. It was he who insisted that I invade Spain, then when I kicked out Ferdinand, the Spanish king, he invites the man to live in his chateau in Valençay, a chateau that *I* gave him. You saw all the guards outside?''

David nodded. ''I wondered about that.''

''Only the royalists used to hate me,'' Hersh said, moving back to sit heavily at the desk once more. He coughed, a nagging, chronic cold. He took a throat pastille from his tortoiseshell case and popped it into his mouth. ''Now everyone hates me . . . and they call themselves patriots.''

''Well, you did declare yourself Emperor,'' David said, removing the greatcoat and laying it across his lap. ''That is, to some, an admission of purpose.''

''It was necessary for the line of succession,'' Hersh said as he sucked the pastille. ''The world had to know that the French government would not simply depend on one man. And now I have a son, an heir.'' He pointed to a portrait above the mantle, by Horace, of a small child in uniform. ''The King of Rome. I shall succeed myself.''

''Not with a mortal, you won't,'' David said.

A darkness crossed Hersh's face that David couldn't quite figure out. ''I feel things are beginning to unravel,'' he said. ''Something's wrong here . . . with all this. Am I waking from the dream?''

''You're living the mortal cycle. You're not a dreamer anymore, you're human. If you don't like this . . . skim away.''

''It was worse in the timestream, David. You know what it's like there . . . everything is disjointed and nothing makes sense. At least here there's an illusion of reality, of meaning. We've tried to pin the Russians down here, but they refuse to stand and fight. They're always withdrawing, always moving. When you finally catch them and attack, they never surrender. They must be killed, one by one, like machines. They are fortresses that must be demolished by cannon. It *means* that much to them. The ultimate stakes make the contest ultimately meaningful. No, David, there's nothing for me in the timestream to equal that.''

''And what of Josephine?'' David asked, watching the lines deepen around the man's eyes.

''She has Malmaison,'' Napoleon said after a moment.

''Her gardens,'' David said, thinking of many happy hours spent in the great woman's company.

''Our gardens,'' Hersh said, words choking. ''I . . . visit

occasionally. She takes very few visitors, not even her old friends. She pines, I'm afraid. I let my host have his way with that. If only my precious flower had been able to bring forth an heir. . . ." He left the words drift off, and stared down at the desktop before him, breathing deeply.

David stood, uneasy, gazing around the room. The Tsar had left nothing behind to skim except a big empty room and a wall map of his huge country. He walked to the window and gazed out over Moscow. It was dark now, very dark. There was nothing to see.

"What happens when your host dies?"

"I like being mortal, David," Hersh said. "I'm not like you; I don't live with a lot of lofty ideas about life and happiness. I'm a soldier and I picked the ideal soldier's life. I can't stand what's happened to my dreams, but I wouldn't trade them for anything. I've been trying to accomplish something, and that's important to me, even if it's a meaningless display to you."

"Will you die with your host, then?" David asked, turning to him.

"Perhaps," Hersh said. "I suppose you think I'm a fool."

"Oh, no," David said softly. "I envy you. God, how I've tried to think in those terms. I just don't have the courage to do it."

Hersh stood and retrieved a large pasteboard case full of papers from under the desk. "Perhaps it's just not your time yet."

"There's no such thing as time," David countered.

"To us, there is," Hersh said, and pulled a letter out of the sheaf of papers he held in his hand and gave it to David. "Silv left this."

"Silv!" David said, and grabbed the letter from him. It was addressed to Hersh. He opened it. "When did you see her?"

"I didn't," Hersh said. "I found this among my papers one day. I don't even know how long I carried it before finding it."

"I don't—"

"Read."

David looked at the papers in his hand. The first was a note to Hersh, asking him to give the letter to David. David put the note aside and read the letter with trembling hands:

* * *

MY LOVE,
I felt I owed you an explanation. The night I
disappeared from Malmaison, I was quite fright-
ened. I had been trying to remember something that
had been extremely important to my childhood, hav-
ing to do with a drug I had invented. It was gone,
just gone. I should no more have forgotten that drug
than my own name. Then I realized—brain death
was setting in. We were wrong about the timelessness.
Time passes slowly in the stream, but it does pass;
synapses must spark, electrons must flow; nothing
stops, even for immortals. My brain cells are dying
slowly, taking a little more of my memories with
them as they go. Slow death, as my mind winks out
of existence cell by cell.
I can't be with you anymore. I simply can't bear the
thought of you having to watch me go a piece at a
time. I am satisfied where I am. Please don't search
for me . . . for what's left of me. I couldn't stand your
pity.
Don't try to trace me through the letter. I delivered it
deviously and you won't be able to track it. Don't
try. Know that I love you dearly. I pray that my very
last memory will be of you.
                                              SILV

David reread the letter. If Silv was dying, so was he. There
was an end, at least to him. Caulaincourt's mouth went dry.
Poor Silv, dying alone. He wondered if the process had begun
on him yet, if whole bits of his past were simply snuffing
themselves out without his even knowing it.

He looked at Hersh, and they shared an understanding that
neither one of them had known before. Hersh would die
alone, too, the last of them. Now he knew why the man's face
had darkened when he had mentioned mortality.

"What are you going to do?" Hersh asked.

David slowly refolded the letter and put it back in the
envelope, then stuck the envelope in Caulaincourt's pocket.
"I'm going to find Silv," he said. "Now more than ever, she
needs me."

Hersh brightened, his face breaking into a grin. "Did you
hear yourself?" he asked, laughing loudly. "You said, 'she
needs me'!"

"So?"

"You're giving, David!" he said, running to David and catching him in a big hear hug. "You care more about somebody else than you do about yourself. Great Gods!" He raised his hands to the ceiling. "Maybe there's hope for me, too!"

David smiled with him. "I never thought there'd be so much jubilation over my death sentence."

Hersh laughed again. "Oh, David, for such a smart man, you sure are stupid. Death...it means nothing. Living...living with yourself; now, that's something to be proud of!"

There was a commotion just outside the door. It burst open and Murat rushed in, his hair hanging down wildly in his face, his eyes wide with fear. He was out of breath.

"The city..." he said, pointing back the way he had come. "It's horrible...the city..." He was gasping, trying to get his breath.

David and Hersh rushed to the window and looked out. The dark night that David had seen wasn't a dark night at all. It was smoke choking everything out. The city, all of Moscow, was in flames.

"Someone should have watched the troops more carefully!" Hersh yelled. "Why didn't—"

"Your Majesty," Murat gasped, still breathing hard. "It wasn't the troops...all the firefighting equipment has been taken from the city. The Russians...they did this themselves!"

Both David and Hersh turned back to the fire. Huge orange flames lit the night as far as they could see in all directions. It was an overpowering sight, the death of such beauty, the obsession of character that would lead to its destruction. The city was crying out its emotion, its hatred of the invaders.

Hersh was shaking, tears in his eyes. David put an arm around his shoulder and pulled him close. "It ends here," the emperor said, orange light dancing on his sallow face. "We'll have to fight our way out of this damned country now. It's a small step from the sublime to the ridiculous, such a small step."

"You wanted to be human," David said. "This is what it means."

He looked up then, and David had never realized what a frail creature he really was, like a delicate glass figurine. "I want to see my wife," he said in a small voice. "I want to see my child, to hold the King of Rome."

"Skim to them," David said.

Hersh shook his head. "I got us into this. The least I can do is try and get us out."

"Now who's being unselfish?"

Napoleon nodded slowly. "I've had a good teacher."

And as David stood there watching the uncontrollable blaze, an idea occurred to him as to how he might find Silv.

"No, no," Sigmund Freud said, setting down his coffee cup. "The word is *intrusion*, not *association*. It's the concept of preconscious ideas interjecting themselves into conscious thinking. It's basically the cornerstone upon which all of my psychoanalytic theories are based."

"And you developed the concept with Breuer?" David asked, sliding his chair in a bit farther under the umbrella to avoid Vienna's bright summer sunshine.

They sat around a large table at the Café Metropole on the wide, lazy Ringstrasse Boulevard. Farther down the block the monstrous Vienna State Opera House and its neo-Renaissance architecture dominated the street. Beyond that, the four-hundred-fifty-foot tower of St. Stephen's Cathedral reached to the heavens in gothic splendor, standing quiet watch over the tomb of Frederick III.

The year was 1902, Napoleon was nearly a hundred years gone, and the pace of an industrial world hadn't caught up with the slow-moving casual elegance of the city on the Danube. David had intruded himself into Freud's small circle of students, dubbed the Vienna Psycho-Analytical Society, Freud himself two years away from publishing *The Psychopathology of Everyday Life* that was to bring him a measure of deserved fame.

"Breuer, yes," Freud said, staring at David with intensity. "I was studying his techniques of hypnotism in the treatment of hysteria. We were analyzing a woman named Elizabeth under hypnosis, when she began to form her own intrusions in a free flow. I stupidly asked her some questions and she berated me for interrupting her train of thought."

The five other students around the table laughed at the story, Freud looking surprised. He stared at them in perplexity until they quieted down.

"It was then," Freud continued, "that I was struck with the notion that has been my life's work ever since: that all vital phenomena, including psychical ones, are rigidly and lawfully determined by the principle of cause and effect.''

"So, then, every thought is important, and should be reported to the physician," David said.

"Within reason," Freud replied, and absently sipped his coffee. The breeze carried the smell of pastry as carriages traveled slowly up and down the boulevard. "If the physician doesn't exercise some control over the direction of the patient's intrusions, you'll find that they can merely be decoys to help conceal the real cause of neurosis from both patient and physician."

"So, in other words," David said, "the physician directs the patient, through *Einfall*, intrusion, toward a predetermined end."

Freud smiled, pursing his lips. "Sexual ends," he said. "Knowing where the neurosis comes from to begin with, helps one to direct the thinking back to that."

"What if you're not looking for a source of neurosis?"

"Then you have no need for a patient!" Freud said, and the assembled laughed, the master joining them this time.

David pulled at his stiff collar, his dark suit heavy with sweat. Though Vienna was casual, it still wasn't southern California. After the laughter abated, he pressed on. "What if you are looking for a specific point, a life direction, for example? And you want to search for it psychologically."

"Like a detective?" Freud said, then narrowed his gaze. "I've never thought of such a situation before. You're speaking of a combination of environmental factors that would point to future decisions."

"Exactly," David said, thinking of Hersh. It had struck David, seeing as how Hersh and Silv had come from the exact same controlled environment, that he could do associative tests with Hersh that might be able to show where Silv had gone. "How could one go about something like that?"

Freud set his cup down and leaned back in his chair, his hands behind his head. "This is pure speculation, obviously, and theoretical in that I can see no situation in which it could be needed. But . . ." He drew out the last word, making the students laugh again. "It seems to me, that if one made out a list of words to associate with that were totally directed toward the end you were searching for, that with the proper control by the physician, a real direction could be ascertained

...just like when we direct the patient toward the sexual reasons for his neurosis.''

"It could work, then?''

Freud straightened and leaned upon the table, pointing a finger toward David. "Yes. *If* the physician is talented enough to determine the proper direction of his questioning.''

"Thank you, Dr. Freud,'' David said. "You don't know what this means to me.''

The great man's eyes twinkled. "Does it mean enough for you to pay for the coffee today?'' he asked.

> *The peace we now see*
> *will run*
> *till the next war begins whereupon peace*
> *will be ushered in*
> *at the end of the next war.*
> —Carl Sandburg

> *Before him, did ever a man gain an empire simply*
> *by showing his hat?*
> —Balzac

David stood with the fifth line regiment of French regulars and barred the Grenoble Road, the mountain pass that would be remembered in history as the *Route Napoleon*.

His host was an amiable enough young man named Roger Chappe, once of the Imperial Guard, now recently back from exile. They were there on the unpleasant business of keeping the once Emperor of France from becoming so again.

After the Moscow debacle, the string had unwound quickly for Hersh. A new politics, made possible by the very existence of Napoleon, was taking over Europe. The old monarchies were beginning to dissolve, replaced slowly by an enlightened proletariat that wanted no more of Napoleon's empire than it did of the ancient regimes. Times were changing, and it seemed to David, the Emperor had begun to outlive himself.

An alliance of nations had been formed that wore down what was left of the Grand Army, finally culminating with the surrender of Paris and Napoleon's abdication on April 12, 1814. The great man was sent to exile on Elba, and Louis XVIII was put on the French throne.

David was in the front ranks of the grenadiers, the white cockade of the royalists in place of the tricolor on his hat. It was March, the air still cold, the mountain road bare and hard. The snow-covered Alps stretched around them, a physical wall to divide nations. Colonel Delessart was moving through the lines, calming the troops; for before them, one hundred yards down the road, stood Napoleon himself at the head of a column of a thousand of his personal guard, incredibly, marching back to retake his throne.

It was a return from the dead, and David smiled to think that this was right up Hersh's alley. Who else would have the courage and blind faith in the will of his people to think he could escape exile, march without an army into enemy territory, and come away victorious? David could see them down the road, Napoleon in his familiar gray campaign coat, sitting atop his mule.

"Do you hear that?" Rapp, the man next to him, asked.

"It sounds like music," David said. "I can't make it out, it's..."

"'La Marseillaise,'" someone whispered in the rank behind, and as the guard moved closer its sounds became clearer.

David felt his eyes tear, others openly weeping. "La Marseillaise," the sound of the Revolution, the song of the people, had been banned when the royalists took power again. It tore deeply into most of them, a song of freedom to rend their hearts. David knew, then, that Napoleon's day wasn't over yet.

"Courage, men," Captain Randon of Grenoble called from his horse. "He hasn't many men. We can end this here."

"What about us?" Rapp said, his cheeks streaked with tears. "Don't we count?"

"He's raised the tricolors," David heard his host say, and Hersh began riding toward the regiment, leaving his small force behind, their muskets trailing.

"He's coming alone!" someone called, and the music swelled, electrifying the regiment.

"Muskets ready!" Randon called, and about half the regiment made a dispirited gesture at raising their weapons.

When he drew to within range of their guns, Napoleon dismounted and walked toward the regiment on foot, his head high, bearing proud. David now wept without shame. His feelings for Hersh were indescribable at this moment. His former patient, alone and unprotected, was walking proudly into the path of Death, confident that his record of deeds and his personality itself would not consign him to the ashes. It was an act of pure madness and pure faith, and a thrill ran through David that could only be described as religious.

"There he is!" Captain Randon yelled. "Fire! Fire!"

The man drew closer, and the guns leveled at him but remained silent. Napoleon moved close, within twenty feet, and drew apart the lapels of his overcoat.

"If you want to kill your Emperor," he called in a loud voice, "here I am!"

Randon had jumped from his horse, and ran to the men in the front ranks. "Fire!" he screamed, grabbing at their muskets. "Fire!" The man moved to David, his face red with rage. "Fire right now!" he demanded.

David pulled out his ramrod and dropped it down the barrel of the empty weapon, holding it in the air and rattling it around. "Just see if I want to kill you!" David screamed, then turned to the regiment. "Long live the Emperor! Long live the Emperor!"

The shout was picked up immediately, the men pulling off their shako caps and sticking them on the ends of their bayonets. They rushed to Hersh, waving their shakos above their heads, cheering the last hurrah of the Grand Empire.

Everyone on both sides broke ranks, rallying to the Emperor and embracing one another. Men were breaking into their haversacks and pulling out their own tricolors. They threw down the cockades and became Napoleon's soldiers once more.

David shoved through the confusion to Hersh, the two men embracing upon discovery.

"You have found me on a very great day, my friend!" Hersh yelled above the noise.

"On purpose, I'm afraid," David said. "I followed the emotions here. I need your help."

"Fine, fine!" Hersh said. "Let us continue our journey and we'll talk."

Order was brought to the ranks, the infantry joining Napoleon's Polish lancers, doubling the size of his "army" to nearly two thousand. Grenoble and its royalist garrison would be the first test of wills on the march to Paris, and Hersh wanted to face it as quickly as possible. He was testing the water for dreams.

A mule had been procured for David, and he rode at the head of the column with his former patient.

"So, what do you think of all this?" Hersh asked once they were underway. "Do you think me still insane?"

"Insane, but not delusional," David said. "This world is yours. You know exactly what you're doing."

"That makes me feel better than you can imagine . . . and for a very special reason."

David looked at him. Though tired looking, the man still had a twinkle in his eye. "What reason?"

"My secret," the man said. "Maybe I'll tell you sometime."

"What made you come back this way?" David asked.

Hersh shrugged. "It was simple enough," he said, "and, perhaps, necessary. I looked at it like this: if the people and army don't want me, at the first encounter thirty or forty of my men will be killed, the rest will throw down their muskets, I shall be finished, and France will be quiet. If the people and the army do want me—and I hope they will—the first battalion I meet will throw itself into my arms. The rest will follow."

"Quite a gamble, Monsieur Hersh."

"France does not want the Bourbons," Hersh replied simply. "The spirit of republicanism still lives. Louis didn't bring back the monarchy, he merely ascended *my* throne."

"Your throne has cost you a great deal. I understand Talleyrand handed Paris over to the allies."

Hersh smiled sadly. "To Talleyrand, treason is merely a matter of dates. He gave away a city that could have been saved, and it was he who declared Louis king of France. Like a cat, he lands on his feet. My Empire has suffered more from Talleyrand than from a thousand princes of Austria."

"You don't seem bitter."

He shook his head. "I've always done just what I've pleased, haven't I? I suppose I shouldn't get too angry if others do the same. They all deserted me—my own family, my marshals, my people—but, as you know, David, forever is a long time."

David could see riders approaching farther down the road. "There's something about your philosophy that I don't quite understand."

"It's the destiny of cause and effect, David," Hersh said. "The reason why I fought, why I had always to fight, was simple: I achieved my throne by conquest. Should I defeat the King of Spain, he returns beloved to his capital and lives with the loss. Should I be defeated, my reign is finished and I am

no more. I was trapped by that concept. So, I tried to set up a
dynasty to help me attain peace and rule still, but events were
already moving too fast . . . Do you know that the Empress
Marie and the King of Rome have been spirited off to
Austria?''

"She was not even allowed to share your exile with you,"
David said. "I'm sorry."

Hersh waved it off, his own attention caught by the closely
approaching riders. "Here's my point: Those who shared my
dream saved themselves when the dream was finished. That's
the way it should be. My kings ran their kingdoms, my
marshals became royalist generals. But . . . if the dream could
be made to live again, they would return to my side, happy
and loyal. That is the nature of sharing someone else's
fantasy. Already, Murat, who had fought against me at the
end, has come back. My brothers will come around. Pauline
and Madame Mère lived at Elba with me. Who knows, I may
yet hold the King of Rome in my arms." He straightened up
in the saddle. "Ah, my Polish major has returned."

It was seven in the evening, the night march undertaken in
order to reach Grenoble before it could be reinforced. Major
Jerzmanowski and four lancers rode quickly up to the Emperor.

"Sire," the man said in perfect French. "A large column
of infantry is marching south up the roadway. They're in
battle formation."

The Emperor seemed unruffled. "Thank you, Major," he
said. "How far behind you are they?"

"Thirty minutes perhaps," the man said.

"Good. They shan't detain us long. Have the men form
defensive formations."

"Yes, sir." The major rode back to the column, orders
hurriedly given. The line broke quickly, soldiers taking up
positions in the dead winter fields that spread out around the
roadway.

"What now?" David asked.

Hersh shrugged. "We'll see who else shares the fantasy."

"You're not afraid of this, are you?"

The Emperor shook his head, smiling. "I've learned a lot,
David. I've learned that Napoleon is just as crazy as Hersh,
and that craziness is only a problem when everybody else
thinks you're crazy. When everyone else agrees with you,
you're perfectly healthy! We're about ready to see just how
crazy my dream really is, and I'll venture that the people of

France will legitimize my insanity. If they don't, I'm no worse off than I was at Elba.''

''Unless you're dead.''

''I've said it before, David. There are far worse things than being dead.''

''This is scary,'' David said. ''You're beginning to make sense.''

Hersh laughed. ''Not totally,'' he said. ''Did you know that I tried to commit suicide again after abdication?'' David just stared at him in the darkness, watching the man's breath puff white in the cold air as he laughed. ''But, then, something happened that changed everything.''

''Yes?'' David prodded when the answer wasn't forthcoming.

''My secret, remember?'' Hersh said. ''Listen.''

David listened. The sound of drums beating a marching cadence drifted to them on every breeze. The infantry was rapidly closing on the dream.

''Just a few more minutes,'' Hersh said. ''What kind of help did you want from me?''

''Have you ever heard of free association?'' David asked.

''It sounds like a trade guild,'' the Emperor answered.

''I want to read some words to you,'' David said, ''and you will respond with the first word that comes to your mind. This is normal practice in psychiatry, but you and I never used it because we had the perfect recall of Silv's drug that made it all unnecessary.''

''I thought you said I wasn't delusional anymore?'' Hersh asked with suspicion.

''It's not for you,'' David said. ''Since you and Silv were raised in a similiar environment, I thought that the answers you give to the questions might be on a par with the answers that she would give . . .''

''And if I give the right answers, you might be able to figure out where she's hiding.''

''Exactly.''

''I'll be proud to help you . . . tonight, after we take Grenoble.''

David smiled and reached across to pat Napoleon on the leg. ''Why not?''

''And here they come,'' Hersh said, pointing down the road.

They marched four abreast, the formation tight and perfect.

These were not conscripts, but hardened veterans, ready to follow orders whatever they might be.

Behind, David could hear orders being passed up and down the hidden lines by the lancers. Everything tensed around him. The thud of boots and the clink of bayonets was heard from all around. The moment was golden.

Down the road, the army drew closer. One of Napoleon's staff ran before the Emperor's mule and called, "Who goes there?"

"Seventh regiment of the line!" a voice shouted back, and a lone rider, preceded by a drummer, broke from the column and marched slowly forward.

"Seventh regiment," Hersh said, straining to see who was approaching. "I know who that is. It's La Bedoyère! He used to be Lannes's aide-de-camp! Now we'll see."

Colonel La Bedoyère drew within ten feet of Hersh and David, who still sat their mules. He dismounted, and Hersh did the same. David sat his mount, watching.

The colonel approached with his drummer and Napoleon walked up to face them. The colonel saluted, then clenched a fist and put it right through the drum—the sign of surrender.

"My sword and my life, I pledge to you," La Bedoyère said, and handed Hersh the regimental colors. "Welcome home, Sire."

"Ha!" Hersh said loudly, and took the man in his arms, kissing him on the cheeks. The cheer rose spontaneously from both camps, and the soldiers rushed one another, repeating the earlier scene.

And David sat there, shaking his head while the dreamer's army doubled again. The Emperor turned to look up at David while the soldiers swelled around him. "This morning I was an adventurer," he yelled. "Tonight I am a reining prince!"

And so goes reality.

Within minutes they had resumed their march, reaching the Grenoble gates by nine that night. Grenoble was a key city in the Alps, its center defended by stone walls and two thousand well-armed troops. But when Hersh arrived, thousands of peasants were marching on the walls with torches and pitchforks, yelling, "Long live the Emperor!" The garrison troops, infected by the growing dream, began climbing down the walls and deserting to Napoleon's side. By the time the gates were knocked down, there was no resistance left, and Grenoble surrendered without firing a shot.

The townspeople flocked to the Emperor, carrying him on their shoulders to the Hôtel des Trois Dauphins, where he was taken upstairs to the best bedroom in the city and given the panels of the broken-down Bonne Gate as a souvenir.

David walked amidst the jubilation of the town, bathing in the excitement of created reality. Napoleon's return was true only because so many desperately wished it to be true. It may have been only a last gasp, but never was a sunset so glorious.

He joined Hersh about ten, after supper, when the last of the well-wishers and confidants had slipped away. The man was lying in bed with his stockings down and spots of wine on his unbuttoned waistcoat.

"There you are," Hersh said, sitting up and running a hand through his wispy hair. "I've just gotten some news. The bastard, Louis, has already fled Paris, leaving it open for us. I shall rule again!"

David shook his head. "Unbelievable," he said. "I thought I understood so much about life, but I'd only ever looked at it under a microscope. You once said that it was a small step from the sublime to the ridiculous, but perhaps the reverse is true also."

"Unfortunately, it's not." The man drew his legs over the edge of the bed. "Berthier went with him," he said. "That's a blow. I'll need another chief of staff."

David sat at the small wooden table off to the side of the room, noticing how unhappy the departure of Berthier made Hersh. For the dream to work, he needed everyone to share it. The fact that someone so close could refuse to feel the ripples bothered him tremendously, and David realized that a dream this large was a great deal more fragile than he had known. Hersh knew, though. He understood perfectly.

The Emperor stood, exhausted, and David saw the reality of what such a life takes out of a man. He was no more fit than the Napoleon he saw in Russia, just more positive. Perhaps the idea of starting with a clean slate took away the inevitability of defeat.

Hersh walked slowly to the table and sat across from David, bringing a candle with him. He set it between the two and stared hard at his former physician. "I'm ready," he said.

David's heart leapt. If Hersh's large dream was possible, why not David's small one? If he understood Silv enough, it seemed possible that he could find her, even given the whole world and all time. He reached a shaking hand into the side pocket of his uniform and pulled out the paper he had scribbled on when he had stood in the front lines of the fifth regiment.

"Are you sure you're not too tired?" David said.

"No, let's go," Hersh said.

David pulled the candle a little closer to him and laid the paper out flat on the table. "I'm going to read a word to you," he said. "I want you to relax, and simply say the first thing that comes into your mind, all right?"

"Sure."

"Napoleon's going to have to submerge himself. I want this to come completely from Hersh."

"No problem," Hersh said quickly, and smiled. "Let's go."

"Okay," David said, his voice quaking. "First word, mother?"

"Whore," Hersh said, David writing it down.

"Okay, God?"

"Me."

"Freedom?"

"Death."

"Religion?"

"Politics."

"Woman?"

"Whore."

"Sex?"

"Battle."

"Body?"

"Count."

David looked up. "Count?" he said.

Hersh shrugged. "Body . . . count. You said to say the first thing."

This wasn't working at all. Hersh may have come from the exact same environment, but his upbringing wasn't anything like Silv's, his mind certainly working along its own unique channels.

"Color?" David asked.

"Red."

"Escape?"

"Death."

"Damn," David said, slamming down his pencil and leaning back in the chair. "This was a stupid idea. There's no way I'm going to pull anything about Silv from your mind. I was so hoping . . . oh, well. I don't know where to go from here.''

He came forward again in his seat, using his arms as a pillow on the table. "I've searched for several lifetimes," he said. "There's just nowhere else for me to go."

"I think you're going about this the wrong way," Hersh said.

David raised his head and stared at the man. "What do you mean?"

"Why are you asking *me* these questions? I mean, I understand what you're saying about environment and everything, but, you know, I'm able to live with Napoleon because we share the same environment of mind."

"You mean genetics," David said.

"Right. You and Silv share a mind. I'll bet you share a lot of similiar attitudes."

David put his hands up. "I never thought of this," he said. "My whole orientation is toward environmental factors. Psychiatry doesn't take genetic factors into account. But, God, you could be right."

"Why don't we just switch," Hersh said. "Let me ask you the questions."

David shoved the paper across to him. "I've got nothing to lose," he said. "Let's give it a try."

Hersh smiled. "If you see Silv," he said, "tell her I said hello."

David leaned back in the chair and closed Rapp's eyes, forcing the man completely into the background. "I'm ready," he said after a moment.

"All right," Hersh said. "Here we go. First word, mother?"

"Duty," David said.

"God?"

"Nothing."

"Freedom?"

"Solitude."

"Religion?"

"Study."

"Woman?"

"Man."

"Sex?"

"Skimming."

"Body?"

"Water."

"Color?"

"Blue."

"Escape?"

"Swimming."

"Happiness?"

"Peace."

David's mind began to drift, his psyche floating off on his responses in measure to the feelings evoked by the questions. And as he drifted, he realized that he had known the answers to his questions all along but had just never connected it all up.

"Water?"

"Eternity."

The rest of the questions were drifting on high tides through his mind, for he was already traveling, already skimming off, like a rock on a lake, to find his other half. He was thinking with his heart and with his dreams.

David walked along the rocky shore just far enough off the shoals that he could feel the salt spray from the breakers on his face, just above the upturned collar of his canvas jacket. He nearly stumbled, regained his balance, and continued moving toward the Portland Head lighthouse fifty yards in the distance.

His host was named Silas Luper, sailmaker on the liner *Bohemian*. His ship had just pulled into Portland harbor with a full load of Irish immigrants, and Silas was walking up to Portland Head to check out firsthand the light that had many times guided him into safe harbor. Silas was an artist of sorts, a drawer of lighthouses and harbors, and Portland Head, with its hundred-foot tower and attached whitewashed cottage and outbuildings, had often attracted him.

David was hoping for something else. He was hoping for Silv. This was the logical place for her, close by the raging waters that were her religion, aloof in her tower with her privacy. This place drew David. He could pray that it had the same effect on Silv. He picked up his pace as he closed in on the lighthouse. If this wasn't it, he had nowhere else to try.

He liked Silas, felt good within this simple man. Silas also loved the sea as if it were a god, his pencil and charcoal renderings of it his way of paying homage. He was a man of few needs and of great personal fortitude. He was craggy and set in his ways, but he was also yearning for something more.

At the moment, he was tolerating David.

Why don't you go steal somebody else's soul?

I'm not stealing anything, only visiting.

Well, I just hope you don't eat too much.

The lighthouse stood at the promontory of the head, the highest point in the harbor area. He climbed the steep incline instead of using the road, and came up near the cottage. Portland stood in the distance behind, a bustling nineteenth-century trade city, its harbor full of two- and three-masted schooners, as small as toys so far away. Before him lay the ocean, raging and free. He smiled as he spotted Alden Rock, the most dangerous spot in the harbor place. Even that monster, from this distance, looked small and harmless. What a place, this light! So peaceful and removed. A place where a man could get up a good lungful of air and sing all night if he chose to.

"Hello!" he called at the cottage window, but no one answered. He looked around a little, then put a hand to his eyes against the afternoon sun and looked up the length of the light. A woman stood on its outer deck, her skirts blowing free in the wind, her long hair whipping around her face. A woman who understood this place, what a wonder she must be.

He ran to the base of the tower, David hurrying him inside in his excitement. The stairs spiraled up the inside wall of the light. "Is anybody there?" he called through cupped hands so he wouldn't surprise her.

Within seconds, she was staring down at him from her lofty perch, her face set in perplexity even from so great a distance.

"May I come up?" he called.

"No," she called down. "Come back another time."

Silas, being basically a shy man around the opposite sex, would have left right then, but David would have no part of it. He took the body full and began climbing.

"Please go away!" she called down, and her voice contained an edge of hysteria.

I'm not one to tell the spirit world what to do, but maybe we should be getting on our way.

Nonsense. She wants to see us.

But she said . . .

She wants to see us.

"I'm coming up!" he called as he climbed, and took the stairs two at a time, no hard job to one used to bandying about in the rigging like a monkey.

He reached her within minutes, smiling as he moved up to the lens room. "A long climb," he said.

"Who are you?" she asked, frightened.

"It doesn't matter," he said, then walked around to study the Fresnel lens with its concentric series of glass rings. "Never saw one of these up close ... only from the other side." He nodded toward the sea.

"Your name," she said. "Your name. Is it Silas Luper?"

David gasped. It had to be her. No mortal could have known his identity; only someone who could see the future would know. He cocked his head. "Now, how could you know that?"

"I've known ... and I've dreaded your coming for years."

It was Silv, it was! He looked her up and down. This host was no Thérèsia Tallien, but with Silv's spunk to give her impetus, she could be something special. He could feel it. Silas liked her, too.

"What are—" she began, and David jumped at her, taking her into his arms, his hands running up and down her body.

Oh, Silv, Silv, Silv ... recognize me!

What are you doing?

It's all right, believe me.

Believe you! You want to get me strung up!

"No!" she screamed, and David began to worry that it wasn't Silv after all. He eased his hold on her and she kicked free, running out to the rail.

He charged after her. God, what had he done? She could fall. She reached the rail and stopped, looking straight down.

He grabbed her again, spinning her around. Her face was ashen and she looked deeply into his eyes. "Could you love one already dead?" she asked.

Relief flooded through him and he began laughing. It *was* Silv. He pulled her close, bringing her back inside the light to draw her to the floor beside him.

"We all die, Silv, even me."

"David," she said, eyes wide and staring. "You've found me!"

"My heart did," David said, and pulled her close, her own embrace as fierce as his. "I love you. I searched for you a hundred years and I'd search a hundred more."

"Please go away," she said, lips trembling. "Please. I don't want you to see me this way."

"What way?" he demanded. "What way? Less than perfect? Don't you see there's no such thing? I'm dying, too. We've got to embrace life while we can."

"Oh, David, I'm frightened."

She was shaking in his arms, her fear and her need trying to tear her apart. And his own need swelled, his love and desire the only reality that existed at that moment.

"Make love with me, Silv," he said sternly, voice hoarse. "Right here, right now." His large hands found her breasts, and she pulled his lips hungrily to hers, her own dormant passions no longer containable.

Callused hands were clumsily undoing the buttons on the front of her dress as she pulled at the rope that held his pants up. Neither were doing very well.

He stopped working her buttons and smiled. "It's a sailor's knot," he said, and slipped it right off.

She smiled her wicked smile and put her hand on his crotch. "And this must be the anchor."

He laughed loudly. "You haven't changed a bit!"

"Neither have you. Are you sure you want to be near me?"

"Face it, lady," he said. "After all we've been through, you're stuck with me."

"But . . ."

"Listen," he said, putting a hand to her lips. "We're both in the same boat. We need each other. We want each other. We love each other. Goddamn it! When it all comes down and all the shouting and crying is over . . . what the hell else is there? Please. I'm begging you. Share the time we have left with me. We deserve it, don't we? A little happiness . . . just a little happiness."

She was crying softly, like a child afraid. She took his craggy face in her hands and kissed him with wet, trembling lips. "I do love you so," she whispered, and began working on her own buttons. "Mind of my mind. I've loved you since you were twelve."

David started pulling his own clothes off, then stopped. "Should we introduce our hosts?" he asked.

"Certainly," Silv said, pulling her dress off her shoulders, her slip bright white and frilly with lace. "Carla James, this is Silas Luper, the man you're going to marry."

"What!" David and Silas said at the same time.

Silv shrugged, then smiled that wicked smile again. "Sorry to let the cat out of the bag," she said. "When I . . . moved in with Carla, I checked her history and found that she married an itinerant seaman named Silas Luper in 1856, the year after the Fresnel was installed. I didn't want to horn in on her life after that point, so I figured I'd just stay around until then."

I ain't marryin' nobody!

You can't fight city hall, pal.

David reached for the woman, helping her out of her dress, and Silas was as excited as a schoolboy on his first date as he watched her beauty unfold before him. David felt contentment at last, and Silas, Silas was in love even before he got his pants off.

And they made love in the top of the light as if they had invented it. Their love had the passion of experts and the thrill of amateurs. Their love was shared memories and the mystery of the oceans. It was all sailor's knots and lonely poetry and nights at Malmaison. They made love for hours, then they went downstairs and Carla fixed them both supper.

They made love again in bed that night as the light pulsed out its rhythm to the night, the fog bell tolling because of the mist. And it never occurred to Silas that he should go back to his ship or leave this place ever again.

> *And as the evening darkens, lo! how bright*
> *Through the deep purple of the twilight air,*
> *Beams forth the sudden radiance of its light*
> *With strange unearthly splendour in its glare!*
>
> *And the great ships sail outward and return*
> *Bending and blowing o'er the billowy swells;*
> *And ever joyful, as they see it burn,*
> *They wave their silent welcomes and farewells.*
>
> —Longfellow

David sat quietly while Silas sketched Alden Rock and Henry Longfellow, who sat upon it composing an ode to Portland Head light. It never ceased to amaze David how such large, clumsy hands could turn blank paper into a work of art by simply smearing charcoal onto it. It was creation of the highest order, and he stood in awe of its magic.

He leaned against the light, getting the morning sunshine,

his fingers leaving places on the paper unsmeared to catch the sun's highlights on the water. He took the long-stemmed pipe from his mouth and banged it against a nearby rock to clear the ashes. He set down the sketchbook and began the methodical job of slowly boring out the pipe, then refilling it. It was a ritual to Silas, a memory repeated to habit, a familiarity that never failed to bring him peace.

Silas Luper was happy and content.

For the first time in his long life, so was David Wolf.

Silas Luper and Carla James had been married several months before. It had been their own idea, David and Silv staying out of the decision completely, though they had never doubted the destiny of the situation.

Silas and Carla were very much in love. They had both had unhappy lives until they'd met, and both found the fulfillment they had lacked within each other's eyes. It hadn't been totally easy, both were set in their ways, but the final outcome was never in doubt. These people belonged together.

David and Silv had been very careful in allowing the relationship to nurture outside of their control. They hadn't wanted a repeat of the Antoine-Thérèsia relationship and all its inherent pain, so they were careful early on to spend a great deal of time skimming together and leaving the two lovers alone for weeks at a time. It had worked beautifully.

Both Silas and Carla were good-hearted people who sincerely liked David and Silv and were not adverse to sharing minds with them. In a sense they even felt a certain responsibility toward the skimmers for bringing them together to begin with.

It was a successful relationship all the way around. They were four minds, sitting out the raging oceans of life, taking a kind of emotional rest. It wouldn't last, of course. A Civil War was boiling on the horizon, and even Silas's old ship, *Bohemian,* was destined for a tragic rendezvous against the very rock that Longfellow was sitting upon; but they all accepted that eternity must be found in the moments and appreciated while they last.

Silas finished filling his pipe and stuck it in his mouth, striking a match on the whitewashed stone of the light. He puffed leisurely for a moment, then picked up the sketchbook again.

This is really quite good.

Bah, you're no critic. You like anything.

I like anything you do. You have a great talent.
It's just my thank-you to God, that's all. Nothing more.
Isn't that enough, though? Isn't it?

A great deal of time had passed in one place or another. He and Silv had spent alternating periods skimming and living at the lighthouse with Silas and Carla. Silv had gotten progressively worse, her memory fading in larger chunks day by day. David, also, had begun to lose sections of his mind. Medical school was gone completely, as was his first marriage. There seemed to be no rhyme or reason to the things that would disappear, and there was no pain connected with the loss— some things simply wouldn't be there anymore when he searched for them.

They had traveled time together and even space. They had found a genetic host once who had been an American astronaut, and they had walked and played golf with him on the moon. Silv had shown an interest in the space program, something that had disappeared from world culture sometime in the early twenty-first century through lack of interest and money. They'd gone under the North Pole in a submarine and had reached it above ground on dogsled. They'd been to Walden Pond and to Russia under Stalin. They had traveled far and seen everything there was to see, but, always, the happiest times were at the lighthouse where the simple joys, the simple memories, could be savored and stored up in the heart.

They had spent an amount of time with Hersh, Silv and Napoleon finally solidifying a relationship that had never had a chance to develop properly. Hersh's dream had, of course, ended at Waterloo, and it was during his exile at St. Helena that they usually visited with him. It could have been a time of quiet contemplation for Hersh, but the impatience of his character simply couldn't or wouldn't adjust to the confinement, and he wasted away.

As for David, he was doing well. He was content, a word signifying much. He had spent several hundred years as a citizen of the timestream, and through it had learned that the less complicated a thing is, the more beautiful. He and Silv complemented and made whole one another. They loved and laughed and shared everything together, and if there was still a little corner of David's life that wasn't completely satisfied, that was part of the package and just fine, too.

In his time at the lighthouse he had known life and lived

life the way billions of people had taken for granted since the dawn of time—and to him it was a miracle.

"David?"

"Around here," he called, taking the pipe out of his mouth and tapping it on the rock out of habit.

Silv moved around the lighthouse to sit next to him. She stared at the picture, tucking her flower-print dress up under her legs. "Good piece of work."

"Thanks." He leaned over and kissed her on the cheek.

She pointed down to Longfellow. "You should give it to Henry when you're finished."

"Good idea. I'll make a present of it. He might be able to use it to wrap up the fish he catches."

"Oh, you," she smiled, and slapped him playfully on the shoulder. "David? Are you in control?"

"I'm here . . . yes. What's up?"

"Something we need to talk about. It . . . involves all of us somewhat."

He touched her arm in concern. "Is something wrong?"

She smiled sadly, taking his large hand in both of hers. "We . . . well, Carla and Silas are going to have a baby."

"A baby," David said softly, and he could hear Silas screaming inside him.

Let me out, for God's sake!

David submerged, Silas grabbing Carla with strong arms! both of them giggling like schoolchildren.

David drifted with it lazily. In essence, it wasn't his child or Silv's, but, realistically, it was part theirs too, just as they were part of it. David had affected the life cycle to become his own ancestor. He was a living part of eternity.

"David?" Silv called him back again. "David?"

"Yes?"

He looked at Silv, both of them controlling their hosts.

"What are we going to do?" she asked.

He didn't understand what she was talking about. "What's the problem?"

"Can we . . . do we have the right to stay here now?"

"You mean leave, leave the baby?"

"It's not ours, David."

"I know that, but . . ."

"No. You don't understand. This is going to be a very special, very personal time for them. We'd be intruding."

*No, David. Don't think that way, We're all one here. It's
your baby too.*

I really appreciate that.

*There's nothing to appreciate. We share all things. Carla
agrees, too. This doubt is all coming from your woman.*

"Are you sure that's all there is to it?" David asked.

"I don't know. Carla says I'm foolish. I just want to do
what's best for the baby. We have no right to mess up its
life."

David took her in his arms, holding her close. "We do
have a right," he said. "A right to parenthood, a right to love
and care for a child. How can that be wrong?"

"I don't know," she said again, her head buried in his
shoulder. "We're dead, David. I just don't think that we
could or should try and bring forth life from that place."

He pulled her to arm's length. "It's not our baby. It's
theirs. Don't be scaring Carla with your invented fears. We'll
be . . . like godparents, that's all. It'll work. God, think of
how wonderful it will be. A child to hold, to teach about
life."

"You make it sound so easy."

He kissed her hard on the lips. "It is easy. What could be
easier?"

She looked back down at the poet, shaking her head. "I
don't know."

He took her by the chin and lifted her face until they were
eye to eye. "Do you want the baby? Do you want to be here
for it?"

She tightened her lips to keep the sob in, but her glistening
eyes gave her away. She nodded, unable to speak.

"Then, let's do it," he said, kissing her. "It'll work out, I
promise."

"No promises, all right?" she said. "We'll take it a
moment at a time. No promises, no expectations."

"Fair enough," he said, giving her another quick hug. "It'll
work out. You'll see." He stood, pacing quickly, excitedly.
Silas was already planning on taking his son out sailing as
soon as he was old enough.

Fatherhood, the ultimate infinity. David couldn't be happier. What he couldn't do alive, he was able to accomplish
dead. He realized the fundamental change in his character. He
had never wanted children before, had never wanted to bring

them into the insanity of the world. But now he knew. For all the inherent problems, life had its moments.

This child would have everything. Think of the firsthand knowledge of history he could be taught and . . . David's mind turned to Hersh. Maybe news like this could cheer him in his exile. His own wife and son had been taken from him, never to be seen again. Maybe this would help.

He turned to Silv. "Let's go visit Hersh," he said, waving his hands around. "I've got to tell someone, I'm bursting! He's the only one we could . . ."

He stopped talking—she was staring at him, her face filled with horror, her eyes wide and frightened.

"What is it?" he said, kneeling in front of her and taking her hands. "What's wrong?"

"Who's Hersh?" she asked in a small voice.

Not every end is the goal. The end of a melody is not its goal, and yet if a melody has not reached its end, it has not reached its goal. A parable.

—Nietzsche

The storm was incredible. It raged, a thing wild beyond recollection; it battered the Maine coast with wind and water and God's fire from the sky. David stood on the deck at the top of the light and screamed into the dark night of the storm as it lashed him with cold, stinging rain and roared in his ears to drown him out. Lightning flashed, grounding on Alden's Rock, shattering the black into cobweb streamers that formed a daisy chain across the whole sky. Behind him, the Fresnel focused the light sharply, pinpointing it into the storm, only to have it sucked up again by the blackness.

"Why not me!" he screamed, holding tightly to the rail. "What's wrong with me!"

He was speaking of death.

The wind sang again, trying to shove him from his perch to the peace of the jagged rocks so far below. But he held on, despite himself. He always held on.

"Silas!" Carla yelled from below, her voice rolling up the tower like more thunder. "David! Will you come down here? You're scaring me to death."

Come on, David. I'm not ready to die up here.

Reluctantly, David reached out for the doorframe, grasped

it firmly, and used it to pull himself back inside, keeping his head turned from the blinding glare of the light as it winked on and off. The fog bell was ringing loudly, but no one would hear it through the storm.

"I'm coming down!" he called, still shading his eyes.

"Thank God!"

He began the long walk down the spiral stairs, Silas shaking with the cold. It was early November, no time to be braving the elements in New England.

Carla waited for him at the bottom of the stairs, her stomach great with child, serious concern evident on her face.

"How could you, David?" she asked, when he had reached the bottom and taken her in his arms.

"I'm sorry," he said. "I apologize to both of you. After tonight I'll never interfere in your lives again."

"You don't interfere," Carla said, wrapping a tarp around both of them. "You know we want you here."

They ran out of the light and across to the cottage, the rain lashing at them. When they got inside, David went right to the kitchen to stand before the huge brick fireplace that formed the core of their lives. The smells were of gingerbread and melting candle wax and the string of apple slices hanging up to dry before the fire. David looked around at the simple wooden table and cupboard, his mind smiling on the many hours of yarn dyeing, sausage making, and cider bottling that had gone on there. He would never see the like again.

Silv was gone, just a memory, and David once again felt lost. He had been splitting his time between depression and revisiting things that had been, but it wasn't fair to Silas or Carla. They shared his grief during a time that should have been the happiest of their lives, and he felt responsible for it. As four, they were complete. As three, David was not only getting in the way, but ruining their lives. As much as he wanted fatherhood, he knew he'd not be staying for it.

"Why don't you get out of those wet clothes," Carla said, moving to hang the copper teakettle over the fire. "You'll catch your death."

"Dreamer," he said, and felt bad immediately when she gave him her stern look in return. She was beautiful in pregnancy, her face glowing, her clumsy amble somehow as graceful as a dance. He stared at her, trying to set the image for good in what was left of his mind.

"Will you change?" she said again, prodding in her gentle way.

"Silas can . . . in a minute," he said, and watched her face drain of color.

"What do you mean . . . Silas can?"

"You know what I mean," he replied. "I've got to leave. Tonight."

Carla looked at the floor for a minute, then back at David. "You really don't have to," she said in a small voice.

"Yes, I do,"he said. "Now that Silv is . . . gone. It's just not the same—for me or for either of you."

Now wait, David . . .

No, Silas. It's time. We both know it.

"Won't you wait at least until the baby's born?" she asked, putting on her apron.

He shook his head, glad that the rain on his face hid his tears. "I—can't," he said. "Not without her. Not at all without her."

She moved to the cupboard, taking down plates for the gingerbread and coffee cups for the tea. "Where will you go?"

He moved closer to the fire, staring into its prolonged death and thinking about Hersh and his love of fire. "I have everywhere and nowhere to go," he said. "I'm searching for the end of the road."

"Will you stay for tea?"

"I've got to go now, while my resolve is still strong."

"Will you come back?"

"No."

She persisted. "Will you let us know where and how you are?"

"I'm going where people don't come back, Carla," he said. "It's the hardest decision of my life. Don't make it any harder."

She put the utensils on the wooden table and moved to take him in her arms, trying to give her mother's strength to him. "We'll miss you terribly," Carla said, staring up at him. She looked different to David ever since Silv had left. She was obviously the same woman, but some special light was gone from the eyes. This woman wasn't his anymore. He kissed her tenderly, lingeringly.

"Raise your children with love," he said, pulling away from her, needing to be strong. "Teach them to appreciate the small things and not worry about the big ones. Life has a way of working itself out.''

She nodded, smiling. ''You're a good man, David Wolf,'' she said. ''Know that you have touched our lives for the better.''

He nodded, and they shared a look. They had given much to one another, and in the gaze, everything was said. Then he turned and looked through the doorway next to the fireplace. The buttery. The last place he had ever seen Silv.

''Good-bye,'' he said, and turned from her, moving into the room off the kitchen.

Good-bye, Silas. Life has been good with you.

We'll be the worse for your loss, David. I hope you find what you're looking for.

I'm not exactly sure what that is, but I hope so, too.

He walked into the buttery, with its long shelves of utensils and washtubs and cutting boards. Silv and Carla had been in there the month before, putting up preserves, when he had come in with a load of wood for the fire and heard crying.

He closed his eyes.

He remembered.

''What's wrong?'' he asked Silv, walking in and wrapping his arms around her huge stomach from behind.

She broke from his grasp and turned to him, her eyes red. She pulled up a corner of her apron and wiped her cheeks. ''I just can't do it anymore, David,'' she said. ''I'm so sorry, but I just can't.''

''Can't do what?''

''Stay here anymore.''

''Now, wait, Silv . . .''

''No!'' she said evenly, cutting him off. ''Listen to me this time, please.''

He nodded, and moved a few steps away from her. The counter was full of cranberries, an iron pot full of them already boiling in the kitchen. The acrid smell was one he'd never forget.

''Our time together is finished,'' she said. ''It's been the happiest time . . . no, the only time, in my life. But it can't go on any longer.''

''Why?'' David asked quietly, like a child.

''I've lost everything,'' she said. ''Can you understand that? My entire past is gone. I can feel my mind slipping away more each day. It's horrible, this dying by inches. I just don't have the strength for it anymore. I wanted so to see the baby, to hold it, but that's just not my destiny.''

''Are you sure you can't hang on a while longer?''

''Hang on to what?'' she asked, her face pleading. ''There's nothing left for me to hang onto. Everything but what lives in this house is gone from my memory. It's frightening. I can physically feel it going. I'm a walking corpse. It's time to let go.''

He swallowed hard, finally understanding her plight fully and feeling ashamed for his denial of it. He was losing memory, too, and dealt with the problem by ignoring it. ''Where will you go?'' he asked, numbed inside.

''Home,'' she said. ''My death is calling me, I can feel it. It's finally over for me.''

''God, I can't stand the thought of you going.''

''Please stop making it hard for me.'' She turned, a bit angry, and stared out the side window at the autumn of gold and red that had graced their landscape. ''I don't feel real anymore. I'm afraid that one day I'll wake up and simply be gone, nothing of me left at all. That's no way to die. I want to face it. I *must* face it.''

He walked to her, smelled the natural perfume of her hair. He felt so protective of her. She seemed so alive. ''Are you afraid?''

She turned to him, looking up. ''Not really,'' she said. ''It's the natural thing . . . I can't quite explain it.''

He shook his head. ''I've felt that same thing in others,'' he answered. ''I know what you're talking about.''

She took his arms, gripping tightly. ''Then, let me go, David. You've given me everything. Now give me the freedom to die.''

He pulled her to him. ''Our love has conquered time. Maybe it will conquer this. Perhaps we'll meet somewhere else,'' he said.

''You don't believe that,'' she said, her hands flat on his chest, alternately pushing away and pulling him close.

''I don't know what I believe,'' he said. ''This is the only real thing that's ever happened to me. I can't believe that it could end.''

''Then, maybe it won't,'' she whispered, and stood on tiptoes to kiss him softly on the lips. She touched him once on the face, then the light died in her eyes.

She was gone. Just like that. Her existence only a memory, a light flickering out.

As the body of Silas Luper and the soul of David Wolf braced itself against the washstand, David the skimmer bid a last good-bye to life and jumped into the timestream, searching for death himself, his fine elusive friend.

The past is the present, isn't it? It's the future, too. We all try to lie out of that but life won't let us.
— Eugene O'Neill

"But I don't want to go in with that man, Momma," Naomi Williams said. "Please don't make me."

"Just do what you're told, girl," Martine Williams said, looking down at her thirteen-year-old daughter. "There's a Depression going on. We've all got to do our part."

Naomi looked at the closed door to her mother's room and thought about the man waiting on the other side. He was fat, and his wide yellow tie had grease stains on it. His hair was slicked black with oil and he snorted all the time. Why was Momma making her go in there with him, and dressed in her nightgown?

It was the summer of 1937, the hottest Kansas City had ever known. The tiny apartment was hot enough that only the roaches could be comfortable, and her brother, Joey, was in the hospital from eating the sweet-tasting flakes of old paint that had peeled off the wall.

"But what am I supposed to do?" the girl asked, her face feeling strange from all the makeup Momma had put on her.

The woman knelt before her and looked the girl in the eye. "You do whatever Mr. Stavis wants you to do, understand? He likes little girls your age and is very nice to them if they're nice to him."

"I don't *want* to be nice to Mr. Stavis, he smells bad!"

"You'll do what I tell you to do!"

"I won't! I won't!

"Stop it!" Martine said, slapping her across the face. "You ungrateful little shit." She looked at the closed door and lowered her voice. "I've been laying on my back for years to put food in you and your brother's mouth. The least you can do is return the compliment."

Momma had grabbed her arms hard and was shaking her. "You're hurting me, Momma!"

The woman released her, shoving a strand of bleached blond hair out of her face. They stared at each other in silence, the only sounds the traffic on the Quay River bridge outside the open window.

"You need to do this, honey," Martine said. "We have to get the money for your brother's hospital. If we don't he might die, and it would be all your fault."

"Oh, no!" Naomi said, tears coming to her eyes. "I didn't do anything to Joey!"

"If you don't go in an' be nice to Mr. Stavis, it will be the same as if you had killed Joey," Martine said, and stood, smoothing her skirt. "It's up to you." She turned and walked into the kitchen, staring out the open window.

"Hey," came the thick voice from behind the door. "I'm'a ain't got all day!"

Martine flared around and stared at Naomi. "Well?"

The girl looked at the closed door and thought about her brother dying in the hospital. She was scared and shaking, but Joey . . . Joey. . . .

"I'll be nice to Mr. Stavis, Momma," she said in a tiny, frightened voice.

"Good girl," Martine said, and moved to take her by the hand and lead her to the door. She knelt before Naomi again and checked her makeup and the slight redness on her ear where she had been slapped. "You look real pretty, honey. Mr. Stavis will think so, too. Now remember: anything he wants."

"Yes, Momma."

"If it hurts a little bit, it will feel better later."

"Yes, Momma."

Martine's eyes twinkled. "I'll tell you what. After Mr. Stavis leaves and you've been nice to him, we'll take thirty cents and go see that Clark Gable movie."

"In the fancy theater on State Avenue with the refrigerated air?"

"Nothing but the best for my little girl."

Naomi threw her arms around Martine's neck. "Oh, thank you, Momma. I love you."

"I love you too, sweetheart," Martine said, and stood, opening the door to the bedroom.

Mr. Stavis lay on the bed without his shoes and jacket on. He was smoking a big, green cigar.

"About time," he said, pulling his legs off the bed.

"She's a real sweet girl," Martine said. "And untouched."

The man smiled wide, showing gold teeth. "That's what I want," he said. "Come'a in here, pretty girl."

Martine gave Naomi a shove, then quickly closed the door behind her. The girl stood, petrified, at the foot of the bed.

"Well, come here," Stavis said, loosening his tie. "I'm'a not hurt you."

She walked slowly to within his grasp. His fat hand snaked out and grabbed her by the arm, pulling her up to him. "You a pretty one," he said.

"Thank you, sir," Naomi said.

"Yeah, thank'a me." The man laughed, his dark eyes leering. He put the cigar down and began pulling on her nightgown. "Let's see what you got under here, huh?"

He ripped her gown off, his tongue lolling out of his mouth as he pulled her up on the bed and ran his hands all over her body. She was shaking wildly, totally out of control.

David sat within her, anger coursing through his mind. He dared not speak or do anything that might make things worse, as Stavis pulled roughly on her small breasts, laughing as she cried.

"Look'a what I got here," the man said, hoarse, and the fly was open on his pants, his erect organ poking through the material all purple and slimy.

Naomi stifled a scream as the man climbed up on the bed with her, and David couldn't stand the procession of horrible images that ran through his mother's mind. And as she screamed, he screamed too, jumping back into the stream.

He fled blindly, emotionally, and settled into the first calm he felt. He was in a damp, dark shed, tapping a wooden wine keg.

He felt shame and deep sorrow over his feelings about his mother. What arrogance was within him to forgive himself for what she'd done to him, but not to forgive her? How he was so quickly able to blame her without even trying to know the horrors she had gone through herself.

Sometimes the timestream was beautiful and sometimes ugly, and ofttimes the beauty and horror were merely states of mind. What the timestream was, for good and all, was honest. What his own mind did to that honesty was subvert it to fit into the patterns he most wanted to believe. It's called reality, and it's invented from moment to moment in the mind of the beholder.

I'm sorry, Momma. I'm so sorry.

A rat scurried across his feet, and he heard his host curse. Where was he?

He was putting the newly filled bottle of burgundy on a small table and pouring something from a glass vial into it. It was arsenic! He was poisoning wine!

He sank in more fully, still reeling from his mother's emotional Harpies. He hadn't intended to take another human totally after he'd left Silas, but this bore inspection.

Louis? Louis Marchand?

David. So, you've come for the end.

God. His emotions had drawn him back to Hersh. He was at Longwood House, St. Helena island, Napoleon's dank prison of his last days. He was inhabiting the body of Louis Marchand, the servant he had taken before on previous visits to Hersh. Of the incongruous band of strangers that had entered exile at St. Helena with Hersh, Marchand was the most loyal, the most dependable. Yet, here he was, poisoning the wine.

What are you doing?

God's work. I'm helping that poor man out of his degradation.

By killing him?

Out of love, David. What he suffers here is far worse than Death's gentle kiss.

You don't have the right to make that determination.

I've claimed the right. The suffering has to end.

David made to stop the man, when he remembered Hersh's admonition that there were things worse than death. A premonition? He backed off, knowing Destiny when he saw it.

Marchand corked the bottle and carried it across the dirt floor and out into windy twilight, moving across the yard to the house. Longwood House was a moldy, leaking excuse for a residence, chosen by enemies who wanted to humiliate the Emperor of France. It was a fit residence only for the rodents that populated it.

How is the Emperor?

Dying. He may not last the day.

Aren't you afraid someone else may drink the arsenic?

The Emperor is the only one who drinks from this bottle. He doesn't trust the others to have access.

They moved into Longwood House proper, a converted cow barn of yellow stucco containing twenty-three rooms. The English had chosen this prison well, an island of rock in the south Atlantic. Longwood itself lay on a barren plateau five miles by winding hillside road from the port of Jamestown. Despite frequent rain, the land resisted civilization. The grass was unfit for grazing and the few gumwood trees that grew were permanently bent by the constant southeast trade winds.

Remembering Hersh's escape from Elba, the English had three thousand men garrisoned at St. Helena, their primary purpose to watch the Emperor in his daily routine. A wall surrounded the estate, upon which five hundred red-clad English soldiers stood and kept Longwood and one another within constant visual contact. They relayed messages about the Emperor by semaphore. Around the bleak, windy plain rose dark, jagged volcanic peaks, one of which held Alarm House, where the English fired cannons to announce sunrise, sunset, and the arrival of ships. They could also announce escape.

The handful of exiles who chose to share Napoleon's life sentence with him were a strange group. Hardly any from the old days were there. They were hangers-on, camp followers, what in David's time were called groupies. Altogether, over fifty people lived at Longwood, most of these servants.

They moved through the large sitting areas, where Fanny Bertrand watched her three children running around the thread-bare furniture. Her husband, Henri, was not of the others' ilk. He had been with Napoleon in Egypt, and was grand marshal at the Tuileries. He stood at this moment arguing at the front door with Hudson Lowe, the English governor of the island.

"He must be seen at least once a day!" Lowe said sternly, strutting like a peacock in his stiff-collared uniform. "These are my rules, and I must follow them."

"He's dying, General," Bertrand said. "He will not be trying to escape."

"Suppose he's just pretending to die?" the man said angrily.

"Then, he is surely one of the world's great actors."

Is it always like this?

Always. The governor drove the Emperor indoors a long time ago with his constant harassment.

It saddened David to think that Hersh's last days would be much like his first, controlled and humiliated. No wonder he reacted so badly to life here. That is, if Hersh, indeed, intended to stay in this body.

They continued through the house, passing groups of silent servants and assorted guests, all of whom were waiting... waiting. Hersh occupied two rooms in the far corner of Longwood. Louis moved to the door of the Emperor's bedroom and entered without knocking.

Napoleon lay in a canopied four-poster, or rather his shell did. David had to bite his lip to keep from crying out. The man was totally without color, his eyes sunken in emaciated flesh. The familiar reek of desperate sickness hung in the room like a fog. The Corsican doctor, Francesco Antommarchi, stood at his head, trying to give him a mixture of water, orange water, and sugar to no avail.

The man looked up when Louis entered, his eyes falling on the bottle under his arm. "There'll be no need for that," he said. "The Emperor is no longer able to drink."

David walked to the bed to take Hersh's pulse. The man's arm was like a sheath of rolled-up papers. David could barely find a pulse. Even the body heat was beginning to depart.

Napoleon fluttered heavy eyes at Louis, then opened them to focus. "Someone," he rasped. "Someone... David?"

"I'm here," David whispered.

"You've come back to me."

"I'm always with you, old friend."

He motioned for David to lean down closer, then whispered, "Get that quack out of here while there's still time. I want to talk to you."

"You need your strength," David said.

Hersh signed loudly. "For what? For what do I need my strength? Where I'm going strength means nothing."

"So you *are* going to go."

"I always... told you I would."

David straightened and looked at the young doctor. "He'd like to talk to me alone for a moment."

Antommarchi pursed his lips, nodded. "I think I'll get everyone together." He looked at a pocket watch. "It will be dark soon. I think I'll bring everyone in quietly."

"In a few minutes," David said.

The man nodded and left the room.

David moved back to sit on the bed with Hersh. "Your host dies today," he said. "You're sure you want to die with him?"

Hersh tried to smile, but it turned to a painful grimace. "Why, when I'm the one who's dying, do I always feel sorry for you?" He rested a hand weakly on David's arm. "Listen, my friend. I was never cursed with your yearnings. One life has been enough for me."

"But don't you fear. Don't you wonder?"

"Fear for me was in the living," Hersh said. "And my wondering about death never proceeded beyond idle speculation. For you, it's an obsession. And, I think, an unhappy obsession."

"All obsessions are unhappy," David said, smiling. "Silv's gone, too."

Hersh nodded. "She told me, the last time you two visited, that she was feeling the pull toward death. She made me promise not to say anything to you, because of the way you are. We said our good-byes then."

"Your identity slipped from her mind sometime after that," David said, and he thought of Silv, felt the emptiness that had stayed behind when she had gone.

"She's beyond the pain now," Hersh said. "Remember the good times." He coughed, painfully, and David used a damp linen cloth to wet Hersh's lips.

The man closed his eyes for a minute, David fearing that he was breathing his last. He looked around the room. A small garden made by Louis in his spare time sat just outside a door leading to the bedroom. On the wall hung portraits of his beloved Josephine, Marie-Louise, and the King of Rome, who was destined to die of consumption before reaching adulthood.

"David," he sighed, then opened his eyes again.

"I'm here," David said.

"You never guessed my little secret, did you?"

"The secret at Grenoble?" David asked, and smiled at him. "No."

Hersh tried to sit up, but didn't have the strength. "That was me on the Grenoble Road, all me."

"What do you mean?"

"Napoleon talked me into finding out Silv's formula a long

time ago," Hersh said. "He made some up at Elba, and left one night, just like that."

"You mean he's off skimming?"

"He never came back."

"Where do you think he went?"

Hersh tried to lick his parched lips. David wet them again with the cloth.

"He was always interested in Alexander the Great," Hersh said. "That's where I'd put my money."

David shook his head. "Fascinating."

There was a light knock on the door. A second later, Dr. Antommarchi poked his head inside.

"Not yet, please," David said, and the man disappeared without a word.

"We were so much alike, him and I," Hersh said. "In the quad, we had to move fast. There were thousands of miles of connecting tunnels between quads, and the ability to move quickly from one place to the next was to great advantage. We adapted that style in our European wars and it worked to perfection. After Napoleon left, I got the chance to try it all on my own. I failed . . . failed at Waterloo, but it was close. I missed by inches. I didn't quite have his genius for strategy."

David took his hand and kissed it. "Watching you march up the Grenoble Road was one of the most extraordinary moments of my life," he said. "You had his greatness, every bit of it."

"Liked that, huh," Hersh said, and coughed again. The effort to speak was taking whatever strength he had left. The end was quite near. "Those are memories I'll take beyond the pale with me."

"You've got to answer a question for me," David said. "Why Talleyrand? So much of your failures were his fault, why did you let it happen?"

"Oh, David," the Emperor said, his voice a whisper. "You would have had to grow up as Hersh to understand that. I was an upstart, a mere soldier who pretended greatness . . . something that came naturally to Monsieur Talleyrand." He waited a moment, building his last strength for small fits of talk. "He was . . . everything I admired. I felt that if I could only be l-like him . . . the world would be mine." He stopped again, gasping slightly. "You saw me at Saint-Cloud the day we seized p-power. I was like an ignorant child. Talleyrand always knew what to do. I loved him, I think, sexually." He tried to smile, but the effort was too much and his mouth fell slack. "When he treated me as an equal, I was grateful and . . . happy. When he cheated me, I got angry, but forgave him because I used him as my g-gauge of legitimacy. So . . . you see . . . I was never totally able to accept myself and my position in life."

"You accepted yourself enough to change the world," David said. "Your Napoleonic Code of Law survived as the norm in much of Europe even until my day."

"Do you know w-why I succeeded? You taught . . . me. You and the timestream." He coughed, painfully. "I learned events don't mean anything. H-history is a wheel . . . turning in on itself, never going anywhere. Mankind is doomed to repeat the same mistakes over and over again. Why?"

David thought about that. "Because, though the world changes, emotions don't, and the passions keep creating the same end results over and over."

"Very good," Hersh said, and took several raspy breaths. "Events are meaningless, emotions are real. Understanding this, I was able to arouse the passions of millions."

"It was the reason that you played "*La Marsellaise*" on the Grenoble Road!" David said.

"Long after the events of that day or their . . . implications are forgotten, the m-men on that road will . . . feel me in their hearts whenever they hear that song. I live through the emotions, David, and the emotions are eternal."

He stopped, resting again, his pain-filled eyes searching David's for the compassion that resided there as if he could take that to the other side with him. "I feel the . . . infinite in myself. All else is meaningless. What is the future? W-what is the past? What . . . are we? What magic liquid is it that shuts us in, and hides from us the things we ought most to know?" He wheezed loudly. "We move and live and die in the midst of m-miracles. But the emotions remain, they are constant."

Antommarchi opened the door again, took a horrified look at Hersh, then said to David, "I think now is the time."

David nodded, and the man left again.

"So," Hersh said, "the vultures come to devour the corpse. A bad bunch, most of them, not nearly as hearty fellows as shared my previous fantasy. They bicker constantly, like children. You know, I think they've poisoned me to get rid of me, but I'll tell you a secret: they're doing me a great favor.'' He wheezed loudly, a scarecrow hand grasping at his chest. "You are the last, my friend," he said, his voice so weak David had to put an ear near his mouth just to hear. "Seek the emotions; don't eat yourself alive . . . with . . . questions."

Hersh sank into the bed, almost as if he were drowning in it. David stood. It was nearly five, the room darkening by degrees as night descended on Longwood House. Fanny Bertrand came in first, bringing Hortense her daughter, and her three sons, one of whom was named after Napoleon.

The children made a scene, crying and kissing the Emperor's hand. Young Napoleon even fainted, and whether this outpouring of affection was real or orchestrated, David couldn't tell and no longer cared. But they made such a ruckus that they had to be taken out into the garden.

After that came the French servants, then the hangers-on, most notably Count Montholon, a Talleyrand clone if ever David saw one. Altogether, sixteen people entered the bedroom.

Hersh was all but gone now, delirious, the sun outside setting all pink and orange on his empire. He stirred one last time, uttering the final words of his life.

"France . . . armée . . . tête d'armée . . . Josephine. . . ."

In the distance, the cannons at Alarm House sounded retreat, and the sun vanished in a burst of light. Hersh sighed once, embracing the void, then all was quiet. A roomful of people stood, watching, waiting. All at once, Hersh's eyes opened wide.

Antommarchi moved to the body and closed the eyelids. It was over. The body of Napoleon Bonaparte was dead, used up, at age fifty-one.

As those around him cried and moaned, David watched the man with some happiness. He had lived his life as he chose, accepted the unconditional terms of that life, and embraced the darkness unafraid. What more could anyone want?

He moved out of the room and walked the silent, dark halls of Longwood House. He could hear the rats scurrying through the walls, totally oblivious to the hopes and fears of the people who shared the house with them. Funny, the arsenic that killed Hersh was originally bought to kill the rats; but for fear of them dying in the walls to a dreadful smell, it was never used.

Forget events, forget life and death, Hersh had told him. Concentrate on the emotions. They are eternal.

Time is meaningless.

"You have to pull the knob toward you as you turn the key," Mrs. Wilcox told the detective as he struggled with the door. "Here, I'll show you."

"No thanks, lady," Ed Henderson said. "We can take it from here."

His partner, Detective Sergeant Dominick, took the woman by the arm and professionally moved her down the long flight of stairs leading up to the garage apartment.

The woman, a washed-out, prissy blonde named Maureen, moved a few feet away from the stairs then turned and took up a permanent position there. "Dr. Frankel was such a quiet man," she said. "He always paid his rent up a full year in advance. Can you believe that?"

"That's something, all right," Herm Dominick said, starting back up the stairs.

"Do you think he's been murdered or something?" the woman called to the detective's back.

He turned halfway up the white wooden staircase. "People turn up missing all the time, ma'am," he said.

"Can I rent out his room and keep the rest of the money? There's six more months' worth there."

"Up to you, ma'am."

"Herm," Henderson whispered urgently from the top of the stairs. "I think somebody's in here."

The man ran up the stairs, his short-barrel .38 out of his hip holster with the safety off.

He reached the landing, both men staying to the side of the plain wooden door.

"When I got it open," Henderson said, "I heard somebody moving around in there."

"Okay," Dominick said softly. He looked back down the stairs to see the landlady already partway up the steps again. He waved her back frantically, then looked at his partner. "We announce it, then go in, okay?"

Henderson nodded, his nickel-plated .45 pointing into the Oklahoma sky.

"Police officers!" Dominick yelled. "Open up!"

Nothing.

The two men shared a look, then Henderson kicked at the already-open door. With a screech, a cat came flying through the opening, sending both men into a terrified crouch. The animal was down the stairs and gone in seconds.

Dominick heard giggling at the bottom of the stairs and saw the blonde shaking her head.

"If you'd have asked, I'd have told you," she called up to them.

They holstered their guns and moved into the small apartment, stepping over the little mountain of letters that had been pushed through the slot in the door. The first thing was the smell of cat crap. Henderson made a face and looked around the living room.

It was an innocuous room with plain furniture. All the right things were there, but it looked like nobody really lived in it. It was bland, no character.

While Ed moved around the living room, Dominick disappeared into the kitchen. A small bookcase sat off to the side. Ed went to it and looked at the titles. It was filled with books about Hitler and the killing of Jews during World War II. There must have been fifty or sixty volumes on that topic, and nothing else.

"Got anything?" he called to Dominick.

The man came into the living room shaking his head. "The kitchen's a mess," he said. "It looks like nobody's been here for weeks," he said. When the cat got hungry it tore up anything that smelled like food. Wrappers are all over the place in there."

"Well, that checks with Missing Persons," Ed said. "The hospital reported him gone, but only after a few weeks. Everybody just assumed he was on vacation."

"You find anything?" Dominick asked.

"Take a look at that bookshelf," Henderson said, pointing.

Herm went and took a look. "Wow," he said. "This guy must have been a real ghoul."

"Yeah," Ed said. "He was some kinda kraut or something during the war, something like that. All them fuckers were loony."

"They shouldn't'a let 'em come over here," Dominick said. "Weird fuckers."

Ed was chuckling.

"What's so funny?"

"Hey, meatball, Eye-talians was krauts too back then."

"Fuck you, Ed."

"Yeah. Let's look the rest of the place over."

They checked the bedroom and small attached bath with a tub and no shower, but there was nothing in the tidy, barren apartment to show any indication of anyone really living there at all.

Dominick came back and sat on the living-room couch while Ed picked up the stack of mail from the floor and looked through the usual collection of bills and circulars.

"A shame it stinks so bad in here," Herm said. "We coulda stayed around for a while and watched the tube or something before goin' back."

"Yeah," Ed said idly, then stopped going through the stack of letters, stopping at one made out in a shaking scrawl with no return address.

"Wonder what we got here," he said, and tore open the envelope. He read quickly, then reread. "Son of a bitch."

"What?"

He carried the letter to the sofa and handed it to Herm. It read:

TO WHOM IT MAY CONCERN:

A man I met thousands of years ago told me something I'll never forget. He said that God is time. As I've moved through the ages and the pains and triumphs of man since then, I think I begin to understand. I live in a Hell of my own choosing. I have taken as my God the time of pain and called it real. I have embraced pain as one embraces a lover, for my God ruled my life.

But time! Time is moments. God is the God of all time and not just the time of pain. The emotion of the moment exists! The emotion of all moments exists! If you find this, it means I am gone. You now must choose your God. I beg you to listen to me. There is freedom in your life. There is happiness. There is forgiveness, most of all forgiveness.

Choose life, please listen to me. Choose life.

The moment exists. It does!

All is one.

Don't grieve for me. Create no more pain.

* * *

"Jesus," Dominick said, refolding the letter and putting it back in the envelope. "Jesus Christ."

"I told you them krauts was loony, didn't I?" Ed asked, not really expecting an answer.

Dominick moved to the door. "Put that damned thing down and let's get out of here and get the stink blown off our clothes."

"Sure," Ed said, dropping the letter and all the letters on top of the kitchen table.

They moved out of the tiny apartment and into the afternoon sunshine.

The letter, along with the report of Sergeants Henderson and Dominick stayed in the active files of the OCPD and the OSBI for a period of time, then the whole mess was photostated and stuck into inactive, then into deep inactive, in the computers, which were eventually purged of such memories.

> *In short, whatever forms exist,*
> *Impermanent and transitory,*
> *Are illuminated in contemplation,*
> *By the power of each mind.*
>
> —Lama Mipham

Liz Wolf geared down to second and wheeled the Porsche into David's driveway, gravel crunching loudly beneath the tires. It felt strange, coming to this house again, the place where so much had happened in the last two days. As she pulled up behind his old Cadillac, she couldn't shake the feeling that she was touching something denied to most people, something clear and unmuddied.

The trouble was, she didn't know if that was a good thing.

On the phone he'd said that he'd beaten it, that somehow he'd survived Bailey. But, if that were true, why did she still feel the images of death left by Silv's mind? She walked toward the front door, and no matter how she tried, she couldn't escape a sense of fear and loss. Seeing David would help, knowing that he really *was* all right.

"Elizabeth," a voice called. "Elizabeth Wolf?"

She jumped, startled, and turned at the front door to see a weathered, aging stick of a man, who'd apparently come out of the bushes. He wore jeans and a plaid work shirt, his skin thick and wrinkled like leather. He looked at her with deep, sad eyes, a half smile crossing his face.

"W-who are you?" she asked, drawing back. "How do you know my name?"

He took a step forward, raising a hand. "Now . . . don't get scared," he said. "I don't mean you no harm."

Liz backed against the door, her hand feeling for the knob. It turned in her hand. "Now, I don't know who you are, but . . ."

"Don't go in there!" he warned loudly, then softened. "Please . . . wait for just a minute." He backed away from her, farther into the drive. "See? We'll talk from this distance if you want."

"Who are you?" she demanded.

"My name's Sonny," he said in an easy Oklahoma drawl, "Sonny Wolf. I—I guess I'm your daddy."

She just stared at him. If he was truly who he said he was, she was looking at the man she had hated since she was a baby. "What are you doing here?"

The lanky old man jammed his hands down in his pockets and stared at the gravel beneath his feet. "I guess you could say that I come with him . . . with your brother Davy."

"David invited you here?"

"Not exactly invited, honey."

"Don't call me that," she said, a chill going through her. "You have no right to be familiar with me, even if . . . especially if you're my father."

He nodded. "Fair enough."

Her hand went to the door again. "Well, let's tell David you're here."

"I think he'd want me to talk with you before you go in there," the man said.

"Why?"

"So's you'd understand better, I guess. Don't you have some knowledge about this . . . traveling and stuff?"

Liz felt her insides tighten up, a deep fear welling within her. "S-some," she said, taking a few faltering steps in his direction. "Where's David?"

"Partly in there," he said, pointing toward the house. And then the finger turned and touched his own head. "Partly in here."

"David's . . . in you?" she asked.

He nodded. "I think he wants me to tell you a few things."

"Why doesn't he just tell me himself?"

The man who called himself her father looked at her then,

and his eyes carried a hint of eternity. She'd never forget the depth of his eyes. "He . . . can't, hon . . . Elizabeth. He don't know how anymore."

"I don't understand."

"I'm not sure I do either," Sonny Wolf replied, "but I'd like to try and explain if you'll listen to me for a few minutes."

She stared at him, and it was difficult to believe that a monster lived within this kindly shell. She tucked her summer skirt up under her legs and sat on the front step, patting the place beside her. Sonny smiled with black teeth and sat down happily.

"Mind if I chew?" he said, and took a package of Red Man out of his back pocket.

She shook her head. In this place of miracles, anything was possible.

Sonny took a big wad of tobacco and tucked it in his left cheek, then stared for several seconds into the rapidly darkening twilight sky before speaking.

"Your brother's come back here to die, Elizabeth. His body's laying inside right now." He turned and stared at her, his face guileless, studying hers.

The words tightened in her mouth, her chest constricting painfully. "Have you . . . did you . . . ?"

He shook his head and chewed vigorously. "I been waiting out here for you. That's what Davy wanted." He turned his head and spit into Bailey's flowerbeds. "He came to me several weeks ago. I was working on a rig down near Galveston, when all of a sudden—whoosh! I was thinkin' about things I ain't never thought about before." He laughed. "Hell, I wandered right off the job and set in my trailer house for three days 'for' I had any idea what was going on."

"I'm not sure what you mean by that," she said.

He turned and studied her again. "Davy, the Davy you knew, doesn't exist anymore. He's more . . . feelings than anything. Don't even know how he found me. Maybe it was some sort of animal instinct or something. But after living with his brain for a while, I began to figure it all out."

The man spit again and stood up, putting a hand to his stooped back. "Not too great at squattin' anymore," he said. "Gettin' old, I guess." He walked around for a moment.

"Would you please get on with it?" Liz asked, her insides jangling. "I can't stand this."

He stopped walking and nodded at her. "His body's dead, but his brain ain't. He's been traveling through the mind places, through people, through feelings. He's a good boy, Elizabeth. He's made me feel like I'm good, too." The man's eyes misted up and he spit a long streamer on the ground in counterpoint. "He wants you to know that no matter what you see in that house, his life's been more than that, much more. He's traveled for lifetimes and more lifetimes, forgetting about *things* and living with feelings. He's been animals, run and flown with them in prehistoric forests." He clenched his fists in front of him. "I could smell the orchids, big as a basketball, and see the deep green forests. And then he became the forests and I could feel how they feel."

Sonny Wolf stood transfixed, staring into space blankly. "I could feel all life, flowing like an oil pipeline, all of it connected by the emotions. I found out that all memory is the remembering of emotion, that's all. All emotion is the same emotion; bad things—hatred, fear, anger, lust—is just the emotion turned inside. And he lived like the trees and the birds, and I guess he started in losin' what he'd been before. Out of the shell, he stopped carin' about what the shell cares about. The body, it dies. The feelings, though, Elizabeth, they last forever. And Davy's just feeling now. He wants you to know, he couldn't be happier."

Liz lowered her head and began crying softly. "We never . . . really had a chance to be close," she said, and didn't jump when he came and put a hand on her shoulder.

"He had a child," Sonny said.

She looked up at him, taking strength from his angelic face. "A . . . baby?"

Sonny laughed. "Craziest thing," he said. "It was my great-grandma, Sylvia Luper. She was a wild thing, too. Born in a lighthouse somewhere up in Yankee country, she spent her whole life on a houseboat on the Mississippi. Shit . . . she was somethin'." He spit again. "Davy wants you to know that you'll have a child, too."

"M-me?"

"You remember a woman, name of Silv?"

Liz nodded.

"Well, you're her grandma, plenty of times removed down the line."

Liz stood, smoothing her skirt. Her feelings were indefinable as numbness set into her brain and body. She was seeing at once the infinite past and the eternal future and it was more than she could deal with in the course of a moment. She knew she'd miss David, but why did he choose to come back in this man from their past, this . . . and then it struck her.

"You've done all this on your own, haven't you?" she asked. "Coming up here, talking to me. David didn't make you do any of it."

He smiled. "Davy can't make anybody do anything," he said. "And wouldn't if he could. He's just feelings now."

"Then . . . why?"

"You're my daughter, Elizabeth. My blood. I did it for you."

They stared at one another for a long moment. "C-call me Liz," she said in a small voice.

"Oh, baby," he replied softly, and it was a start. "There's so much I want to tell you."

"We'll take the time," she said. "Get to know one another slowly. I've been hurt . . . a lot."

"We'll go with the feelings," he said, and in that, she saw truth.

He moved past her, up the step and to the door. "I'm going in to say good-bye now," Sonny told her. "You want to wait out here for me?"

She shook her head. "I'm going in, too."

He nodded and opened the door, moving into the big living room. Liz followed, seeing David's body immediately on the floor, blood all over his chest. His dead eyes were staring at her.

She heard her voice scream his name from a distance, and Sonny was holding her back as she tried to run to him.

"It's all right," he said gently. "He's happy. You're grieving for yourself."

She stopped fighting him then and looked into those eyes. Emotions turned inward, he had told her. And she tried to think from David's viewpoint.

"I never knew you much," Sonny told David's body from a distance of five feet. "But you come out good, boy. Whatever your momma was, she somehow done right by you. You taught me a lot about lovin' and hatin', and I thank you."

Liz had no words. She'd undoubtedly cry them out in her sleep for many weeks, but since the grief was for herself, it would probably be cleansing. And the way things had turned out, she wondered if Sonny had been David's present to her, to help her out of her own problems.

"Good-bye," she heard Sonny say, then saw the old man put a hand to his head and collapse to the floor.

Then there was a second, a glorious second, where she felt David within her, opening up his world of feeling to her. He *was* happy. He had learned the secret that he had spent his whole life searching for, and was going contentedly to the other side.

And the feeling passed, leaving only residue behind. Each mind having to find its own brand of peace.

The thing that had been David Wolf slipped easily into the still-warm body on the floor and opened itself to the experience. It was familiar, this place, and David was struck with a rush of old memories connected with this body.

The pull had drawn him here, the ultimate knowledge that the song cannot be known until the melody is finished. It was the perfect and natural place to be, and his longing was stilled forever.

And as he happily embraced the void and its dark, numbing waters, he crystallized one last thought: It wasn't the fear of death that motivated all that lived; it was the fear of life.

The blackness took him and drew him down.

David Wolf had come home.

At last.

To discover the final truth.

Life is a struggle leading only to death.

But death is just another moment in a world full of moments. . . .

The sun warms, then is cooled by the ocean breeze and the salty foam of the breakers as the man makes his way toward the lighthouse at a place called Portland Head.

The man is searching, searching for the moment of eternity, as he enters the light and climbs its winding stairs to where the woman waits.

She stands, watching for him as she has always stood and always will. He finds her, at last, the moment made more poignant by the long separation. They are as young as springtime and as old as wisdom. When they fall into one another's arms, infinity flows through them, a pipeline to the ages.

David smiles at Silv, and the gesture is a symbol for all time, linking them with everything that has gone before and is yet to come. They make love, their happiness and desire a total feeling, an eternal giving that can never be taken away from them. The moment exists for all time, to be visited and revisited over and over and over without dimming, without decay.

They laugh and relive the moment, the pristine, eternal moment, and the feelings are ever strong. The moment is.

And they are creating a new life this moment, the union of their love extending beyond their own existence to affect the futures and the memories of countless new generations.

And so the cycles go, renewal and rebirth, happiness regenerated. All love is a memory. As long as memory exists, love can never die. Eternity in a moment.

Choose life.

AFTERWORD

MEMORIES is a book about truths, both literal and emotional, and, as such, was an intensely personal write. The truth of the little Corsican's life tongue-and-grooved perfectly into my own sense of reality and I strove for accuracy as much as was possible in the story.

The words, with small exceptions, are Napoleon's own words, the activities described all took place during a thirty-year span of the Emperor's life.

The interpretations, however, are my own.

ABOUT THE AUTHOR

Mike McQuay, author of MEMORIES, has led a diverse life. Beginning at age fifteen, he worked in a wide range of professions including musician, retail business owner, airplane mechanic, banker, bartender, factory production line worker, film pirate, and speech and public relations writer, before settling on fiction writing as a livelihood.

McQuay has written more than twenty novels and short story collections in the last ten years, ranging from children's books to science fiction to mainstream. Among many other titles, he is the author of ESCAPE FROM NEW YORK and THE M.I.A. RANSOM, both from Bantam.

McQuay is married to novelist Shana Bacharach. They live in Oklahoma City with their three children and three cats. McQuay, 37, is Artist-in-Residence at Central State University in Edmond, Oklahoma.

RETURN TO THE UNIVERSE OF
STARTIDE RISING

THE
UPLIFT
WAR

BY DAVID BRIN

David Brin's epic *Startide Rising* swept the Nebula, Hugo and Locus Awards. Now this master storyteller returns us to this extraordinary, wonder-filled world. Drawing on the startling events of *Startide Rising*, he tells a tale of courage, survival and discovery. As galactic armadas clash in quest of the ancient fleet of the Progenitors, a brutal alien race seizes the dying planet of Garth. At stake is the existence of Terran society and Earth, and the fate of the entire Five Galaxies.

Buy The Uplift War and all of David Brin's novels, on sale June 15, 1987 wherever Bantam Spectra Books are sold, or use the handy coupon below for ordering:

THE CONTROVERSIAL NEW NOVEL BY THE AUTHOR OF BUG JACK BARRON AND CHILD OF FORTUNE

LITTLE HEROES

By Norman Spinrad

Here is an extraordinarily powerful novel of sex, rock and revolution driven by a relentless beat. It is the near future. Tens of millions live on the streets. The City teems with Uzi-toting enforcers, kibble-munching streeties and wireheads plugged in to the latest electronic high. And somewhere along the line, rock and roll has lost its soul—or rather sold it to a mega-corporation that churns out passionless synthesized hits. From the highest towers of the corporate world to the sex-and-thrills bars, to the death-infested streets, an explosion is about to take place. And a handful of little heroes are going to set it off.

Buy **LITTLE HEROES**, *on sale June 15, 1987 wherever Bantam Spectra Hardcovers are sold, or use the handy coupon below for ordering:*